Between Husbands

&

Friends

Between Husbands

&

Friends

NANCY THAYER

PIATKUS

For more information on
other books published by
Piatkus, visit our website at
www.piatkus.co.uk

Copyright © 1999 by Nancy Thayer

First published in Great Britain in 2000 by
Judy Piatkus (Publishers) Ltd of
5 Windmill Street, London W1P 1HF
email: info@piatkus.co.uk

First published in the United States in 1999
by St. Martin's Press

The moral right of the author has been asserted

A catalogue record for this book is available from the British Library

HBK ISBN 0 7499 0533 6
PBK ISBN 0 7499 3172 8

Typeset in Bembo by Palimpsest Book Production Limited,
Polmont, Stirlingshire
Printed and bound in Great Britain by
Mackays of Chatham plc, Chatham, Kent

This book is for my friend,

my sister,

Martha Wright Foshee, B.S.H.A., R.N.

She saves lives.

'He wishes to be far away, either at sea or on the shore. *In between*, he realizes, *is the most difficult of all places to be.*'

—*The Sea Man* by Jane Yolen

Between Husbands

&

Friends

JUNE 1998

IT'S A SOFT, lazy morning with the early June sunlight tumbling into our kitchen where the four of us move in a carbohydrate-high daze after indulging in Max's triple-fruit pancakes. I'm loading the dishwasher, Margaret's finishing the cold rice salad we're taking to the Cunninghams', Max holds Jeremy on his lap, reading the *Boston Globe* comic section aloud, simulating tough-guy growls or femme-fatal falsettos so extravagantly that Jeremy's in hysterics and even Margaret grins.

'I'm going to organize the beach bag,' I tell them, and hurry up the stairs. We'll spend most of the day outside, so I head for the children's bathroom to search through the cabinet for the new bottle of sunblock I *know* I bought, when all at once the bag drops from my hand. My heart hammers fast and hard. Hot blood churns up through my chest, floods my face.

I slam the bathroom door, lean against it. What the hell is going on? Am I dying? I'm thirty-seven, way too young for hot flashes. Anyway, these things can't be called *flashes*, they're more like *explosions*, as if my heart is full of time bombs.

I hate this, I *hate* this. My heart trips and gallops. My fingertips are numb. My lips are icy. I'm afraid.

I drop to the floor, curl up into the smallest possible mass, wedge myself into the corner, the cool ceramic tiles like walls, like barricades behind my back. I bring my knees to my chest, drop my forehead on my knees, cross my arms over my head, like someone in a crashing plane.

'Mom?' Jeremy wanders up and down the hall, calling for me. Oh, God, I hope I locked the bathroom door when I came in here. I don't want him to find me like this, but at the moment it's beyond my powers to crawl over there and check to see if the lock is snapped. 'Mom? Dad says it's time to go.'

I can't answer. I hear him shuffle off.

I can't sort through the commotion in my head. Is it anger? Is it that I feel pressured – trapped? It feels like fear.

But what do I have to fear? I mutter to myself: Be reasonable, Lucy. If it's the job offer from Jared Falconer, well for God's sake, you can deal with that. If Max feels really strongly about it, then don't take it. If you feel even more strongly that you want it, then *do* take it. You can work it out, you and Max. And the children will be just fine. Margaret's fourteen. Jeremy's going to be in first grade this year; he'll be in school most of the day. It's Max, isn't it? You're afraid of Max, afraid he'll disappear into one of his effing depressions.

'Mom? Are you in there?' Margaret taps on the door.

'Be out in a minute,' I call.

Okay, my voice works. I drag myself up to the sink to splash cold water on my face. I stare at my reflection. My heart slows. I'm okay.

Occasionally I've had other bizarre spells, fits of dread that seize me in the middle of a clear bright day, and I never can figure out what's going on, and then two days later something happens: My aunt dies, a friend's child is hit by a car. That doesn't mean I'm psychic any more than it means I'm psychotic. Mostly it just makes me uncomfortable.

But these are, I think, panic attacks, and they've been happening a lot recently. I've got to do something about them. If it's the job offer, I'll talk it out with Max and make a decision. That should stop them.

Get a grip, I order my reflection. 'All right, I'm ready!' I call, and fly out of the room, grab up the canvas carryall, and head down the stairs like any normal mother.

In the kitchen Max has Jeremy sitting on the counter while he ties his sneaker. Over his shoulder, he asks, 'You okay?'

'I'm fine.'

In one easy movement, Max lifts Jeremy up onto his shoulders. 'Okay, crew, time for blastoff.'

When the four of us crowd our way through the front hall, Midnight and Cinnamon fly into their usual Kamikaze Cat routine, streaking back and forth, ears back, tails bristling, tripping us. As we step out into the bright light of day, Margaret morphs from contented daughter of the house to blank-faced sophisticate, so that anyone passing by won't think she actually has a family.

We set our bags in the trunk, then pile into the Volvo station wagon, Max behind the driver's seat. I relax, roll up the sleeves and undo the buttons of my blue cotton shirt, letting the sun fall on my throat and chest. I lean my head back. The heat feels good.

I look over at my husband, who's dressed for a day off in shorts and a cotton T-shirt, an old present from his staff that reads on the front: 'How many editors does it take to change a light bulb?' And on the back: 'One, but first he has to rewire the entire building.' Six days a week his newspaper has him, pretty much heart and soul, but on Sundays he belongs to us, and when he's really with us as he is today, he lights up our lives.

We drive through a town flooded with morning light, past houses and lawns shining as if freshly washed, out toward the country.

'Daddy,' Jeremy calls, 'can we do the ant song?'

'Sure. Let's see. How does it start?' Max tosses me one of his lightning-white smiles, then begins to sing: 'The ants go marching one by one, hurrah, hooray, the ants go marching one by one, hurrah, hooray!' He throws his head back, letting his rich baritone roll out into the air. His teeth are a beautiful milk white against his tan, and his black hair glistens and curls like the pelt of a vigorously healthy animal. This is my Max at his best.

'The ants go marching one by one, the little stopped to suck his thumb!' Jeremy croons.

I add my vague soprano to the mix. 'And they all go marching down, into the ground, to get out of the rain!'

Jeremy pokes his sister. 'The ant song!' he yells at her.

Margaret rolls her eyes at him and presses the earphones tightly against her head, but by the time we're on three – 'the little one stops to take a pee' – she's yanked the earphones down around her neck and joined in. She loves this stupid song as much as we do, and we've been coming to the Cunninghams' for summer Sundays forever, and she really doesn't want to miss a thing, not even her brother's maniacal laughter because we all said 'pee.'

By the time we finish the song, we're turning off the main highway onto a winding, pot-holed, empty stretch of secondary road through farmland.

'Dad!' Jeremy calls. 'Can I drive?'

'All right,' Max says, and slows the car. Jeremy undoes his seat belt and climbs over into the front seat, his wiry little body seemingly composed entirely of elbows and knees. Max pushes back his car seat to make room for Jeremy on his lap, reminds Jeremy where to put his hands, and off we creep at fifteen miles an hour, with Jeremy concentrating so hard he's got his tongue stuck between his teeth. Occasionally the car wavers over too far to the left, but Jeremy's doing a pretty good job as we bump along.

Just before we reach the Cunninghams', an old red truck approaches from the other direction, clanking and shuddering.

'Dad?' Jeremy queries.

'You can do it,' Max tells him. 'Keep your eyes on the road. Don't look at the truck. Look toward the right side of the road.'

We all hold our breath while Jeremy steers the Volvo. We're even with the truck, and then it's behind us, and Margaret cheers, 'Well, done, Germ!' and Max tousles his son's hair. 'Yes, Jeremy. Good job.'

The road bends. Thickets of trees and shrubs loom above, forming a green-black tunnel, and then we go around a curve into the sunshine. The Cunningham farm spreads out beneath the blue sky.

'We're here!' Jeremy yells.

'Can you make the turn into the drive?' Max asks.

'Sure.'

The road runs parallel with a long fenced pasture where Chip's beautiful gelding Gringo grazes beneath a tree. The horse raises his head, watches us go by, swishes his tail disdainfully, and returns to his grass. Seven-year-old Abby's there, too, in jodhpurs and a sleeveless plaid shirt, waving enthusiastically. She's on her pony Brownie, and Princess, the other Shetland, stands in readiness at Brownie's side.

The Cunninghams' historic brick Georgian mansion rises up like a set for *Masterpiece Theater*. Max helps Jeremy make the turn past the neat circle drive at the front of the house to park on the white gravel at the side. We spill out of the car. The golden lab, Sugar, waddles out to greet us, her tail wagging.

Chip lopes toward us, a tall blond man wearing only swimming trunks and sneakers. His shoulders are burned, his skin glimmers with sweat. No doubt he's been working in his vegetable garden, or cutting brush away from his various trails through the woods.

'I just drove!' Jeremy crows.

'I saw you. You did great.'

'Can I ride Princess?'

'Absolutely. Abby's got her all ready for you.' He takes Jeremy's hand, turning to tell us, 'Kate and Matthew are in the house.'

Max opens the trunk, and we fill our arms with the bowl of rice salad, beach bag, and a carryall holding two bottles of white wine and one of apple juice which we carry through the back door into the cool kitchen. Kate's there, barefoot, wearing a black bikini. She's bending over the long pine table, lost in thought, her face somber, even sorrowful.

'Kate,' I say.

She jumps, startled, and in an instant transforms herself. 'You're here! Hi, guys! Margaret, look what I just made!' She waves her hands like a game show hostess, displaying a rectangular cake turned into an American flag by raspberries, blueberries, and white icing. She's got icing on her cheek and elbow, but her eyes are pouchy and red-rimmed.

'That's cool, Aunt Kate,' Margaret says.

'Thought I'd practise for the Fourth of July.'

'What a girl.' I hug her.

'Where's Matthew?' Margaret asks, looking around. Matthew outgrew the ponies long ago and never took to riding as Abby has.

'Where do you think?'

Already Margaret has gone off into the den, drawn by the sirens' song of MTV. The Cunninghams and Max and I decided long ago that when our two families get together the kids are permitted to watch all the television they want, but they have to join us at the table for dinner, *when* dinner's ready, no matter what's on television then.

'Chip's been mowing,' Kate tells Max. 'I think he wants to take a dip in the pond.'

'I'll join him,' Max says, and heads out the door.

Through the high windows I see Chip tightening the cinch on Princess, then making a brace of his hands onto which Jeremy eagerly steps. Jeremy climbs onto the pony's back and grabs the reins. In the sunlight Jeremy's brown curls take on a paler glint; by the end of the summer his hair will be bleached almost blond.

Abby kicks her pony, and they set off at a trot, Princess at her flank, Jeremy trying to post. Jeremy often has coughing spells after riding. He's probably allergic to horses, and guiltily I hope he is. I'm always nervous when Jeremy rides. Even a pony is huge, compared to my little boy.

'I put beach towels out on the patio,' Kate calls.

Max joins Chip. The two men walk along the path between grasses and wild daisies to the pond, one tall, blond and lean, one short, dark and stocky. A giraffe and a bull. Good friends.

I say, 'I think I'll have a swim, too,' but Kate puts her hand on my arm.

'Wait. I want to talk.'

'Kate, not now.'

'Lucy, please.' Her face flushes and tears well. 'Lucy, he's dying.'

Her grief is so painful. I take Kate in my arms and hold her as if she were my child. 'Oh, honey.'

'Chip won't let me talk about it. He's so inflexible! And intolerant, and just plain ignorant, too!'

'Chip's just worried,' I assure Kate. 'It's understandable.' I pull out a chair. We sit facing one another. 'Tell me.'

'He's so thin,' Kate cries. 'And his skin—'

For several years Kate has been doing hospice work, visiting a young man named Garrison who has AIDS. Chip fears that Kate will somehow become infected, or will carry the disease home to her children. They've had many royal battles over this. Kate insists on sticking with her work with Garrison. Chip retaliates by refusing to listen to one word about the dying man. It doesn't help that Kate has, if not fallen in love with Garrison, at least come to love him deeply, and not only platonically. To Kate, Garrison is as handsome as a wounded god, brilliantly funny, creative, sympathetic, intuitive. She tells me there is a deeply complicated sensuality in caring for him. She brings him expensive treats: iced mango sorbet, Dom Perignon and Stilton, chocolates from Switzerland. Each bite he takes is a thrill, an event. She cuts his nails. She combs what hair he has left. She touches him as much and in as many ways as she can, sometimes she even gives him facials. She rubs his back. Often they sit listening to music – Garrison likes opera – holding hands.

'I want to bring Oscar here,' Kate says, weeping. Oscar

Wilde is Garrison's Yorkshire terrier. 'I promised Garrison I'd give him a good home. And Oscar knows me, trusts me. He won't be so bereft. Or we can be bereft together.'

'What does Chip say?'

Kate snorts. 'What do you think? He doesn't want Oscar here. Says one dog is enough. Right, as if we don't live on a fucking *farm!*' Kate rises, grabs tissues, blows her nose, sits down again. 'Chip says Oscar would upset Sugar. Make Sugar jealous. God, Sugar's so fat and lazy, she needs a younger dog around to get her moving!'

'Sugar's not the point, Kate. It's that Oscar is Garrison's dog, and Chip is jealous of your relationship with Garrison.'

'Yeah, well, he damned well should be!' Kate sobs. 'Garrison loves me in a way Chip can't even understand! Garrison loves me with his soul. Oh, God, how will I live without him?' Grief overwhelms her. Kate bends double, her entire body shaking with sobs. She sinks to her knees on the cool tile floor.

I glance around. Matthew and Margaret are still in the den. Outside the children sit enthroned as their ponies try to much grass. I can't see the pond, but the men must be there.

'Kate.' I kneel next to my friend and wrap my arms around her. 'Honey. I'm so sorry.'

'If he goes into the hospital, I want to spend as much time with him as possible.'

'Okay. I'll look after Abby and Matthew.'

Kate shakes her head. 'I know. And I want to tell Chip I'm with you.'

'No. Kate, I'm already lying to him.'

Chip hates it when Kate is with Garrison, so for the past six months Kate's told Chip that she sees Garrison twice a week, during the day, while the children are in school. In fact she's been visiting him four or five times a week and telling Chip she's with me. Kate asked me to help her by perpetuating the lie and I have agreed; it is a *good* lie, I believe. It does no one harm, and it helps Garrison and Kate.

I haven't told Max about this. He hates lies. It's surprising, how easy it is to pretend to be doing something with large chunks of my day, and my own husband doesn't know. In a guilty way, I kind of like this. It gives me an illusion of freedom. Still, I don't like the thought of extending the magnitude of the lie. That would increase the chances of getting caught.

'Every day but Sunday. Lucy, don't shake your head, *listen* to me. Garrison is dying. He'll be gone by the end of the summer. He has no one else who can care for him like I do.'

It's true. Garrison's lover died of AIDS two years ago. His parents disowned him when he came out to them. He has many friends, but some of them just can't handle this particular illness, and others are just so busy making a living.

'I thought we could pretend to be taking a course together. At the community center. A summer course, just six weeks. Exercise or basketweaving, it doesn't matter, Chip won't want to hear about it. As long as he thinks you and I are together, he'll be fine.'

'I don't know, Kate. That's more complicated.' I'm thinking aloud, trying to find a solution. 'I haven't had to say anything to Max about all this yet, and Chip thinks you've been coming to our house. But if we're supposed to be going out, in public, taking a course . . . why, think about it, Kate. Other people would have to be in the course, people we all know, who Chip might run into. It just wouldn't work.'

Kate rises and rinses her face with cold water. 'I have to see Garrison every day.'

'You need to tell Chip that. You need to tell him the truth.'

'It will initiate World War Three around here.'

'I know. It will be hard. But it's the only way. And maybe it will make things better between you and Chip.'

Kate flashes me an angry look. I've overstepped an invisible line, insinuating that things between the Cunninghams are less than perfect. Oddly, the more I stand up for Chip, the more it seems to free Kate to complain about him, and the reverse is true; if I criticize Chip in the slightest, Kate jumps to his defense. I can understand this; it's the way I feel about Max and my children. But it's easy for me to champion Chip. Very easy.

'Mom?'

Matthew and Margaret stand in the doorway.

Every time I see the boy his bones seem to have grown. His collarbone almost pokes out of the tanned skin of his shoulders. Only a month older than Margaret, Matthew looks much older: Tall already, five feet ten at age fourteen, he will surely be as tall as his father soon. Matthew doesn't seem comfortable with his early height and the attendant stretch of his long arms and legs; he trips on the untied laces of his sneakers (but still won't tie them). His blond hair is clean, but too long and badly cut. It hangs over his eyes and around the sharp planes of his face; clearly he's using it to hide behind. His chin is spotted with acne and the beginnings of a paltry beard. I know his parents have advised him that the oil from his hair will only exacerbate the acne; I'm also sure that he chooses to ignore their advice.

Matthew wears a tattered T-shirt and baggy madras shorts; Margaret wears a faded button-down shirt of her father's and a pair of her enormous jeans. It's a good guess that she's trying to hide her body. Over the past year her breasts have sprouted like tubers, like squash, large and firm, organically incontrovertible evidence that she's growing up. I know Margaret is now absorbed with the vision of herself as someone quite distinct and separate from her family. She wants to travel, she wants to have boyfriends (she wants to have *lovers!*), she wants all the adventures awaiting her in the wide world.

Although if Margaret has her way, she might find sufficient adventure right here. She must notice that in spite of his shield of hair, Matthew is as drop-dead handsome as his father. Perhaps that's why she holds her face so poker-straight, as if she's numb.

'Hi, Biggies,' Kate greets Matthew and Margaret. She's gotten her face and voice under control. 'Want to go up to the pond?'

Margaret shrugs.

Matthew says, 'Sure.'

'I made a gallon thermos full of iced tea and one of lemonade. Could you carry them, Matthew?' Kate is all business now, assigning tasks, handing me the basket of fruit, Margaret the bag of chips. 'Dad already set the lawn chairs out.'

We head out the door, our arms full.

WE WALK ALONG a freshly cut path toward the pond, through a stand of evergreens long ago planted as a wind block. Abby and Jeremy sit on their horses in the shade of a huge maple at the far end of the pasture. The sun beams steadily down without a single cloud to block its strength.

When they bought the farm, Chip had several loads of

sand delivered and dumped at one end of the pond to form a beach, and it's here that he's set up the beach chairs. He and Max are on the other side of the pond, working on the dock that extends into the water. One of the rubber inner tubes that supports it has come loose and they are refastening it.

Kate sinks onto a towel and begins applying suntan lotion. I peel off my jeans and shirt, sink down next to her, and do the same. Matthew walks over to the men and talks a moment, then drags his T-shirt over his head, tosses it aside, runs out onto the dock, and belly flops into the water.

Margaret spreads her towel out and sits next to me. I bite my lips to keep from asking, 'Aren't you hot?' After a while, with a little moue of resignation, as if she's being forced against her will, she unbuttons her shirt and steps out of her jeans. She's wearing a one-piece bathing suit, and her figure is so slim and nubile that tears come to my eyes. She is lovely. She is what men have been writing poems about for centuries. Her hips are narrow, her thighs long and sleek. My beauty. She is a jewel. When I tell her this, she retorts, 'Yeah, Mom, just what I want, compliments from a middle-aged woman.'

She wades into the water, dipping her palms to catch water up and splash it on her shoulders.

Kate leans close to me. 'Look at her,' she whispers. 'She's beautiful. Man, Lucy, she's really blossomed over the winter!'

Margaret takes a deep breath and strikes out in a long easy crawl for the middle of the pond. Matthew sees her, grabs a silly alligator-shaped float that the Littlies love, and heads her way. They collide in the middle of the pond and surface and splash and shriek, suddenly transformed back into the child-hood buddies they've been for eleven years.

Kate lies back and closes her eyes. I join her. The sun

soothes me, makes me drowsy, hypnotizes me. This could be any summer day here or on a Nantucket beach, when our families are together. Good fortune, normal life.

A commotion of hoofbeats and laughter makes me lift my head. Jeremy and Abby are galloping full speed across the pasture and screaming with glee as they go. Jeremy sits the horse well. I remind myself that he's a year younger than Abby; that's why he looks so small beside her. Abby is a tidy child, with her brown hair neatly braided and tied with ribbons that matched the tartan of her shirt. She has a pug nose sprinkled with freckles and her father's bright blue eyes; she looks brave and bold and good, like a miniature model for a book titled something like *Abby Cunningham, Air Force Nurse*.

'Mom!' Jeremy yells from the other side of the fence. 'Did you see that?'

'You were great, Jeremy!' I yell back. 'You were flying!'

'I love this horse!' Jeremy tells me, and begins to cough.

It's a moist, webby, mucousy cough that shakes Jeremy's body. It's the cough I was dreading. Rising, I walk to the fence on the pretense of petting Princess.

'Good girl,' I tell her, stroking her velvet nose. I try to keep my voice, my face, serene.

Jeremy's cough continues. It seems so out of place here on the farm, in the green grass, beneath the blue sky and the bright sun. Jeremy is almost folded double in the saddle.

I want to lift my little boy down into my arms. I want to pat his back and carry him to the house and hold him while he coughs. But I can feel my husband's attitude from clear across the pond. Don't baby him! Let the boy grow up!

'Want a sip of water or lemonade?' I ask.

Jeremy shakes his head. He can't even speak. His face has

taken on the frowning, deeply concentrated look that comes with his worst coughing spells. He is six years old. He can't get his breath. I'm going to call the pediatrician first thing Monday morning.

Finally the coughing subsides. Jeremy gasps for breath. The skin beneath his eyes is blue.

'Let's go to the barn,' Abby says. 'It's too hot to ride.'

I know for Abby it's never too hot, cold, windy, or rainy to ride, and I'm grateful to her for her thoughtfulness of Jeremy.

'I'll come help you unsaddle the horses,' I tell the children.

By the time we're in the barn, Jeremy is coughing again. It's impossible to ignore it. 'Jeremy, I'm afraid you're allergic to horses,' I tell him as I lift him down.

He doesn't want to be allergic to horses; he pushes away from me, indignant, as if my words are the cause of his coughing. I kneel next to him, trying just to be there, not to pressure him, as his cough subsides.

The barn is cool and shadowy and clean, but the air dances with dust motes. Abby swings down from her horse with the effortless fluid movement of an old pro.

'Why don't you go outside and sit under the tree in the shade,' I suggest. 'I'll help Abby.'

Jeremy's too exhausted to argue. Just outside, beneath a dusty lilac bush, he sits down, draws his knees up, folds himself into a ball of a boy, like a turtle drawing its head into its shell. I listen. His coughing has stopped.

The ponies mutter and step sideways and swish their tails, eager to be out of their gear and back into the pasture. I unbuckle the cinch of Princess's saddle. She turns her head sideways and eyes me balefully. She knows she can intimidate me. She shakes her beautiful spoiled head, shivering her white mane, making her bridle clank.

'I'll do that, Lucy.' Chip comes into the barn. He must have swum across the pond; his wet hair lies plastered against his skull, and beads of water slide down his long torso. He smells of dark, leafy damp, like tea, and of something sweet, like rum.

'Thanks.' I step back.

Chip has already spent so much time in the sun that his shoulders and back are spotted, pink patches of burned and peeling skin dotting a layer of deep bronze tan. Under his ministrations Princess subsides, standing with her head low and her eyes closed, as if concentrating on the touch of Chip's hands.

I have a sense of being enclosed, for a moment, in this cool and shaded place where sight is a secondary sense and touch and smell are paramount. Putting my hand on her haunches, I move around Princess to help Abby. I lift Brownie's saddle off and carry it into the tack room. Chip comes in and settles Princess's saddle onto the rack. This small room smells healthy, masculine, of leather and saddle soap. Chip lifts the saddle from me, and as our hands touch I think how soft skin is, how inviting, more supple and enticing than hide or hay or the smoothest leather. Chip and I are almost naked in this confining room; he wears swimming trunks; I, my two strips of red bikini.

Chip and I look at each other.

'Here's Brownie's bridle!' Abby enters the room, leather and metal in her hand.

'Thanks, Pudding,' her father says, turning away from me to take his daughter's gear.

I fetch Princess's bridle and put it away. Chip and Abby lead the ponies out to the pasture. Jeremy has regained his equilibrium and races off toward the pond with Abby. Chip and I follow them up the path, more slowly.

'Lucy.'

We pause by the low privet hedge. I look at Chip. My pulse throbs in my neck.

'I know it's none of my business,' Chip says, 'but I think Jeremy's cough is worrisome.'

'I agree. It's been getting worse and worse this year. I'm going to call Dr. Calder Monday.'

Max is in the pond, racing with Margaret and Matthew while Kate, Jeremy, and Abby stand cheering from the shore.

'I'd be surprised if it were just a matter of allergies,' Chip says. 'When I took the kids to the Disney movie two weeks ago, Jeremy had a coughing attack.'

'I didn't know that.'

'I told Max.'

'Max didn't tell me.' I snatch at a long strand of grass bobbing my way and shred its fuzzy head between my fingers. 'He thinks I baby Jeremy. Thinks I'm turning him into a mama's boy.'

'Want me to say something to Max?'

'I'd be grateful. On certain subjects he won't even listen to me.'

'Max won!' Abby calls. 'Daddy, come on. It's your turn to race.'

Chip leaves my side in a flash, running across the sand and diving into the pond. The Littlies scream with delight. I lie down on my stomach on my beach towel next to Kate. The sun massages my shoulders. Together we watch our husbands and children race and splash in the cool fresh water of the pond, and we have no idea how much our lives will change before the storms of autumn.

1987

I'VE ALWAYS BELIEVED that real friendship is as much a pure gift from the inconstant gods as is love. I had several close friends in college, but distance separated us after graduation as they went off to law school in California, med school in Iowa, or business school in Pennsylvania. I married Max, got pregnant, and moved with Max to western Massachusetts where he had his first job on a small newspaper. I had just begun to get to know some of the young mothers in that small town when Max took a better job in Northampton, and a year later, a new one in Worcester. I didn't mind all the moves; it seemed right to be moving. I was elated with everything. At night Max and I plotted and gossiped like children, toasting each other with cheap champagne each step of the way, secretly amazed to be perceived, so early in our lives, as capable adults. Margaret was an easy baby, Max was happy, and if I missed a female voice I could always call my mother. We were exactly where we wanted to be, doing what we had dreamed of doing. We were going to make a difference in the world, one newspaper reader at a time.

When Max took the job as editor in chief of *The Sussex Gazette*, we bought our first home. Sussex was just starting to boom, becoming yet another bedroom community for the prosperous Boston doctors, lawyers, and executives who wanted their families to live in a historic, idyllic small town. Of course, as they descended on the town, buying up old houses, old farms, they drove up the prices and sent Main Street into a tailspin of yuppie transformation from which it has never recovered. The community exploded with heated confrontations about the dump, a proposed road through the cemetery, renovations for the library, development versus conservation, all good copy for newspapers. *The Sussex Gazette* subscription rate soared and has continued to grow steadily over the years.

The newspaper was owned by Ann and Paul Richardson, a wealthy couple in their early seventies who lived in a townhouse on Beacon Hill and in Fairfields, a farm in Sussex where Ann kept her horses and rode, and where they held an annual Memorial Day barbecue and an elaborate Christmas party for the newspaper staff. Tall, white-haired Paul Richardson was debonair, charming, and mildly flirtatious in a way it seemed that only men of his generation knew how to be. Bony, angular Ann had a nervous, bossy, peremptory air about her. I admired the Richardsons and had no problem holding my own with them at the necessary social functions, but I knew they were not going to become close friends.

MAX WANTED to make *The Sussex Gazette* not just good, but the best small-town weekly in New England. We both wanted to make a difference, however small, in the world. Perhaps we were idealistic to the point of comedy. Certainly we were young.

The first day Max went off to work as editor in chief, he appeared before me for his morning coffee dressed in what must have been his fantasy of what a small-town newspaper editor should look like: button-down shirt, cord pants, L. L. Bean boots, bow tie, and . . . a *sweater vest*.

'Are you going to start smoking a pipe?' I asked him. He had tried to subdue his wild dark curls with mousse, and he'd cut himself shaving, so that a little red spot of blood bloomed near his left ear. I adored him.

'I want the community to have a reliable image of me,' my husband replied. 'Do I look too much like a horse's ass?'

It was hard on us both, how much Max wanted to succeed, how close to the brim of his soul his aspirations surged. I loved him for his optimism and his openness, but by now I knew the other side of the coin, how, when he failed himself, he could plunge into a desperate depression.

'You look handsome,' I assured him. 'Handsome and intellectual . . .'

'I don't want to look like an intellectual! I'll scare people off.'

'I take it back. I don't mean intellectual. I mean *intelligent*. You look handsome and intelligent and mature.'

So he went out the door, and from that moment on his family and friends knew what to give him for Christmas. By now Max has a stunning collection of bow ties and sweater vests, probably enough to wear a different one every day of the year. It says something, I think, about his success as an editor and a leader that many of the young men who have interned under him have taken to wearing sweater vests themselves.

.   .   .

THE NEWSPAPER OFFICES are in a split-level house at the edge of town, but when we first moved to Sussex, it was in our home where much of the real work got done. I wrote my column here on the kitchen table while Margaret gnawed and drooled on her playpen. I surveyed people by phone from here, and it was here where people gathered to discuss political issues, zoning issues, ideas for features . . . and all the gossip.

Max's reporters and ad salesmen, college graduates only three years younger than we were, burst in on Sundays or in the evenings with fresh rumors and local news flashes. When Max wasn't working, he was attending committee meetings, serving on boards, donating free time he didn't really have to local charitable causes. Gradually, as we came to know them, members of the civic league, directors of boards and trustee-ships, lawyers for conservation foundations found their way to our house, where they sat around having informal forums. Neighbors strolled in, pretending to need to borrow sugar, really curious about all the activity, and stayed to argue against a tax increase or to flirt with one of Max's reporters. Friends dropped their children off while they raced to the grocery store or the gynecologist to see if they were pregnant again, or arrived full of indignant energy about the latest stupid decision by the board of selectmen. Soon every-one stopped in all the time, casually, unannounced.

We could afford to buy our house because it had been the home of an elderly couple whose children didn't want to deal with the legacy of a house marked by benign neglect: brittle venetian blinds, worn rugs, rusty appliances, faded drapes. Their children just wanted to get rid of it and get the money; we bought it as is. With a lot of elbow grease and the help of our friends, Max and I scoured and painted all the rooms. I washed the windows and put up the fine old cream linen drapes that had been languishing in my parents' attic. As we worked, I looked out the windows at all the beautiful flowers and thought how old Mrs. McIntyre must have hoarded her money and her energy to buy and tend the iris, tulips, daffodils, rhododendron she lavished around this backyard. She must have made it through the long winters in her dark house by anticipating spring.

We ran out of time and money before we could replace the former owner's old wall-to-wall carpet; it still spread over the living and dining rooms, a shaggy olive green expanse that seemed to absorb small objects as well as dirt; it gave us the illusion of being outside. This provided an odd sense of freedom. I certainly didn't care if the thing got soiled or stained; we planned to have it ripped out as soon as we could afford it. I shampooed it thoroughly, then simply felt grateful that it never showed any sign of grime or wear, and our friends felt totally relaxed when their children spilled drinks or their infants had a moment of projectile vomiting.

We were all so young then, and our children were young, and crawling or toddling. I had all the sharp edges of the fireplace and the coffee table cushioned with bubble wrap and tape. In the warm weather I kept a pitcher of strawberry daiquiris in the refrigerator and boxes of popsicles in the freezer. In the winter I made Irish coffee laced heavily with liquor and topped with whipped cream with which I also embellished the hot chocolate for the children. The adults sat on the floor and sipped their drinks while their children munched animal crackers and apple slices. Friends changed their babies' diapers while discussing whether to get up a petition, then rushed off, late for dinner, leaving their children's soiled diapers curled like cauliflowers growing from the green carpet. Children cried when their bits of He-men or Barbies disappeared in the oceanic rug, and I handed them Lifesavers to quench the tears. We discussed everything: political candidates, a runaway dog, divorces, affairs, gothic baby-sitters, abortions, crucial dinner parties, babies, disastrous haircuts, diets, failure to be given tenure, elation over a promotion. We complained and wept and laughed and cursed about it all.

It's odd, but those were amazingly sexy days. At least I thought so, *felt* so. Perhaps it was because of all the children I held and nurtured, passing their heavy, flushed bodies back and forth so that my arms touched the arms of other daddies as I bent close enough to breathe and smell and feel the heat of another man's warm, ever so slightly boozy breath. Perhaps it was because being parents of young children brought out the beast in us. Our most extreme emotions boiled just beneath our skin: adoration and vigilance and fierce possessiveness. I had to be alert all the time, so all of my senses were turned up to their fullest capacity, and I couldn't modulate my senses or censor them. One moment I'd experience a hot flash of panic when a child fell off a chair or shut her fingers in a door, and then someone's husband would walk in the door and flash me a smile, or someone's daddy stood just a little too close to me as I warmed a bottle for him at the stove, and lust would drench me, leave me weak.

LATE ONE FROSTY December night during our first year in Sussex, when Max was asleep, I slipped from our bed, pulled on a robe, and went quietly through the dark house to the kitchen. I made a mug of herbal tea and carried it with me for the companionship and warmth.

I didn't want to sit in the living room where the Christmas tree would incline my thoughts toward duties. I checked on Margaret, who was sleeping soundly, and went whisper-footed up into the attic.

Does every woman at some point in her life wander through the sleeping house, looking in at her husband and children, and wonder what she's doing here, in this particular life?

I think so. I think we all carry the girl we once were within us, and from time to time we need to commune with her, our early self. We need to find a quiet spot where no one can see or intrude, and just as we used to giggle with our best friend behind a closed bedroom door, we sit down with the girl we once were and laugh and exclaim: Can you *believe* all this? A house, a husband, a child, a microwave, and you're not even thirty! I thought you'd be in Afghanistan, teaching English and having a hot affair with a Mongol.

Perhaps I'm more restless than others. The best way I can account for this is the Zodiac. I'm a Gemini. The Twins. I have two equal sides, in my case, the domestic and the wild. And in my life I had two equal role models, my mother, the consummate homemaker, and my mother's sister, Aunt Grace, who left me her Nantucket house. The two sisters came in the middle of a family of five children with not enough money or space; they hated the rush and tussle of their home and longed for life with subtlety, fluency, and silence.

Hope, my mother, married my father, several years older and already established as a statistician in a large insurance company. Mother ran her home like a top, keeping every faucet clean, each fuse reliable. She became a capable, much-sought-after committeewoman, sitting on boards for charities, libraries, and hospitals, and she gave cocktail parties and birthday parties and elaborate dinners with a zest and flair that came from genuine pleasure. My mother loved her life, adored my father and me, and found the quotidian tasks of daily life absolutely delightful. She was a rare woman, and I've often regretted that I wasn't blessed with more of her qualities. When my father retired in his early sixties, my parents moved to Arizona, where they play golf and tennis and hike; my mother is on the board of the local opera, library, and historical museum.

Aunt Grace looked like my mother (and I look like both of them), with flyaway blonde hair and green eyes. Like my mother, Grace had a rare gift for appreciating life, but she took a completely different route than my mother. Grace got a Ph.D. and became a professor of English literature at a small women's college. She never married. She travelled every summer, usually to England, sometimes with a man, sometimes with a woman, sometimes alone. She was a raving feminist, and her greatest desire was to write a book about Dorothy Wordsworth. Perhaps not surprisingly, Grace and my mother were closer to each other than to their brothers, my uncles, who spread to all the corners of the map and seldom appeared in our Connecticut home. Grace and my mother wrote each other often, and then phoned each other weekly, and I loved it when Grace came to visit. Mother and Grace would sequester themselves on the screened porch with glasses of tea and cigarettes, and laughter would curl through the afternoon like their cigarette smoke.

Mother didn't like to leave Daddy, so it was Aunt Grace who took me on trips, every summer from the age I was nine. Two weeks: first, to national parks in the United States. Later, when I entered my teens, to France and Italy and England and British Columbia. Aunt Grace supplied me with the novels and poetry of each region and gave me mini lectures about them every night over dinner. She was an enthralling speaker, partly because she had no qualms about discussing the sexual episodes in the books which my mother would have ignored.

When my aunt was in her fifties, she bought the large old Victorian house on Nantucket, planning to retire there and write. Every August my parents and I stayed with her for two weeks. My mother did all the cooking and cleaning – she wanted to, she enjoyed it, and she made no secret of her opinion of what Grace considered a decent meal. Grace spent most of the day in her study, working on her books. My father taught me to sail, and on Sundays all four of us would get into Grace's old Jeep and bounce out to Great Point for a picnic.

It was a fortunate childhood, I know. And it was a gesture beyond benevolence when Grace left her Nantucket house to me. In a way it made sense: Her brothers and their children, her other nieces and nephews, had seldom visited her there. But she could have left the house as part of her estate; it could have been sold and the profits equally divided. No, Aunt Grace meant something by leaving me the house, and I wanted to honor that, not simply by taking my own family to summer on Nantucket, but by paying attention to the part of my soul that had been nurtured by my aunt, and to the yearnings and questionings and dissatisfactions and hungers in my soul that came, that had to have come, from genes I shared with Grace.

. . .

IN THE MIDDLE of that December night as I sat in the attic, it seemed I was accompanied by the spirits of the young girl I once was, and by my Aunt Grace. What would they think of my life? Would they be disappointed in how domestic it was, how ordinary? Was I disappointed? By twenty-six I had gone through labor and through a terrifying spell when my husband was so depressed he hadn't talked to me for eight days. If I had not become heroic, at least I had become brave.

The unfamiliar crossings of the shadows in the attic pleased me. It was a safe landscape, demanding nothing, yet somehow mysteriously electric, alive. I thought about the McIntyres who had lived in the house before us. I imagined the ancient, secret routines of mice or sparrows in the eaves, making nests, making babies, feeling in their feathers, fur, and pin-narrow veins the dawn or an approaching storm long before we humans heard about it on The Weather Channel. For a moment I was not Lucy West, mother and wife, part-time journalist for the local newspaper, concerned citizen. For a moment I was a young woman, still capable of doing anything at all.

In the silence of the attic I realized what I needed: a friend to talk this over with, a real friend, who wouldn't be shocked or censorious, who would laugh with me, who would make me laugh. I'd met plenty of nice women and smart women, interesting ones, but with none of them had there been that *click* that happens when you meet someone who thinks the way you do.

'That's what I want for Christmas, Aunt Grace,' I said aloud into the night. I saluted her with my mug, then went back down the stairs to my bed.

·   ·   ·

IN MAY THE Little Red Schoolhouse held an open house for all prospective parents and children. Max and I had decided that we wanted Margaret to start preschool that fall. She was three, and she was an active, sociable, curious child who loved to be with people. If she attended preschool every morning, that would free me up to write more articles for the newspaper, which would help Max, provide me with a bit of pocket money, and give me a chance to write.

Twenty mothers and four fathers arrived for the open house, all with their three-year-olds, some also carrying infants and toddlers in packs on their backs. We listened to the introductory spiel from the head, Anita Walton, and to the brief but glowing testimonials from preschool parents, which were not really necessary, since through the casual town grapevine we knew that this was the best preschool in the area.

The exterior of the Little Red Schoolhouse was a cheery barny kind of color, but it had never been a schoolhouse; it was just a normal ranch house with a large fenced backyard full of playground equipment and its living room, dining room, kitchen, and bedrooms turned into the Main Room, the Quiet Room where children napped, the Table Room where they had snacks and engaged in finger-painting or modeling with clay, and the Story-Telling Room.

Several assistant teachers supervised the children as they explored the Main Room and its toys while the parents talked with the head teacher and with one another as they sipped a punch that tasted suspiciously like Kool-Aid and nibbled on homemade cookies. I'd lived in the town for almost a year, and I knew many of the parents, so it was a comfortable morning for me. I was having a good time, and gregarious Margaret was with her friend Amy Granger, near the doll cradles. I wore twill slacks and a blue cotton sweater. Most of the parents wore similar clothes, comfortable, washable garb.

But one woman stood out, and I surreptitiously studied her. Tall, thin, blonde, she lounged against the wall in a pale violet linen sheath, looking as if without the wall she'd fall right on over with boredom.

'Who is that?' I whispered to Sandy Granger.

'Kate Cunningham. Isn't she gorgeous?'

'She looks like a model.'

'She *is* a model. For Smith and Smith. You must have seen her in their catalogues.'

'I *say*,' I murmured, affecting a British accent. Smith and Smith was a revered women's New England clothing store specializing in a certain kind of just slightly dowdy old money look. Their models wore pearls with their simple white shirts and plaid golf slacks. Their heels were never over two inches high, their hems never above the knee. They were always posed against the brick walls of Ivy League colleges or the masts of sailboats with a yacht club launch in the background.

'Her husband's a lawyer with Masterbrook, Gillet, and Stearns.'

'Perfect.' Masterbrook, Gillet, and Stearns was the oldest, stuffiest, most elite group of lawyers in Boston.

'They just bought the Seldon farm,' Sandy continued, naming the most expensive property in Sussex county, one hundred acres with pond, horse barn, hills covered with maple sugar trees, and a two-hundred-year-old farmhouse that it was rumored Paul Revere had slept in.

'Wow. Is she nice?'

'I have no idea. I've never met her. Whoops.' Sandy was off

like a shot to referee in a tussle of little boys.

All around us women were exchanging inventive recipes to make vegetables palatable to their children or comparing pediatricians. Out of the corner of my eye I saw elephantine, competitive, hyperactive Jiffer Curtis barreling toward me, no doubt to tell me that her daughter had just learned to recite the alphabet in four different languages. I turned and made my way through the miniature chairs, tables, and people to the window supporting Kate Cunningham.

'Hi. I'm Lucy West. My daughter, Margaret, is over there.' I pointed to the spot where Margaret was gathered with a gaggle of little girls.

'Kate Cunningham. My son, Matthew, is over in the corner, trying to decide whether to eat the modeling clay or stick it in his ears.'

Sure enough, there was a boy with white-blond hair and his mother's fair skin, standing all by himself, facing the wall, intensely scrutinizing the wads of clay he held tightly in each fist.

'My husband and I try to tell ourselves that Matthew has a *scientific* nature,' Kate Cunningham continued. 'We reassure ourselves that he really is capable of socialization, that he'll learn at some point to talk to other children, that someday he'll have friends and get married and not grow up to be some misanthropic insectologist living in an apartment with twelve thousand jars of bugs.'

I looked over at my daughter, who had Lulu, her own doll, in one arm while with the other she sorted through a pile of baby dolls, discussing their prospective merits with several other little girls. 'Max and I worry that Margaret will get pregnant at twelve and have a baby every year.'

'I'd rather have the bugs,' Kate said in a low, husky,

conspiratorial voice, and we both laughed. 'Do you have any other children?'

'No.'

'Just no? Not "not yet"?'

I leaned closer to Kate, drawn to her intensity, to her lack of pretense.

'I don't know. We weren't quite ready when we had Margaret. I mean, we'd just gotten married, we had no money, we hadn't gotten our marriage established, really. I'm sure we'll want other children, but not yet. In the meantime, I spend too much time feeling *guilty* for turning Margaret into the dreaded Spoiled Only Child, but I don't want to have another child just because of guilt.'

'Oh, *guilt*.' Kate sighed. 'It's *exhausting*, isn't it? Jesus, when Matthew was two weeks old, I had to cut his fingernails. Well, I accidentally sliced into his fingertip! He turned *purple* screaming! I felt so guilty I nearly went down and stuck my own hand down the garbage disposal in penance.'

'Oh, God. I know.' A kind of demented laughter swept through me. Emotions welled up inside me, surprising me; I hadn't realized how much I had been tamping down.

Kate went on. 'Now we've bought this farm so he can have a puppy and fresh air and I'm sick with guilt because he doesn't have any neighbor children to play with. *It doesn't fucking end.*'

I nodded. 'I know. They never told us this before we got pregnant, did they?'

Other mothers were collecting their broods now; it was time to leave. Children whined and resisted as their mothers attempted to lead them out the door. One woman tried to detach her son from a toy race car; he squirmed and fussed then burst into a full-scale rage. Anita Walton and her assistants were gathering up paper cups and napkins.

I said, 'I wonder, since you mentioned the farm . . . my husband is the editor of *The Sussex Gazette*. I'd love to do an article on your farm. What it was like before, what you're planning to do with it now.'

Kate Cunningham looked at me, and a shield dropped down over her face. 'I don't think so.'

Oh, no, I thought. She thinks I came over to speak to her because I want to do an article on her. To use her.

Then I thought: And she's right. That was one of the reasons I came over. That, and because I was escaping Jiffer Curtis.

I hadn't suspected that I might like her, that I might feel something in common with her.

'Look,' I said, desperately, 'would you like to come over for coffee sometime? You could bring Matthew. He could play with Margaret. They could look for bugs in the backyard.'

Kate shrugged again. 'Perhaps.' She headed off toward her son.

I wanted to weep. This was the most interesting woman I'd met since I'd moved to Sussex, the first woman I'd felt that private instantaneous *click* of connection with, and I'd insulted her.

'You asshole,' I muttered to myself.

'Did you say something?' Anita Walton asked pertly.

'I said I have to go,' I responded snappily, and crossed the room to take my daughter's chubby hand.

THAT NIGHT, IN bed, I told Max about my encounter with Kate Cunningham. We were lying facing each other, heads on pillows, in the dark. We could talk like this for hours, knowing we ought to go to sleep, but wanting to confide just one more thing. The bed was the core of our relationship: we made love here, I had nursed our daughter here, here we plotted how the newspaper would approach the town's gossip, politics, and business. Sometimes I felt like our bedroom was the warm center of all of Sussex.

'I liked her so much, and I'm afraid I offended her.'

'It's common knowledge that the Cunninghams bought the most historic property in town. It's not offensive to want to write about it. Maybe she's just a bitch.'

'No, Max,' I insisted. I didn't know why, but I wanted my husband to like Kate Cunningham, or at least not dislike her. 'I think it was that she thought I approached her under false colors. Trying to be her friend, and then suddenly becoming press. Intrusive.'

'I wouldn't worry about it,' Max said, yawning. 'Anyway, they're going to begin renovations on the Congregational Church. That can be our historical focus this week.'

I lay awake long after Max's breathing had deepened. I envied my husband's ability to fall instantly into sleep. I always had to wrestle myself out of consciousness, and often the sound of his easy, profound slumber would make me so frenzied with envy that I'd have to stumble from the bed clutching my pillow to collapse on the living room sofa, where I'd twist and turn, trying to get comfortable, suddenly waking to a new morning.

JUNE 1998

THE CHILDREN HAVE only one more week of school, so we have only one more week of these crazy mornings when we're all in the kitchen bumping into one another as we get ready to rush off into our day. Jeremy's cough has disappeared; he's eating well and he's full of energy. I'm busy with the complicated work of French-braiding Margaret's hair while Max stands at the counter, fixing Jeremy's lunch.

'Dad,' Jeremy moans. 'You put apple slices in. I don't want apple slices!'

'Apples are good for you, buddy. You like apples.' Max uses his most cajoling voice.

'Not at lunch I don't like apples! Not slices! They get all brown and yucky! I want apple cookies!'

From under the table comes a wet retching noise.

'Gross, Mom,' Margaret says, announcing the obvious. 'Midnight barfed again.'

'Midnight barfed!' Jeremy echoes, giggling.

Max is a master conciliator, at home as well as at work. 'Jeremy, I tell you what. I'll put apple cookies in if you'll promise to try one apple slice, okay?'

'Okay . . .' Jeremy drags out the word to express his reluctance.

'*Voila, ma belle*. Your *coiffure* eez *parfait*.' I kiss the top of Margaret's head lightly and turn to pour myself another cup of coffee.

Margaret asks, 'Can a cat have an eating disorder?'

'The limo leaves in five minutes, kids,' Max tells them.

The phone rings. Margaret dives for it, answers, hands it to me.

Kate's voice is bright. 'So, are we still on for today?'

I turn my back to my family. My voice is low and even. 'Kate. Don't do this.'

'Great! I'll come to your house and then we'll go to the community center to register.'

'Kate. Come on.'

'Mom!' Jeremy yells. 'I can't find my baseball cards.'

'Kate, I've got to get the kids off to school.'

'Right, I'll pick you up,' Kate chirps. 'About one, okay? You're a doll. See you!'

I hang up the phone and tell Jeremy, 'Your baseball cards are in their albums. You put them there last night, remember?'

'Oh, yeah!' Jeremy grins and streaks from the room.

'Are you okay for driving Jeremy to T-ball after school?' Max asks, coming out of his study with his briefcase in one hand and a sheaf of faxes in the other.

'You bet.' Without warning, my stomach sends up a huge bubble of fear. My heart races. I'm going to faint.

Margaret asks, 'Mom, did you sign my permission slip for the museum trip?'

'It's on the refrigerator. Pig magnet.' My lips are cold. My fingertips are icy, too. A band tightens around my chest.

Grabbing some paper towels, I kneel beneath the table and concentrate on breathing.

'Mommy, what are you doing?' Jeremy asks.

'Cleaning up Midnight's breakfast.'

My family talks and moves as if on the other side of a looking glass. On the other side of the universe.

I think: I'm having an aneurysm. At the same time I notice with an eerie sense of responsible calm that I hadn't spotted all the marinara sauce Jeremy spilled last night; the back leg of his chair is streaked and sticky.

Margaret's legs plant themselves near my vision. On this sunny June day she wears a loose long-sleeved button-down shirt of her father's, baggy jeans, and heavy black Doc Martens. 'Can I ask Jenny to spend the night Friday?'

'Sure.' My heart slows down. Like a tide, the pressure in my chest and head slowly but definitely recedes. My breath comes more easily. 'As long as you both understand you've got to practise piano Friday afternoon.'

'I know.' Margaret sighs. It's *her* choice to take piano lessons and to perform in the summer concert, but recently Margaret is putting distance between us, making me responsible for anything slightly unpleasant in her life.

I rise carefully, not wanting to upset my equilibrium. I toss out the cat puke, wash my hands, smack kisses onto my children's foreheads.

'Come on, guys.' Max bends down to kiss me goodbye, then herds our children out the door to the car.

I stand in the familiar messy kitchen, as exhausted as if I've just returned from outer space.

Grabbing up the phone, I punch the speed dial button for Kate's number.

'*We're sorry we can't come to the phone right now . . .*'

I slam the phone down.

Immediately it rings. I snatch it up. 'Kate?'

'Sorry, no, it's Jared Falconer. Is that you, Lucy?' His voice is deep and rumbly.

I stand frozen like a deer caught in the headlights. 'Oh. Hello!'

'I was wondering if you've had time to think about our offer.'

'Jared, honestly, I haven't. I haven't even mentioned it to Max yet. With school ending and everything . . .'

'I don't want to rush you. Take your time. We wouldn't expect you to start until September.'

'That's good. That's helpful.'

'Would you like to come in and meet some of the staff?'

'Perhaps later . . .'

'Good. Just give me a call. Nice talking to you, Lucy.'

I stare into space, biting my lips, drumming my nails on the counter, then give myself a shake. I pour my cup of coffee down the drain, make some herbal tea, and go out the back door.

Sighing, I collapse onto a lawn chair. The sun beats steadily down. Bees buzz among the iris. I hear morning doves. Mourning doves? It's a haunting, yearning sound.

Our backyard, now that I take the time to really look at it, could use some TLC. Its uses have changed so rapidly over the years, filled first with sandbox and plastic wading pool, then the playhouse Max built for Margaret, and now the badminton net and croquet wicks for Margaret and her friends and soccer and soft balls for Jeremy. I haven't really done any gardening here, and all at once I'm swept through with a wash of gratitude for the house's former owner, Mrs. McIntyre, who planted all the perennials that splash the yard with color.

We did transplant one of Mrs. McIntyre's rose bushes, which a neighbor's fast-growing holly tree had put in the shade. I knew little about plants then (I know little now), but I must have done something right, for after it was transplanted, the leaves dried and the bush looked dead, and then, that same summer, new leaves sprouted, an entire new stem, tender and juicy, off the tough, gnarled, woody base.

Other than that, we never paid attention to the backyard because about the time we bought this house, Aunt Grace died, leaving me her grand old Victorian on Nantucket. Over the years we rented out the Nantucket house in June and July and September, using the rent money to pay for taxes and necessary repairs, saving the month of August for ourselves and, later, the Cunninghams. So when I think of summer, of outdoors, of sunshine and fresh air and respite from all the pressures of daily life, I think of Nantucket, not this backyard.

In many ways I am more myself in Nantucket than here. Or at least a different kind of self. Freer. More sensual. Less constrained. Certainly I have acted that way.

Here I sense a kind of watching, a kind of *awareness* in all the windows of all the houses around me. I have no privacy in this backyard. I have no privacy in this town, really. Always within me is a deep urge, a little gem of discontent, a desire to do something different, something wild . . . what? Dance naked in the moonlight? Well, perhaps. Is my yearning for a little recklessness related to that queer little attack I just had? Is one part of me, subconsciously aware that I'm terminally ill, telling another part of me to gather my rosebuds while I may?

Whatever I want to gather, I can't do it here, where the neighbors might see. I love Sussex. I love it that our children know the police chief, the postman, and ancient Evangeline Champion, the town eccentric who wanders the streets in the formal gowns she wore to college dances sixty years ago. Margaret and Jeremy drink delicious water from the town reservoir and eat fruit and vegetables fresh from the nearby organic gardens. They can walk to a friend's house safely; they can ride bikes through the town. I rarely begrudge the newspaper or any of the town committees we're on the time that we spend there.

But I do feel a certain obligation to be a responsible citizen in every way, and sometimes I resent that. As I grow older, that sense of responsibility seems to fit me better, much like a large dress I've been wearing for years and am at last growing into.

And secretly I find that alarming. I wear L. L. Bean and outlet Gap, but in the closet of my private life lurks a tight black miniskirt, the secret uniform of at least one true part of my soul. And only Kate Cunningham knows.

It's funny, but if I had to say whom I'm closer to, who knows me better, I'd have a hard time choosing between my husband and my best friend.

Oh, of course I'd say Max. We've been married fifteen years, since college. He's seen me in sexual extremes and in labor and having a tantrum in an old bathrobe. We have two children.

But Kate's seen a hidden side of me, a side Max doesn't know. The wild side of me. It always has been Kate who has egged me on to enjoy whatever little bit of wickedness I've got left in this aging old responsible body. Of course, I've returned the favor.

But neither Kate nor Max knows everything about me. I have some pretty serious secrets from them both. I haven't

talked with Kate about the job offer. She'll go gaga, she'll
insist that I take it. And whether I do or don't take the job,
she'll understand. In many ways she understands me more
than Max does. But how long can I continue to lie for her?
Is a secret the same as a lie?

SUMMER 1987

THAT FIRST YEAR in Sussex, Max nearly lived at the newspaper. I understood. And I was content, feathering my nest, raising my chick, writing obits or articles when Max needed me to, yet having plenty of time to dote on my darling daughter.

Still I was eager for warm weather. I wanted to feel the sun on my shoulders while Margaret and I planted flowers around the house. So it was a drag when the first week of June came grizzling in all cold and rainy. Margaret developed a gluey head cold that made her fussy and clingy. She whined all day, wanting me to hold her, carry her, read to her, and then pushing me away when I tried to wipe the green mucus that bubbled out of her chapped nose. Her silky dark curls became damp and matted. Patches of red bloomed on her cheeks. She fought me terribly when I tried to take her temperature, even though I tried to make it into a game. Outside the rain drizzled down the windows while the wind battered and whipped the tender new leaves of trees and flowers. I think I read *The Cat in the Hat* forty-seven times that week. I slopped around in jeans, moccasins, and sweatshirts, tissues tucked in every pocket, singing nonsense songs to cheer Margaret as I fixed dinner with her riding my hip like a baby monkey.

By Friday night, Margaret's cold abated. Saturday the sun came out, the temperature shot up, and Margaret's body was once again inhabited by her real self, a happy, busy, independent little girl.

That spring Max had agreed to be umpire for the Boys' and Girls' Club's minor league, two teams of nine-to twelve-year-old boys who played every Tuesday and Saturday afternoon. I thought it would be fun for Margaret to watch her father; I thought it would be bliss simply to get out of the house. I put on a flowered summer dress and put Margaret in a yellow playsuit. She in turn dressed Betsy, this week's favored doll, in yellow, too.

'Okay, Sunshine, let's hit the road!' I said to Margaret.

'Okay, Sunshine, let's hit the road!' Margaret said to Betsy.

I buckled her into the car seat and sang 'Take Me out to the Ballgame' all the way to the school playground.

The roads leading to the playing fields were lined with cars. I parked, unbuckled and lifted my sweet-smelling child from her car seat. Now she squirmed and refused to be carried, insisting on walking, each of us holding one of Betsy's tiny hard plastic hands. As we neared the metal bleachers, my heart lifted at the sight of the broad green fields spreading beneath the cloudless blue sky.

'See Daddy?' I exclaimed, pointing. 'He's standing behind the catcher, there, by the fence.'

'See Daddy?' Margaret asked her doll. 'Wave to Daddy, Betsy.'

I knew everyone there, at least by name. Some of the men were in T-shirts and jeans. Many had come directly from work and stood rolling up their shirt sleeves and undoing their ties while they watched. Some of the women wore short-shorts already; others, not able to believe that the cool weather had finally ended, were in jeans and sweatshirts. I felt light and feminine in my flowered dress; the chance to don it was probably the true reason I'd come out to the ball game. I was yearning for flowers, loose fabrics, the sun on bare skin. But I'd been a good mother; I'd rubbed my daughter's chubby limbs with sunblock, and dabbed some on her little pink nose.

'Margaret!' Amy, one of my daughter's play group friends, spotted her, raced toward us, and led her off toward a group of little girls.

I joined Amy's mother. 'I intended for this to be a chance for Margaret to see her daddy in action.'

Sandy Granger smiled. 'And I thought Amy would want to cheer for Tom.' She nodded toward her nine-year-old son, playing shortstop for the Yankees. 'She does have occasional spurts of enthusiasm. Whenever the crowd applauds, she yells "Go, Tom!" whether he's on the playing field or not.'

I laughed. 'They're probably too young. We won't stay long, but it's nice to get out in the sunshine.'

Amy had brought a blanket which she spread beneath the bleachers. She and Margaret and two other little girls settled there, whispering busily. I sat down on a bleacher and leaned my elbows on my knees. Max wore a chest guard and a face mask. He didn't see me; his concentration on the game was total. I liked the authority of his decisions, the way he bellowed when he yelled 'Ball!' or 'Stee-rike!'

The pitcher was good, throwing more strikes than I thought a kid his age was capable of, and the batters who were struck out did commendable jobs of controlling their

quivering chins and teary eyes. All the little boys were so cute
in their uniforms, the Red Sox in red, the Yankees in blue.
Some of the boys were all knees and elbows while the older
boys were beginning to acquire paddings of prepubescent
fat. The bat boy was the cutest, perhaps only seven years old,
and not much bigger than the bat.

'Come on, Mikey! You can do it, Mikey!' The mother
next to me screamed so much her voice was hoarse. 'I can't
help it,' she told me. 'He struck out in the last inning when
the bases were loaded. If he doesn't get one hit in this game
he'll be one miserable little son of a gun.'

The sun fell like a blessing on my face, the sky was blue
and infinitely high, the air fresh and fragrant with the smell
of new-mown grass. In the further field, a mixed-sex soccer
game was in process. The players were college age, all of them
tall, lean, and already tanned. As I watched one young
woman in a red shirt and very short shorts swivel and dart
between two young men, I found myself wondering how she
could do it. How she could concentrate on the game. I
would have been paralyzed by sensual sensations. I was nearly
paralyzed by sensual sensations now, a married mother
watching children play ball. It was warmth of the day, the
fragrance of the grass . . . it was the proximity of the other
men, all heights and sizes, watching with their arms folded or
lounging back on the bleachers, suddenly yelling, 'All right!'
I loved men, I thought, and it suddenly hit me that I'd like
to sleep with them all

Just then Matthew Cunningham streaked past the bleachers, his mother in hot pursuit. Kate grabbed her son up,
seized the popsicle someone else had discarded from his
hand, dumped it in the trash, then came toward me. She
wore another simple linen sheath, this time in lime green,

and her blonde hair was tied back with a green ribbon. She wore sandals. Her toenails were painted the same color as her perfectly shaped fingernails. The polish matched her lipstick.

'The boy down the road plays on the Yankees,' she said, bouncing Matthew on her hip and wiping his face with a tissue from her pocket. 'Matthew adores Gary. I *thought* he'd be fascinated to watch Gary play.'

I laughed. 'My husband's an umpire. I thought Margaret would like to see him, and look where she is.' I pointed to the shady area beneath the bleachers where Margaret and Amy were exchanging their dolls' clothes.

'Which one is your husband?'

I pointed. 'At home plate.'

At that moment someone called time out and Max lifted off his face mask and wiped the sweat off his face. His hat had mashed his black curls down around his head.

'He's cute,' Kate said.

'Yes, I guess he is. He looks even better when he's not covered with sweat.'

'Oh, I kind of like them that way,' Kate said, and before I could respond, Matthew squirmed. She set him down, he raced off, she followed.

I watched the game. The pitcher caught a line drive by simply lifting his hand in the air. Then he had two strikes on the next batter, a boy so thin he looked like he was made from coat hangers, when the thin boy whacked the ball so hard it flew over the heads of the outfield and into the soccer game. There were two runners on base; the thin boy hit a home run; everyone screamed and jumped up and down until the bleachers shook. The pitcher struck the next batter out and ended the inning, but damage had been done. The Yankees were behind. This was good training for real life, I thought; this would teach kids all sorts of things: team spirit, self-control.

The pitcher raced off the field, his mouth clenched, looking ready to cry.

'Wally.'

I turned to watch as a young man about twenty approached the wire fence near the wooden dugout.

'Come here. I want to talk to you.' The young man's voice was low but husky and strong. He wore jeans and a white T-shirt. His shoulders were wide, his stomach flat, his thighs long and thick.

He must have been the pitcher's older brother. The pitcher took off his cap and I could see that they both had thick sandy hair and handsome, wide, all-American faces. The brothers faced each other through the fence.

The older brother hooked his hands into the wire. His arms were muscular and the blond hair on them glittered in the sunlight. 'Don't let it get you down. It happens to everyone.'

'I sucked, Dan,' Wally said.

'Yeah, you did, but just for a few seconds. The rest of the game you've been brilliant.' Dan squatted to get on a more even level with his younger brother. 'Remember what the coach said about concentration. Forget what happened. Focus on right now.'

When had Max last worn jeans? I couldn't remember. It was cords or flannel in the cold weather and khakis in hot. What was it about jeans that was so sexy? Dan, brother of Pitching Wally, was oblivious of the way his jeans outlined the sleek thick curve of his thighs and the tidy bulging packet at his crotch.

What would it be like to spend an afternoon alone with

him? To run my cool palms against the hot length of his back? To lift his T-shirt and see the sun catch fire in the twists of hair on his chest and belly and groin? Embarrassed, I forced myself to look away from the young man.

As if pulled there by her own magnetism, my gaze landed on Kate's face. She was smiling at me, a smile full of mischief and insolence. She wiggled her eyebrows and glanced over at Pitching Wally's sexy brother, then glanced back at me and nodded. She knew exactly what I was thinking. She was thinking it, too. I laughed out loud, and for a few more seconds I felt free of my responsible, reliable, good-citizen persona. It was like lifting off the earth, like being weightless, like breathing an atmosphere made of the driest champagne. It was a little bit like falling in love.

A FEW DAYS after the baseball game, Kate called to invite Margaret and me to their farm.

'Wear old clothes,' she told me. 'And warn your little girl that we've got an overaffectionate puppy.'

Wear old clothes, Kate had said, and we were going to the country, and it was a hot summer day. Still, the memory of Kate and her cool perfection in her linen sheaths intimidated me. While Margaret napped after lunch, I tried on just about every item of clothing I owned, trying to find something that would look casual but chic. I settled on a pair of khaki shorts and a white linen shirt. When Margaret woke, I persuaded her to wear a pretty polka dot sundress and multi-colored sandals.

The Seldon farm – now the Cunningham farm – was tucked away on a hill to the south of the town of Sussex. I took a narrow two-lane road which angled off Route 169 and turned right at a vacant and dilapidated general store and gas station onto an even narrower road deeply rutted and bordered so thickly by trees and brush that we were suddenly enclosed in a dark green tunnel.

'Mommy, the trees are trying to touch each other,' Margaret told me, and she was right. The wild tangle of growth on either side of the road brushed the roof of our car and made scraping sounds against the sides.

'Daddy won't be pleased if the paint's scratched,' I muttered. I was just slightly unnerved by the solitary road.

Then we went around a bend and the whole world seemed to open up before us. The brush was gone. Neat fences enclosed sweeping pastures and fields, and up on the right, a majestic brick house stood, lilacs and roses and mock orange and morning glories embroidering its trellises.

Kate was waiting outside, holding the leash of an exuberant golden lab pup. Her blonde hair was pulled back in a ponytail; she wore shorts and a tube top. Her exposed midriff was as sleek, smooth, and flawlessly slim as a Barbie doll's.

I stopped the car in the gravel circle drive and helped Margaret undo her seat belt and jump out. She and the puppy were almost the same height, and Margaret stepped back, behind the protection of my legs, and peeked out at the dog, who whimpered eagerly and wriggled all over.

Kate squatted down to my daughter's level, keeping one arm tightly wrapped around the fat creamy pup.

'Hello, there. You must be Margaret. I'm Kate. And this is Sugar. She won't bite, but she likes to jump up on people.'

Margaret smiled but stayed behind my leg.

I bent to pet Sugar. 'Hello, you sweet thing.'

Sugar quivered and whimpered.

'Margaret? Try petting her.'

Kate held the puppy tight while Margaret stepped forward, stretched out a chubby hand, and touched the dog's ear. Sugar extended her neck and licked Margaret's face with a long pink tongue.

'Oooh.' Margaret giggled. 'She likes me!'

'I'm going to let her off the leash,' Kate said. 'If she jumps up on you, just say "down" in your meanest voice, okay?'

'Okay.' Margaret kept hold of my hand. 'Where's your little boy?'

Kate's brows drew together, but she said brightly, 'We're playing hide and seek. Want to help me find him?'

'Okay,' Margaret said.

'Let's go in the house,' Kate suggested. She led the way, around to the back of the house where a door led into a low-ceilinged, dark kitchen. The windows were small, the walls white plaster and dark beams. 'This is the oldest part of the house,' she told me. 'These four rooms were built in the eighteenth century.'

A round claw-footed table held a blue and white vase of pink peonies. A pine dry sink was set with bottles of whiskey and vodka and gin as well as several exquisite cut-glass decanters; a pine corner cupboard held what looked very much like Spode china.

'Beautiful fireplaces,' I murmured, stunned. There were more valuable antiques in the kitchen than in my entire home.

'This used to be the borning room,' Kate continued, leading us on. 'This is supposed to be the room where Paul Revere slept one night.' She indicated a small plaque set in the wall. 'The former owners put it there; we didn't. I don't know whether to keep it or not.' Her eyes darted around the room, as if she were looking for something out of place, and her movements were brusque. 'Matthew, honey!' she called suddenly, then sharply turned and left the room. I followed. Her shoulders were rigid with tension.

The front of the house was Georgian, with high ceilings, long windows, and deep sofas. The rugs were thick Persians. Great porcelain vases holding ferns and other greenery had been set in the fireplaces.

Kate dropped to her knees by a sofa and lifted the dust ruffle. 'Matthew?' When she rose, her face was pinched. 'Let's go upstairs. He might be in his bedroom.'

'Wow,' Margaret said when we entered the ultimate little boy's bedroom. It was an enormous room, with sunlight streaming through the long windows onto the thick carpet. Two walls of shelves held books and every conceivable toy. A small desk was laid with pads of paper and crayons. Trucks and cars and trains were scattered across the floor.

Kate crossed the room and opened first one closet door and then the other. 'All right,' she said to herself. 'All right.' To me, she said, 'You can come into my bedroom if you want, on the condition that you tell no one about the mess it's in.'

'I promise.' I grinned and followed her across the hall, expecting to find more perfection.

The room, a mirror image of Matthew's, was large and sunny, with a marble fireplace and elaborate brocade draperies and a massive four-poster bed. Yet I immediately felt at home in it: Clothes were scattered over the chaise longue and the bench at the end of the bed, books were piled on the bedside table, and the bureaus and dressing table were cluttered with every kind of cosmetic imaginable. The woman who inhabited this room was a woman I could like.

Once again Kate knelt. She looked under her bed, then

rose in a fluid movement, dashed to her closets, and yanked open the doors.

She looked at me. 'The little shit. Excuse me.'

'Who?'

'Matthew. Come on. We've got to find him.'

Margaret was still in Matthew's room, slowly picking up each toy and studying it with the awe of an anthropologist scrutinizing ancient treasure, before returning it to its place and moving on to another toy.

'We're going outside now,' Kate said. 'You can come back here later. I promise.'

Something in Kate's voice was so harsh, in spite of her glittering smile, that Margaret looked scared and guilty. Quickly she came to me and took my hand.

Kate led us down the back stairs. There, in the kitchen, sat Matthew, out in the open on the fireplace hearth, picking at a scab on his knee, his strawberry-blond hair glimmering in the light, his head tucked to one side, as if he were deep in thought. He looked up at his mother, his face wary.

Kate crossed the room in three strides, grabbed Matthew by the shoulders, and yanked him up.

'Where have you been? Don't you *ever* do that to me again, do you hear me?'

Matthew raised his chin defiantly and glared at his mother, who suddenly folded him against her in a bear hug and began to weep.

'Matthew, why do you do this? You know how it scares Mommy when you hide. I told you you could stay in your room today when our guests came. I told you you didn't have to see them if you didn't want to. I thought we had a pact. Didn't we have a pact? Didn't we?'

She held her son away from her so that she could see his

face, but Matthew kept his expression stony and he would not speak.

'What am I going to do with you?' Kate said with anguish in her voice.

Mother and son glared at one another, deadlocked.

'Sugar made weewee on the floor,' Margaret said into the silence.

Kate let go of her son and actually pulled at her hair with both hands. 'I can't stand this,' she said to the ceiling. 'I just can't stand this.'

But Matthew was looking at Margaret. 'Is weewee pee?' he asked.

'What's pee?' Margaret replied.

Matthew walked over to the corner of the kitchen where Sugar stood, tail blithely waving, pink tongue lolling from her mouth, next to a puddle of urine. 'That,' Matthew said pointing.

'That's weewee,' Margaret said.

'That's pee,' Matthew said.

'So weewee is pee,' Margaret giggled.

'Pee is weewee!' Matthew crowed, laughing hysterically.

'Peewee!' Margaret chortled.

Kate's eyes met mine. She smiled. 'Want some popsicles, kids?'

'Yes!' they both answered.

'Want alcohol, Mom?' Kate asked me. 'I know I do. It's almost four o'clock. That's late enough for me.'

Something light, I said. Kate opened a bottle of sparkling wine. She put a triangle of brie and some wheat crackers on a cheese board and carried them outside. We sat in wicker lawn chairs and watched Margaret and Matthew roam from the jungle gym to the swing set to the sandbox. The puppy beat a path between the children and us, enticed by the smell of the cheese until all at once she collapsed next to Kate, nibbled on her tail, curled up, and slept.

Kate asked, 'Did Jiffer Curtis phone you? About joining the committee for the fund-raiser for the Little Red Schoolhouse?'

I paused. Jiffer Curtis was enormous and enormously wealthy. She sat on all the important boards and terrorized people into generosity. On the other hand, she was dictatorial, paranoid, and mean-spirited. No one had warned me about her when I came to town, and I'd come away from all associations with her humiliated and exhausted.

I took a deep breath. 'I'd steer clear of Jiffer Curtis if I were you. She's an effective fund-raiser, because she terrorizes people into giving her money. She's a Valkyrie, and if you get on the wrong side of her, you'll regret it, and it's easy to get on the wrong side. And if you tell anyone what I've just told you, I'll deny it.'

Kate threw back her head and laughed, and all at once she seemed younger. 'Town politics. Ugh.'

'It's not all bad.'

'Okay, what boards *should* I join?'

I considered. 'Anything run by Sandy Granger. She's rational and organized.'

'Sandy Granger. She was at the preschool open house, wasn't she? The one who looks like a chipmunk?'

I laughed. I hadn't thought of it before, but Sandy did look like a chipmunk. Matthew ran over to us.

'Can we have another popsicle? Please?'

'No.' Kate was definite. 'Absolutely not.'

The little boy stared at his mother, quivering like the needle on a lie detector, gauging the strength of her response.

'All right.' He sighed dramatically, slumping off. A moment later he and Margaret were giggling.

'I know you think I spoil him,' Kate said. She hadn't combed her hair after pulling on it and it stuck out all over, only part of it still sleeked back in a ponytail.

'I wasn't thinking that.'

'I know he has too many toys. But there are no other kids out here except for Gary Gordon. He's nice but he's nine years old and a mile away. I *do* spoil Matthew. Whenever I have to work, I always bring him a really good present. It was a good plan in theory. I thought he'd connect getting a toy with having a baby-sitter, and eventually he'd become accustomed to being left with sitters. Eventually he'd look forward to it and be glad when I left. But it hasn't worked out that way at all.'

'Margaret operates differently. She doesn't hide. She doesn't even make a fuss. What she does do, when I lean down to kiss her good-bye, she pats my face sweetly and whispers, "Mommy's so pretty. Pretty Mommy, stay with baby Margaret."'

'Ooh, clever girl.'

Matthew and Margaret sat on the edge of the sandbox, heads bent together, discussing something quite seriously. They began to make paths in the sand. We watched them for a while.

'*That's* the way it ought to be, all the time,' Kate said.

'I'll drink to that.' We clinked glasses and sipped our wine.

We sat in silence, enjoying the golden afternoon, the peaceful sounds of happy children.

Then Kate asked, 'Did you ever think you'd end up like this? And so young?'

'What do you mean?'

'I mean married. Monogamous. Spending most of your waking hours doing exactly what your mother used to do. Housework. Groceries. Obsessed with a little child's every breath and movement.'

'I guess I am surprised to find myself so settled, so young. I think about it a lot. I imagine where I'd be if I hadn't gotten married. If I'd gone on to grad school.'

'Parallel lives. Dream lives.'

'Right. But I wouldn't change it. I wouldn't give up what I have.'

'No. Nor would I. Still. And it's not the professional stuff that I yearn for. I can always do that, no matter how old I get. It's the stuff that happens only when you're young and nubile.'

I just glanced at her. We were verging onto hazardous grounds.

'I mean,' she continued, 'when I think of that beautiful boy we saw at the baseball game. The one who was being so nice to his younger brother?'

I grinned. 'I remember.'

'Didn't you just want to run your hands over that beautiful body? Press up against him? Lick the sweat off his shoulders?'

I laughed, shocked, and uncomfortably thrilled. I closed my eyes and remembered the man. His muscles. His white T-shirt. 'I wanted to kneel before him and put my hands on his thighs and unzip his jeans.'

'Yeah,' Kate said.

'I can't believe I said that.'

'Why not? It's what everyone thinks. All the time. You know your husband lusts after other women.'

'I guess.'

'All men do. All women do.'

'So how do we manage to stay faithful?'

'Fantasies, I guess. That's what they say. Use the fantasies. How many men have you slept with?'

I shifted in my chair. Took a sip of wine. Her question threw me. 'Well.' This was a little bit like going too far too fast on a first date. 'Probably too many.'

'I've slept with too few.'

'What's too few?'

'Two. My high school boyfriend and Chip.'

'Too late now.'

'You think?'

'You're married. You have a child. And how would you feel if Chip had an affair?'

'He doesn't need to. He's slept with hundreds of women.'

'He is handsome.'

'Don't I know it.'

'Is he a good lover?'

'Define good lover.'

'Well . . . he takes his time. Focuses on you.'

'That's bullshit. All that therapeutic stuff. It's not the thought that counts with me. It's that electrical *zap*. Pure body chemistry. And the excitement of the new.'

'Mommy!' Suddenly Margaret was stumbling toward me, wailing. 'Sand in my eyes! Ow!'

I lifted my daughter into my arms. 'Let's go in the kitchen and wash your eyes out.' Glancing at Kate, I said: 'To be continued!'

Margaret fussed and writhed as I washed out her eyes, then clung to me like a monkey, burrowing her head into my chest. She was tired. She'd had an exciting afternoon.

'Time to go home,' I told her.

'No, Mommy, please. Just five more minutes,' Margaret wailed, while Matthew stood with his arms folded, his lower lips stuck out and his face stormy.

'We'll come back,' I told my daughter. 'And Matthew, we want you to come visit us. Soon.'

As I was buckling Margaret into her car seat, Kate asked, 'Do you still want to do a story on this place for the newspaper?'

'I'd love to,' I answered honestly.

'Okay, then. Let's fix a date.'

'Could I bring a photographer?'

'Sure.'

'Sometime next week?'

'All right. I want to get the cleaning lady in here first.'

I laughed. 'Yes, really,' I said, 'I believe I saw a dust mote on your escritoire.'

Kate didn't laugh. 'Believe me, if the wives of the lawyers Chip works with spy an unplumped pillow in any public photograph of our home, I'll hear about it.'

'God, how awful,' I said.

'Just part of the joys of being part of Masterbrook, Gillet, and Stearns,' Kate said.

'Well, you can stop in at our house any time for an antidote,' I told her. I drove away, singing a nonsense song to Margaret.

JULY 1998

EACH MONTH HAS its familiar routines; on the first Monday in July, I'm alone in the peace of my house. I've driven the children to Camp Arbor, where Margaret is a counselor and Jeremy is, as Margaret was, a camper, a member of the Birch tribe. Max is at the newspaper. Midnight has eaten and vomited and eaten again, and both he and Cinnamon are asleep in the middle of our queen-sized bed after a hard night prowling around outside beneath a July moon. I'm waiting for Stan Cutler, the handsome twenty-five-year-old computer whiz with whom I run a desktop publishing business called Write?/Right. We create newsletters for nonprofit groups, brochures for the local health spa and the local counseling center, advertisements for the Lowenski Farm and Greenhouse, the Little Red Schoolhouse, Amelia's Catering Service. And now we have the retirement home brochure, and I'm delighted. Max should be, too. In just four years Margaret will be in college; we've got to find a way to pay the tuition.

I often wonder what it would be like to work in a real office, in the company of a large staff, instead of in a converted downstairs bedroom in the midst of the mess of my home. I'd feel more professional, I'm sure, because I wouldn't have Jeremy's kindergarten artwork or the family grocery lists mixed in with my business papers. But with a room of my own in the heart of my home, I can wander out to do the laundry while I mull over a project, and I can get to the kitchen as often as I'd like. Most important, I'm here at home if a child gets sick.

Stan and I are working on a big glossy pamphlet about Sunset Estates, the local retirement home. It's a challenge to make wizened arthritic old geezers with catheter bags in wheelchairs look and sound as if they're in the prime of their lives, and in fact we've decided not to take that approach, which is, after all, false. Misleading. We're trying to convince the owners of the home to let us present the facts straight out and clear: This is a facility where your beloved aging relative will be gently lifted and turned by strong and cheerful employees several times a day to prevent bedsores. This place is not a first-class hotel, it is a first-class nursing home. It is clean. The employees are kind. The patient will not recover enough to tango across the dance floor of a cruise ship with a newly discovered passion for life, but he will be attended to each day with such care that he will be in as much comfort as possible.

'Lucy?' Stan bangs on the door, then enters without waiting for me to answer. Short and slight, with horn-rimmed glasses, a goatee, silver studs in his tongue, lip, and nose, rings in his ears, Stan wouldn't frighten any little old ladies on a strange street at night. He can't help it; he projects an aura of preoccupied benevolence. Stan is kind, and also brilliant, and I've never been with him when I didn't have the sense that most of his amazing mental energies were currently engaged somewhere in a sphere I knew nothing about. When he has time, Stan is writing a sci-fi novel. He is always reading one.

'Sorry I'm late. I was talking a friend through a computer glitch.'

He's wearing a paisley shirt and extraordinarily baggy jeans; his entire body could fit in one leg. He treads easily past the laundry baskets which have made it only as far as the downstairs hall, past a doorknob hung with a pink cotton sweater of mine which Margaret tried and rejected on her way out the door. Around a set of matchbox racing cars Jeremy sent streaking down the hall this morning.

'Have you had breakfast?' I always know the answer to this question. Stan scarcely can remember that eating is a daily human function necessary to power his brain.

Stan stops. He considers. 'Ummmm.'

'I've get you a bowl of fresh fruit and some muffins.'

There are two chairs in my study: a swivel typing chair for me and a wooden desk chair which Stan has perched on. I set a tray in front of him, on top of various file folders on the table, then sit down behind my desk.

'Thanks.' Stan takes a few bites of fruit. 'Lucy—'

'So,' I begin. 'I've been looking at your photos of Sunset Estates—'

'Wait.' Stan swallows, clears his throat. 'Something else first. You know all this fuss about the Lamb property?'

'Of course I know all about it.'

How could I not? It has consumed our town for the past few weeks. When Horace Lamb died a few months ago, he left eighty acres of prime property to the town, which in turn was offered a healthy sum for it by the CDA Development Corporation, who wants to build a 300,000 square foot office complex there. That plan is opposed by the conservation groups in town, who want the town to sell it to them to be used as a nature sanctuary.

Max's editorials on the issue have been in favor of the developers, a rare stance for him. He argues that the construction and maintenance of this complex will provide jobs for the people who really need the work, and will eventually make it possible for more people to live here in Sussex without having to drive for hours into Boston each day. The land is not particularly beautiful; no endangered species live there; part of it is swampy, buggy, a breeding place for mosquitoes. His opinions have caused some of his enemies to become more friendly, and some of his friends to feel betrayed.

Stan says: 'Guess who one of the major shareholders in CDA is.'

'Tell me.'

'Paul Richardson.'

This is a blow. 'I don't believe you.'

'Believe me.'

'How did you find out?'

'It's not that hard. Let me show you.'

Stan comes around behind my desk, bends over, taps some keys, accesses the Net, taps some more. His fingers are so long and flexible I almost believe the human body secretly, all through the millennia, has been developing genes to link us with computers. The monitor goes blue, green, yellow and green, as different sites emerge and dissolve. The CDA Corporation is owned by Marco Gilotto, Henry Frick, the GenSen Corp., and Fairfields Co. More tapping and a new display appears on the screen: Fairfields Company is owned by Ann and Paul Richardson and by Eva and Peter Richardson.

'Fuck,' I say.

'Right.' He draws his fingers through his goatee, leaving a furrow. 'I'm sorry.'

'No, we need to know. I'm glad you found out. Look, I'd better call Max right now.'

I dial the paper and chat a few seconds with Melanie, Max's current secretary. Then Max comes on and I give him the news.

'Let me talk to Stan.'

I'm glad to hand the phone to Stan. What will Max do now? He'll have to review his position. Does he really believe a new office complex will serve the best needs of the Sussex community, or was he lured into this opinion during his weekly phone conversations with Paul? Has Paul told Max that he has a financial interest in seeing the land developed? If he hasn't, Max is going to feel betrayed, he's going to be furious. He's going to feel like all kinds of a fool.

'The Net,' Stan says.

What matters most to me right now is not the public property, but the private state of the mind and soul of my husband.

'Fairfields,' Stan says.

And if anything could pull the rug out from under him, it is this, that the man whom he has admired above all others, the man whom Max thought was his comrade in serving the community, the man whom Max has looked upon as a mentor and model, has been using Max to serve his own financial greed.

I'd always known Max would be constantly engaged in controversy. That's the stuff newspapers thrive on. Max loves a good fight.

'You bet.' Stan hangs up.

But now Max will blame himself for not doing more homework, for not finding out himself that Paul Richardson is connected with the CDA Corporation. And whether he confronts Paul or not, Max will doubt his alliance with Paul from now on. He'll have to be less trusting. He's always known that Paul is manipulative, but I don't think he suspected ever before that he was one of Paul's pawns.

Stan and I work on the brochure for a couple of hours. He's the graphic artist and I'm the writer, but we've gotten pretty good at critiquing each other's work. We scrutinize photos, go over the copy one more time for redundancies.

'By George, I think we've got it,' I say after a while. 'Do you want to run it by Mrs. Mackey?'

'You do it. She likes you better.'

'All right.' I look at my calendar. 'I'll call and set up an appointment with her tomorrow. Then I'm giving it all to you, right?' I put my arms behind my head and give my back a good stretch. It's a little after noon. We drift out of my study. 'Want some iced tea?'

'Sure. So you guys leave for Nantucket August first?'

'Absolutely. We've had our ferry reservations since January.'

In the kitchen I take down two tall narrow glasses, fill them with ice, take a pitcher from the refrigerator. The ice cracks and snaps as the amber liquid surrounds it.

'What about the posters for the church fair?'

'You don't need me for that.' I hand him a glass. 'I've got fresh mint in the backyard.'

We step outside. I'm surprised at how dense the heat is. Stan sits on the back step. I pick some mint, murmuring, 'Thank you, Mrs. McIntyre,' rinse the pungent green leaves under the outside faucet, slip them into our glasses, then settle down next to Stan. I'm wearing a T-shirt and shorts and I stretch out my legs in the sun.

'Aren't you hot in those jeans?'

'No. They're really cool, I mean temperature-wise. Sort of like a protective bell of air.'

I doubt this. Stan is just less aware of things like heat and cold. And wouldn't all that metal on his face attract the heat?

'Has Ciara found a job?'

'Yeah, out in the Berkshires. She's threatening to go there.'

'Unless?'

'Unless we get engaged or something.' He sounds dismal, a doomed man.

'Max and I got married at twenty-three.'

'Yeah, well, it's all right for some people.'

'Honestly, Stan! Ciara's a beautiful, intelligent, wonderful young woman. She's got a great sense of humor and she adores you.'

'It just seems like it would be *The End*.'

'Well, it would be, of part of your life. But it would be *The Beginning* of a new phase of life.'

'I like things the way they are.'

'Don't you want children?'

'God, not yet.' He sips his tea. 'I'm having too much fun. I'm just barely an adult.' He sighs. 'You probably always wanted kids.'

'I did. But Max did, too, Stan. It's not just a woman's thing. Max loves his kids.'

'I know he's a great father. Coaching sports and all that stuff. I just don't think I could do it. Would want to do it.'

'Hey, there are all kinds of fathers. You wouldn't have to coach sports. But you could play awesome computer games with your children.'

Stan thinks about this. 'Maybe so. Kids have faster reflexes than adults.'

'Think how smart any child of yours and Ciara's would be,' I say, and then my heart explodes in my chest. It's like a bomb going off. It knocks against my ribcage so loudly I'm sure Stan can hear it. The blue sky, the hot day, the green grass, Stan's baggy denims all seem to contract and recede into a kind of halo around me.

My iced tea lies on the ground, a curling worm of spilled liquid staining the grass a darker green, the ice cubes glittering in the sunlight. My hands push against my chest. I'm trying to squeeze air out, I'm trying to hold my heart in.

'Lucy?'

Stan's face looms up close to mine.

'Can't breathe,' I say.

'I'll call an ambulance.'

'No!' I grab his arm. 'Just sit here with me.' His arm is pleasantly unfamiliar to my palm, longer and wider than my children's, narrower than my husband's, and furry, almost gorillalike.

'Your hand is freezing,' Stan says.

'I was holding a glass of iced tea,' I reply reasonably, and my heart slows and the rhythm of my breath becomes more regular. I take my hand from Stan's arm. 'I'm okay now.'

'What happened?'

Bending over, I pick up my glass. 'I don't know. I couldn't catch my breath. Maybe I'm allergic to something. Developing asthma.'

'You'd better see a doctor.'

'I probably just need lunch.'

'It's not a normal response to stop breathing because

you're hungry,' Stan points out.

He follows me into the kitchen and leans against the wall, watching me tear lettuce and rinse it. 'Want some salad?' I ask. 'And I've got some great rolls.'

'You just fed me.'

'Several hours ago.'

'Thanks, but I've gotta go.'

I open a can of tuna, then bend over to squeeze the water into the cats' dishes. Instantly Midnight and Cinnamon race into the room, their tails high, bristling with self-importance. 'I'll call you tomorrow, after I talk to Mrs. Mackey.'

'Right.' Stan heads off down the front hall, then comes back into the kitchen. 'Lucy.'

'Yes?' I'm shaking a glass jar of salad dressing.

'You know Max is going to be okay about this CDA thing, don't you?'

I'm surprised, touched, and slightly on guard.

'Of course I know that. Max deals with knottier problems than this every day. It's just part of his job.'

Stan holds up his hands as if in surrender. 'Hey. Me friend.'

'I know that, Stan. And I'm grateful.'

'It's just that I think maybe you had an anxiety attack. Outside. On the steps. When you dropped your tea.'

I hesitate before answering, considering his suggestion. 'Maybe.'

'You can look up information about anxiety attacks on the Net,' Stan says. 'They're not unusual, you know.'

'You're sweet,' I tell Stan, which I know is the perfect thing to make him cringe. It reminds him that he's younger than me, that I'm more capable. I have a husband. I have children. 'And I will check into it if it happens again.'

'Cool.' He turns to go.

'Stan. Jared Falconer has offered me a job.'

Stan turns back. 'Wow. You going to take it?'

'I don't know. I've got the summer to decide. I, um, I haven't told Max yet.'

'Why not?'

'Well, you know. I mean, the salary's absurdly high.'

'Max seems strong enough to deal with that.'

'And everything would change.'

'Everything changes all the time anyway.'

'Yeah, you're one to talk.'

'You'd have to commute.'

'I know.'

'I'd have to get a new partner.'

'I know.' I look at Stan. 'What do you think I should do?'

'Man, I don't know. You better talk to Max.'

'You're right. I will.' And I will, but I don't know when.

SUMMER 1987

BY THE TIME Margaret was three, I felt like a complicated, accomplished adult. Being pulled in two directions by a husband and baby seemed right for the Gemini I was, calling forth from me qualities of competence and ingenuity I'd never known I had. I could rock a baby in one arm and write an obit with the other. I could talk on the phone to the high school superintendent while changing a diaper. I could appear as a sweet, storybook mother when I kissed my little girl goodnight, then morph into a sex goddess as I walked into my bedroom. I could speak effectively for the environment at a town meeting, then go home to color princess paper dolls on the floor with my daughter. Suddenly I had so many roles to play that I felt like a small-town TV station that just got cable.

Yet I was . . . I won't say *bored*. I wasn't bored. But part of me, the girl in me, was not satisfied. Kate was a god-send to me with her sarcasm and trenchant remarks and good honest lust. That we had children of the same age who actually liked to play with one another seemed like a good omen for the future.

It would be far too much to hope for that our husbands would like one another. I toyed with the idea of inviting the Cunninghams over for a casual dinner; Max could barbecue swordfish, I could serve my mother's lemon cream pie, Matthew and Margaret could play in the yard. But when I met Chip Cunningham at a cocktail party, I ditched the idea fast. If Kate looked like a model, her husband looked like an effing god. Tall, blond, slim, and handsome, he had the floppy blond hair and narrow patrician face of old Boston money. Just looking at him made me feel short, impoverished, and tongue-tied. He was three years older than I was, too, *over thirty*, which at the time made him seem much more sophisticated and mature.

It didn't help that he was so reserved. Kate had told me that this characteristic of his drove her crazy; it was the major source of all their arguments.

'I'm so glad to meet you at last. Kate talks about you all the time. Well, she would, wouldn't she, she's your wife,' I babbled when we shook hands.

'I'm glad to meet you,' he replied calmly.

'Margaret loves playing with Matthew.'

'Yes, Matthew's quite smitten with your daughter.'

Max was at the drinks table, getting a vodka tonic for me; I wished I could take a huge inhibition-loosening gulp of it right now. Kate was talking with Andrea Cobb.

'Kate tells me you're a lawyer.'

He nodded. His gaze was kind but intense.

'Do you get to do exciting things? Will I see you on television?'

'I'm not that kind of a lawyer.'

I waited for him to expand on this information. He didn't. He was so unbelievably handsome. As if in defense, my mind sent every lawyer/shark joke I knew spinning through my head.

Desperately I said, 'I've seen your farm. It's really beautiful.'

'Yes, we were fortunate to get it.'

He didn't look bored or contemptuous; in fact, he seemed quite kind. He just was so *quiet*.

'Kate tells me you'll be buying some horses.'

'Probably.'

Max arrived then, and I nearly flung myself upon him in relief. 'Max, this is Chip Cunningham, Kate's husband.'

They shook hands and muttered a few polite things about Matthew and Margaret.

'Your property abuts the Jenkinses, doesn't it?' Max asked.

Chip nodded. 'Right.'

I watched carefully as I slugged back my drink. I truly hoped these two wouldn't hate each other. Max was as handsome as Chip, but he was *shorter*, and at the moment it seemed like a liability.

Max said, 'I heard that old man Jenkins is getting ready to sell.'

'Really. Do you know how much land he's got?'

Max wrinkled his brow, considering. 'I'm pretty sure it's over a hundred acres.'

Chip squinted, as if he could see the land lying out before him. 'I wonder how it lies. How much of it fronts the road. And you know, I think the stream that runs through our property begins on his land.'

'Have you met the Jenkinses?'

'Just the wife. She brought us a homemade pie when we moved in. Seems very nice. I've been so busy at the office that I haven't had time to be neighborly.'

Max nodded sympathetically. 'Abner Jenkins told me I could take a walk through his land sometime. Want to go with me?'

'God, that would be great. I really don't want to buy any more land, but I would like to see what it's like, and of course I'm concerned about who buys it. I'd like to see the countryside remain country up there. It would be a crying shame if someone tried to develop it.'

The two men launched into a conversation about development around Sussex. I stood dumbfounded, and utterly infatuated with my husband. He was wonderful. He was irresistible. He could make anyone talk.

I glanced over at Kate, who was listening to Olivia Carlton gab about the church fair. Kate nodded toward our two husbands and gave me a thumbs-up sign. Another miracle had occurred.

THAT SUMMER WAS Max's first year at the paper, and he didn't want to spend much time away from it, no matter how often I reminded him that he needed a vacation. This was complicated by the fact that Max had an irrational, deep-rooted, powerful fear of flying. He'd been on planes only twice in his life, and each time was such an excruciating experience that he vowed he'd never fly again. Because of this, he had to take the two-and-a-half-hour ferry trip to the island instead of the fifteen-minute flight on the little commuter planes. That, added to the two-hour drive from Sussex, meant over four hours of traveling each way. I couldn't blame him for not coming every weekend.

So I invited Kate and Matthew to spend a couple of weeks with Margaret and me on Nantucket, in Aunt Grace's house.

She jumped at the chance. Our husbands would try to come down for a week at the end of the month.

ON A STEAMY Monday in August, Kate and I drove down together in my Volvo station wagon. It was just a little over a two-hour ride, but Matthew and Margaret were keyed up, impatient, and whiny. It seemed we stopped every fifteen minutes to use the bathroom. During the ferry ride they were still wired, wanting to race each other around the open decks and up and down the stairs, wanting to pet every dog they saw, wanting to do everything but sit still.

'What were we thinking?' Kate said to me. We decided to divide up, taking the children to opposite ends of the boat.

Once we got to the island, we still had chores to discharge before we could relax. Kate went off to the grocery store while I made the beds and opened up the house. The children weren't hungry; they'd filled up on pizza, hot dogs, and pretzels on the ride over. We had a makeshift dinner of cheese and crackers with our blissfully cool vodka tonics while the children played like demented aliens in the backyard, and the alcohol must have warped our thinking because at bedtime, when Margaret and Matthew pleaded to sleep in the same room, we agreed. An hour later, we separated our exhausted and overstimulated children, settled their fretful little bodies in their own bedrooms, staying with them, singing lullabies, until they fell asleep.

It was almost eleven o'clock when we finally collapsed downstairs on Aunt Grace's deep chintz-covered sofa.

'It can't be like this all summer,' Kate sighed.

'The first day is always hard.'

'I've always dreamed of spending a summer on Nantucket.

I never imagined it like this.'

'You weren't imagining it with a three-year-old.'

'I wonder if I'll ever feel young and wild and free again.'

'I don't believe that's in the job description of mother-hood.'

'Well, I can't stand it. I'm not kidding, Lucy! I can't stand it!'

I thought a moment, then said, 'I think I have an idea.'

KATE AND I schlepped our cooler, beach umbrella, beach bags, and two children away from Jetties Beach, over the sand and the narrow boardwalk toward the parking lot. We'd spent almost six hours by the water and everyone was stoned from too much sun. We'd tried to give the children a rest by insisting they lie on the blanket for a while, but they hadn't slept. They'd amused each other by making fart noises with their mouths. Now they were cranky. We adults weren't exactly vivacious.

I drove; Kate supervised the kids from the front seat. Matthew didn't want to wear his seat belt; it pressed on his sunburn.

'Keep it buckled,' Kate insisted.

'Noooo,' Matthew whined, twisting and kicking the back of my seat.

'I've got sand in my bum crack!' Margaret wailed.

'Bum crack!' Matthew echoed, then laughed maniacally.

Back at the house, we dumped everything in the front hall then rushed off to our separate bathrooms. Margaret and I stepped into the shower, pulling the glass door shut, enclos-ing us in a blissfully slick white world, a technological man-made miracle, less dazzling, more snug than the seaside. As the cool water sluiced down over us, we peeled off our sticky swimsuits, exposing skin as shockingly white and ultranaked as worms under rocks. Specks of sand trickled down around our feet. We'd both been wearing bikinis, and now we were as striped as zebras.

'Mommy has bo-bo hair!' Margaret sang out, pointing at my crotch.

'And Margaret will have hair there, too, when she's a big girl,' I told her. 'Now close your eyes. I'm going to wash your hair.'

'My head hair.'

'Your head hair.'

The creamy muffins of Margaret's bottom broke into goosebumps when I began to massage the shampoo into her scalp. I adjusted the water temperature. Steam rose around us. The baby shampoo foamed in my hands like the froth that had laced the shore.

'Now you wash Betsy,' I told my daughter, and she did, as I shampooed my own hair.

When our tanned skin was squeaky, free of the grit of sand, I turned off the water, pulled on a toweling robe, and wrapped my little girl in a towel.

'Oh, don't we feel all healthy and clean!' I hugged her. She smelled fresh, as if all her pores exuded sunlight. I combed her hair. Her scalp was paler than her forehead. I dressed her in shorts and shirt, and she lay on my bed, dressing her doll while I pulled on shorts and a jersey.

Kate was already in the kitchen, chopping vegetables. In the three days we'd been here, we'd been virtuous, eating enormous fresh salads and giving the children tortellini and thin slices of chicken.

'What can I do?' I asked. I liked it that Kate felt so at home in my Nantucket house. It was one of the things that drew me to her, how easily she could take charge – or let me have it.

'Milk for M & M,' she said. 'Their macaroni and cheese is heating.'

An outraged squeal came from the living room. Our children got along as well together as we did, but even the best child gets tired, and we had tried our best to tire these two today.

'All right, you go first,' Matthew snapped.

They were playing an ersatz version of Candyland. We let them play until we heard the petulance edging their voices. Then we herded them into the kitchen and fed them. We took them to their separate bedrooms and read them stories and kissed them and tucked them into the soft clouds of their beds. We turned on the night-lights, turned off the overhead lights and went out into the hall, leaving the doors open slightly.

Then I changed clothes and went off to get the baby-sitter.

THIS WAS TO be our antidote to too much adult responsibility: an evening touring the local bars.

We showed Sadie, the baby-sitter, where the children were, and the food, and the emergency phone numbers. We promised we'd be home by midnight. We hurried out to the car.

I drove.

Kate said, 'I'll bet this will be the only Volvo station wagon in the parking lot.'

'I'm sure.' Already I felt more relaxed. It was just after nine and the air was soft and dark and inviting, like the pelt of a purring cat.

We went to the Muse, a bar outside of town on the Surfside Road. They had live music on weekend nights and tonight there was a local group performing.

We parked between a classic red Impala convertible and a Jeep Wrangler. We stood in line to pay the cover charge, squeezed between a clutch of already drunk college boys and two couples with mousse-backcombed hair (men as well as women), and gold chains around their necks and wrists (men as well as women).

'I don't know about this,' Kate whispered.

But when we stepped inside, our spirits rose. The good hard beat of rock music pounded through the room. The dance floor was jammed and so was the bar. The faces of hundreds of males of all sizes and ages stirred in the shadows.

Kate, taller than I and more aggressive, cut a path through the crowd to the bar. I followed.

'Two margaritas, ice, salt,' she yelled at the bartender.

The air of the room was redolent with a complicated and entirely grown-up funk of tanned skin, alcohol, aftershave, and cigarettes. I sipped my drink; it tasted sweet and smoky. Kate squeezed and slid through the crowd to the edge of the dance floor. The drum beat was like a primitive pulse, irresistible.

We watched the band: five guys in jeans and torn T-shirts. The lead singer's dark hair hung in wet hanks around his face. His chin and cheekbones were so sharp they could have cut paper.

'Love this!' Kate shouted at me, her words torn away in a thunder of music.

'Me, too!' I was downing my drink awfully fast, trying to

hit my inhibitions with a knockout punch of alcohol.

Everyone on the dance floor looked young to me, and cool and glamorous and carefree. I was twenty-seven, and I felt ancient. The dancers looked buoyant; I was a wife and mother, weighted down for life.

Then a male body blocked my view of the dancers. A big guy, under thirty, with a lobster-red face and sun-bleached hair and brows leaned close to me. He yelled something at me. My first reaction, pathetically enough, was confusion. It took me a moment to understand that this stranger wanted me to dance with him. For a moment I teetered on the edge of rectitude, sobriety, propriety. Then Kate hit me between my shoulder blades and knocked me into the present.

'Get out there!' she yelled. 'Give me your glass!'

I slugged back the last of my margarita, handed Kate the glass, and followed Lobster Guy onto the dance floor. For a few moments I only swayed and shuffled timidly, but my partner was one of those men who, although blocky and chunky and solid, seemed to connect, batterylike, right up to the music. He beat his hands as if he had invisible drums in front of him and shook his head and muttered and shouted out 'All right!' He was demented. What did I care what he thought of me? I dropped my defenses and let the music flood in, churning my blood.

I looked over at Kate and grinned. And realized with a jolt of totally immature satisfaction that someone had asked *me* to dance first.

Not long after that I saw Kate being led to the center of the mob by a tall and really cute guy. I waved and grinned at her, then dove back into the electric frenzy of music.

Lobster Guy was inexhaustible. I danced for hours, until my hair and shirt and underwear were soaking wet and clingy. Sweat slid down my neck and into my bra as softly as kisses. How long had it been since I'd danced like this, been free like this, at once totally myself and also part of the music? No little hands tugged at me. No proper matrons were watching me. No one here needed me, and it was like being young again, when I could dance all through the dark night and step out into a morning as crystal-dewed and new as Eden.

Now at twenty-seven I was responsible for that world. Sometimes it felt like I was responsible for the very turning of the sun. Most of all I was responsible for the health and safety and happiness of my daughter, and that was overwhelming. Here it was all heat and beat and freedom.

It was twenty after twelve when I looked at my watch. Across from me Kate tilted her pelvis toward her partner in what looked like a Zulu mating ritual. Her hair had come totally loose from its clasp and hung in wet limp strands around her flushed face.

'We have to go home,' I yelled at her. 'Baby-sitter.'

'No!' she shouted.

'Yes!' I took her hand and dragged her off the dance floor.

'Not fair, not fair!' she yelled at me, stumbling against me. The fresh air outside hit us like a slap in the face.

'Oh, God,' Kate groaned. 'I feel like Cinderella.'

'You're going to feel like Frankenstein's monster in the morning.'

We fell into the Volvo. I drove home at a virtuous twenty miles an hour. With great earnest sobriety I paid the baby-sitter and drove her home. When I got back to the house, I found Kate passed out on the sofa. I smiled, covered her with a light blanket, and let her sleep.

JULY 1998

'You look cool, Mom,' Margaret says. She's lying on our bed, watching me dress for a posh summer cocktail party.

'Thanks, kid.' I'm wearing tight black slacks, black high heels, a sleeveless turquoise linen shirt.

'And I like your hair like that.'

Now I'm suspicious. My hair looks like it always does in the summer, a curly unruly mess. 'So you're all set for tonight?' When Margaret baby-sits Jeremy, we pay her the going rate; in return she has to pretend he's not her little brother.

'Yeah.' She hears a car door slam and looks out the window. 'Dad's home.' She wriggles off the bed, busies herself with smoothing out the light cotton quilt we use for a summer spread. 'You know, Mom, Jeremy's watched *The Little Mermaid* about a hundred times.'

'So?' I'm carefully lining my eyes.

'So it's kind of not fair. There's a really good movie on HBO I'm going to miss so Jeremy can watch his dumb old video.'

'You're baby-sitting.'

'I know. But still . . . why can't we have two TVs in the house? Everyone else does.'

'Listen, kid, sometimes I think one set is too many.'

'Mom.'

Max rushes into the room. He looks hot and tired and miserable. 'Give me a minute to shower and change.'

'You'd better shave.'

'Not enough time.'

'You look a little rough.'

Margaret protests, 'Mom, he looks great like that. Urban chic.'

Max slams the door on our discussion, shutting himself in the bathroom. 'Hello to you, too, Dad,' Margaret says sulkily to the closed door. Since Stan told Max about Paul Richardson's involvement in the CDA corporation a few days ago, Max has been gloomy, taciturn with me, uncommunicative with Margaret and Jeremy. I can deal with his bad spells, but I hate it that he's beginning to let them affect the way he treats his children.

Downstairs I kiss Jeremy, go over the rules for the thousandth time with him and Margaret, and then Max comes down the stairs, handsome in his navy blue blazer, his black curls glistening from the shower.

'Have fun, Dad!' Jeremy cries.

I can see the effort it takes Max to make his way through his dark self-absorption to answer, 'Thanks, son. Be good.'

As we ride together to the Curtis's home, I ask, 'Are you okay, Max?'

He sighs. 'Don't start.'

'Max, you're beginning to take it out on the children.'

'I've got a lot on my mind. That's reality. They have to learn that.'

'Is there anything other than the CDA business troubling you?'

He makes a kind of snorting noise. 'Does there need to be?'

'Have you talked to Paul about it?'

Max turns on the radio, plays with the dial, finds a talk show.

'Max.' I reach over and touch his hand. 'Don't shut me out.'

He moves his hand away from mine and turns up the volume on the radio.

JIFFER CURTIS, OUR hostess, has opened her house and her expansive, elaborate garden, as a fund-raiser for the hospital. Young men dressed in white button-down shirts and khakis stand at the front door of her mansion, waiting to park our cars. Max chats to them all; we know these boys; Max coached them years ago in Little League.

As we walk around the side of the vast brick house, the sky turns dark and ominous with clouds, and a breeze begins to stir. I stand for a moment, just taking in the view: The garden is a masterpiece, formal, tended, with high and low hedges making little rooms here and there, and clever topiary standing like statues near the fish pond and the gazebo and the teahouse. Everyone in town is here, looking gorgeous. I love this town.

Max doesn't stop but heads straight for the drinks table. By the time I make it through the crowd I see that our hostess has cornered him.

'I don't see,' she trumpets furiously, 'why you don't do more with your editorials to support the hospital.'

'Jiffer. There are seventy-three nonprofit organizations in Sussex alone,' Max points out reasonably. 'I have to be fair.'

'But surely the hospital is the most important!'

'And that's why I'm so glad they have you to head their fund-raiser,' Max says, smiling. He takes her arm and leans toward her as he continues to speak in his charming, rational way.

Why can he do this? I wonder, watching him. Why can he summon up so much energy for his fucking newspaper and community, and so little for his own family?

A breeze sweeps past. I shiver. One fat drop of rain plops down on my nose.

'What a bother!' Jiffer exclaims, glaring at the sky. 'I'd better tell the caterers to move things inside.' She waddles officiously away.

Max and I join the throngs pouring into the enormous house and make our way through the 'library' where a television set the size of a twin bed reigns supreme, to the billiard room.

Chip and Kate are here talking to John Galware, the dentist, and his wife, who've just returned from two weeks touring along French canals. With one smooth, elegant turn, Chip cuts me out of the group so that we're standing face-to-face, his back blocking us from the others.

'You look sensational tonight, Lucy.'

His low voice and intense gaze stir me, hold me captive. Outside, the storm gathers strength. Rain beats against the window panes, and a few brave souls who waited too long rush in through the French doors, laughing like children and breaking into our brief liaison.

'I'm drenched! Lucy, darling, hello! And Max!'

We're kissed, hugged, greeted, then the wave of friends

moves on to other rooms, taking the Galwares with them, leaving Chip and me with Max and Kate.

'New jacket?' Max asks.

Chip smiles. He's wearing a beautifully cut cream linen blazer. 'Nice, isn't it?'

'It's all right for some,' Max responds, his voice bantering. 'Those who can afford hand-tailored clothes.'

'Come on, you wouldn't wear it if you could afford it,' Chip says. 'It would spoil your intellectual image.' He looks at me. 'How do you like your lit class?'

My eyes flash to Kate's.

'Lit class?' Max asks.

'It was Lucy's idea,' Kate says shamelessly. 'She's thinking of working on her aunt Grace's book about Dorothy Wordsworth, but felt she needed to review all the poetry and stuff.'

'I didn't know you were doing that,' Max says, turning to me, his brow wrinkled.

I feel Kate's eyes on me, a fierce grip. One false move on my part and she tumbles into an abyss.

'I just decided,' I say. 'Classes just started.'

'But how can you handle the kids and Write?/Right?'

'It's only two hours a week in the late afternoon,' Kate interjects, leaning forward. 'Tuesdays and Thursdays at the community center.'

'But what about Nantucket?'

'I don't have to finish it. I'm not taking the course for credit.' It's odd, how Max's reaction, his disapproval, makes me get my back up. I find myself strenuously defending a lie. 'I just wanted someone to get me started. I need a syllabus and a reading list.'

Kate says, 'Lucy and I can continue to read while we're on

Nantucket, and we can discuss the readings with each other.'

'But what about the kids?' Max asks.

'Duh,' I say. 'They're at camp.'

'In the late afternoon? I thought camp ends at three.'

Kate laughs. 'Did I say late afternoon? I meant early afternoon. Lucy and I discuss metaphors and similes on the way to picking up the kids.'

'I'm glad you're doing this, honey,' Max says. 'I think you've been wanting to work on this Dorothy Wordsworth thing for some time.'

I smile up at my honest husband, suddenly flushed with love for him because he has forced his way through the weighted dark of his soul to wish me well.

I feel Chip's eyes on me, judging.

'Kate!' I say brightly. 'Want to play billiards?'

'You bet.' She sets her drink on the table and rises and follows me to the other side of the room. As we take our cues from the cabinet, she whispers, 'I owe you big time for this.'

'It's got to stop, Kate,' I hiss in return.

'And it will stop,' she retorts, stiffening her spine. 'And sooner than I'd ever want. When Garrison dies.'

I look at my friend in her sleek black dress. Her eyes are shadowed and sorrow has bracketed her mouth with parentheses.

'You break,' I tell her, as we move toward the green table and the striped balls.

SUMMER 1988

THE AUGUST THAT Matthew and Margaret were four, Kate and I once again headed for Nantucket. This time the plans were that Kate and her son would stay for three weeks. The men would join us for a week at the end of the month.

Probably.

Max was immersed in his newspaper, in his responsibilities to his town. Over the past year he'd become an expert on every aspect of Sussex, from the dog catcher's illegitimate baby to the background of the new board members of the Sussex Bank. Nothing escaped his interest – he cared about the septage treatment facility, where every single high school student was headed for college, who was raising money to have the Methodist church painted, who was getting married or divorced or having babies.

This didn't leave him a lot of time or energy for a home life. I didn't mind, most of the time. Max was nearly delirious with the sense of being exactly where he wanted to be, at the heart of an American town as it sped at warp speed through the last part of the twentieth century. I was content in a more languorous way, loving the freedom I had to spend time with my daughter or to prepare elaborate meals for dinner parties. Each week I wrote an article or two for the paper, filling in whenever Max needed. I helped out at the Little Red Schoolhouse two mornings a week. I talked to Kate about ten times a day on the phone. Where I was needed, I was there. My life was full.

KATE WAS CRANKY during the drive down to Hyannis, and on the ferry she curled up and slept, leaving me to watch M&M, who were hyper with excitement and wanted to run as fast as they could all over the boat, tripping over feet and dogs. The three of us stood at the deck, watching the island come into view, but Kate headed on down to the car.

'Hey,' I said to her when we were back in the Volvo, disembarking from the car deck, 'what's up with you?'

'I'll tell you tonight.'

This time we'd taken a morning boat so that we could get the frazzled rush of stocking up on groceries and making beds and organizing the house over with on the first day. It seemed an eternity until we had the children tucked away, having threatened direly that if they got up once more we wouldn't take them to the beach the next day. When Kate and I finally collapsed together on the screened porch, Kate rose one more time, went into the kitchen, and returned with Dove bars. One for me. One for Kate. Kate, slim, glamorous Kate, never ate ice cream.

'What's going on?' I asked.

'Smith and Smith called me yesterday. They're letting me go.'

'You're kidding! How can they? Why?'

'They want younger models.'

'But Kate. Why? You haven't gained a pound or a wrinkle anywhere!'

'It's not your kind eye that's judging me, it's their camera.'

'When did this happen?'

'Just two days ago. I haven't even told Chip yet.'

'Well, he won't care, will he? It's not as if you needed money.'

'No, not that. But he did like the cachet it gave me. The way it added to his image. Hot-shot lawyer with a model for a wife. I feel like I'm letting him down.'

'Aren't there other modeling jobs?'

'Oh, sure. My agent's already lined up some for the fall, mostly benefit fashion shows. But still . . . '

'This really sucks, Kate. I'm sorry.'

'Thanks.' We sat in silence, then she said, 'It's not like it's where my heart's at. I never wanted to be a model. My first job just fell into my lap when I was at college at B.U., and I've continued doing it ever since. In a way I'm relieved. I won't have to diet so much.'

'Still,' I said, 'it's an insult.'

She nodded. 'It is. And it hurts. It's like someone's stopped loving me.' She began to cry, softly.

'Oh, Kate. No one important has stopped loving you.'

'I know. I know. But I'm getting old, Lucy, and I hate it. I'm getting old and ugly.'

I burst out laughing. 'Please! Let's not get carried away!'

But I suppose that getting carried away was exactly what Kate needed, why she did what she did, that summer.

WE HAD AGREED to give ourselves another night of dancing. We'd been planning it all year, really. Sometimes at enormous cocktail parties in Boston, we'd see a handsome stranger, and we'd whisper to each other, 'I wonder if he ever goes to Nantucket.' We joked about making up cards to carry in our wallets to hand out to any sexy guys who caught our fancy:

The Muse. Nantucket.
August 21. See you there.

Once we were on the island, we thought about dancing constantly. We'd planned to wait until the last week, a reward for being perfect mommies, when we were all tanned and relaxed from the sun.

But we couldn't wait. When, that first weekend, both our husbands called to say they couldn't come because of crises at work, we hired a baby-sitter for Saturday night and went out.

THE MUSE WAS more crowded than before. You couldn't get to the bar without squeezing through ten thousand young male bodies. By the time we had our beers, our foreheads were damp with sweat and our voices were already hoarse from yelling at each other. The band had a female lead singer, and she was great and crazy, wailing and screaming, shaking her spiky black head and hitting her undulating hips with a tambourine.

This time Kate was the first to be asked to dance, by a tall guy with a long pony tail. The beat of the wild screaming music was so contagious that I downed my beer and was practically dancing with the bottle when someone came up and pulled me out onto the floor. I almost fainted when I got a better look at him: This man was ugly and mean-looking, I realized with a thrill of horror. His teeth were bad, crooked and discolored, and his face was terribly pitted from what must have been a hideous case of acne. He wore jeans and a black T-shirt and heavy steel-toed cowboy boots. He smelled as if he hadn't bathed in days. A tattooed snake writhed up his forearm. When he smiled he looked like he was about to bite me. He was one scary dude, and I couldn't believe I was dancing with him. I entirely loved it that I was.

We danced all night. He bought me a beer. His name was Herb and he worked for a moving company. He and his buddies had just delivered a vanload of furniture to the island and were leaving on the morning ferry.

I told him I was a senior at Northeastern, working here this summer as a chambermaid for a hotel.

He believed me. He totally believed me. I couldn't wait to tell Kate. I felt gorgeous and young, and I hated it when I looked at my watch to find that it was after midnight.

I said good-bye to Herb and wound my way through the crowd. Kate was still with Ponytail, and they were both drenched with sweat, their clothes clinging to them.

She and Ponytail were staring at each other as if entranced. I had to grab her and pull her near me to get her attention.

'It's after twelve. We've got to go.'

'You go on!' she shouted. 'I'll come home later.'

'The bar has to close at one.'

Kate turned and gave me a look that I couldn't interpret. 'I'll come home later,' she said, enunciating each word distinctly, as if it were a code.

'Kate—'

'Just leave the front door unlocked.'

'All right.'

When I stepped out into the night air, the quiet and coolness unnerved me. It was as if a pressure were lifted from me, and I stumbled. I'd alternated beer and Perrier all evening, but my legs were weak and wobbly.

Where was the Volvo? To the right? To the left. There, at the far end of the lot. I went toward it on Jell-O legs.

I opened the door and collapsed onto the seat. It was bliss to sit, and for a few moments that was all I did. I was slightly uneasy about leaving Kate at the bar, but she was a big girl, she could take care of herself. She wasn't drunk. She'd get home okay. And I had promised the baby-sitter we'd be back by midnight. I put the key in the ignition.

At home, all was quiet. Sadie could walk home; good thing, since I didn't want to leave sleeping children alone. Kate was still dancing. I smiled. I couldn't blame her.

I checked on the children one more time, then fell on my bed, exhausted. My teeth could wait until morning to be brushed. My entire body felt like a lead weight. I went out like a light.

I WOKE AT three in the morning, sitting up, heart pounding in alarm. It wasn't that I'd heard something. It was more that I hadn't heard something. I went through the house without turning on a light; I knew the house well and the summer sky was bright with moonlight that fell through the windows in silver strips.

Kate wasn't in her room. I checked Margaret and Matthew; they were fine. Kate wasn't downstairs, passed out on the sofa, or in the kitchen having a drink of water. She wasn't in the house.

'Damn it, Kate!' I whispered. What should I do? What

could I do? Call the police and report a truant mommy? I knew from rumor, not experience, that there were parties on the beaches every summer night; perhaps she had gone off with someone. That had to be what she was doing. I imagined her dancing on the sand, the ocean lapping nearby, streaked with moonlight. I was sure that was what she was doing. Wasn't I?

I took two aspirin and curled up on the sofa, fuming. How irresponsible of her, how selfish, how arrogant! Here I was, feeling like her mother, worried that she'd been in a car wreck or abducted by drunks. I curled down into the cushions, resting my head on the arm of the sofa. Could I describe the guy she was dancing with to the police? He was tall. He had a pony tail. Black hair, or maybe brown; it had been too dark to tell and I hadn't really paid attention. He was cute, there was a helpful clue. I moaned. Most of the young adults had to work; wouldn't they have gone off to bed by now?

Had Kate gone to bed with that guy?

My eyes flew open, as if I could see her.

Kate wouldn't go to bed with that guy. She loved Chip. She had a happy marriage.

What if that guy were assaulting her in some way? Perhaps I *should* call the police.

But they wouldn't do anything. Not yet. Kate wasn't really missing. If she wasn't home in time for breakfast with her son, *then* I'd call the police.

I looked at my watch. It was almost five o'clock. My mouth was stale and my skin felt like leather. My eyes burned. I was dizzy. I needed a shower. I needed to brush my teeth. I desperately needed to sleep.

I closed my eyes and let my body sag into the sofa. I was

almost asleep when I heard a car approach. I shot straight up in the air and went to the window and looked out. The car passed on by. I returned to the sofa.

'LUCY,' SOMEONE SAID softly.

I opened my eyes. Kate was bending over me. I was sprawled half on, half off the sofa, and my neck and shirt were wet with drool.

I sat up, wiping my chin with my hands, pushing back the straw that had once been my hair, trying to orient myself in this world. 'Where have you been?' I looked at my watch. 'It's six-thirty. Where the fuck have you been?'

'Lucy, we just went to someone's house.'

I stared at her. Kate looked different. She was somehow different. She was shining.

'I've been frantic with worry about you,' I said. 'I couldn't sleep.'

'So I see,' she said wryly.

'Damn it, Kate, this is not funny! I almost called the police! I thought you'd been kidnaped or assaulted or something!'

Instantly her expression changed. 'I'm sorry, Luce. I was having so much fun, I just didn't think.'

'I guess you didn't.'

Kate sat down next to me, and put her hand placatingly on my arm. Her clothes were rumpled and disarrayed . . . but then, so were mine. Her cheeks were rosy. She smelled like sex.

Kate smelled like sex.

'Where did you go?'

'I told you. Someone's house.'

'To do what?'

'What do you think? To dance. To hang out.' She stood up. 'I'm going to take a shower.'

I rose, too. 'Kate, you can't just walk off like this. We need to talk.'

She turned. The smile on her face was somehow indulgent. Condescending. 'All right. Talk.'

'I don't think what you did was right. I had no idea where you were. You didn't call me. You could have called me. I was really worried.'

'Come on, Lucy, don't be so stuffy. I'm a grown-up.'

'I know that. And I'm not being stuffy. You left your son here, didn't you think about him?'

'Sure I did. I knew he was with you. I knew he was safe. So I had fun. I had a wonderful time, Lucy, and I don't regret it. I'm sorry that you worried about me, but get over it. I'm here now.'

'And all you're going to say is that you went to someone's house?'

'I don't owe you an explanation.'

'I think you do.'

'Well, I've told you all I'm going to tell you. I had a wonderful night, and I'm not going to spoil a second of it by sharing it with you when you're in such a pusy mood.'

I stared at Kate, my heart pounding. 'Jesus. I don't even know you.'

'Mommy?'

We both turned. Matthew was at the bottom of the stairs, looking into the room at us.

'Hi, honey,' Kate said. 'Did we wake up you?'

'Uh-huh.' Matthew rubbed his eyes.

By now the room was bright with sunshine.

'You know what, Kate?' I said, my voice falsely cheerful. 'You left me alone to care for the kids without consulting me. Now I'm returning the favor. I'm going to bed now. I'm going to sleep as late as I want.'

'Fine with me,' Kate said, her voice edged. 'I'm not sleepy anyway. Come on, Matthew. Curl up on the sofa with me, honey.'

I looked in on Margaret one more time; she was sleeping like an angel. I shut my bedroom door, stripped off my clothes, and fell into bed. This time when sleep reached up to claim me, I let it take me under.

I WOKE AT one o'clock in the afternoon, feeling groggy and hung over. The sky was overcast; the air cool. I looked out the window and saw Margaret and Matthew playing Frisbee in the back yard. By the time I had showered and washed my hair and brushed my teeth, I felt better. I wanted coffee. I wondered how Kate was holding up.

I found her in a rocking chair on the back porch. She wore sweat pants and a long white shirt and had her hair pulled back in a pony tail. No make-up. She looked fabulous. She looked radiant.

'Good nap?' she asked.

I nodded. 'How are the kids?'

'Happy as larks. I took them to the library and to get videos. Walked them all over town.'

I settled onto the wicker swing and sipped my coffee.

'Want to talk?' Kate asked.

'Please.'

Kate looked out at the back yard. The M&Ms were picking berries from a shrub and mashing them into the

Frisbee, muttering imprecations over the mixture.

Kate said, 'I slept with him.'

'You didn't.'

'I did.' Kate met my eyes. 'Lucy, it was wonderful.'

'I don't believe this.'

'Believe it. I did it, and it was the best thing I've done for myself in years.'

'Kate . . . Kate, who is he?'

Kate laughed, a throaty, smug, delicious chuckle. 'His name is Slade. He's twenty-four. He likes to ski and swim. He just goes where the action is and works as a waiter and has fun. He is completely irresponsible.'

'Not too irresponsible to use a condom, I hope,' I snapped.

'Don't worry, Mom. We used a condom. I should say condoms.' Kate leaned toward me, her face glowing. 'Lucy, it was just astonishing. I've never had sex like this. I've never felt so free, so totally carried away. *We made love all night long.*'

Margaret and Matthew came up to the porch, went in the house, and returned carrying a doll and some pots and kitchen utensils.

'Betsy's sick,' Margaret said. 'Matthew's a doctor. He's going to give her some medicine.'

'That's good, sweetie,' I said. I would have said it if they'd been carrying the Cuisinart outdoors. I was too stunned to think.

It was true that Kate and I had developed a kind of conspiracy, not so much against our husbands as in the aid of being female. Over the past year as we'd become closer and closer, we'd complained about our husbands' faults and made fun of certain particularly amusing habits.

But we loved our husbands. We were happily married. If

our sex lives were sometimes less than amazing, it was understandable. Anyone with young children had to forfeit a bit of
quality sex.

'I don't know what to say,' I finally admitted.

'You're shocked.'

'Yes. I am.'

'I've never done it before, Lucy. Never been unfaithful to
Chip. And it can't hurt him. He doesn't ever need to know.'

I thought about Chip. Over the past year he and Max had
become friends; but then Max could be friends with just
about anyone, and was.

Of course Max and I had discussed Chip and Kate
thoroughly, just as I was certain they'd discussed us.

Why doesn't Chip talk more, I'd asked my husband. *He's a
lawyer, after all.*

He's not a trial lawyer, Max pointed out. *Chip's one of those
guys who reads the mind-numbing fine print in eighty-page
contracts.*

I think Chip's vain, don't you? I'd continued. *I mean, the cost
of his suits, his shoes. And everything is so perfect.*

He's not any more vain than Kate, Max retorted, protecting
his gender. *And don't forget, he works for one of the most prestigious firms in Boston. Image is crucial. It's a responsibility.*

I couldn't live like that, I'd sighed, and snuggled close to my
cozy husband.

Chip was happiest when we were doing something
physical. When the men came to Nantucket the summer
before, Chip had rented a sailboat for the day and had been
in his element, hauling up the heavy canvas sail, tying intri-
cate knots in the rope, trimming the sails. His play with the
M&Ms was the best; he chased them, held them by their
ankles and flung them around in circles, spent endless

amounts of time supporting them in the salty waves of the harbor as they tried to learn to swim or float. In the evenings, when the children were asleep, Chip initiated card games or board games, while Max wanted to watch the news and discuss world events. I had assumed that because he was such an athlete, he would be a good, vigorous lover.

'Aren't you happy with Chip?' I asked Kate.

'God, yes,' she said. 'This has nothing to do with Chip.'

'Has he had affairs?'

'Of course not! Look, last night hardly qualifies as an affair.'

'What would you call it?'

Kate leaned back against the rocker and closed her eyes. She smiled. 'Therapy,' she said at last. 'Let's call it therapy. Just what I needed, and ever so much less expensive.'

MAX AND CHIP arrived the next weekend. We met them at the ferry. Max swung Margaret up in his left arm, grabbed me with his right, pulled me to him, and kissed me soundly on my mouth. 'I've missed you,' he said, his breath warm and stirring against my neck.

Chip lifted his son up on to his shoulders, and perhaps it was because he had to steady the boy by holding on to both legs, or perhaps it was just the way Chip was – reserved – but I noticed that he only leaned forward and pecked Kate chastely and briefly on the lips.

While we'd waited for the ferry to pull in, our children tugging on our hands and wriggling all over like excited puppies, Kate had said to me in a calm, even cavalier tone, as if reminding me to pick up something at the grocery store,

'Don't tell Max about my little fling, okay?'

I didn't respond. I had to think about that. I told Max *everything*.

'I don't want him to think less of me, Lucy,' Kate continued. 'And you know he would.'

It was true. He *would* think less of her. And he might begin to wonder about me. About what it was I was looking for when I danced at the Muse.

'Okay,' I said to Kate. 'I promise.'

That was the first time I made a choice between my husband and my best friend.

JULY 1998

MARGARET'S HELPING ME chop vegetables for tacos. She's just returned from the Cunninghams' and all she can talk about is Matthew's new electric guitar.

'I think we're ready,' I tell her. 'Will you call Jeremy and your dad?'

She knows by now that I don't mean she should stand in the middle of the room and bellow. Off she goes, while I set glasses of ice water at each place. The ice seems to make my fingers tingle ... but now my lips are tingling, too. I take deep breaths. I will not allow another effing panic attack to overwhelm me, not now.

Max enters the kitchen, Jeremy riding on his shoulders. We sit around the table, passing salsa, cheese, tomatoes, and Margaret is still going on about Matthew's electric guitar.

'So is Matthew giving up piano?' Max asks.

'No. He's going to do both. Classical piano and electric rock.' Carefully she spoons green peppers onto the tidy layers of her taco. 'He's going to form a band with some other guys. Tony Rondo and Jason Cutler. It's going to be really cool.'

'Mom,' Jeremy asks, 'who's Jared Falconer?'

Surprised, my first response is to wait for the anxiety attack to knock my breath out of my chest. But nothing happens. Perhaps the heat and spice of the tacos provide sufficient antidote to the cold of panic. I swallow and wipe my mouth. 'How do you know about Jared Falconer?'

'He left a message on the machine for you.' Jeremy looks guilty. 'I forgot to hit the Save button.' His taco shell shatters before he can fill it and his chin crumples.

I take his broken shell, put a whole one on his plate, and help him delicately spoon in the filling. 'That's all right, honey.'

'Why did Jared Falconer call you?' Max asks.

'I've been meaning to tell you.' Jumping up, I find myself spontaneously moving into diversionary tactics. 'You know what would taste good with this? A beer. Want one?'

'I'll take one,' Margaret says.

'Yeah!' Jeremy laughs, exposing a mouth full of food.

'Close your mouth when you chew!' Max, Margaret, and I chorus, laughing with disgust.

I open a beer for myself and one for him, pour them into glasses, set them on the table. 'Jared Falconer asked me to join his firm.'

'When did he do this?'

'Um, just a couple of weeks ago. I was going to talk it over with you, but I wanted to think about it first.'

'What kind of firm, Mom?' Margaret asks.

'It's a prestigious advertising and public relations firm in Boston,' Max says. 'Did he talk about salary?'

'Only generally.' I can feel myself blush. I sit down and slug back some beer. 'I told him I need some time to think about it. He said I can let him know in September.'

Max says, 'So they're not just filling an empty slot. They want you.'

'I never thought of it that way, but I guess you're right. They liked the fund-raising I did for the animal shelter.'

'It's quite a compliment,' Max says.

'That's true. But it might not be the best thing for me. Commuting to Boston and all. I'd probably have to wear suits. High heels.'

'That would be cool, Mom,' Margaret says.

'What do you think?' I ask Max.

He considers. 'It would change your life. Our lives.'

'I know. And I'm very happy with my life just as it is. On the other hand, we've got Margaret's college tuition to plan for.'

Jeremy begins to cough.

'It's all the driving that bothers me. I've been so lucky, working at home.'

Max rubs Jeremy's back. 'Okay now?'

'Okay, Dad,' Jeremy says.

'We've got a lot of time to talk about it,' I say. 'Things have a way of coming clear when we're on Nantucket.'

LATER THAT NIGHT, Max sits on Jeremy's bed, leaning against the headboard. He's just finished reading *Caleb's Friend* for the ten thousandth time. Jeremy checked out this book so persistently from the library that I finally ordered a copy for him to have for his very own. He looks at it every night before he goes to sleep.

It's about a real boy who becomes friends with a mer-boy. They never speak – the mer-boy can't, and can't understand words either – but they manage to communicate, to tap into something profound and enduring in the other's soul. It's a beautiful book, but melancholy, and I wonder what it means that Jeremy loves it so.

Maybe Jeremy thinks he's part merman. Certainly he loves the water as if he were. His joy at being in the ocean has strengthened my sense that we are right to keep the Nantucket house. I am an enthusiastic if graceless swimmer, and Margaret has had lessons since she was two years old and likes the water well enough, but Max is a Taurus, a land animal, preferring to keep his feet on land. Or he did, until the first summer that Jeremy toddled, shrieking with glee, into the shallow waves at the Jetties. Jeremy is one of the few children I've seen who didn't cry when he first got his face wet, and when a wave knocked him off his feet, rolling over him so that for a moment he was under water, out of our sight, he came up grinning, blowing water out of his nose, and dancing a little jig of happiness. He could swim well by three; he didn't need lessons, but looked around him, saw other people, imitated their movements, and set off. Max has become a stronger swimmer, and has even taken lifesaving lessons, just to try to keep up with his son, and I know he's proud of his new skills, glad to feel more at home in the water. In the winter, Jeremy and Max go off to the high school pool two nights a week and on Saturdays, to keep improving their strokes. Of course this all delights me; it makes our Nantucket house seem even more integral to our life.

Jeremy's longing to really swim, like the big boys do, out beyond the sand bar. Tonight he looks too small to fight his way across a pool, let alone a harbor. His brown curls glint with gold lights and his nose and cheeks are sunburned from his days at Camp Arbor. He's lost his right front tooth and all of his teeth look too small, out of scale with his face. His cough has dried up; he is a normal healthy boy, tired after a summer day, and fiercely protective of his secret relationship with the boys in the book.

I'm leaning against the door frame, looking in at my guys, pleased with what I see. Jeremy will be on the short side like his father, and if he ever gains any weight, he'll be stocky, too. He has taken up his father's habit of taking a deep breath and nodding sharply, once, between one matter of attention and focus and another, and as I watch, both father and son inhale and nod. They've finished reading. Time to move on.

'All right, son,' Max says. 'Time to get some sleep.'

''Night, Daddy,' Jeremy responds, sliding down onto his pillow. His book stays in bed with him.

'Good night, Jere-Bear,' I say, entering the room. Jeremy reaches up his skinny arms for a goodnight hug.

Max turns on the night-light. We pull the door not quite closed, open enough so he can see the light in the hallway.

Margaret is also in bed, also reading, so deeply engrossed in a gothic mystery that she only offers her cheek for a quick kiss and keeps her eyes on the page. I love this; I feel Max and I have done at least one thing right: We've turned our children into addicted readers.

''Night, Magpie,' Max says, kissing her forehead.

'Night, Dad.'

'Don't read too late,' I warn her, and she nods absently. I could have spoken in Russian and received the same response.

Max's in the study, reading a fax.

'It's late,' I tell him. 'Come to bed.'

'In a minute.'

It's been two weeks since Stan dropped the bomb about

Paul Richardson's involvement with the CDA Corporation. Max's making an effort to interact with the children, but with me he can't dissemble quite so easily.

Entering the study, I approach Max and stand behind him. I wrap my arms around his waist and rest my head against his back. I feel the muscles in his shoulders move as he adjusts the pages of the fax.

I have a book waiting, too, a good book. Over the fifteen years of our marriage there have been plenty of nights when I've chosen to read a book rather than make love, or even when I've resented having to put a book aside because my husband's hand was on my thigh. We haven't made love for two weeks, and this is an early warning sign. I can feel Max slipping away from me.

'Do you want to discuss the Jared Falconer thing?'

'Not now.'

'Then do you want to do this . . .' I move my hands down to his groin.

'Not now,' he grumbles, twitching his shoulder irritably.

'Now,' I say. Standing on tiptoe, I nibble at the skin behind his ear. He has shaved today and his skin is only slightly bristly with evening beard.

'I've got to make some notes.'

'You can do that later.'

'Come on, Loose,' Max says, suddenly moving away from the table and away from my touch. 'I told you I have work to do.'

This is where I usually give up. It's at junctures like this that I've thought, Oh, fuck it, and walked away. But not tonight. I feel like some kind of mythological heroine, leaning over a well or a cliff, trying to grasp her lover, to haul him back up from his fall into the depths.

'Max. Honey. It's nine-fifteen. Let's take the phone off the hook and give ourselves twenty minutes. We haven't had twenty minutes for quite a while.'

I don't know about him, but the pitch of my voice is seducing me. My need seduces me. I reach out and put my hand on his wrist. I do love this man. After all these years I am intensely attracted to him. I love the electric bristle of the curly black hair on his arms.

Sighing, he turns and pulls me against his chest. 'Lucy, please. Not now.'

'Don't shut me out,' I say.

'I'm not shutting you out,' he protests gently. 'I've just got a lot to get done.'

I look up into his eyes. 'Max, I'm worried about you. I want you to see someone. I want you to try antidepressants.'

He laughs. 'Hey, just because I don't want to make love one time doesn't mean I'm depressed.'

'No, but it could be a sign. Added to all the other signs—'

'There *are* no other signs. I'm just tired and overwhelmed with stuff from work. After a week on Nantucket, after this damned humidity drops, I'll be fine.'

'It's just so hard to live with you when you're depressed.'

'I'm not depressed!' Max insists.

'Well, *I* am,' I mutter as I leave the room.

SUMMER 1989

CHIP BOUGHT A sailboat, a beautiful twenty-foot sloop that sliced gracefully through the water and responded, he told us, with an almost sentient quickness. The second Friday in August, Chip and Max brought the boat to Nantucket from the Cape, and on Saturday we all went sailing. Chip had the best of intentions for all of us, and eventually the children came to love sailing, but that first time out was misery.

It was a blustery day. Margaret and Matthew were energetic, wriggling, goofy, five-year-olds, and they hated the rubbery confinement of life jackets. The wind whipped Margaret's hair into her face and batted the sheets against Matthew's head. The dazzle of the sun off the water hurt their eyes. They wanted to hang over the sides and dangle their hands in the bubbling water, but Kate and I clutched on to them for dear life, knowing how easily one sudden move of the boat could send a small child into the sea. Sniveling with boredom, the little ones crouched down in the cabin while Kate and I watched them fiercely to be sure they didn't get clubbed by the boom or tangled in the sheets. And all the time Chip was too happy and busy to notice, and Max was crewing and having a great time himself.

When we got back to shore, Kate and I took the children off to Children's Beach, where they ran and splashed in the water, releasing their pent-up energy. The late afternoon sun seared our windburned skin, and we were thirsty and hot. We arrived back at the house with two tired, sandy, cranky children, to find Chip and Max reclining in chairs in the backyard.

'What's for dinner?' Chip called.

'Whatever you and Max find at a takeout,' Kate shot back, as we ushered Matthew and Margaret upstairs to shower.

Sunday morning the men left early to spend the day sailing alone. Kate and I took the kids to the beach, but about an hour after we got settled, clouds came scudding in, the air turned pearly with mist, and the temperature dropped. We had to lug all our paraphernalia back to the Volvo, back to the house. We showered and changed and walked into town to buy books and little treats. The streets and shops were jammed with families doing the same thing on this cloudy, cool day. We picked up videos. We played numerous games of Candyland. That evening the men came back, smelling of salt and wind and sea, expansively pleased with themselves and invigorated from sailing on a day full of wind. They barely had time to shower and dress before jumping into the Volvo so that we could drive them to the ferry.

Max put his bag in the car, then sat on the front porch, holding Margaret on his lap, spending a few moments just with her. I ran up to the bedroom to pull on a thick cotton sweater, when I heard Chip and Kate in the hallway.

'Is this the way it's going to be?' Kate asked.

'What do you mean?'

'I mean, are you going to spend every weekend sailing and ignore me and Matthew?'

'I didn't ignore you and Matthew. Didn't we all go sailing yesterday? And I invited everyone again today.'

'Chip. Your son is five years old. Sailing bores him. All he can do is sit. That boat is too big for him, too dangerous.'

'Look, Kate, I don't want to miss the ferry. I'll call you and we can talk about this, okay?'

I couldn't hear her answer, but her face must have expressed something clearly because all at once Chip's voice took on a tone of exasperation. 'Jesus, Kate, what is it with you? I can't do anything right these days!'

I held my breath, feeling fascinated and guilty. Should I pop out into the hall now, pretending I hadn't heard anything, or remain hiding here, where I couldn't help but overhear even more?

I didn't have to decide. Without a word Kate stamped down the stairs, and after a moment, Chip followed.

KATE WAS HAVING an unsettled year. She'd been approached by an Italian designer who wanted to open a shop on Newbury Street and wanted her to work there as a saleswoman. She'd agreed. It was a posh, snobby place, with a doorman out front and a pair of brass-ornamented glass doors that opened only if the saleswoman on the inside pushed an electric button.

I'd visited the shop. Once. The few clothes displayed cost thousands of dollars and the other salespeople were condescending to the point of rudeness.

'How can you work there?' I'd asked Kate later. 'How can you stand being around those horrid people?'

'They're all right, once you get used to them.'

'But what kind of people shop there? Who spends two thousand dollars for some hideous piece of fabric that looks like my grandmother's rug?'

Kate bristled. 'You just don't understand couturier fashion.'

'Damn right I don't.'

'Look,' Kate shot back. 'Your last article was all about how great the school concert was, and you know that that poor Miller child never got anywhere near the notes he was supposed to play. And Kenny Freeman's piano solo was just pitiful.'

'What's your point?'

'That we both deal in illusion. And you have no more right to insult my work than I do to insult yours.'

I opened my mouth, then shut it. Why was I so upset, anyway? Why did I care where Kate worked?

'Kate, I apologize. I think I'm just defensive because you've entered a world I don't feel comfortable in. So it makes me feel like I'm losing you, or that somehow we're not as close as we have been.'

'Well, that's just silly,' she snapped, then relented and hugged me. 'Oh, Lucy, you know you'll always be my best friend.'

BUT HER JOB did signify the difference between us. *I* was thrilled to shop at a sale at Talbot's. *Kate* bought dresses costing as much as our monthly mortgage. She was on the board of a number of prestigious organizations, and she and

Chip had a social life in the winter that was far more glamorous than anything Max and I would even aspire to. Neither Max nor I was particularly interested in money, so it never became an issue. In fact, when Max and I lay in bed, talking about our friends, we always felt more concern than envy for the Cunninghams. I would have found all the socializing and the pretension boring and distasteful, and I knew Chip was always on the edge, trying to keep in favor with the formidable powers that ran his firm and established the hierarchy.

It surprised me, that summer, when Kate expressed *her* concern for *me*.

It was a rainy night and the children were watching a video while we sat in the kitchen, finishing a bottle of red wine.

'Don't you ever feel resentful,' she asked, 'that you have to work for Max? That you have to do what he tells you? That you're helping him achieve his goals but achieving none of your own?'

I was stunned. 'I never think of it that way, Kate. I *like* what I do.'

'But you've told me . . . ' She gestured toward Aunt Grace's living room, with its shelves full of books.

'Oh, Kate, I've got the rest of my life to write books. I'm not interested in that sort of stuff now. I'll tell you what I really would like to do.'

Kate leaned close.

I whispered, even though the children couldn't possibly hear: 'I want to have another baby.'

Kate moaned. 'I know. I can't believe it, but so do I.'

We spent the rest of the evening thoroughly discussing it: when would be the best time for Matthew and Margaret to have a sibling, how we would change our houses, our schedules, what baby furniture we had tucked away in our attics, the best baby-sitters in Sussex, the best pediatricians.

We always got to the heart of things on Nantucket. During the other eleven months we were rushed with our daily lives, and even though we talked several times a day on the phone, it was always about details, emergencies, necessities: town meetings, children's raincoats, doctor's appointments, birthday cakes, new shoes. On Nantucket we had the leisure to begin conversations that would last the whole month long.

THE NEXT WEEKEND both men were to arrive on Friday night, and to my disappointment, though not surprise, Max called to say he wasn't coming. Another newspaper crisis. He was impatient and energetic, caught up in the moment, and I smiled to myself even as I assured him we'd miss him. Max was in his element.

'Hey,' I said to Kate, 'Max isn't coming this weekend. Why don't you let me take Margaret and Matthew to a movie, and you and Chip can have an evening alone together?'

'Sounds good to me,' Kate said.

We'd always been easy with each other about responsibilities, efficiently dividing up the housekeeping tasks, generously taking over the care of the other's child to give each other time off to shop or simply lie in the hammock and read. If Margaret ran into the house with a splinter in her foot or a skinned knee, she addressed whichever adult was nearer and took comfort and direction from either mother. It was as if we were a family during the month of August, two adults who both happened to be mommies, and the daddies were only visitors, arriving in their strange, heavy, somber work clothes from another world. The daddies didn't know in which cabinet the Band-Aids were kept, or which store carried the penny candy. They cooked only when they felt the urge, usually if they'd gone off on a charter fishing boat, returning with bluefish. They never cleaned or vacuumed or went to the grocery store. Kate and I did that while they spent time with their children.

Friday night I took the children out for a spaghetti dinner at Vincent's and to a movie, and then to walk around town listening to the street singers. All this was to give Kate and Chip the entire evening at home, to dine in peace and to spend as much time making as much noise in the bedroom as they desired.

It was almost eleven when we got home. The house was quiet. Kate came out from her bedroom in a long shirt and shorts.

'Daddy's sleeping,' she told Matthew as she led him to his room. 'You can wake him up in the morning.' She shot me a wry look that made it clear they hadn't had a wildly passionate evening.

SATURDAY I WOKE to find a note: Chip and Matthew were off on a bike ride, Kate had taken Margaret into town. The morning was mine. I poured myself a mug of coffee and called Max. He was already at the paper.

'All hell's breaking loose,' he told me. The high school guidance counselor had been accused of rape by a junior. The town was taking sides. It was possible that the counselor had also falsified some references to colleges. It was a terrible mess. The newspaper's phones were ringing constantly. We talked about the counselor, the girl's family, the lawyers, the evidence, the need for great caution in reporting this, and suddenly it was noon and Matthew and Chip and Margaret and Kate were bounding into the room. I told Max good-bye; he'd call on Sunday to talk to Margaret.

'We ran into each other in town,' Kate said. 'We've brought lunch.' She spread a variety of sandwiches out on the kitchen table. Something abrupt and edgy in her movements made me look from her to Chip.

'So, what do you think?' Chip asked. He was patiently scraping mayonnaise off a sandwich for Matthew.

I bent over Margaret's plate, cutting her sandwich into small pieces, thinking, Whatever it is, Chip, if you can't tell just by the way Kate's mouth is set that the answer's no, you're thicker than I thought.

'Why don't you take Lucy,' Kate asked through clenched teeth.

'Take me where?' I asked brightly.

'Sailing,' Chip said. 'This is a perfect day for a sail. Kate doesn't want to go. I need someone to crew. Want to come?'

'I—' Actually I had no idea whether I wanted to go or not. First I thought of Matthew, then Kate, then Margaret.

'Go,' Kate said, plonking down into a chair. She lifted her long hair, tied it into a knot, let it all fall down again in a cascade of blonde light. 'Please. The kids need naps and so do I.' Kate looked at me. 'Go.'

THE SAILBOAT SKIPPED over the choppy water as we sped between the cut in the Jetties and out toward the northeastern part of the island and the wide Atlantic. High above us the August sky spread in cloudless blue, but toward the northeast whipped-cream clouds were piling up. Dozens of motorboats and sailboats dotted the horizon like a million Monet canvases flickering in the wind.

Everything was new to me and excitingly unfamiliar: the rough bite of line as I sheeted in the jib, the impatient flap of the sails, like wings of a great bird lifting off into the sky, the greed of the boat to move, so that it seemed we spent as much time reining it in as letting it go.

Chip was totally engrossed in the sail and infinitely patient with me as I bumbled around taking directions from him, usually having to ask him what he meant. The wind was capricious and unsettled, blowing steadily, suddenly gusting. We skipped across the waves, the bow lifting and falling wildly in the churning water. The low green and gold shoreline raced past us as we headed out into water that was the rich, brilliant blue of great depth. I was secretly afraid, and very grateful that we hadn't tried to bring the children.

Chip sat out hard on the side of the boat, using his weight to balance the heeling of the vessel. He was grinning from ear to ear. It occurred to me that I'd never seen him look quite so young and happy. The stiff restraint with which he carried himself at all times had lifted off, and he was moving fluidly. He was exactly where he wanted to be, and it was exciting to see him. Exciting and oddly intimate. This was a man I didn't know; this was his secret heart, exposed.

If Kate weren't my best friend, if I weren't so happily married . . . I slammed the lid tight on the thought.

When I looked back at the water, I saw that it had darkened, had become as indigo blue as the sky just before night falls. I looked up. Storm clouds were advancing toward us like an implacable battalion, bearing the wind. The dark surging sea frothed with whitecaps. All at once I was frightened.

'We should go back!' I shouted at Chip.

He looked surprised. It was as if he'd forgotten I was there. I saw him evaluate the situation. The wall of clouds rolled relentlessly forward, blocking out the sun. The air grew chill. The water deepened to a green-black.

'Right,' he said. 'Ready about. Hard-a-lee.'

I scrambled for the next few moments, ducking under the boom, then settling back and sheeting in the jib sheet. We planed across the water, the waves slapping against the bow. We were far from shore now, but speeding back, and I grew a little more comfortable as the land enlarged.

Rain began to fall in large, fat, icy drops. The wind whipped it sideways so that it stung my skin. A gust came roaring up, Chip yelled something at me that the wind ripped away, and the little boat lifted up on the crest of a wave, rode the air for a few wild moments, tilted sideways, and plummeted toward the water. This was way past my experience with sailing, and I was frightened, but Chip was laughing.

'This is great, isn't it?' he yelled, and was too busy with the boat to wait for my response.

I wrapped my arms around myself. If I were on land, I'd love this. This was the sort of weather that drew Margaret and me from the house in our rubber boots and rain slickers to dance along the beach, stretching our arms out for maximum impact from the wind, throwing our heads back to catch raindrops in our mouths, shrieking with exhilaration.

Now I hunkered down in the cabin, cold and wet and worried. It was a relief to see all the other boats heading in; we looked like a regatta. When we slipped back through the cut in the Jetties and entered the calmer waters of the harbor, I felt my muscles unclench. If I had to, I could swim from here to shore. In only moments we were back at Chip's rented buoy. I helped Chip lower and roll the sails. We took a launch back to shore, where I actually thought about kissing the ground.

As we walked to the car, Chip hugged me against him with one arm, a side-by-side, jovial, comradely sort of hug. 'How'd you like that?'

'It was a little too much for me,' I confessed.

'Were you frightened?' he asked as we arrived at the car.

I nodded. The weather had changed so quickly; when we came out I'd worn only a bathing suit and a T-shirt, both of which were completely wet. I found a towel in the backseat and wrapped it around my shoulders like a shawl.

'God, I'm sorry, Lucy.' Chip turned on the heating, even though he seemed perfectly comfortable in only his wet swimsuit and visored cap. 'I grew up sailing. I forget that it's not second nature to everyone else.'

'You really love it, don't you?'

'It's a lifesaver.'

This admission knocked the breath out of me. I'd known the Cunninghams for two years now. Max and I had shared countless meals with Chip and Kate, and many August nights and days we'd all lived together in the Nantucket house like one big family. I knew when Kate was premenstrual; I knew what television shows gave Matthew nightmares; but I knew very little, really, about Chip. About Chip in the first person, as opposed to Chip, husband of Kate, about whom I did know a little. I knew that most men were not like Max, like Max in his normal, real self. Most men did not talk so readily and often and enthusiastically about whatever it was that was on their minds. But Chip was especially reserved, which seemed odd, given his profession. Or perhaps it was because of his profession that he was so reluctant to discuss private matters.

'A *lifesaver?*' This implied that his life was in need of saving. That perhaps he didn't like his work, or something, as well as I'd thought.

He hesitated, then said, 'Sailing is straightforward. Like working on the farm or riding. Pure action. No words. I get sick of words.' Chip stretched out an arm and turned on the radio. 'Let's see what the forecast is. Looks like a real storm is settling in.'

That was as close as I was going to get to Chip today, I thought lazily. The heater blew warm air onto my goose-bumped skin. Torrents of rain cascaded down, drumming on the roof of the car, spraying the windows. The windshield wipers ticked steadily, soothing pendulums in a turbulent world. I considered asking Chip if he and Kate were having problems, but decided against it. The tension between them was no worse than it had been at times between me and Max. I was Kate's friend; she would confide in me if she wanted me to know anything.

But, *lifesaver?* I was fascinated.

THAT NEXT WEEKEND the men did not come down, and Kate and I went to the Muse. I danced until my clothes were transparent with sweat and my hair clung to my skull. At midnight I drove home alone. This time I fell asleep without fretting about Kate, but I did wake up and look at the clock when I heard the front door open and close.

Five-thirty.

The sun was up. Its light was dazzling. Birds were yammering away in the yard like maniacs. I pulled my pillow over my head and went back to sleep.

'I DON'T SEE why you're so upset,' Kate said.

Our voices were low and reasonable, because the M&Ms were near. We could have been discussing our fall wardrobe.

It was raining. Matthew and Margaret had built a fort in the dining room out of chairs turned on their sides with blankets and pillows over them. Kate and I sat in the kitchen over coffee.

'For one thing, it makes me feel odd,' I said. 'It makes me feel I don't understand you. Don't *know* you. For another, I hate keeping secrets from Max.'

'How can you not understand me? You of all people in the world should understand me. Don't tell me you never lust after any other men.'

'Well, of course I do, but I don't act on—'

'Don't tell me that sometimes you don't regret marrying so young.'

'You know I feel that way sometimes.'

'Don't tell me you don't get sick of being so damned good.'

Margaret and Matthew came into the kitchen. My daughter still wore her pink nightgown and her brown hair curled wildly up and outward like the tendrils of some sun-starved plant. Matthew wore his Red Sox jersey and his Star Wars pajama bottoms.

'Mom, can we take the pillows off your bed?' They chorused their question simultaneously.

'Sure,' Kate and I replied.

'Yay!' The children raced off for the stairs.

I said, 'I do get sick of being good, Kate. But that doesn't mean I really want to be bad.'

'And you think that sleeping with someone other than my husband makes me bad.'

'I didn't say that.'

'You implied it.'

'I don't know what I think, Kate, except that it makes me uncomfortable and worried.'

'Maybe because you want to sleep with another man, too. Maybe because the corollary is knowing that Max would like to sleep with another woman.'

'Kate, we'd all like to sleep with other people. The point is that we don't. Once we're married, we don't. Just like, once we're adults, we don't live on a diet of chocolate, vodka, and corn chips.'

Kate smirked. 'That reminds me.' She rose, went to the freezer, and took out a Dove bar. 'I worked off so many calories last night, I deserve this.'

'I don't want to know the details.'

'I meant dancing.'

'Oh.' After a moment, I got a Dove bar, too. I sat down across from Kate. The M&Ms were dragging pillows into the dining room and into their fort. I watched for a moment, remembering the completely consuming joy of being five years old and constructing a fantasy world. The satisfaction of a shadowy cave with imaginary lions outside and a pillow smelling of my own scent next to me. A carpet as a jungle floor, a crystal pool, a pit of vipers. Being thrilled with fear, and at the same time profoundly safe.

I had lost all that, the bliss of a pretend world. I had grown up.

'Kate,' I said. 'I lied. I do want to know the details.'

She told me, while we licked the melting chocolate and the sugary ice cream.

AUGUST 17, 1998

IT'S OUR THIRD day on Nantucket, and when I awake to the summons of the alarm clock, I lie for a moment watching the breeze billow the white cotton curtains, filling the room with the fragrance of salt and roses. I stretch, feeling happy and relaxed in every vertebrae and cell.

One of the many familiar pleasures of our August vacations is the unscheduled pace of our waking. Unlike the nearly synchronized routine of our work and school day mornings, when we all have to be dressed, fed, and out of the house by a certain precise moment, our Nantucket mornings belong to each of us. We can rise early and jog down to the ocean or sit with a cup of coffee and a novel on the back porch or stroll into town for a huge breakfast. If the men are here, a delicate languor suffuses the air as Kate and I tiptoe from our bedrooms to let the men sleep late, or lie in bed talking to our husbands in whispers that make the moment richly intimate.

All the children become sloths, twisted in their sheets, snoring, twitching, or as still as statues. Usually the Littlies, Abby and Jeremy, wake first, with puffy faces and damp hair, to wander into the kitchen or onto the porch, yawning jaw-cracking wide yawns, and crawl into someone's lap, their bodies warm with heat and sleep. Then Margaret rises, showers, and dresses, bringing into any room she enters the sweet light floral fragrance of her perfume. Finally Matthew stumbles down the hall, Neanderthal man not yet evolved, not capable of evolving until after breakfast. If he devours last night's pizza, cold, for breakfast in front of the television, we let him, because once he eats, he really wakes up, and usually he's the first one to announce that it's time to head for the beach. According to the weather, we unhurriedly plan our day, a day built around sunshine and families and friendship and pleasure.

BUT THIS MORNING the alarm wakes me, and suddenly I remember why, and my body clenches with fear. My heart starts to race, then steadies.

Today I have to take Jeremy to Boston for some tests at Children's Hospital. Wally Calder, our pediatrician, made the appointment for me. 'Because of Jeremy's recurring respiratory problems,' he said. 'And because he's having trouble gaining weight.'

'What do you think could be wrong?' I asked.

'Let's see what the tests show,' he'd answered with maddening vagueness.

I pretended I wasn't worried when I told the others that Max and I would be taking Jeremy up to Boston for the day.

'Probably he's allergic to something,' Kate said sensibly.

'Yes, and with my luck it's common house dust,' I retorted, and we'd both laughed, laughed so the four children watching us could see how unafraid we were.

Now I moan, 'Seven o'clock,' and roll across the bed to wrap an arm and leg around my husband. I wear a white T-shirt and bikini briefs, and the blue and white striped sheets are cool and silky against my bare skin. 'It's too early. I don't want to get up.'

Max lies next to me, as still as a rock except for the slight rise and fall of his chest. At home he sleeps nude, but here he wears both boxer shorts and pajama bottoms to bed, to keep from traumatizing anyone if he has to get up in the night. There are three big bathrooms in the house; still, with eight people it's best to be conservative.

'We have to get up, sweetie,' I remind him, cajolingly.

He sighs and sits up on the side of the bed. His black curls are rumpled, his jaws blue-black with beard. His shoulders slump. At the moment of waking, he is thinking of work, I can tell.

I sit next to him. I put my hand on his warm shoulder. 'I want Jeremy to be okay.'

'He'll be okay,' Max says.

'Promise.'

'I promise,' Max says, yawning, pulling on his terry cloth robe.

I slide into a flame-red kimono, a present from my peripatetic parents after a visit to Hawaii, another of summer's joys. The satiny fabric against my skin and the luxuriously impractical sweep of its wide sleeves and long skirt against my limbs reminds me that summer mornings can be voluptuous and self-indulgent.

Max shakes his head like a spaniel coming out of water, and wakes fully. 'We should hurry. I'll make coffee. You get Jeremy ready.'

Sunshine floods the smallest room, its gold drowning out

the night-light's white-silver glow. Jeremy lies on a twin bed
with blue sheets and duvet patterned with sailboats and
whimsical fish. He's breathing easily, deeply, his chest rising
and falling regularly. He's slept through the night without
waking, but he seems to need more sleep than other children
and I hate to wake him now.

'Hey, big guy,' I say softly, sitting on his bed and touching
the tip of his nose with one finger. 'Time to rise and shine.'

He stirs beneath the sheets, his body so thin and knobby
it makes me bite my lip, one pain counteracting another.

He opens his eyes, looks around, sits up, coughs. I pat his
back lightly while we wait for the cough to subside.

'Are we going on the fast boat today?' he asks.

'Absolutely!' Both the Steamship Authority and the Hy-
Line have added high-speed ferries that make the crossing
between Nantucket and Hyannis in just one hour. We've
never gone on the fast boat before, and this treat makes the
trip to the hospital seem part of an adventure. *Fun*.

'Hey, buddy,' Max says, coming into the room. He tries to
give Jeremy a mug of coffee, sweetened and thickened with
milk, just the way I like it. 'Daddy!' Jeremy scoffs. 'I don't
drink coffee!'

'Oh, right! Then this must be for you!' Max hands it to
me, then sits down next to me on the bed and pulls Jeremy
onto his lap. 'Let's see, you want tea, right?'

Jeremy giggles. 'I don't like tea!'

'Oh, I forgot: You want pineapple juice.'

'No, Daddy!'

My coffee sloshes in the mug as Jeremy wriggles in his
father's arms. I rise, lean against the wall, and sip it as I watch
them. Jeremy wears a short-sleeved baseball jersey with
number 5 – his hero, Nomar Garciaparra's number – printed

on it and a pair of cotton socks with vaguely dirty soles.

'You don't want pineapple juice, you don't want tea, you don't want coffee, what do you want?' Max teases, and Jeremy explodes in a frenzy of giggling, knowing what's coming.

'Daddy!'

Max says, 'I know! You want to be tickled,' and sets to work while Jeremy squirms and shrieks with laughter.

'Sssh,' I say, 'you'll wake the others.' From our bedroom, the phone rings. 'I'll get it,' I say, but I know it's for Max.

'Lucy?' It's Roland Cobb, Max's associate editor and second in command. 'I hate to bother you, but I need to speak to Max. We've got some problems with the computers.'

I hand the phone to Max and set about getting Jeremy up and dressed and ready for the day. We're in the kitchen eating cereal when Max comes in, the phone still in his hand.

'Do you think you can manage in Boston without me?' he asks.

I hesitate. 'Sure.' Jeremy is next to me, I don't want to show any fear, any concern, but *damn*.

'I'll be there in as soon as I can,' Max tells Roland. Clicking off the phone, he says, 'I think I can take care of things today. I might even beat you back, but don't count on it.'

'Are you going on the fast boat with us this morning, Daddy?' Jeremy asks.

'You bet,' Max says, ruffling his son's hair. He's talked with both children about his flying phobia. Sometimes people just have these idiosyncrasies; it's irritating and irrational, but nothing to be ashamed of. If he had to fly, he'd do it, of course, but as long as he can take alternative methods of transportation, he will.

Kate enters the kitchen, yawning and disheveled and still looking like a Victoria's Secret model in her floating peach gown and robe, her blonde hair tumbling around her face. 'Want me to go with you, Lucy?'

Yes! I think. But I'm superstitious. The comfort her presence would give, and my selfishness in wanting that comfort, might move a balance on an invisible scale. 'No, thanks. We'll be fine, won't we, Jeremy-Bearamy?'

'Sure, Mom,' he says around a mouthful of cereal.

'Well, then I'll have dinner waiting,' Kate says. 'Not lobster. Chicken.'

'Or maybe lasagna.' Margaret, clad in shorts and a T-shirt, comes into the kitchen, and with the ease of someone who's completely adored, she settles next to Jeremy, picks him up, and hugs him against her. 'Want lasagna, Germ?'

Jeremy nods, his mouth too full to speak.

'Oh, honey,' I tell Margaret. 'You don't want to make lasagna. Not on a day like today. Look at it! It's a perfect beach day.'

'There will be a zillion perfect beach days, Mom.' Margaret says.

'I don't know what time we'll be back,' I say, and I hear the shrillness in my voice. Don't be so nice, I want to warn my child. Don't make a big deal out of this. This isn't an emergency. There isn't any crisis. This is just a simple trip for tests. Everything is okay.

Then I think: But what if Margaret has made her own bargain with God? What if she promises to miss this golden day and stay inside and cook, what if she offered that in trade for Jeremy's good health? We've always been so close, my daughter and I, until this past year, when she's turned fourteen and become reticent, even secretive. But she loves her brother and would do anything for him.

'If you want to make lasagna, Margaret, please do. We'd love to have it, wouldn't we, Jeremy?' I bend to kiss my daughter's head. 'You're sweet to offer.'

I head to my bedroom to dress for the day.

As I climb the stairs to the bedroom, I lift the skirts of the flame-red kimono to keep from tripping on them. My head is bent down, and so I feel Chip's warmth, enter the electric zone of his presence, before I see him.

He's coming downstairs, dressed for the day in khaki shorts and a polo shirt faded to an antique blue that matches his eyes. He smells fresh, of soap and aftershave, and I feel hot and sluttish, still in my robe, my teeth unbrushed.

'Hey,' Chip says.

I stop one step below Chip. Chip moves down so that we're side by side on the staircase, which is wide, but suddenly not wide enough.

'I'm getting ready to take Jeremy into Boston for tests,' I remind him, sounding prim. 'And Max has to go back to Sussex. Just for the day. Yet another crisis.'

'Want me to come to Boston with you?'

Still, after all these years, I can't read Chip. I can't discern the motive behind his offer.

'No, thanks. We'll be fine.' Lifting my kimono like a heroine from a gothic romance, I flee, barefooted, up the stairs.

1990–1991

I'VE OFTEN WONDERED what sorts of trouble Kate and I would have gotten into if we'd let our misbehavior increase with each passing summer, but the summer that the M&Ms were six we broke the cycle. Since Max didn't fly, we visited my parents only in the winter, during school vacation, when we drove for three days down to Tucson, saw sunshine, cacti, and mountains for three days, then drove for three days back. It wasn't the most satisfying way to visit, and that summer my parents decided to fly up to stay in Aunt Grace's house on Nantucket for the month so they could have some extended time with their granddaughter, and with me, and with Max when he could get there. Kate and Chip took Matthew to Europe for a month, and when we all reunited the last weekend in August, we were such an affectionate, prattling, lobster-eating mob that we didn't have a moment even to think of separate mischief.

I missed Kate terribly that month, missed being able to pick up the phone to whisper childishly about how my father's insistence on smoking cigars in the house or my mother's time-consuming, nearly anal perfectionism with each one of our meals was driving me into a state of scarcely controlled lunacy. But I had to wait until my parents flew back to Arizona and Margaret was settled in school to really talk with Kate, and then we talked every day, ten times every day, catching up on lost time.

THEY SAY THAT close friends, or women who spend a lot of time with each other, have their periods on the same days of the month. Some quirk of nature, I suppose, and just the sort of thing that caused Kate and me to discover, the Halloween the M&M's were six, that we were both pregnant, and both due in May.

During that winter and the approaching spring, Kate and I were as close as sisters. We were in that stage when our girth and weight made us feel regal, and the movement of the new life within us made us feel honored. Our husbands, mere men, seemed amusing, nature's joke, so much booming hairy physical matter needed to produce and protect tiny drops of sperm, while we carried an entire child with us.

Kate wanted a girl; I wanted a boy. We dreamed together: when we gathered together on Nantucket the next summer, our babies would be three months old and probably sleeping through the night. Margaret and Matthew would be seven, the perfect age. They could entertain themselves, yet they would still hold our hands. Chip and Max could go off sailing all they wanted. In our indulgently arrogant states, we considered anything but taking care of babies and children pitiful tasks. We were boats ourselves, grandly swaying around behind the bulging prow of our pregnancies.

Through the long dark winter nights I yearned for the coming summer. The men could sail. Kate and I would spend the warm afternoons reading storybooks to our children or idling through the sun-dappled streets, babies tucked on our backs, children holding our hands, to buy ice cream cones. We would watch Margaret and Matthew splash in the mild waters of the Jetties beach while on the shore we would lie beneath the shade of a beach umbrella, taking care to keep the new babies' tender skin from the harsh rays of the sun. In the evenings while Matthew and Margaret played flashlight tag in the large backyard, Kate and I would lounge on recliners, the babies kicking in their playpens at our sides, and we would gaze up at such a high bright sky that it would seem we were looking up through time and space to all eternity.

I went into labor in the middle of the night of May 11, three days past my due date.

At three a fierce cramp awoke me, and at once I knew what was happening, as surely as if it was the hand bar of a roller-coaster car pressing against me: Things were in motion now, and there was no stopping this ride.

I lay in bed for a while, timing the contractions – three minutes apart – by the green numbers on our digital clock until it became too uncomfortable for me to lie still. So I rose silently, knowing I wouldn't wake Max; by now he was used to my slipping from bed at night to pee or sneak a snack in the kitchen.

It was a warm night. The windows were open and no wind rustled outside. Our sleeping house had that atmosphere I've often sensed before, of its own peaceful vigilance and benevolent life. The rooms welcomed me, the four walls wrapping around me like a parent's arms, the air a gentle breath of security and memory and, tonight, expectation.

I stood for a moment in the baby's room, just smiling. It was a beautiful room, a perfect room, with everything waiting: diapers piled on the changing table, a musical mobile over the crib. During Margaret's infancy our lives had been so turbulent that while she didn't quite sleep in a packing box, neither did she have a pretty room with everything pristine. We were just starting up the newspaper and had no time to devote to coordinating wallpaper with crib bumper pads. Margaret hadn't suffered, hadn't noticed, really, but I was looking forward to having it all just right for once. We hadn't done amniocentesis, didn't know whether the new child was a boy or girl, so the room was done in yellow and pale green. I hung onto the bar of the crib during a long contraction and touched the cloud-soft yellow blanket folded at the end of the bed. In just a few days our baby would be sleeping here.

'Soon, baby,' I said.

Then I went to my daughter's room, looking in as she slept. Fascinated with the idea of pregnancy, Margaret had taken to mimicking me, binding a baby doll to her tummy with a scarf, waddling and sighing and sitting with her legs apart just as I did. She didn't want to wear her pregnancy to school, for which I thanked the fates and gods, but she raced to her room when she got home to fasten it on and when she went to bed at night, she carefully positioned her own baby doll on top of her stomach, beneath her pink flowered nightgown.

Now, in the warmth of the night, Margaret had kicked off her covers and lay sprawled on her flowered sheets, her slim arms extended out as if she were making snow angels in her dreams. Her baby had fallen to one side and lay with its little bald head and one arm hanging perilously over the edge of the bed. As quietly as I could I slipped into the room and moved the doll to a safer spot between Margaret and the wall. As I did, another contraction seized me, taking my breath away, paralyzing me for a moment.

I'd been in labor for a long time with Margaret, but my Lamaze coach had told me to expect that, and Max had stayed with me every moment, spooning crushed ice between my chapped lips and rubbing my back so assiduously I was surprised to find I had any skin left there the next day. If I had felt distanced from my husband during pregnancy, I'd been reunited with him during labor. I had been very much aware that I was doing this for *us*, having this baby for *us*. Max wanted children, wanted *my* children, *our* children, and the birth of our first child was thrilling for him, and terrifying as well. I knew he would have seized the pain and endured it himself if only he could have. And the look on his face when Margaret came squawking out into the world, pink and flailing, a smear of brown hair like icing across her head, was something I would treasure all my life. The radiance of motherhood, the glow, the ecstasy, none of that compared with the look on my husband's face when he held his daughter in his arms. I loved him so much then that I thought my heart would break with joy.

Still, I reminded myself as I waddled slowly from Margaret's room, still there was that pain to get through. My body had not forgotten that. Would never forget that. Over the past few years, during my menstrual period when I was swollen and bloated and then seized by a particularly ferocious cramp, I would close my eyes and sink deep within myself, shutting out all sounds and sensations from the outside world. Remember, I would think, with a kind of perverse pleasure. Just remember how this clenched power pulled me down into a cauldron of pain. Yet I had borne it, and oddly relished the thought of going through it all again.

In the kitchen I leaned on the table for support, huffing and puffing, and then all at once I was quite pleased with myself, for my water broke, wetting the kitchen floor rather than one of our good carpets or the bed. Now the contractions were two minutes apart, and powerful. The second baby came more quickly than the first, that was the general rule.

I woke Max. I phoned Nanette Berry, our dear friend and practically a third grandmother to Margaret. She lived next door and had insisted that we call her day or night. In only a few minutes she was at our house, her white hair still caught up in a hairnet.

'We promised Margaret she doesn't have to go to school the day we have the baby,' I told Nanette. 'And she likes hot oatmeal for breakfast; I keep the brown sugar in a glass canister between the flour and white sugar, and I don't know what she'll do about having her baby, I hope she doesn't shock you, I've been fairly explicit with her, but I've had to, there's so much on television these days . . . but she can watch TV, you'll have to be sure she's got decent programs . . .'

'We'll be just fine,' Nanette said, patting my shoulder. 'Just go. *Go*. And God bless.'

By the time we got in the car I was caught in the grips of such remorseless agony that I couldn't even speak to Max, except to pant, 'Yes,' every time he asked, frantically, 'Are you okay?' He had called ahead, and when we arrived at the hospital someone was waiting with a wheelchair. As I maneuvered my aching body into the wheelchair, a wave of nausea overcame me and I vomited hugely onto the pavement. That hadn't happened with Margaret's birth, and it left me weak.

This birth was progressing much more quickly than the first. No sooner had the nurses gotten me out of my street clothes and into a Johnny than my entire body arched and I knew I was already in transition. Max suddenly appeared next to me, clad in green scrubs, his eyes brilliant and eager and young, a boy's eyes, a child's eyes just before Christmas.

He took my hand. 'I love you, Lucy. I love you.'

I gripped it and squeezed. 'Me, too.'

The pain jumped to quantum force. My vision blurred. A nurse attached something to my abdomen.

'I can't find a heart tone,' she said, then a wave of pain rose up and washed her away from my senses.

'Can you do something?' I heard Max ask.

'The birth is progressing,' the doctor muttered.

I had remembered the pain, but I had forgotten the *urgency* of childbirth. I, who could do five things at one time, was trapped in the immediacy of pain and could do just one thing: endure. I needed things to slow down. I had the terrifying sense of things being beyond my control. I could feel by the movement of the bed beneath me and those around me that I was being wheeled into the delivery room, but all I could see, really, was a dizzying blur of light and color.

'The baby,' I called to Max.

'He'll be all right,' Max said. 'You're almost there.'

'I can't do it this time.'

'Sure you can.'

'It hurts too much.'

'No heart tone,' the nurse said.

'The baby's head is crowning,' the doctor said.

I knew how lions felt when a net was flung over them, trapping them, I knew their murderous anger and their savage fear, and I arched my back and felt my jaw stretching as I bellowed in pain.

Max was still holding my hand. His eyes were shining with

tears. 'You're wonderful, Lucy, you're my wonderful woman.'

The doctor said, 'One more push,' and taking an enormous breath, I clutched Max's hand for strength, and gave another, final push.

Relief swept over me like a white tide. Other sensations returned as the primal pain faded: My legs were trembling, my throat burned, my abdomen was heavy, sodden like a canvas bag.

And there was an odd silence at the end of the table. A long moment, like a gasp in the room.

Then there was low murmuring, and a kind of electric mist rose up, surrounding me, as Max turned toward the doctor and asked, 'Boy or girl?'

'It's a boy,' the nurse said.

But the doctor had left, had gone across the room and was bending over something on another table.

Max left my side. Went toward the doctor. I couldn't hear his words or the doctor's, but I could detect in the very tone of their voices that something had gone wrong.

'What's happening?' I called.

A nurse said, 'Push. Let's get the placenta out. You can do it, honey. Push for me. That's a good girl.'

Across the room Max made a noise from deep in his belly, a tortured groan not unlike the sound he made when climaxing.

'Max? Where's my baby?' I lifted myself up to lean on my elbows.

A nurse approached and took my hand. 'There's a problem, dear.'

'What? Tell me. My baby—' I tried to wrench myself off the table.

The doctor stood next to me. He put his warm hand on

my upper arm. 'He had a knot in his umbilical cord. I'm sorry.'

'I don't understand. I want my baby.'

'You've lost the baby, dear,' the nurse said, touching my other arm, and the touch was one of control, not concern.

'But this is a hospital, for Christ's sake,' Max yelled. 'You're a doctor! You're a nurse! *Do* something. You can do something, can't you?'

'The baby wasn't breathing when he was born. We couldn't resuscitate him.'

I shrugged off the nurse's hand. 'Give me my baby.'

And they did.

They put in my arms a perfect child, a little boy with every finger and toe, with eyelashes, with a swirl of brown hair, with skin of dark blue.

'We don't know why it happens,' the doctor was saying. 'It's always something beyond our control.'

'No,' I said. 'Wait.' It could not have happened so fast.

'Oh, God,' Max sobbed. Tears streamed down his face. He stood next to me, nearly bent double with grief.

'Wait,' I said again. I looked down at my little boy, my perfect child. 'He was moving last night. I felt him move last night.' I pressed my face against his, and wrapped my hand around the back of his tiny head.

'Sometimes this happens,' the nurse said. 'A knot in the cord.'

'But why? Did I do something wrong?' I ran my hands over my baby, trying to warm him up, caressing his limp limbs.

'No, dear, of course not.'

'Should I have come to the hospital sooner?' That was it; I was so confident of my child-bearing skills, so smug, waiting till the last moment, and had been struck down for my pride.

'We never know why this happens.'

I looked down at my son. 'Baby,' I whispered to him. 'Baby, *please.*'

'I'm so sorry. This is the worst thing anyone ever has to bear,' the doctor said. 'We'll leave you and your husband alone with him for a few moments.'

'And then what?' I asked.

His eyes dropped away from mine. 'Then we'll have to take him.'

AUGUST 17, 1998

JEREMY LOVES THE fast boat. He can't decide where to sit, in the posh lounge with its carpet and plush seats, or out on the deck where he can wave at the sailboats and fishing boats and ferries we speed past. The glittering turquoise water ruffles up sparkling white foam in a long wake behind us.

We walk with Max to the lot where he keeps his van. He drives us to the airport where I pick up my rental car, a dark blue Taurus.

'I'm sorry I can't go with you,' Max says.

'Hey, we'll be fine,' I tell him, full of bravado in front of our son.

We kiss good-bye in the parking lot and go our separate ways. Max drives faster than I do; he'll be in Sussex before I'm in Boston, even though his distance is slightly longer.

The day is a clear bright hot blue. Jeremy plays an electronic baseball game while I drive up Route 6 to the Sagamore Bridge over the Cape Cod Canal, and around the rotary to Route 3. The traffic moves steadily. We end up behind a huge U-Haul van that progresses at a constant sixty miles an hour. Good enough for me; I turn on the soft rock station. Near Braintree, we stop at a McDonald's so Jeremy can pee, just in case traffic into Boston is congested. But we move right along, no breakdowns or road work slowing us, and before we know it, we're turning onto Massachusetts Avenue and the roads to Boston's Longwood medical complex.

I steer the car into a ramp and stop to take a ticket from the machine.

As we wind up and up through the vast, low-ceilinged parking garage, Jeremy whispers, 'I'm scared, Mommy.'

'Why, honey?' I reach over for his hand.

'How will we find our way back to the car?'

Relief blots a wide cold spot on my chest. He means he's afraid of this particular space. We don't have anything like it in Sussex, and it is kind of scary, so dark and full of echoes and shrieking brakes.

'Each floor has a number. See?' I point one out as I maneuver into a tight parking spot. 'We're on floor 3.' Next to the number is a picture of a zebra. 'Or we're on floor zebra, whichever is easier for you to remember.'

'Zebra,' he says. But he holds my hand while we walk to the elevator and then across the street.

It is shocking to come to this enormous complex after the low-silhouetted natural spread of Nantucket. To reassure him, I remind him, 'It's just the big city, Jere. You know. Like the Alewife parking garage, when we take the T into Boston to ride the swan boats.'

'I know,' he says quietly, clutching my hand.

Thank heavens, Children's Hospital is a child-friendly place. The lobby is large and airy and colorful and when we enter it, Jeremy's eyes light up. He runs first to the large aquarium, then to the bright, entrancing Chitty-Chitty-Bang-Bang kind of perpetual motion machine like the one at the Museum of Science. Kids and people are everywhere; it's like a museum.

I approach the information desk, overlooked by a lifelike sculpted giraffe. A woman with a beautiful smile instructs me: We want Farley 4.

ON THIS LEVEL, where the pulmonary testing is done, the hospital floor is patterned with large bright triangles and squares, elementary, friendly, familiar shapes.

Allen, the pulmonary technologist, wears street clothes: jeans, a striped rugby shirt. With his buzz haircut and contagious cackling laugh, he seems like one of the young men who coaches Jeremy's T-ball team, and Jeremy is only a little nervous as they attach the gauze pads and electrodes to his arms.

Jeremy seems unconcerned, more curious than frightened. He chooses to sit on a chair rather than my lap; still he leans toward me, and allows me to keep an arm around his thin body.

There are toys in the lab room where we sit, but Jeremy wants to know about the process, wants to hear the real, grown-up words about what's being done to him.

'Pilocarpine stimulates the sweat glands,' Allen tells him.

'Pilocarpine,' Jeremy repeats, syllable by syllable.

'We've already weighed the gauze pads; when the time is up, we'll weigh them again to see if there's any change; this difference would be in sweat, from which we measure the salt content.'

'I have *salt* in my body?' Jeremy asks, eyes wide.

'We all do. Human beings have lots of minerals in our bodies.'

He is such a beautiful boy, with fine gold-glinting brown hair that curls in loose lazy swirls and huge eyes, thickly lashed. ('Not fair, Mom!' Margaret has often chided me. 'Why did you give Jeremy those long lashes and not me?' As if I had some control over their genetic inheritance!)

Now his eyes widen in response to the electric currents.

'Feels like when your foot falls asleep, doesn't it?' the lab tech asks.

'Like when I hit my crazy bone,' Jeremy tells him. He looks up at me. 'It kind of itches.'

'Good boy.' I nuzzle a kiss into his hair. His scalp smells clean and slightly salty, as if we were still at the sea.

'Time's up! You did great, Jeremy.' Allen detaches the electrodes. 'I need you to keep the gauze on for about thirty minutes, okay? You don't have to stay here. In fact, you ought to go check out our entertainment center. Just come back in about half an hour.'

Jeremy holds my hand as we find our way back through the corridors to the elevators and then down to the main floor. The entertainment center is a large open area with a stage. Several children are playing in the long stage curtain, hiding in its folds, and Jeremy runs over to join them. I sit down at one of the low tables. Whenever Jeremy looks for me, I wave, as if we're at a playground.

SPRING 1991

ABIGAIL ALISON CUNNINGHAM was born three nights after Maxwell Junior was born. Kate was in labor less than three hours. Abby weighed eight pounds, one ounce, and had a full head of sleek, nearly white hair. She was perfect.

Kate told me all this over the phone. I went home the day Kate went into the hospital and while I could have summoned the energy to return to the hospital, I had no inner resources of strength left which would have allowed me to see her new baby without weeping for the loss of my own. It seemed that I wept all the time.

My body craved its baby, my arms yearned to hold my child, the milk in my breasts pushed and swelled, wanting to be sucked. My body, which had been blooming and blushing like a full summer rose, seemed blighted. Now it was only a skin full of useless fluids and tears. Alone behind a locked bathroom door, I dug my fingernails into the skin of my traitorous belly, my moans hidden by the noise of the shower. Hideous body. Vile body. Evil body. To have carried a little boy for nine full months and then to choke the life from him at the moment of his birth! My body was abominable. I was detestable. I thought I would go mad with my grief-driven thoughts trapped beneath my treacherous shell.

I let my daughter observe some of my sorrow. It seemed appropriate to do so. She should know that this baby was loved, that his death was something of great significance. She was only seven, though; it was hard for her to understand. Impossible for anyone of any age to understand, really. She didn't cry when we told her. But she was subdued over the next few days and weeks, and she watched her father and me closely. When I lay in bed weeping, she would come and lie next to me, studying my face. After a while she would pat my hair or my arm. 'It will be all right, Mommy. It will be all right.'

She was my living child. I owed it to her to agree with her, to show her that life could go on, that she was loved, that I was happy in her presence.

'Yes, Pudding,' I would reply. 'It will be all right.' And I would pull her to me, and the warmth of her small perfect body against mine soothed me for a while, and for her sake I would talk of other things: her school, Brownies, ballet lessons.

LIFE HAD TO go on. Laundry had to be done. Food had to be bought and prepared and eaten. Margaret's schoolwork, words written in huge crayon letters, pictures of flowers and bunnies, had to be admired. I had to wash my hair and clothe myself and leave the house to drive my daughter to visit friends. I had to answer what seemed like hundreds of well-intentioned phone calls: 'Yes. Thank you. It's very kind of you to call.'

I had to pretend that I wasn't furious with Max, who left

for work early in the morning and stayed there until late at night. He was using the paper as a refuge from his grief, and I felt abandoned, left to suffer on my own. He did spend a dutiful amount of time with Margaret, taking her off for little. forays to the library or to buy an ice cream cone. In front of our daughter, he did a sufficient job of behaving as if all would be well. But I needed him to weep with me.

As time went on, I ceased being angry at Max and instead became worried about him. He stopped shaving and his beard grew in, a motley mixture of black, brown, and red, coarse and unattractive. It didn't suit him, and it bothered me. It was like trying to kiss thistles, and I knew that was one of the reasons he'd stopped shaving, to put up this rough barrier between us. He became busier and busier, as if hiding from his grief, like a frantic animal trying to cover over a well of sorrow that lay open beneath him, an endless dark pit growing deeper with each day.

For a few days after Abby's birth, Kate phoned me again, and we talked briefly, until I cut the conversation short, pretending I had chores to do. After that, I kept the answering machine on and blocked all Kate's calls. I just didn't have the energy to deal with her sympathy or with her joy.

Perhaps in every close friendship there is an element of, if not competition, then comparison. Perhaps that is one of the things that makes a friend belong especially to us. Somehow, in the secrecy of our hearts, a scale must balance. Kate was more beautiful than I, and much wealthier, but I was smarter than she was, and happier in my life.

Now the balance had been destroyed forever.

When Abby was a month old, Kate phoned. I stood looking down at our answering machine while she said, 'Lucy. I want to see you. I want you to see my baby girl. I want to see Margaret. I want her to see Abby. I'm coming over tomorrow. You don't have to make tea or even get dressed, but you do have to open the door and let me come in.'

I picked up the phone. 'All right.' I added, 'Come around four. So that Margaret will be here.'

While I dressed for Kate's visit, my emotions roiled so turbulently that I longed for some kind of valve to squeeze, to let some of the pressure out. Why did I lose my baby? Why didn't Kate lose hers? Why did she insist on coming here, to display her perfect daughter in all her newborn glory? Why couldn't she leave me alone? I never wanted to see Kate again.

The woman who stared back at me in the mirror was a hag. I had lost a great deal of weight and my loose sundress hung on me. Everything drooped, hair, face, shoulders, empty breasts, empty belly. My skin was gray. I put lipstick on for the first time in a month, and the result was glaringly unpleasant, like wax lips on a dummy.

'They're here!' Margaret was keeping watch from the living room window. She couldn't wait to see Matthew again; he was her best friend and she'd seen him only at school for the past month. And she was excited about seeing the new baby, the girl baby. 'They're coming up the walk!' Margaret announced. 'Oooh, Kate's got a little bundle in her arms. A little pink blanket. Oooh, I can see a tiny hand!'

Kate knocked. Margaret raced to the door and threw it open, dancing up and down in ecstasy. 'Kate! Matthew! Let me see your baby!'

I said hello to Kate and Matthew, and when I smiled, my lips trembled with tension. Kate was more beautiful than I'd ever seen her in all her life. She'd gained weight with her pregnancy, and her full cheeks curved much like those in the old Dutch masters paintings. Her skin was luminous. Her hair shone. She was radiant with happiness.

She settled on the sofa, lay her daughter in the ridge between her thighs, and unwrapped the pink blanket, exposing a small, perfect child in a creamy dress. Abby's tiny feet were bare.

'It's too hot for her to wear booties,' Kate explained to Margaret, who pressed close to Kate, looking down with awe at Abby. Matthew sat next to his mother, smiling at his sister.

Margaret asked, 'Can I touch her?'

Kate said, 'Of course.'

I sank onto the edge of a chair and watched my daughter reach out her hand to gently touch a tiny wriggling foot. I could see that Abby was awake, alert, trying to focus.

'She's so soft,' Margaret said. Her face was tender with adoration.

'Oooh,' Abby cooed in a sweet high voice and waved her little fists in the air.

Margaret leaned closer to the baby. 'Hi, baby,' she said gently. 'Hi, Abby.' She reached out to touch the little girl's hand. The baby responded with another coo and waved all her limbs like a starfish. Her tiny fist opened, then closed on Abby's finger.

Margaret looked up at Kate, her eyes shining. 'She likes me.'

'She likes you a lot, Margaret.'

Kate gave my daughter a one-armed hug. She looked over at me. It was only when our eyes met that I realized that tears were streaming down my face. A look of complete understanding fell over Kate's face. Her forehead furrowed and she bit her lips.

'She needs to sleep now,' Kate told Margaret, even though Abby was obviously wide awake. 'Matthew brought you a present.'

'The Lego circus!' Matthew yelped, holding up a bag in his hand.

'Why don't you and Matthew go play in your room for a while,' Kate suggested. 'We'll call you when Abby wakes up.'

'I could hold her while she sleeps,' Margaret suggested eagerly. 'I could sit here and be very quiet and hold her.'

'You go play for a while,' Kate said. 'You can hold Abby when she wakes up.'

Margaret knew that tone of voice well. 'Okay,' she said, unable to hide her disappointment. 'Come on, Matthew.'

The M&Ms left the room. We heard them chatter to each other as they went up the stairs. We heard the rattle of the toys being dumped onto the floor.

Kate put a cushion on the floor. She laid her baby daughter on the cushion. She came over to where I sat on the chair and knelt next to me.

'Lucy,' she said, and wrapped her arms around me and we held each other and sobbed, our tears soaking into each other's hair.

AUGUST 17, 1998

As THE PULMONARY technologist gently removes the gauze and plastic from my son's arms, he asks, 'Did you find the entertainment center?'

'Yeah,' Jeremy said. 'I met a kid who has a brace on his leg.'

'You'll see lots of kids like that around here. There. You're done with this part, Jeremy. It's going to take about another half hour to develop.' He looks at his watch. 'If you're hungry, there's a great Au Bon Pain.'

'Can we see the aquarium, Mom?' Jeremy asks.

'Sure.' I take his hand and we walk together down the hall, over the bright squares and triangles.

At Au Bon Pain we buy sandwiches, juice, and cookies, but I'm not really hungry and Jeremy is eager to get to the large aquariums in the lobby, so I wrap our food and pack it in a bag; we can eat it later, during the drive back down to Hyannis.

'Wow, Mom! Look at this!'

The fish Jeremy likes is brilliant, nearly fluorescent, yellow, fat, flat, and silky, like a tulip with eyes. Jeremy presses his face close to the glass.

'What kind of fish is this, Mom?'

'I don't know. We'll go to the library and get a book and find out.'

He runs and turns, following the fish as it speeds back and forth.

'Are there fish like this at the Jetties?'

'I don't think so, honey. I think these are tropical fish. They need warm water.'

'Can we get one?'

'Perhaps. We'll have to do some research. We certainly can't have an aquarium this large, and it may be that this kind of fish needs a lot of space.'

My voice cracks as I talk. Our half hour is almost up. My throat and mouth have gone dry.

THE WALLS AND carpet of Fegan 5 are a soothing periwinkle and gray, and next to the office is a waiting room filled with a child's dream of toys. Parents sag on chairs, reading magazines or holding their children while other children play as happily as if at home in a day care center. I smile at a woman with a three-year-old in her arms; she smiles at me, as if nothing in this place is dangerous.

A young woman with a mole next to her nose and earrings like lilies approaches us. She's smiling, too.

'Hi, Jeremy. Mrs. West? I'm Serena. I volunteer here, and I thought maybe I could play with Jeremy. Dr. Hall would like to speak with you. Dr. Hall's office is right down that way, Jeremy. Your mom won't be far away.'

But he's not frightened. I am.

It's absurd, how nervous I feel in this office, and how *subordinate*. Like a kid facing a test. Or worse, like a student facing the principal, knowing she's been caught, knowing she's in big trouble now.

Dr. Hall shakes my hand. He's a small man with salt-and-pepper hair and a firm handshake. He gestures to a chair.

I sit, smoothing my skirt over my thighs.

His office is small. Three walls are lined with bookcases crammed with books, medical texts, thick doorstops of journals. Behind him a window shows a perfect rectangle of blue sky. His desk is piled with a confusion of papers, computer printouts, manila envelopes, Xeroxed articles, pens, memos, writing tablets, chains of paper clips.

He is wearing a gray suit, white shirt, navy tie. He must be in his forties.

He begins to speak, 'I'm very sorry to have to tell you this, but Jeremy—'

I've always loved watching storms hit Nantucket. I've left the warmth of the house to drive to Surfside where I'd stand on the beach watching the ocean surge, swell and crash, roaring angrily, full of a nearly personal and certainly living power. The wind would buffet me, knock me backwards, nearly push me over, making my raincoat shiver and crackle against my body while rain spattered like pellets against my face.

The noise and expansive power fascinated, exhilarated, and somehow *owned* me like nothing else could. I'd stand watching wave after wave roll inexorably toward me, hands shoved down into the warmth of my pockets, nose dripping, eyes tearing, face soaked with salty spray, until my face grew so cold I couldn't feel it and my teeth chattered and my body shook like a flag whipped in a gale. Still I couldn't seem to get enough of it, I was like a screaming adolescent fan at a rock concert, shaken to my core, losing all reason and shudderingly glad to lose it, grateful ... *thrilled* ... to be clutched and claimed by such ferocious power.

Eventually I would become so cold that it was painful, or someone else would arrive at the beach and want to talk, or I'd remember an appointment, and I'd force myself to turn my back on the ocean. I'd sit in the car, turning the heat on full blast, dripping water everywhere, my skin flushed with warmth, my body glowing and humming like a great engine that had just been refueled.

But in the early part of this decade a series of storms hit Nantucket Island with an unexpected violence. For two years in a row, these storms rose up in the autumn with a destructive fury that was unanticipated and unchecked. First came the thundering waves that swept away a long expanse of beach on the northeast side of the island. Then came the second attack, the real onslaught, unimaginable waves like marauding hordes, attacking the homes on the shore, smashing down on them, destroying them, carrying them out in ruins into the victorious sea while their owners stood on the shore, weeping or watching with numbed helplessness.

We were there for that weekend. We saw the second storm, the storm that raped the shoreline and ravaged the homes. We watched while waves rose up like colossal mouths, white teeth biting down into rooftops, crunching porch railings, chimneys, trellises, shutters, and doors into sticks and swallowing them into the ocean's voracious maw. I did not feel exhilarated then; I felt cowed.

I had always been taught to take care when I was on Nantucket. To wear my life jacket when in a boat, to swim close to shore and with friends, not alone, and not at Surfside, where every summer the friendliest, most playful waves heartlessly tossed some unsuspecting swimmer down on the sand, snapping his neck. I had liked to flirt with the ogre-hearted ocean, I had liked to wade in its cool, glittering waters, tempted, but safe.

Now as I sit listening to the kind and articulate Dr. Hall, it seems I feel my chair tremble beneath me. I know I am at the very edge of my life. The floor resonates with the vibrations of an approaching force. I clutch the arms of my chair. An invisible wave, the dark, heartless side of nature's gifts, rises up in the room and plummets down over me, pulling me down into its frigid, roiling gloom.

'Cystic fibrosis . . .' Dr. Hall says.

His lips continue to move, but somehow the words don't quite reach my ears. Now I know why I've been having anxiety attacks. All along my body has been warning me. Still, it's too much. I'm sitting deadly still, but I feel as though I'm thrashing through thick water that moans in my ears and makes the universe tilt. Which way is up? I am nauseated.

'Inherited genetic defect . . . both parents . . .'

His words swim past me like the fish Jeremy admired in the aquarium. What is it they say? The sins of the fathers are visited on the children? How about the sins of the mothers? Obviously the sins of this mother. But this is beyond fairness, beyond justice, beyond bearing.

'Your son is not in crisis now, however . . .'

Jeremy, I think, *Jeremy*. My God. What have I done?

JULY 1991

AT THE END of July, almost three months after little Maxwell was born, I went to the offices of *The Sussex Gazette*. It had been a long time since I'd been there. Weeks. Months. Perhaps almost a year. As the newspaper's circulation had grown, so had its staff, and even though there was the normal amount of transience, Max did have a loyal quartet – reporter, photographer, business manager, and copyeditor – who kept the paper running smoothly. I wrote an article only occasionally, in an emergency.

Over the years the ranch houses around the newspaper had been transformed into beauty shops and photography studios, and the willowy saplings had broadened out into substantial shade trees, giving the area a prosperous air. What had once been the front lawn had been converted into a parking lot with tubs of flowers on either side of the front door, and as I pulled in, I could see through the large picture window a warren of computer-topped desks, swivel typing chairs, and people talking on phones or bent over notepads, chewing on pencils.

I took a deep breath and pushed through the door into

the main room. The air was full of chatter, which stopped abruptly when Dora Gilbert cried, 'Lucy!' The plastic clatter of computer keyboard keys ceased. People looked up at me, as surprised to see me as if I were a ghost. Carrie O'Connell was the only one who continued working. 'The dog's name was what?' she asked the person on the other end of telephone.

I had just had my hair cut, and it looked as good as it ever would in the humid summer, curling around my face. I wore lipstick. I had a tan from taking Margaret swimming. My yellow flowered sundress was loose around me, but not grotesquely so. I didn't look like a madwoman. Still, most of these employees had not seen me since Maxwell's birth, and even though they'd sent letters of condolence, I could tell they were now struggling with how to approach me. Should they mention my misfortune or not?

'I just dropped in to see Max for a moment,' I announced brightly.

'He's in his office,' Dora said.

'I know the way.' I smiled at her and walked confidently on by.

Max's office was divided from the rest of the large room by glass walls; I could see him bent over a filing cabinet. I knocked and entered at the same time, and once in the room, I shut the door firmly behind me.

He looked over his shoulder, saw me, and turned so sharply that he hit his knee on the filing cabinet.

'Lucy. Are you all right?'

'Of course I'm all right. I just wanted to talk with you a moment.'

He looked wary. 'Sure. Sit down.' He gestured at a scarred wooden desk chair.

I sat, moving the chair slightly to position it so that my back was to the outer office. 'Could you sit, too?' I asked, smiling.

Max went to the wide leather chair behind his desk, the only other chair in the room. He leaned forward, arms folded on his blotter. The sleeves of his red and white striped shirt were rolled up to the elbows. He wore a white cotton sweater vest. A blue bow tie. But his beard was about three inches long now, and ragged.

I tried to be positive. 'You look patriotic today.'

'Do I?' He looked down at his tie. 'I guess I do. What's up?'

'Max, I want you to go to Nantucket with me in August.'

He blinked. 'That's why you came in here today?'

'We don't seem to be able to talk much at home.'

'Honey, listen—'

'No, Max. You listen. What you're doing isn't fair.'

'What I'm doing?'

'Working all the time. Ignoring me. Shutting me out.'

'Come on, Lucy. By now you should know that working all the time goes with the territory of—'

'You haven't talked to me, *really* talked to me, since Maxwell died.'

'This is hardly the place—'

'You haven't held me, we haven't made love—'

'This is not the place for such a personal discussion!' His face flushed red with anger and embarrassment.

'It seems to be the only place,' I calmly pointed out. 'You never talk to me at home.'

'All right. I'll talk to you at home. But not here. Not now.'

'Tonight?'

'Tonight.' His mouth thinned into a exasperated line.

'Max.' I leaned forward and spoke softly. 'Max, I love you.

I need you. Margaret needs you. I won't let you go into another depression. I can't.'

He rose. 'Not here, Lucy.'

I sat firm, crossing my legs, folding my arms over my chest, glaring at him.

He sat down again. 'I'm not depressed.'

'Not here, you're not. Here you're managing just fine, here you've barricaded yourself from your emotions with all this, this—' I waved my arm to indicate the glass walls, the activity in the outer office. 'But at home you're another person. You're silent and miserable and closed off. It's hurting Margaret. It's hurting me.'

'I have a reason to be miserable.'

'So do I. But life has to go on. For our daughter if not for each other.'

We stared at each other, deadlocked.

Max's shoulders sagged. He rubbed his hand over his jaw. 'What do you want me to say? I'll try.'

'I think you should see a therapist.'

'I said I'd try, Lucy. I don't need a damned therapist.'

'I want you to promise to stay with us a full week on the island. You need to lie in the sun and build sand castles with Margaret. You need to sail with Chip.'

'You think it's going to be that easy? A week on Nantucket?'

'I didn't say it was going to be easy. And if you don't think a week on Nantucket will help, then why are you so dead set against seeing a therapist?'

'A therapist won't bring back my son.'

I looked down at my hands. My son, too, I thought. I wanted to say a hundred different things to my husband, but all I could think of was that Maxwell had had curly black hair, like Max's. Even in his newborn state, he had resembled Max clearly. His loss shot through me like an arrow of grief.

I leaned forward. 'Max,' I whispered. '*Help me*. I can't do this alone.'

He looked away. He cleared his throat and swallowed. I wanted him to come around the desk and hold me. He had not been able to hold me since Maxwell's birth. 'All right,' he said at last. 'I'll try.'

His phone rang and he snatched it up.

I sat a little longer, regaining my calm, until I could walk back out through the office, dry-eyed.

AUGUST 17, 1998

MARGARET HAS MADE lasagna. The house smells of garlic and olives, a hearty aroma, a comforting one. Jeremy runs straight through the house to his sister.

'I'm going to get an aquarium!'

'Cool.' Margaret picks her brother up and carries him to the stove. 'Look what I made for you.'

'When can we eat?'

'We were just waiting for you to come home.'

'The plates are on,' Abby says, coming in from the dining room. She's carrying a tray with the worldly ease of someone who works as a waitress when she isn't in school. 'Now what?'

'Give everyone glasses,' Margaret tells her, and Abby hastens to obey. Our two families are tangled with skeins of idolatry: Jeremy adores Abby, who admires and copies Margaret, who in turn worships cool, perfect Kate. 'Wine glasses for the adults.'

Matthew stands at the counter, slicing tomatoes for a salad. This simple fact takes my breath away. Never before in his fourteen years has he shown any interest in cooking. And I don't believe it is cooking that brings him to the kitchen now.

Matthew wears a tattered T-shirt and baggy madras shorts; Margaret a short blue-checked sundress. Her long chocolate-brown hair is held back with a pale blue headband. I loved headbands on my daughter, they made her seem serene and collected . . . and young.

But Margaret is no longer a child. Any implication that even a remnant of childishness remains turns Margaret into a fury.

Matthew and Margaret had been buddies all their lives. How will adolescence change that? When the two were infants, Kate and I had joked about them marrying, but now I find that thought disturbing.

It doesn't matter now. This will certainly be the last summer our two families would share a house. Possibly the last night.

'Hey.' Kate comes into the room, one finger bookmarking a paperback. She wears loose white trousers and a blue T-shirt. 'How did it go?' She looks perfect as always, and just for a moment she stands in a shaft of sunlight that backlights her, rings her body with an aurora. She looks like an angel, beautiful, calm, cool, but she is only human, and vulnerable, my best friend, to age and time. To loss. Tears well up in my eyes.

I'm trying hard to remain in control. Especially in front of the children, I must remain calm. I smile falsely, brightly. 'Fine. Is Max home?'

'He just got in on the Hy-Line fast boat. He's upstairs changing.'

'Margaret? Take care of Jeremy, okay?'

'But, Mom, aren't we all going to eat together?'

'Dad and I will come down and eat later.' Reaching into the refrigerator, I take out two bottles of beer. I would prefer straight scotch, straight gin, but with everyone watching I settle for the beer.

Silently Margaret sets Jeremy on the floor. She's chewing the inside of her cheek.

Abby hands my son a pile of napkins. 'Help me put these around,' she says.

'Okay.' Jeremy's game for anything Abby suggests. As he follows her from the room, he announces 'I got attached to *electrodes!*'

'I had to have two cavities filled at the dentist,' Abby counters, undaunted. 'It sounded like a blender in my head.'

Kate trails me out of the room. 'Lucy, what's up?' Her forehead is creased with worry, more fine lines on that flawless face.

'Oh, Kate.' I hesitate at the bottom of the stairs. I want to put my arms around her. I want to sink to my knees and beg her to help me. I want to beg her to forgive me. 'I wish . . . I'm sorry. I've got to talk to Max first.' I run up four steps, then turn back to look at her. She's standing at the bottom of the stairs, watching me. 'Kate. You know I love you, don't you?'

Her frown deepens. She opens her mouth, to protest, to demand that I tell her what's going on, and then she gets it: something serious is up. Something huge. 'Yes. And I love you.'

'I know.' Tears blur my vision and I stumble on the stairs, banging my shin. '*Shit.*'

The door to our bedroom is shut. I open it to find my husband changing clothes. Behind him, the August sky shines through the open windows in a flawless blue. The evening air is so heavy and fragrant it seems as if someone in the neighborhood is making wild grape jam. Birds call as they settle in the apple trees and in the tangled thickets surrounding the house. This is paradise.

Max sees my face and swallows. 'What is it?' he asks.

SUMMER 1991

WHEN WE SUFFER a terrible loss, it seems that the world has stopped. But of course the earth keeps turning, the sun keeps rising, the birds fly north to sit outside our windows, singing blissfully, bird-brainedly, of the return of summer's warmth and light. The summer after Maxwell was born, I woke to each day with a heavy heart. I mourned the loss of my little boy. I would continue to do so, in privacy, in the secret space of my own heart, all my life.

But for Margaret's sake I tried to strike a proper balance between grief and perseverance, between sorrow and the recognition of remaining joys. I loved my daughter. I did not want her to feel as lost in the enormity of Maxwell's death as her father seemed to be. With each passing day Max became more withdrawn, isolating himself into a carefully guarded darkness into which we could not penetrate. He would recover with time. But Margaret needed me now. And I needed her. I decided to take her to Nantucket. I would devote all my time to my little girl. We would build sand castles on the beach, play in the salty ocean, let the sea and wind and sun scour our souls and heal us. I would show

Margaret I could still be happy. We would be happy, together.

Max said he would come, but as usual, he was tied up with work. Chip promised to come, too, later. As usual, Kate and I loaded up the Volvo and made the trip ourselves. Almost as usual . . . Abby was with us now.

Kate nursed her baby while I drove and sat holding Abby on the ferry ride over while I supervised the M&Ms, trailing behind them as they exuberantly explored the boat. When we arrived at the house, we settled Kate and Abby in state in the living room. I carried all our luggage into the house and up the stairs. I made all the beds, Kate's and Matthew's as well as our own, and set up the port-a-crib for Abby. I left the children watching television with Kate while I went off to fight the crowds in the streets and stores for groceries. At home I unloaded the groceries and fixed dinner. By the time I got the M&Ms in bed, all I wanted to do was to fall into my own, and I did.

I woke to a room full of sun. It was almost nine o'clock, and I sat up in bed, slightly dazed. How could I have slept so late?

Most mornings, Margaret woke me. I would awaken to the breeze of her arrival, the slight drift of air as she lifted the sheet from my skin and scooted down next to me, the warmth of her presence. I'd feel the stir of her sweet child's breath against my skin.

'Mom-mee,' she'd whisper to me.

I would feign sleep, playing a game that we'd begun when she was there.

'Mom-mee.' A little song. 'Time to wake up.'

Sometimes I'd peep out at her from beneath my lashes. She would be studying my face, one plump finger hovering above me as she decided just where to touch me, lightly.

Would she lift my eyelid? Or try to tickle me beneath my arm? Or make a buzzing noise and delicately brush my ears and lips, then giggle, 'Mommy, that bee is bothering you again!' Finally she'd cry, 'Wake up, Mom! The whole ocean's waiting!'

Why hadn't she awakened me today? She must still be sleeping.

Or perhaps she was lying awake in her bed, waiting for me, thinking that since Maxwell's death everything had changed. My heart twisted.

I slipped from bed, pulled on my scarlet kimono, and went into her room. Her bed was empty, rumpled, the covers tossed back in a rush.

I headed downstairs.

And there she was, my daughter, seated on the living room sofa in her pink and white nightgown, a pillow tucked beneath her arm, and nestled on her lap and arm was three-month-old Abby. The baby wore only a diaper and a white cotton undershirt. Her pink feet and hands waved in the air.

'Hi, Mommy! I'm holding the baby!' Margaret called proudly.

'Morning, Glory,' I said. I sank down next to my daughter. 'Good morning, Abby.'

We both looked down at Abby, who stuck a rosebud tongue between rose petal lips.

'She's making bubbles, Mom. She's trying to talk. Aren't you trying to talk, you smart little girl?' Margaret was totally in love.

Abby was a good baby. She slept through the night. She never had colic. She looked out at the world with calm navy blue eyes that seemed to understand and approve of all she saw.

'Coffee's ready.' Kate came into the room. She wore shorts and a loose white shirt that buttoned up the front, beneath which her proud, formidable breasts were anchored in a nursing bra. She was barefoot and her hair was pulled up into a sloppy ponytail, but in her ears she wore her one carat diamond studs; she'd worn them ever since Chip gave them to her, a present at Abby's birth.

'Great.' I rose and went into the kitchen. I poured myself a mug, added sweetener and milk, and stared at the selection of doughnuts, croissants, and muffins on the table. Since Abby's birth, Kate and I had spent very little time together. I found it hard to be near her baby; she understood. One night in June we went to a movie, just the two of us. By the time we drove home, her blouse was wet with milk. I dropped her at her house and drove home, my face wet with tears of grief and envy. But three months had passed since Maxwell's birth and death. I needed my friend. I missed her. I had to recover my sense of balance and my sense of humor as well if this Nantucket August were to bring us together again.

I returned to the living room to find Kate seated on the sofa next to my daughter and Abby. I sank into a chair across from them. 'Gorgeous day.' I pulled my feet up beneath me and settled back.

'Yes,' she said. 'Makes me feel lazy.' She traced a figure 8 on her daughter's belly. Abby burbled.

'I feel lazy, too,' Margaret said, looking up at Kate with starry-eyed adoration.

'I got it!' Matthew came thudding down the stairs. His short chestnut hair stuck out in a series of cowlicks. He wore a red basketball jersey that hung down to his knees. He carried a bottle of nail polish in his hand.

'Lovely,' Kate said. 'Pull that footstool over here. No, I'll put my feet there. You can sit on the floor.' She smiled at me. 'Matthew's going to paint my toenails for me. It's too hard to do it myself.'

'Want me to do it?' I asked.

'No!' Matthew was definite. 'I'm going to do it.'

Abby made an airy noise and everyone laughed.

'Abby belched,' Margaret announced proudly.

'She's a good baby,' I said. 'Slept all night.'

'I know. She's a little doll.' Kate leaned over her baby and cooed, 'You're a little doll, aren't you, Abby? Mommy's little doll.'

Abby gurgled and shivered with glee.

Kate looked at me. 'You're not having a croissant?'

'I'm not hungry right now.'

'I've already had one. It's delicious.'

'You can have the other, if you want.'

'You're sure?'

'Sure.'

Kate started to rise, then looked down at her right foot, propped on the foot stool. Matthew was biting his lip with concentration, carefully slipping cotton balls between her toes. 'Guess I'll wait.'

'I'll get it,' I said.

'No, *I'll* get it!' Margaret cried urgently. She looked up at Kate. 'You hold Abby.'

'Thanks, sweetie,' Kate said, and lifted her daughter into her arms. 'Who's the most beautiful girl in the whole wide world?' she asked, nuzzling kisses into Abby's face.

Margaret raced to the kitchen, returning with a croissant on a plate and a napkin. 'Here, Kate.'

'Thanks. Let's see. Put the plate on the sofa on this side,

then you sit next to me on this side and hold Abby again for
me so I can eat, okay?'

Margaret gladly obeyed. Abby was perfectly content to be
transferred from arm to arm. Kate sighed and nibbled on her
croissant. Her son sat at her feet, carefully brushing polish
onto Kate's toes.

I said, 'So, Margaret. Let's have breakfast, then we can go
to the beach.'

My daughter shot me a cautious glance. She edged a
millimeter closer to Kate. 'Are you going to the beach?' she
asked Kate.

'Not today.' Kate yawned. 'It was such a commotion
yesterday, getting here. I'm wiped out.'

I ran my finger around the rim of my mug.

'I'm wiped out, too,' my daughter said. She bent over the
baby, wagged her own head from side to side so that her curls
tickled the baby's face, and chanted, 'Aren't you tired, too?
Tired, too? Tired, too?' Abby waved with glee.

'But don't you want to go to the beach?' I asked Margaret.

She didn't look up at me. Her shoulders shrugged beneath
the pink-and-white nightie. 'I can go later.'

'Matthew? Want to go swimming?'

Matthew bent over his mother's feet. 'No, thanks.'

Abby was beginning to fuss. Her face flushed and little
catching sobs broke into her gurgling. Kate's face took on a
radiance.

'I'm going to have to feed her soon.' She stuck a finger
into her daughter's diaper. 'She's still dry. I need a diaper for
my shoulder.'

'I'll get it!' Margaret exclaimed.

'Upstairs, near her crib. Bring me the Handi-Wipes, too.
I'll be needing them sometime soon.'

Her tongue stuck between her teeth as she concentrated, Margaret gently placed the baby in Kate's arms, then she skipped up the stairs.

Matthew said, 'There, Mom! What do you think?'

Kate scrutinized her red toenails. 'It looks perfect, Matthew. Thanks.'

Matthew climbed up on the sofa, snuggled next to his mother, and made a series of comic faces at his sister. Abby cooed and reached out for him, enchanted. Then her face flushed again and she threw herself backwards and began to cry in earnest.

'She's hungry, honey.'

'Here's the diaper!' Margaret skipped back into the room.

Kate put the diaper on her shoulder, unbuttoned her shirt and unfastened her bra. She lifted her breast into her daughter's mouth, adjusted her arm and legs. Margaret sat on one side, watching every movement with wide eyes. On the other side, Matthew scooted close to his mother, reached out his finger, and grinned when Abby clutched it in her fist. The four of them sat there, completely engrossed in the moment.

I could almost feel the tug of a baby's mouth on my nipple, the answering pull deep in my pelvis. The tingling flood of milk. The relief and the narcotic sensations of pleasure. The knowledge of being pulled into the sweet hot core of the universe.

I rose and went upstairs. No one called my name.

THAT WEEKEND, CHIP came down to visit his family and I went back to Sussex. Max had called to say he was so busy that he couldn't come to Nantucket; he would try to come the next weekend. His voice on the phone had been dull, preoccupied, listless.

My own week had been lonely. Kate and Abby and Matthew and Margaret had coalesced into a kind of hive with the baby at the center. Twice I'd taken the M&Ms to the beach while Kate and Abby napped, but when we returned home they flew from my side to find the baby.

I know there is something mysterious and desirous about a nursing mother. There is something primitive and erotic and compelling about a woman with an infant, and Margaret was caught in the spell. At the back of my mind, I was glad. I wanted Margaret to see – to feel – the primal satisfaction of motherhood, so that she would want to have children, so that she would be a good, involved, mother. It was possible she would not have the chance to observe this with me. I might never have another child. Certainly not if Max continued to be sexually numb.

Perhaps it was the unusual heat of that summer, or the humidity that lay over the island like a press, or perhaps it was the spell of a baby, but the six-year-olds were oddly indolent, happy to lie on the floor staring at Abby, or gazing at picture books, or pretending to be babies themselves. I had nothing they wanted. So when I suggested that I go to Sussex to visit Max for the weekend and leave Margaret with Chip and Kate, Kate agreed happily.

And so did Margaret.

MAX WASN'T HOME Friday night, so I left a message on our answering machine: '*Max, I'm coming home for the weekend, and I'm bringing Nantucket to you.*' In the back of the Volvo, I had a cooler packed with lobsters and ice and Nantucket butter-and-sugar corn fresh off the stalk. I had gotten a bit of a tan on Nantucket and a good rest, lying out in the sun, reading, while Margaret hung out with Abby and the gang. It was a treat, traveling all by myself; I put in tapes of Carl Nielsen's symphonies and heard two all the way through, without interruption. By the time I arrived home, I was relaxed, hopeful, even eager to get on with life.

We always had a local boy mow our lawn and water the flowers every August, and as I pulled into our driveway I noted with pleasure how tidy everything looked. Still, there was an air about the place that spoke of emptiness. Perhaps it was the shades pulled down on every single window. Against the sun?

The house was empty when I walked in. I knew it would be. I knew Max would be at work. I planned to shower and set the table with candles and serve a succulent dinner and woo him back to life.

The living room was slightly dusty and had a forlorn air. I walked through the kitchen and into the den, then stood there, stunned. The floor and coffee table and the top of the television were littered with empty Häagen-Dazs cartons, beer bottles, Cheez-It bags, and candy bar wrappers. Not just a few. A week's worth. As if Max had been glutting himself on junk food.

Within Max lived a secret slob; within all of us, probably. During the week before my period I consume chocolate and salt in bizarre combinations, but shame always drove me to hide the containers. Max was generally a tidy man. Even in the chaos of his office he knew where each article was, and while he might settle into a nest of beer and chips for a baseball game, he picked up afterwards. But this. This room . . .

I had called Max last night to tell him I was coming today.

He had had time to pick up, to go through the room with a trash bag and stuff in at least the worst of the trash. This room was like a message. But what was the message? I can't deal? I don't care?

The bathroom and bedroom were the same. The bed was mussed, one corner of the bottom sheet pulled away, exposing the mattress. A week's worth of dirty clothes layered the floor. Damp towels huddled in clumps in the bathroom.

This was not Max. Even in college he had not been so sloppy. I was angry and alarmed. I brought the cooler in and put the lobsters into the refrigerator, then I began to clean. I picked up a basket of clothes and began a wash. I went through the house picking up trash. I vacuumed, set the table, and showered. I put on a pretty dress that set off my tan and the figure I had regained over the past three months.

Then I waited for Max to come home.

It was after eight when I heard the car pull into the drive. I knew by heart how many seconds it took for him to slam the van door, come up the walk, put his key in the lock, and enter our house. I remained on the living room sofa, curled up with a book, wanting to give him all the space in the world.

'Hey.' He set his briefcase on the floor and dropped into a chair.

Perhaps it was that everyone on Nantucket looked supernaturally healthy, but to my eyes Max looked ill. Pale and pasty-faced, his shoulders slumped forward like a man who carried a heavy burden. His eyes were ringed with dark shadows and his multicolored beard sprouted in shaggily, unkempt tufts. His chinos and plaid cotton shirt were wrinkled and soiled.

'I've brought lobster,' I said. 'And fresh corn. The water's boiling on the stove. Why don't you shower? Dinner will be ready in ten minutes.'

'I'm too tired to shower,' he said.

I lighted the tapers on the dining room table. I bustled around in the kitchen, then carried steaming platters of luscious corn and red lobster to the table. I set bowls of butter before each plate. I'd bought a sparkling Italian white wine and I poured it into flutes.

I flapped my napkin open exuberantly. 'Tell me what's happened in Sussex while I've been gone.'

'Not much.' He bent over his plate, cracking a lobster claw.

'Have they found a replacement for the superintendent of schools?'

'Yes. Guy from Boston.'

'What's he like?'

'Great references. Dottie interviewed him. Said she liked him.'

It was like oiling a rusty door, but smoothed with wine and buttery lobster and corn, Max relaxed. I kept plying him with questions. He answered. It was pretty much like having a conversation. It got us through the meal.

Afterwards, Max helped me carry the dishes into the kitchen. As I bent to open the dishwasher, he turned to leave the room.

'Where are you going?'

'To my study. I've got work to do.'

'You've always got work to do.' I tried to keep my voice light, teasing. I dried my hands on a towel. 'Let's do something else tonight.'

'Lucy.'

I sauntered toward him. 'I want to show you my tan.' I

shrugged one shoulder so that the strap of my dress fell down along my arm and the front of the dress dipped, exposing the line where tan skin met white.

Max sighed. He leaned back against the wall and closed his eyes.

I pressed myself against him. Found the spot on his neck where my head fit perfectly. 'Max.' I wrapped my arms around him. 'Oh, Max. I've missed you.'

He didn't answer. He didn't hold me. His body didn't answer mine. I rubbed against him, and felt no quickening response of lust.

Taking his head in mine, I turned his face to mine and put my lips on his. It had been months since we had kissed. It felt odd, shocking. I ground my hips against his, ground my mouth against his. He remained passive.

'Let's go in the bedroom,' I suggested, and took hold of his hand, and tugged. 'Come on.'

He followed diffidently. It was strange to be alone in the house without Margaret, to be able to leave the bedroom door open. I pushed Max down on the bed and knelt over him. I reached for the zipper of his chinos. When my hand touched his skin, he gasped. I thought he gasped. But when I looked at his face, I saw that he was crying. His face was crumpled with sorrow.

'Oh, Max,' I said. 'Honey.'

He sat up. Zipped up his pants. Took out a handkerchief and blew his nose.

'Max. Talk to me.'

I put a hand on his shoulder, and to my dismay, he flinched. 'Don't touch me.'

'Max . . .'

'I've got work to do.' He rose.

'No!' I rose, too. 'I won't let you walk away from me. I've traveled all day to be with you. Max, don't shut me out like this.'

He stared at me through red-rimmed eyes. 'What do you want me to do?'

'I want you to talk to me. I want you to talk to me about Maxwell's death.'

Against his face crumpled. He turned his back on me.

'Max.'

'I want a son,' he said.

Something in his tone of voice chilled me. Moved me to a strange new realm of fear.

'All right.' I spoke gently, as if he were a wounded animal. 'Go on.'

'What else is there to say?' Crossing the room, he sat down on the little slipper chair, oblivious of the several shirts he'd tossed there. 'You . . . we lost our son.'

'I know.' I sank onto the bed, facing him. Leaning toward him. 'I know, and it's unbearable, but somehow we have to bear it. And go on.'

'I never wanted to tell you how much I want a son,' Max confessed. His face was in the shadows. 'It seemed—' he laughed '—*politically incorrect* to admit how much I want a son. It doesn't mean I don't love Margaret. I love her more than the earth. But still . . . I want a son. I've dreamed about him, my boy, someone to teach baseball and soccer, to take fishing and camping like my father took me. Someone to take to the Red Sox games. To see the Celtics. Someone who looks like me. Someone who *is* like me. A male. A guy. My boy.'

'I didn't know.' I had never been so sad in all my life. 'Oh, honey.'

'Maxwell looked like me.'

'Yes. He did.' We sat in silence for a while, thinking of the baby. Then I said what others had said to me, what the doctors had said, and the nurses, and all our well-meaning friends. What I didn't believe until this moment. 'We can have another baby, Max.'

He shook his head sharply. 'No.'

'What do you mean, no? Of course we can have another baby.'

'Go through nine months of waiting, and have another *dead* baby?'

I was stunned by the bitterness in his voice. 'Max, what happened to Maxwell was unusual. Unpredictable. Statistically—'

'Statistically means nothing. Your record is, one live child, one dead. I don't think we want to see what the third try brings.'

'*My* record.'

Max did not reply.

I sat, letting his words reassemble in my mind, forming a new and terrible pattern. *I want a son. Your record.*

'Max, are you saying that you don't want to have another child with me?'

He hesitated. 'That's right.'

'But you want a son.'

He nodded.

A stream of ice poured down my spine. 'You want to have a son with someone else.'

He didn't respond.

'No,' I said firmly. 'No, you can't do this. You love me, Max, you know you do! You don't want to have a baby with someone else! You need me, me and Margaret. You love us and we love you.' I knelt before him, taking his hands in mine. 'Come on, sweetie. We can have another baby, a baby born healthy like Margaret!'

He stared at me, and there was nothing but sorrow in his eyes.

And a new thought struck me, and I shrank back from Max.

'Are you in love with someone else?'

He swatted my words away. 'No.'

'Max. You owe me the truth.'

'No.'

'Are you interested in someone else?'

He didn't reply.

'Are you seeing someone else? While I'm in Nantucket?'

'No.'

'But there is someone else you want to see. Who? Some hefty wide-hipped cow who could birth entire tribes?'

'Don't be stupid.'

'I'm trying not to be. But you've got to help me, Max. I'm in the dark here. I'm – I feel like someone who's just been pushed over the edge of a cliff.'

My fingertips and lips had gone numb and I was having trouble breathing.

'Do you still love me, Max?'

Max said, 'I don't know.'

SUMMER 1991

THAT WEEKEND WITH Max was probably the loneliest weekend of my life. My husband had entered a dark solitude and shut me out. I was as worried for him as I was for our marriage. I didn't think he was having an affair. He didn't have the ease or glow of a man who was having an affair.

Before I left Sussex to return to Nantucket, I had paid a private visit to Roland Cobb, Max's second in command at the newspaper, and his good friend. Roland told me that even at the newspaper Max was showing signs of depression. He, too, was worried about Max. He promised to try to persuade Max to see a psychiatrist, to get some kind of help. His opinion would be more convincing to Max than mine.

As I drove back to Hyannis, I told myself that when Max felt better, he would think rationally again. He would understand that we could have another child. That we could have another living child.

If staying with Max would have helped him, I would have brought Margaret back to spend the remainder of August in Sussex. But during that sorrowful weekend in August, I was made aware with every moment that my presence brought

Max no joy, no relief. I was terrified; I was heartbroken. I had
been warned that this could happen, that the death of a child
often caused a couple to separate, but I never dreamed it
could have happened to us. To Max and me. We were
soulmates. I had to believe that when Max returned from his
black confusion to find his soul again, he would remember
me.

And my daughter would come back to me, too, I knew. I
understood her completely. She was totally enthralled with
baby Abby. She was like a woman in love for the first time, a
woman possessed, as the profound, instinctive, gripping
magic of infant and mother displayed itself to her day after
day. She could not take her eyes from Abby and Kate. She
wanted to be both of them. She wanted to be in their skin.

She was learning what it meant to be a mother.

She was learning it from Kate.

And Kate. I understood Kate, too. She was punch-drunk
on hormones, blissed out by glands. She moved slowly. She
was in no hurry. She was at the center of a hot, immediate,
pungent, juicy world. She was like a queen, and Matthew and
Margaret trailed her like the attendants she deserved.

One night, during the middle of the week, I said to Kate,
'Want to go dancing some night at the Muse?'

She burst out laughing. 'You must be kidding! With
these?' She glanced down proudly, derisively, at her breasts.
'But why don't you go?'

'Yeah, like I would go without you!'

'I'm sorry, Lucy, but the thought of being in the room
with a bunch of clueless drunks just doesn't appeal to me any
more.'

I considered. 'Well, then, why don't you and I go out to
dinner some night. The Chanticleer. I'll treat.'

Kate shifted on the sofa, stretching her beautiful long legs. She studied her brilliant red toenails. 'Oh, I don't know. I'm so lazy these days, Lucy. I'm perfectly content. Abby's being such a good baby and the M&Ms are being such a help.'

'You've changed.'

'I know. I've lost that old craving for something new and exciting. But that's all right. It's probably natural. We all change as we grow older.'

I considered saying, 'Yeah, but, Kate, what about me? I need someone to play with. I need my friend.'

But it would be demeaning to say that. I didn't want to beg for her company.

So I spent two more lonely weeks in my Aunt Grace's house watching my daughter and Matthew hover around Kate and her baby as if held there by some kind of magnetic force. Chip arrived on Thursday night; he spent Friday swimming with Matthew. Margaret opted to stay with Kate and baby Abby. I spent the day by myself, at another part of the beach, reading the bloodiest paperback mystery I could find. Or, rather, I spent the day staring at the book, where the words ran together on the page into a blurry pattern no less incomprehensible than my life. When no one else was around, I let myself give into great heaving soundless sobs. Before I went back to the house, I immersed myself in the water, so that my wet suit and dripping hair would provide a reason for my red-rimmed eyes.

Then, on Saturday, Chip asked, 'Anyone want to go sailing?'

'You've got to be kidding,' Kate said.

I said, 'I'll go.'

It was the third weekend in August, and very hot and muggy. Kate reclined on a chaise on the porch, reading; Abby drowsed nearby in a wicker cradle; Matthew and Margaret were in the backyard, running through the sprinkler.

'Want to go to Tuckernuck?' He named a small island to the west of Nantucket.

'Sure. I'll pack a lunch.'

I filled a hamper with all kinds of grown-up delicacies, and organized a carryall with towels and sunblock. I pulled Margaret from the rainbow arcs of the sprinkler water to tell her I'd be gone most of the day. She was dripping wet and giggling at Matthew who slid and fell on the slippery grass, and she pecked a kiss in the direction of my cheek before racing back into her game. I told Kate good-bye; she told me, without looking up from her book, to have fun.

HUMIDITY LAY LIKE a white veil over the island, but out on the sound the sky rose above us in a dazzlingly clear halcyon blue. A lazy breeze sent us tacking over tranquil waters. The boat sheered along, tossing up bubbles, like iridescent confetti, as we went. I leaned back to feel the sun on my face while Chip navigated the shoals and shallow waters between the islands and veered toward the northern side of Tuckernuck. We didn't talk. Chip was intent on the sail. I relaxed into the warm day.

Tuckernuck was a small, wild island with no electricity, one telephone, and only a scattering of houses belonging to the few peculiar families who took refuge here when their need for solitude and serenity won over their need for civilization. Near a grove of trees we spotted a cluster of bright color, people walking on the island, and a few sails winked on the horizon, but chiefly we saw sand, sea, sky. Most people liked to picnic on the long bar of sand called

Whale Island, but Chip sailed us to the north and around to the west, into the perfect shelter of Outer North Pond. No one else was here, on land or water.

He maneuvered the boat just to the edge of a shelf of sand, dropped the sail, secured the lines of the boat, and jumped into the shallow water.

I handed him the picnic hamper and towels, then climbed out and waded to shore. The water was as warm as it would ever get, but it was still a shock as it lapped around my skin. It took my breath away.

The sand crunched as we walked to the center of the cove and spread out our towels. On the left, beach plum and wild rose bushes, tangled with vines and speared through with beach grass, provided a low wall to screen us from the water. On the right, a sandy cliff rose perhaps fifteen feet, twisted cedar trees clawing for purchase in the treacherous soil. The sand was warm, the light thick and honey-colored. The wind rustled the natural barrier of bushes but did not so much as flutter the tips of the towels we spread on the sand and anchored with the picnic basket and cooler. I unzipped my florescent yellow life vest and dropped it on the turquoise towel, then began to set out lunch.

Chip settled next to me on a lime green towel, his big feet sticking out into the sand. He was taller than Max, bigger than anyone I'd been around recently. Thick hair on his legs and arms glinted like spun gold in the sunlight and I found myself wondering how much more calcium he would need than anyone else, just to fortify the bones in those long legs. His toes were ridiculously long and crooked and white, like exposed secrets.

'Turkey and brie?' I asked him. 'Or chutney and cheddar.'

I sat cross-legged, aware of the little ball of belly rising from my bikini.

'One of each.'

'How about a nice cold beer?'

'Great.'

I reached into the cooler and brought out a can, beads of ice slithering down its slick sides. My fingers touched Chip's as I handed it to him, his skin hot, a contrast to the cold can.

We sat side by side, munching, scanning the distance. A gust of wind tickled the hairs along the back of my neck. The sun lay steadily on our bare shoulders.

I asked, 'Is that a heron? Over on the other side of the pond?'

He looked. 'I think so. Your eyesight's better than mine.'

'But you can see well enough to sail.' I wasn't really worried.

'Probably,' he teased.

'How reassuring.'

'Know anyone who has a house here?'

'I do. A woman who lives year round on Nantucket. Cindy Harvey. Her parents have a summer place here. I stayed here a few times when I was a teenager. They had a generator, lots of houses do, but there are no electric street-lights, well, there are no streets. It gets so dark here you wouldn't believe it.' I reached into the bag. 'Cookies? Grapes?'

'I'll take some grapes.' He leaned back on his elbows and lifted his face to the sun.

I twisted a clump of seedless red grapes from the cluster and twisted another clump for myself. Perhaps we'd go for a walk, I thought. I could show him where Cindy's house was.

Then, 'So how are you doing, Lucy?' Chip asked.

I blinked. 'All right.' I wasn't sure what he meant. Of the four of us, Chip was the one person who hated introspection and soul-searching. Occasionally he'd enter a debate with Max about politics or some other town issue, but he grew impatient when Kate and I talked about personal matters. Once when the four of us were confined to a car together, riding in to see a play in Boston, Kate and Max and I got into a heated discussion about the nature of God. Suddenly Kate burst into laughter and nodded her head toward Chip, who was gazing out the window in the backseat, his mind clearly elsewhere. 'Elvis has left the building,' she'd said, shaking her head at her husband's inattention.

Chip said, 'I was afraid it might be too hard on you. Living with Kate and Abby. After losing Maxwell.'

Emotions flooded my body. For a moment I couldn't speak.

'And I can bet Max isn't a whole lot of help,' Chip continued.

I swallowed. 'Why do you say that?'

'Hey, I've known the guy for years now. Losing that little boy hit him hard.'

'Max has talked to you about this?'

'Not really. Not much. But I don't need a neon sign to read him.'

'It's a pretty difficult time for us,' I admitted.

'It's a fucking bitch,' Chip said.

'Yes,' I agreed. 'It is a fucking bitch.' And all at once a cataract of tears swept through me, and I folded my arms over my knees and buried my face and wept helplessly.

Chip sat next to me in silence. After a while he put his hand on my back and patted me, a few slow solid masculine thumps. His large hand, firm and warm, was the kindest sensation I'd experienced in weeks.

'Oh, Chip,' I sobbed. 'Max says he doesn't know if he loves me any more. I'm so sad. I'm so lonely. I don't know how I'm going to go on.'

Chip pulled me toward him. I turned and rested my face against his shoulder. There was something in his size, his largeness, that made me feel young again, like a child being comforted by her father, and in those moments I surrendered to every anguish in my body, feeling that somehow this larger man could keep me safe, as if he were really holding my body, together, so that it wouldn't break apart with sorrow. It was an amazing, unexpected, singular feeling, landed on that unfamiliar shore, far from other people, surrounded by sand and sea and sky, naked except for my bikini; I was purely vulnerable, honestly exposed, my elemental self, curled up like a baby, like a shell, in that clear world. My daughter couldn't hear the desperate sounds wrenched from my throat, my husband did not have to bear witness one more time to the disfigurement of my grief. I could let go.

'Lucy, It's okay. It's okay.' Chip stroked my hair.

His caress was infinitely soothing. His shoulder was broad, his arm strong. I pulled away and wiped my tears with my fists. I looked up at Chip, this man I had known for years, and saw such mercy in his face that my breath caught in my chest.

'Chip,' I said.

And as if it were in all the world the only right thing to do, Chip bent and kissed me. His lips were soft, his breath smelled of beer and mustard. He held me firmly, cradling the back of my head in his hand. I had probably never looked more terrible, with my hair tangled from the salt breeze and my face streaked with tears and my belly just three months away from a full-term pregnancy. His touch on my skin was forgiving, and giving. He moved his hand over me as if molding me, and wherever he touched, it seemed my body sprang to life. His touch was like rain after a drought, making seeds stir deep in the dust of my senses.

I wrapped my arms around him. Now the palms of my own hands were aroused and eager, and I touched what I'd marveled at for so long; the curves and knobs of Chip's shoulders and elbows and knees, the adamant length and width of his back, the tender buttons of his nipples, the swelling heat beneath his swimming trunks.

He untied the knot at the back of my suit, and my breasts fell free into the sunlight; their skin was as white as the inside of a shell, the nipples hard and orange-pink, like rose hips. Chip laid me down on my side on the towel, and lay on his side next to me. The sand yielded beneath us as if the earth itself were giving us permission. He brought his mouth to my breast, and gently tugged at my nipple. My breast stung. It was as if a dam stretched beneath my nipples, and Chip tugged again, and the dam broke open, and sensation flooded my body. Overwhelmed, I closed my eyes, nearly swooning into the sand.

I kept my eyes closed while he untied the sides of my bikini bottom. The sand shifted and sifted as he took off his trunks. I felt first of all the blot of cool shadow as he lifted himself above me, blocking out the sun, and then I felt the hot hard shaft of his penis enter me. I shuddered with relief and pleasure. This was real. This was now. I was a naked woman on a solitary beach indulging in the world's oldest form of consolation. I hugged Chip against me, loving the feel of a man's body on me, in me, loving the weight of his

chest and the stir of his breath and the moist pressure of his
mouth and the deep expanse of his cock inside my body. This
moment was as authentically mine as anything in my life. I
was grateful with all my being. The pleasure was intense. I
didn't want it to end. It built, wave upon wave, carrying me
with it in a tide of sensation deep into a whirlpool of bliss.
Tears spurted from my eyes and shook my body. Dimly I felt
Chip reach his own climax. He rolled over, next to me, and
sighed, and reaching out, he took my hand in his. My cheeks
were gritty with sand and tears.

We lay side by side, naked, holding hands, the sun beating
down on us. Eyes closed, I savored the satisfaction of the
body after sex.

'You're a beautiful woman,' Chip said.

I smiled. 'You're sweet.'

'I mean it. Don't you know I mean it?' He turned to face
me. He ran his fingers along the line of my cheek, down my
throat, around my breast. 'You're beautiful in many ways.'

'I only know that right now I feel happy,' I said, yawning.
The sun's warmth on my skin, the gentle lapping of the
water on the shore, the cries of the gulls overhead, the sense
that *now* was eternity lulled me. I slept.

I WOKE TO see Chip walking down to the water. He plunged
off in a strong crawl down the length of the inlet. I watched
for a while, then rose and went to the water's edge. Waves
lapped at my feet. A much less confident swimmer than
Chip, still I walked into the water, gasping as the cold hit my
abdomen, then I lay down in the salty sea pond. I swam a few
strokes, turned over on my back, and floated. Swam some
more. My body felt healthy, strong, supple. I was relaxed, and

the salt pond supported me. When I walked up onto the shore, I felt as if I had been somehow renewed, almost baptized, by the sea.

'We should go back,' I said.

'Let's finish this last beer,' Chip suggested.

We sat on the towels, their edges fluttering at our feet in the growing wind. Chip's long legs stretched beside mine, the golden hair crusted with sand. A slender strip of dark green seaweed clung to his ankle.

Chip said, 'It was good between us. We could be together, Lucy.'

I held the beer to my mouth and felt the wetness from Chip's mouth on the metal rim. I shook my head. 'Don't, Chip.'

'Haven't you ever thought about it? About us?'

'I don't dare.' I handed him back the can and felt the warmth of his fingers on mine. I scooted on the blanket so that I was away from him, facing him. 'I'm married. Kate is my best friend. We all have children.'

'I like being with you, Lucy. I've always been sexually attracted to you, but what I feel for you is more—'

I stood up abruptly. Sand shifted down from my suit onto my feet, making whispering noises. 'We shouldn't talk like this. Hell, Chip, we should be feeling *guilty*. *Remorseful*. You've got a brand new baby. This is all just *wrong*.'

'I don't think so.' Chip leaned back on his arms looking up at me; his long narrow body, all bones and ropy muscles extended before me. The sun hit my body at such an angle that my shadow fell across him in a long stripe, like a brand, as if he were marked by me, as if his body possessed something of mine, something immaterial but real, part of my spirit, part of my soul. I was frightened and thrilled.

'I want to go back,' I said. 'Now. Please.'

The wind had picked up during the day. We sped back to Nantucket over choppy waters. Chip was challenged by the shifting wind, thoroughly engrossed with tacking and adjusting the sails, which made him happy, and made me nervous. He was such a handsome man. How many affairs had he had? Any woman would want to sleep with him, just to touch his perfect body. He was braver than I, more aggressive, more experimental. He was a wonderful lover, too, and he was kind. That he had actually entertained thoughts of the two of us together was stunning, staggering, amazing; it was complimentary and terrifying. All right, so he was less cowed by turbulence than I was; I was still not a complete coward. If I let myself imagine life with him . . . well, I wouldn't do it. I could, but I wouldn't. I would not. We had children to think about, we had Kate and Max.

Lying between Whale Island on Tuckernuck and Smith's Point on Nantucket was a stretch of deceptively innocent water, a rippling aquamarine region that looked like an easy swim in several directions to the soundness of land. In fact the curve and lie of the land and the small opening between the two islands sent a fierce fast current surging along, relentlessly sweeping with it anything that came its way. I had heard that even a strong swimmer could drown here, in these chaotic depths, just yards from shore.

Chip liked a challenge and was good at anything he set his mind to, and we arrived without mishap at last at the inner harbor, took a boat launch to the shore, and headed up to the Volvo. During the sail back we didn't talk, but once in the car I felt enclosed in an intimate space, and needed to speak.

'Chip, about today. I did like it.'

He threw an abashed grin my way. 'I noticed.'

'But I wish it hadn't happened.'

'Really?'

'Really. I want to act as if it never happened. I'm committed to my family. And God knows you can't even consider deserting Kate now.'

He was quiet for a long time. Then he sighed. 'You're right, Lucy. I know you're right. But I want you to know—'

Reaching over, I put my fingers on his mouth. 'No. I don't want to know. Nothing more.'

He took my hand in his and kissed my palm. He said, 'All right.'

We didn't speak again until we arrived back at Aunt Grace's house.

I TOLD MYSELF that what happened on Tuckernuck was a secret, an aberration, something to be taken so lightly it could evaporate into the air, like froth on waves.

Still, I felt stronger when I walked into the house. I felt rejuvenated, capable, alive. Kate and the M&Ms and Abby were in the living room, the children hypnotized by some idiotic television show, Kate reading her paperback.

'How was the sail?' she asked carelessly.

'Great!' I replied over my shoulder as I headed upstairs. I showered and spread a lightly fragrant lotion all over my tanned body, pulled on a sundress and sandals, and went back down to the living room.

'Come on, Margaret,' I said to my daughter. 'Let's get you dressed in something pretty. I'm taking you into town for a shopping spree.'

Margaret looked at me with slightly glazed eyes. Her face had a kind of pouchiness to it from sitting still on a humid day. 'Mom. I want to stay with the baby.'

'You've been with the baby all day. It's my turn to enjoy the pleasure of your company.' My tone was sweet, but firm. My daughter knew that tone of voice. 'Besides,' I added, 'we need to let the Cunninghams alone for a while. They need to spend time together as a family.'

Margaret blinked. Her lower lip quivered. Had I been too cruel, reminding her that she wasn't part of the precious inner circle? If so, too bad. She had to come to terms with it sooner or later.

Still she hesitated. I took her hand and pulled. Reluctantly, she stood. I led her to her bedroom, changed her dress, put barrettes in her hair, realizing as I tended to my child that she was lovely. I had forgotten how lovely she was.

'Let's buy you a pink-and-white striped dress,' I said, turning Margaret around to brush the back of her curly brown hair. 'And a pink-and-white headband for your hair.'

'And peppermint ice cream!' she cried, laughing.

We looked at our faces in the mirror: mother and daughter, identical faces, mine older and thinner and red-nosed, hers chubbier and paler, both of us smiling.

'And peppermint ice cream,' I agreed.

AUGUST 17, 1998

MAX'S CHINOS, BLUE-and-white striped shirt, blue sleeveless cotton sweater vest, red bow tie, lie across our bed, his loafers and socks on the floor near the chair. He's pulling on a faded pair of madras shorts. His chest is bare, and in spite of our week in the sun, his arms and neck are still darker than his torso, giving him the vulnerable look of a creature turned on its back, soft belly exposed.

'Max,' I say, my voice coming out strangled, 'Jeremy has cystic fibrosis.'

He frowns. 'What the hell?'

'Max, I'm so scared. I had to pretend that everything's all right. I haven't told Jeremy yet. I want you to be with me when we tell him. And they have to do more tests. But they're sure, and it was so horrible, driving home Jeremy wanted to sing that stupid, *stupid* camp song.'

Max puts his hands on my shoulders and moves me to the bed. 'Wait a minute, Lucy. Sit down. I don't understand.'

'That damn song about the fly!' Tears shoot from my eyes. 'You know. "There was an old lady who swallowed a fly," and she swallows a cat and a dog and a pig and the refrain is always, "perhaps she'll die!" The doctor's diagnosis shoots through my body like a meteor, and sparks of fear flicker in my stomach. 'Why do they teach children such terrible songs?'

'Okay, it will be okay,' Max says.

'It won't be okay,' I whisper. 'I'm so scared.'

'Here,' Max says, after a while. Looking down, I watch him pry my hands off the beer bottles I've been clutching tightly. He twists the lid off one. 'Take a sip.'

I refuse. My throat is clotted with mucus and terror. 'Jeremy could die.'

Max goes white around the nostrils. 'Look. Start over from the beginning. I don't even know what the hell cystic fibrosis is.'

'It's a disease that affects the lungs and the digestion. It's why Jeremy has had so many colds. Why he hasn't gained weight.'

'Okay.' Max chews his cheek as the information sinks in. 'There's medicine for it, right?'

'There are lots of medicines, to alleviate the various problems. Antibiotics. Enzyme supplements.'

'Okay. Okay. We can deal with this.'

'We have to tell Jeremy, but the social worker suggested that first you and I discuss how to do it.'

'All right.'

'We don't need to tell him everything yet.'

Max's entire face goes white beneath his tan. 'Everything.'

'Max, the average life expectancy of someone with CF is around thirty. Thirty years ago the average life expectancy was eight years.'

Light fades from Max's eyes, drains from his skin. His mouth, his entire jawline, sags. It's as if he's aging years in these few minutes. He fights for optimism. 'There are medical breakthroughs every day.'

'Not every day.' The grief rises up in me again, and the terror.

Max's forehead furrows. 'My God, Lucy. How did this happen?'

A hearty knock sounds at the door. 'Dinner, guys!' Chip calls.

'Later,' I call back.

'Everything okay?'

'*Later*,' Max yells, an edge to his voice.

Max and I listen, almost seeing Chip as he hesitates, puzzled and curious. For a moment I feel very strongly how Max and I are a couple, huddled together here. We hear Chip ambling off down the stairs.

Max says, 'Jesus, Lucy, I'm sorry I wasn't with you today. I had no idea . . . God, I'm sorry you had to do this alone.'

'It's all right.'

'It's not all right. It's unbelievable. It's terrifying.'

Another stick catches in my throat, snags my breath. 'Max. You have to help me through this.'

'Of course I'll help you! Jesus! How can you say that?'

I pull away from him. We are at the core of it. Jeremy's illness is making me fold back and fold back the thick obscuring dark leaves of the past to expose the hard pale knot of truth hiding within.

I fold my arms over my chest. I look down at the old rag rug on the floor, every shade of blue and green blurring at my feet. 'You've deserted me before.'

'I've never . . .'

I look up at him, my husband, this man whom I've loved and lived with for fifteen years. Strands of gray curl among the glossy black of his hair. His jaw and mouth are rimmed with a day-old beard that is almost blue and delineated as sharply around his mouth as if drawn with pen and ink. 'Emotionally, you've deserted me. And physically.'

He blinks. Then he takes a deep breath and nods. 'I know I have.'

'This is as bad as losing Maxwell.' My voice thickens. I dig my nails into my arms. 'This is worse.'

'Lucy, I won't desert you, not this time. I promise.'

'There's something else.' An anesthetizing ice sheets over me, a glacier of dread.

Max looks at me.

Through numbed lips I say, 'The thing about cystic fibrosis is that it's caused by a genetic defect. The parents don't have to have it, but they have to be carriers. A child can have cystic fibrosis only if *both* parents carry the gene. And if one child has cystic fibrosis, his siblings could also have cystic fibrosis.'

'But Margaret has been so healthy.'

'Or the child could simply carry the gene, to be passed on to his children. There's a good chance that the sibling of a child with cystic fibrosis carries the gene. If someone who carries the gene marries someone else who carries the gene, there's a one in four chance that their child will have cystic fibrosis.'

'Is there a test for this gene?'

'There is.'

'So we need to have Margaret tested, right?'

'Maybe not.' I look down at my hands, then back up at Max. I look him steadily, squarely, in the eyes. 'We need to have you tested. And Chip has to be tested, too.'

SUMMER 1991

THE EVENING OF that remarkable Saturday, when Margaret and I were in a shop buying her a pink-and-white striped dress, we ran into friends from Sussex who were vacationing for a week on the island. I'd always found Jana Myers a little too prissy for me, and her daughter was a year younger than Margaret, but Tiffany was rumored to have an enormous collection of My Little Ponies, and when they invited us over the next day, I accepted with alacrity.

Sunday morning I woke Margaret early, dressed her, and hustled her outside. We would leave the Volvo for the Cunninghams to use; we rode our bikes into town for a leisurely pancake breakfast. We strolled around, listening to the street musicians, looking in the shops, buying trinkets, and then we went to the Myers, where I suffered ten thousand deaths of boredom Sunday afternoon as Jana showed me various swatches of chintz; she was redecorating the guest bedroom. Tiffany did have a huge collection of My Little Ponies, and Margaret enjoyed herself so much she pleaded not to leave, reminding me what it was like to be a child, fully immersed in the moment, reminding me how intensely Margaret went at things, how wholeheartedly she bestowed her heart on each moment's immediate passion.

Abby had been her recent passion. And Kate. I wanted to be her immediate passion. So I enticed her with a special treat: since she was wearing her pink-and-white dress, I would take her to dinner with me in the main dining room of the Jared Coffin House, where she knew the Cunninghams and Max and I often ate, always without children. Shameless, I told her that Matthew wouldn't be able to eat in this elegant restaurant with its thick white linen tablecloths and hushed atmosphere for years yet; he was just too rowdy and fidgety. Smug at her own refinement, Margaret behaved like a royal child, sitting straight-backed in her chair, watching me to see which fork to use, taking small bites. I let her order a Shirley Temple, a grilled cheese sandwich, and a hot fudge sundae. Not a vegetable in the lot. She made burping noises as we rode our bikes home in the twilight.

Still, as we pedaled up to the house, my Aunt Grace's house, home of so many nights and days, I felt a slight sadness. This summer so much had changed. I had lost the feeling that I was coming home. The lights burning in every window did not seem welcoming. They only reminded me that the Cunninghams were in occupancy, all four of them.

The floors of the house were crusty with sand. Wet towels and Matthew's wet swimsuit lay in soggy piles on the stairs, a damp T-shirt hung over the newel post. Chip was in the kitchen, cleaning up from what appeared to be a messy spaghetti dinner. From the second floor I heard baby Abby wailing furiously and Kate's terse voice.

Margaret ran ahead of me, light and dainty and delicate in her pink and white, holding the pink My Little Pony I'd bought her at Congdon's. I followed.

The floor of the bathroom the Cunninghams used was heaped with towels. Abby was propped in her carry seat, red-faced and wailing as Kate knelt on the floor, drying Matthew off. Matthew was wailing, too.

'That *hurts*, Mom!' he screamed.

Blood drizzled down both of Matthew's legs from large but not deep scrapes on his knees. Kate was spraying Bactine on the wounds while Matthew danced with fury, his tiny penis flopping up and down. Two large round wet spots darkened Kate's blouse, her milk soaking through.

For one brief moment both Margaret and I halted, stunned and slightly aghast, like characters who'd been living in a Jane Austen novel now presented with something by Dickens. Then Margaret entered the fray.

'Can I hold Abby?'

'Please,' Kate said.

Margaret handed me her pony for safekeeping, swooped down on the carry seat, unstrapped Abby, and picked her up. But Abby was nearly purple with rage and would not be pacified. She squirmed and arched her back and screamed, and Margaret's face fell.

Margaret looked up at me, tears in her own eyes. 'She doesn't like me any more, Mom.'

'Of course she likes you. She's just tired and hungry. Come on, let's go in your bedroom, where it's quiet.'

We went down the hall and around the corner into our wing, which suddenly seemed a haven of peace.

Margaret gently laid the baby on her bed. Then 'Oh, no, Mom!' she cried. Abby had leaked a greasy green diarrhea all over Margaret's pink-and-white dress. 'Oh, gross, gross, ick!'

'It will come out in the wash, I promise you.' I leaned over the baby, undoing her diaper. 'Margaret, run and get me a fresh diaper and some baby wipes and baby powder. Poor baby, such a red bum, no wonder you're angry,' I said.

Abby twisted on the bed, her entire body crimson with wrath, but as I wiped her tender skin and softly dried her and sprinkled soothing cool talc on her, she began to calm down. Now she made pitiful whimpers.

'Poor little girl, she's hungwy,' I cooed. 'Hungwy ba.' Why did we speak baby talk to babies, I wondered, and knew why: It works. Abby settled into my arms, her lower lip quivering, her mouth moving, eyes fixed on mine as she tried to communicate her needs and to take comfort from my concern.

I held her in one arm while I unbuttoned Margaret's dress with my free hand. Then I stripped off the soiled bedspread and sheets and tossed them with Margaret's dress in the wicker basket.

'I want to take a bath,' Margaret was whining. 'I've got poop smell on my front.'

'I'll start the bath water,' I told her. 'You can put this in—' I handed her my best bubble bath and turned on the water, testing it for temperature and ascertaining that it was coming slowly, so that I'd have time to run downstairs before the tub was full. 'But don't get in the bath until I'm here. I'm going to put these things in the washing machine right away. Turn off the water if it gets too high.'

I raced past Matthew's room. He was sitting on his mother's lap, crying like a very tired little boy. I hurried downstairs and into the laundry room only to find both the washer and dryer filled and running. What looked like every towel and beach towel in the house lay in smelly wet heaps.

'It's my fault,' Chip said from the doorway. He was still in

his swimming trunks, his hair dried into a salt-stiffened mop.
He dried a pot as he spoke. 'I insisted that we all go to the
beach. Kate's as white as wax. She needed some sun. Abby
developed a tummyache, Kate thinks from the heat and the
breeze. She's been throwing up and having diarrhea. All over
all of us and everything in the whole house. And poor
Matthew got caught by a wave. He swallowed a lot of water
and fell and scraped his hands and knees pretty badly.'

He looked so forlorn and it was such a terrible list of
normal disasters that I burst out laughing. 'Chip, please don't
bother with the dishes or the laundry. I can deal with them
after I get Margaret's sheets changed and get her tucked into
bed.'

'Do you want me to take Abby?' Chip asked.

I looked down, surprised, at the baby girl who I was
carrying easily against my hip. Abby stared up at me as if I
were some sort of oddity she was trying to figure out.

'Sure. I'll work on the laundry.'

I handed Abby over to her father, and at once she burst
into full-blown tears. I saw Chip's face register disappointment, and as I turned away I felt a corresponding, and
irrational jolt of pleasure: Abby liked me.

I returned to our bathroom and helped Margaret step into
the bath. While she murmured to herself among the bubbles,
I put fresh sheets on her bed, old sheets I had used as a little
girl, pink-and-white sheets. I helped her dry off and slipped
a frilly nightie over her, and we sat in bed together while I
read stories to her and we listened to the noises the various
Cunninghams made crashing around the house.

After I kissed her goodnight, I went downstairs, put a
clean load of clothes in a basket, transferred towels from the
washer to the dryer, and put in a new load of wash. Then I

set to work on the kitchen. Chip had done a fairly good job
of loading the dishes, but the stove top was spattered with
tomato sauce and the floor was littered with bits of
uncooked spaghetti and sand. I swept and mopped away, as
much from a need to keep away from the noise on the
second floor as from a desire to have things sparkling clean.

Finally I went up. I checked on Margaret, who was sound
asleep. In the peace of my bathroom, I took a shower, then
pulled on my kimono and headed downstairs to transfer one
more load of laundry from the washer to the dryer.

The back door was still open. The porch light was not on,
but as I pulled hot dry clothes from the dryer into the basket
I could hear Kate and Chip arguing, her voice shrill, his a
bass murmur. I could not make out their words.

I slammed the door on the dryer and turned the timer,
grabbed the basket of clean laundry, and fled up the stairs. I
left the laundry in the hall; we'd sort it out later. My thoughts
were churning. I shut my door against the turmoil of the rest
of the house, plumped up my pillows, and settled into bed
with a novel. I forced myself to concentrate.

Around eleven, I turned off my light and slipped down
into the clean silky sheets.

I AWOKE WITH a start. It was late, dark. I looked at my
bedside clock. Ten minutes until one. My bedroom door was
opening. Margaret, with a nightmare?

Chip.

He shut the door behind him and turned the lock.

I started to sit up, but he crossed the room in a few brief
steps, pulled back the sheet and climbed into bed next to me.
Lust surged up inside me. His body was hot and large and

smelled like sun.

'This isn't a good idea,' I whispered.

In response, he put his hand on my cheek and studied my face. 'Lucy,' he said.

That was all he said. All he needed to say. I wrapped my arms around him and pulled him to me. The sheets whispered around us as we moved on them. We made no sounds at all. It was lovely and urgent and so quick I didn't come, but that didn't matter. Just having a man's body in my arms was sufficient pleasure. Afterward he curled himself around me. We lay there in spoon fashion for a while. I felt his breathing grow slow and steady.

'Chip,' I whispered. 'You can't sleep here.'

'I'm not asleep,' he said. 'I've never been so not asleep.' He stroked my hair with his hand, left his fingers tangled in it for a few moments, and then rose and left the bedroom.

I lay staring out at the night sky, purple-black, full of stars.

THE NEXT MORNING I packed up clothes for Margaret and me, and over a cup of coffee I told Kate we were going back to Sussex for a few days.

Kate had dark circles under her eyes, but Abby was well now, eating ravenously, her diarrhea over. '*We* should go back,' she said. 'This is your house. We've overrun it like a horde of barbarians.'

I looked her right in the eye. What did she know? What did she guess? 'No, I need to take Margaret and go back to Sussex and do something about Max. I'm not sure what, but something. He's got to come here, he's got to get away from work for a few days, and if he won't do it unless I drag him bodily, then I guess I'll drag him back bodily.'

'Do you think you could bring Matthew's ball and bat and glove when you come? He forgot it and then so did Chip.'

'Sure,' I said, and then kissed Kate on the top of her head and Abby on the top of her head and picked up my bags and called my daughter and we headed out the door.

DOES THE BODY click on and off, like a machine, like a clock, like a lock? Sometimes it seems it does. How else to explain the total absence of sexual confidence I felt before I slept with Chip, and the total assurance I felt afterward? My body had seemed like such a failure that in my heart I had not blamed Max for not loving me, for blaming me, for disdaining me. How did it happen that after I slept with Chip, I knew with a powerful certainty that I loved Max, that I could make Max love me, that I could make Max give me another child, a child I would carry and deliver alive and full of health? I didn't know where the power came from, but it came, and that was enough.

MARGARET AND I arrived back in Sussex in the early evening. We stopped at the house to unpack and make a grocery list, then headed for the Stop & Shop. Driving home, we went past the newspaper offices, and Margaret cried, 'Mommy, there's Dad's van!'

And there it was, alone in the parking lot with one other car, a small red convertible. I looked at my watch. It just was after eight. The paper came out on Thursdays; everyone would be busy today, but not insane. They would not have had to work late.

'Let's go see Dad!' Margaret suggested.

'Good idea.' I turned into the lot and parked next to my husband's van.

The door was unlocked. We went in. The news room was empty, all computers quiet and dark. The light was on in Max's office, but we could see through the glass wall that the room was empty.

'I know where he is!' Margaret whispered to me. 'Let's surprise him!' And she raced away from me, zigzagging around the desks toward the room at the back that had been turned into a staff lounge. Before I could think to stop her, she pulled open the door and called, 'Hi, Daddy!'

Max was standing with his arms around a young blonde woman.

'Daddy Daddy Daddy!' Margaret cried, launching herself at his legs.

The blonde woman turned and smiled at Margaret. She was breathtakingly beautiful. Max looked startled, disoriented, like a drunk suddenly sobered.

'Magpie!' He squatted and lifted her up into his arms.

She wrapped her slim arms around her father's neck, and settled her bum firmly on his forearm. 'Daddy, Mommy took me to eat at the Jared Coffin House! And she bought me a Pink Little Pony! And Abby had diarrhea all over *everything!* When are you coming to Nantucket?'

Max laughed, and the way he looked at his daughter sent a wash of balm through my body: He loved her. He did love her. 'You want me to come to Nantucket to see Abby's diarrhea?' he asked, kidding.

'*No*, Daddy.' Margaret giggled, flirting with her father.

The young blonde woman was ill at ease. She stood at awkward attention, crossing her arms over her chest, then letting them hang at her sides, as if not quite sure what to do.

I waited just inside the door.

'Hey, Vivienne,' Max said. 'This is my daughter, Margaret.'

'Hello, Margaret,' Vivienne said, smiling. 'Pretty dress.'

'And I'm Lucy,' I said, stepping forward. 'Max's wife.'

'Hello, Lucy.' Her smile was strained.

'Vivienne's our newest hotshot reporter,' Max told me. 'Just graduated from NYU.'

I was wearing shorts and sneakers — loose, comfortable clothing for driving and carrying groceries in the heat. Vivienne wore a tight blue top, skin-tight black slacks, and clunky high-heeled black shoes. Her waist looked about as wide as my wrist. Her breasts rode high and firm, pointing out from her chest like ice cream cones.

'I hope you don't find it too boring in our little suburban town,' I said to Vivienne.

'I'm sure I won't,' she replied, still smiling.

Margaret took her father's face in her hands and turned it toward hers. 'I *missed* you, Daddy,' she said. 'Mommy can't play the snorkel game as good as you and she won't carry me on the beach when I get tired like you do. It's not fun without you.' Tears glimmered on the edge of her lashes as she patted his jaw. 'I haven't had a sandpaper kiss *forever!*'

'Well, you'll get one tonight,' Max promised. He lifted his daughter up on to his shoulders. Margaret squealed and clutched at his hair.

'I brought some Bartlett's tomatoes,' I said.

'And blueberries!' Margaret added.

Vivienne said, 'I guess I'd better go. Nice meeting you, Margaret, Lucy. See you tomorrow, Max.'

'Matthew and I did a *one hundred piece* jigsaw puzzle!'

Margaret yammered as we headed outside. 'Can I ride in the van with you, Daddy?'

WITH THE EXCEPTION of the color of her hair, Margaret looked exactly like her father, and when she grew older, it was possible that her hair would grow darker; then she would look exactly like him. I had always known that Margaret loved me, but she worshipped her father. She understood me, because I was female, but she adored her precious father, and from about age three she had developed exceedingly feminine wiles to keep him captivated with her.

Perhaps it was that simple, total, innocent adoration that Max needed. Or perhaps he needed to be drawn down sharply into the immediate world, the child's world, when *now* is what counts and the mind doesn't race ahead to worry about tomorrow. Max and Margaret were nearly inseparable that evening, joking, talking, eating, helping with the dishes. She sat on his lap as they watched television. When she got drowsy, Max carried her up to bed, helped her brush her teeth and put on a nightgown, read her a story, kissed her goodnight.

I turned off all the lights downstairs. Upstairs, I slid a silk nightgown on over my head, and went into the smallest bedroom, the one next to Margaret's.

The nursery. We had wallpapered it in green and yellow and set up the crib. I had washed soft cotton sheets and put them on the mattress. I had folded soft yellow blankets at the end of the mattress. We had hung the mobile Margaret had gazed at above the crib. I had washed and put away in waiting the tiny white undershirts and booties and terry cloth sleepers.

Flush with the success of the newspaper and our lives, Max and I had gone on a shopping spree for the new baby. On the white bureau next to the crib was a beautiful light, shaped like a carousel. I didn't turn the light on but sat in the dark room where moonlight fell through the window in a gentle luminous glow, the leaves of the wild cherry tree shadowed in black tracery on the carpet and wall.

I sat in the rocking chair. In this chair I had nursed Margaret. I had sat here for hours on end comforting her, holding her, nursing her, singing her lullabies.

I heard Max leave Margaret's room. I heard the muffled thud of his feet as he went down the stairs. Was he looking for me? Or was he going to his study, to hide from me.

What is a marriage? What holds a marriage together? For some people, I know, it is the passion, the connection between man and woman that is of ultimate importance, and children are loved and nurtured, but secondary to the alliance between man and wife. Sometimes the marriage and even the family are about the man's career, advancing it in politics or academics or the corporate world, amassing wealth and prestige. In other cases, the entire marriage is about the children, having them, devoting time and energy to raising and supporting them.

What was our marriage about?

Max and I had been married so young. Just one moment out of college. We had thought we would change the world, at least a piece of it, a small town's worth, and we were doing that. We'd talked about that much, about Max's desire to run a newspaper, to be part of the life of a small town. We'd just assumed we'd have children.

Not until this week had Max told me how enormously and desperately he wanted a son, and I was still trying to absorb that information. It was shocking, the thought that my husband had kept such a significant secret from me for all these years. What other secrets had he kept? Was he keeping? In marriage, is a secret a lie?

I leaned my head back against the firm wooden support of the rocking chair and closed my eyes, trying to remember. It seemed to me that Max had been genuinely and completely thrilled with Margaret when she was born. With a daughter. I could envision his face, the radiance and awe that lighted his tear-streaked cheeks.

'My little girl,' he had said, as the nurse put the naked newborn in his arms. 'Hello, Beauty.'

What was he thinking now? Was he contemplating leaving me for the slender Vivienne? Putting a baby into her brand-new capable body? Having a son with her? Had he thought so far ahead that he envisioned our divorce, and joint custody, and Margaret running to him on weekends the way she had run to him tonight?

His own parents were divorced. It had been hard for him. I was certain he would think long and hard before he inflicted that on his daughter.

'LUCY?' MAX STOOD in the doorway.

I hadn't heard him come up the stairs.

'What are you doing in here?' he asked quietly.

We hadn't set foot in this room for weeks, months. It had been a room for the past, for death, for grief.

'This is a pretty room,' I said. 'I'd forgotten that the branches of the tree brush the window.'

Max stood just at the door, not inside the room.

I rose. 'Come in,' I said. 'Sit in this chair. It's so comfortable.'

Max hesitated, then entered. He sat in the chair. Rested his arms along the arms of the chair. 'It is comfortable.' He leaned his head back against the chair and closed his eyes.

I leaned against the crib. The house was quiet except for the familiar, tranquil hum of the central air in the basement. No wind stirred the leaves of the tree outside. The room was dark. We were ghosts to each other, strangers, our skin and clothing black and white.

I lifted my nightgown up over my head and let it fall on the floor at my feet. Max opened his eyes; I saw the liquid gleam.

He looked at me for a while, then started to get up, but I crossed the little room and bent over him and pushed him back down in the chair. I unzipped his shorts and brought out his penis, which, to my infinite relief and delight, was lovely and hard. I don't care, I thought, if this hardness is caused by lust for Vivienne or secret appetites I know nothing about, this is mine now, and I will have it.

The rocking chair was wide, the bottom covered with a cushion, and I was grateful for that cushion as I maneuvered myself onto my husband, resting my knees on either side of his hips, supporting myself with my hands on the arms of the chair. Max's hands fastened onto my hips, and he pushed me down onto him, hard. The rocking chair swayed beneath us. Our bodies were silver in the moonlight. I tightened the muscles of my vagina, clenching him inside me, and very slowly I moved up and down. Max groaned. He put his hands on my breasts. I moved more quickly. The rocking chair creaked beneath our weight. Max put his hands on my shoulders, shoving me down as hard as he could, so that his penis speared up inside me, pushing up further than it had ever gone before. I whimpered with pain, and with pleasure.

Over Max's shoulder, through half-closed eyes, I saw a breeze stir the leaves of the wild cherry tree. With a moan, Max climaxed, his fingers digging into my shoulders. The leaves of the wild cherry tree shuddered. I moaned, too.

Max put his hands on my face and brought my mouth to his, and kissed me like a thirsting man who has found water. I kissed him back, fervently, like a woman who has returned home.

AUGUST 17, 1998

MAX BLINKS. 'CHIP? What do you mean?'

I can't speak. I am so frightened. I'm afraid I'm going to die of fear. My body is made of ice. I stare at my husband, and tears stream down my face.

Max frowns, then rocks back, as if I've hit him. 'What exactly are you saying, Lucy?'

My hands rise to cover my mouth, as if my body is fighting to hold back these words. 'Do you remember the summer Margaret was seven?'

'I can't hear you.'

I force my hands down into my lap. They hold on to each other tightly. 'The summer Margaret was seven . . .'

'Of course I remember it.'

I've got to go through with this. I clear my throat. 'Wait, now, Max, please. Help me with this. I want you really to remember it, how it was that summer.'

'If you mean that I was depressed and morbid and remote and a shit, all right, I remember, and you are saying *what*? That because of that, you slept with Chip?'

Digging my fingers into my palms, miserably, I nod.

Max's face flushes scarlet. 'I don't believe it.'

'I'm sorry. I'm so sorry.'

'You *couldn't*. You couldn't sleep with him and then let me, let us *all* go on as if nothing happened. Jesus Christ, Lucy, tell me you didn't do that.'

I look at my husband.

'Tell me!' Max leans forward, grabs my shoulders, and gives me one quick hard shake, as if to dislodge the words from my throat. When I still don't speak, he lets go of me, rises, and paces around the bed. 'I can't believe what I'm hearing. Let me get this straight. You and Chip had an affair that summer, and for six years after that you've been making fools of me and Kate—'

'It wasn't an affair. Not really, Max. We only were together—'

Max stops. Stares at me, dead white. 'You're saying that Jeremy is not my son.'

'Might not be.'

'Jeremy is Chip's son.'

'I don't know. But it's something that can be easily proven.' I begin to babble, trying to rush us past this moment. 'If you take the cheek brushing test and carry the CF gene, then you probably are his father. Then we would need to have Margaret tested. But because of . . . what I did that summer . . . Chip should be tested, too, in case he also carries the gene. Then Matthew and Abby will need to be tested. They'll need to know if they carry the cystic fibrosis gene. Then we can have paternity tests done to see who . . . who Jeremy's genetic father is. But first we need to find out who carries cystic fibrosis. Because you both could, you and Chip.'

'And if I don't carry the CF gene, that's proof that Jeremy is not my son.'

Oh, God, this hurts. 'Not genetically.'

'Not genetically?' Max strikes his forehead. 'Are you crazy? Is there any other way?'

'Yes. *Yes*. Max, come on.' I rise, stretch my hand out to him, although he backs away. 'Jeremy is your son, no matter whose genes are in his blood.'

'Does Chip know Jeremy's his child?'

'Of course not.'

'*Of course not?*'

'We've never even discussed the possibility. Max, Chip and I were together—'

'Fucked each other—' Max's teeth are clenched. 'Or would you prefer to say *making love?*'

'Only two times. It was just . . . loneliness. Consolation. It was nothing.'

'Right. I believe you. It was so *nothing* the first time that you did it again.'

'I want to explain—'

'All right.' Tears well in Max's eyes and when he speaks, his voice is choked and strained. 'Explain.'

I'm crying too hard to speak.

Max stands over me. 'I can't get this through my head. You slept with me and Chip within the same week? Within the same day?'

'Yes.'

'And when you discovered you were pregnant, what did you think?'

'I thought it was your child. I wanted it to be your child. Oh, Max, Jeremy *is* your child.'

'And it never occurred to you to tell me that this baby might be Chip's? That's impossible. Jesus, does Kate know about this? Does Chip? Am I the only one who's been in the dark all along, some poor miserable cuckold?'

'No one else knows.'

'And you've kept this secret from me every day for six years. Every time we've slept together for the past six years. Every time we've lived with them here on Nantucket.'

'It wasn't like that, Max.'

'Then what was it like?'

'I don't know! It wasn't some precious damned secret held close to my heart. I didn't even think of it.'

'I thought we had a pretty good marriage. I thought we were – ha!' Tears shine in his eyes. 'I thought we were fucking soulmates. It turns out I don't even know who you are.'

'Don't say that. You know me, Max. You know me.'

He stares at me bitterly, his lip curled in a horrible distaste. Then he goes to the closet, pulls down a duffel bag, and begins to throw clothing into it.

'What are you doing?'

He doesn't answer. He continues to pack. He drops his duffel bag on the floor, opens his bureau, and tosses boxer shorts into it.

'Come on, Max, don't do this. You can't leave. You promised me you wouldn't leave. You promised you'd help me through this, remember? Just ten minutes ago!'

His laptop computer rests on a table nestled in a bay window. He slides it into its case, gathers papers together, and stuffs them into a briefcase.

As he heads for the door, I grab him by his arm. Now I'm furious.

'You can't walk away from Jeremy!'

His face is stone, implacable.

'Max, come on. Jeremy is sick. You have to help him.'

'Get his father to help him,' Max says. 'Get Chip.'

Roughly he shrugs off my hand and pulls open the door. He storms through the hall, down the stairs, and out the front door.

'Max! Wait!' I run after him, tripping in my haste and catching my sandal on the stairs, stubbing my toe terribly. 'Max!'

Outside the sky has turned indigo blue. Up and down the street the windows of houses glow golden with light. Max stops on the driveway. He reaches into the back of the Volvo to get something – his windbreaker – giving me time to catch up with him.

He mutters, 'I'll leave the car for you.'

'Max. Please don't walk away.'

He doesn't answer.

'Max, where will you go tonight? It's too late for any planes or ferries. Stay here. Please.'

Max walks away.

I watch his stiff, damnably stubborn back, his proud precious fucking head held high, as he strides off down the road. It is too much.

'Then damn you!' I say under my breath.

'Mom.'

Margaret is standing on the front porch, looking puzzled and scared. Jeremy stands next to her.

'Where's Dad going?' he asks.

'Dad and I had a little fight,' I tell my children as I return to the house.

' 'Cause he has to go back to work?' Jeremy asks.

'Right.' A good lie; it reassures my children. This battle is familiar to them; it doesn't mean that Max and I are really mad at one another.

'Don't you want some lasagna, Mom?' Margaret asks.

I look at my daughter. Her voice is neutral but her eyes are wary.

'Of course I want some lasagna!' I hug her against me, but she pulls away. She suspects I'm lying. I will have to force myself to eat because that, in the idiosyncratic vocabulary of our family, will prove that I'm telling the truth about the argument between her father and me, will reassure her that everything is all right.

In the kitchen, Kate asks, 'Where did Max go?'

'Back to Sussex.'

'Why?'

'I'll tell you later.' I flick my eyes toward my children. Margaret catches my gaze and stares back at me steadily, not giving me an inch.

WHILE CHIP WORKS upstairs, we watch a video together, Kate and I and our children.

Kate is sandwiched between Abby and Jeremy. Margaret curls at one end of the deep sofa, her feet pressed against my thigh; Matthew sprawls at the other end, his long legs extending into the room. This is normality, our two families nestled together, as content and familiar as animals from the same pack, and it seems suddenly precious to me, an ordinary moment suddenly rimmed with sacredness, like the silver of a frame around a picture. I don't think we'll ever be all together like this again.

'Mom,' Margaret says in a low voice, 'you're chewing your nails. Gross.'

By the end of the movie the Littlies are yawning. I take my time putting Jeremy to bed. I want to cuddle his slight body against mine and read him all of *Caleb's Friend*, but he's had a long day. Hugging his book to him, he curls up beneath his sheet.

'Goodnight, Jere-Beer.' I kiss his nose. His skin is cool.

' 'Night, Mom.'

The lamplight shines on his head. His brown curls glint where the sun has bleached them gold. Each separate strand of this hair holds the chronicle of Jeremy's DNA, which contains in its infinitely twining strands the bead that makes him different from other little boys. It registers his curly hair, his big blue eyes, an ability to read at an early age, love of mermen, easy laughter, and the gene for cystic fibrosis, glinting at me like the gleam in Jeremy's hair of gold. It is inseparable from who he is. It's been there all along. It's part of Jeremy. And, I must remember, even though I never knew before today, it is a part of me.

In her room Margaret lies in bed, lost in a book. I kiss her forehead.

' 'Night, Mom,' she murmurs absently.

She is so lovely. She has no idea how much her life is going to change.

'Don't read too late,' I tell her.

WHEN I ENTER the kitchen, Kate hands me a glass with Bailey's Irish Cream poured over ice. 'Okay. Talk. What's going on?'

The only light on in the room is the small bulb glowing over the sink and a gentle illumination from the hall. A hushed fragrant breeze flows in through the screened windows and door. In this moment of peace we stand, two friends as comfortable with each other, as comfort-giving to each other, as a favorite robe. She is so beautiful, my Kate, with her pale blond hair and her nose and cheeks pink from the sun. The lightest, smallest freckles dot her face in spite of all the sunblock she uses. Halfway up her long tanned neck two rings circle, indenting the skin, like age rings on a tree, growing more pronounced with every year. In her ears are the delicate gold and amethyst flower earrings I gave her for her last birthday. She was born in July, a Leo.

I have lied for Kate. I have lied to Kate. Will they balance each other out?

I don't think so. I think I am going to lose my friend.

I ask her, 'Could you get Chip?'

Her eyes widen. 'Lucy . . . '

'Please. I'd like to talk to you both together.'

Kate hurries up the stairs to the little room off their bedroom. Once a sewing room, it's now Chip's summer office, full of laptop computers and cell phones and file folders.

I want to run out the front door. I don't want to do this. How can I do this? I walk into the living room, this fine, shabby, comfortable space with its faded chintz sofas and mantel lined with seashells. I was a little girl here once, a good little girl. I have always wondered if my aunt's spirit somehow remained here, ghostlike, watching. Sometimes I've believed she gave me comfort. What would she think of me now? Certainly I didn't think she was watching when I welcomed Chip into my bed.

Kate and Chip pad down the stairs and into the room in their bare feet.

'What's up?' Chip asks.

They sit side by side on the sofa. I stand in front of the fireplace. The room seems very cold. I wrap my arms around my waist.

I clear my throat. I begin. 'Jeremy has cystic fibrosis. It's a genetic disease related to the pancreas that affects mucus in the body. Especially the lungs and the digestive system. It's not curable. It can be alleviated and worked with, and people live longer now than they used to, but it's still life-threatening; it shortens the lives of those who have it.'

'Shortens the lives,' Kate echoes, stunned.

'The average life expectancy is thirty years.'

'Oh, Lucy, honey.' She's across the room in a rush, trying to wrap me in a consoling hug.

Gently I push her away. 'Kate, don't. There's more.'

Kate grasps me by the shoulders. 'We'll help you. You know we'll help you. Money, anything—'

'Kate, don't. Listen to me, please.' My voice sounds ancient, some primitive rusting mechanism clogged with dirt. 'Seven years ago Chip and I slept together. Twice.'

Chip inhales sharply, the sound of someone hit with a slap of ice water.

Kate flinches. She steps backward and peers at me as if I'm suddenly speaking in a foreign tongue. 'I don't understand.'

'It was the summer Abby was an infant.' I make myself look her in the eye. 'You had Abby, and Margaret and Matthew were seven, and they were fascinated by you and the baby. Remember?'

'Go on.'

'You were this clique, this incredibly elite club, and I was left out in the cold. And Max was . . . depressed. My entire world was upside down.' I look over at Chip. His eyes are closed, his face clenched in pain, and for a bizarre flashing moment he looks like he did all those years ago when he grimaced in ecstasy as he climaxed inside my body.

'Chip?' Kate asks.

But Chip doesn't speak. He's gone as pale as snow.

'He felt left out, too,' I tell Kate. I'm leaning toward her, speaking urgently. Trying to make her remember. 'You weren't interested in sex, in him . . . you know you weren't, Kate.'

'Of course I wasn't! I'd just had a baby!' She looks around, confused, as if she needs to answer the phone or a knock on the door, then she grasps the edge of a chair and sinks down onto it, shaking her head as if to clear it. She studies Chip, who will not look at her. When she speaks, she is still looking at him. 'Are you saying that my *obsession* with my infant gave you two an excuse to fuck each other?'

Chip doesn't answer.

I say, 'Not an excuse. Perhaps a reason.' I pause. 'Remember, Kate, I had just lost my baby. Our son. I thought I'd never have another child.'

'So you were getting revenge on me because I did have a baby?'

'No. It wasn't that at all.' Although as I speak I wonder if I'm lying. It might have been that, partly. It might have been jealousy, spite. I'm capable of that. 'The point is. The point . . . Jeremy might be Chip's son.'

Chip opens his eyes.

Kate just stares at me. She says: 'No.'

'We don't *know* that Jeremy is Chip's son,' I continue. 'Just that it's possible. It's just as likely that Max is Jeremy's genetic father.'

'You slept with them both the same day?'

'Not quite the same day. Jesus, it doesn't matter now, Kate.'

'Oh, I think it matters.'

'The point is, the way cystic fibrosis works, it can only strike a child if *both* parents carry the gene. So Chip, or Max, or both, carries the gene. Chip has to be tested for the cystic fibrosis gene. Max, too.'

Chip ask, 'And if I carry the gene?'

'Then there's a chance that Matthew and Abby carry it as well.'

'Oh, God,' Kate cries.

I hastily say, 'Kate, they can't develop cystic fibrosis unless *you* also carry the gene. I don't know if I can explain it clearly. I can hardly absorb it all myself. The gene hides. It *lurks*. But we have to find out. If Matthew and Abby do carry the gene, and they marry someone who also carries the gene, their children will have something like a twenty-five percent chance of having cystic fibrosis.'

Kate puts both hands to her face. The room fills with a powerful silence.

After a while Chip clears his throat. 'It's possible that Max has it and I don't.'

'Right.'

Kate lifts her head. 'So you should have Max tested. If he has it, then Chip doesn't.'

'Not necessarily. I've thought about this all day, Kate. I didn't want to do this. The thing is, if Max is tested, and if he does carry the gene, there is still the possibility that Chip also carries the gene. If he does, then Matthew and Abby might carry it. I couldn't live with myself if I didn't insist that Chip be tested.'

'Let me see if I'm getting this right,' Kate says slowly. 'If Chip carries the gene, and Max doesn't, then Chip is Jeremy's father.'

I reply, 'And if Max carries the gene, and Chip doesn't, then Max is Jeremy's father. But if they both carry the gene, then we'll run DNA tests to know.'

'You should have come to me in private,' Chip says.

'Right,' Kate remarks, her voice hollow. She doesn't look at him. 'Then you and Lucy could keep one more secret from me and Max.'

'Kate—'

'So let me get this straight.' Kate holds up her fingers, counting. 'You're telling me tonight that first, you had an affair with my husband seven years ago, and God knows how many times over the summers since—'

'Never since, I swear,' I tell her.

She gives out a jagged laugh. 'Yeah, well, I sure do believe you, Lucy. Second, there's a chance that Jeremy is not Max's son, but is Chip's. Third, my two children might carry the cystic fibrosis gene, and their children might be at risk.'

'And fourth, Kate,' I said quietly, 'the one thing we know for sure. Jeremy has cystic fibrosis.'

Chip asks, 'How do we get tested?'

I tell him, 'It's simple. You go to a lab. They brush some cells off the inside of your cheek. It takes thirty seconds. They send it off and you know in two or three weeks.'

'Two or three weeks,' Kate echoes.

'Jeremy doesn't know any of this. Not yet.'

'Poor little boy,' Kate whispers. She looks up at me. 'And what if Chip is his father? What will you do then?'

'I don't know. I can't think that far ahead. We've got to pray that Max is his genetic father. If he is, then perhaps Chip is all right. I mean, he can be tested, and perhaps he doesn't carry the gene, and then your family is all right, home free.'

'No.' Kate's face is drawn and pale. 'I wouldn't say that, Lucy.'

'But healthy.'

'You know, Lucy, I can understand your sleeping with

Chip. What I don't understand is how you could keep it secret from me for all these years. How you could lie to me.'

I stare at Kate. 'I guess I've gotten pretty good at lying,' I say.

A cold moment of dead silence hits the air, as if the oxygen has suddenly disappeared from the room. Then Kate bristles. 'Are you threatening me?'

'I didn't mean it that way.'

Chip says, 'Threatening her?'

'Because you know what?' Kate stands up. She's trembling all over.

Anger has broken through the shock. 'I don't care. You can tell Chip about Garrison. You can tell him about my little summer flings. You can tell him every secret I've ever told you. God.' She laughs, and at the same time tears well in her eyes. 'For all I know, you already have!'

'Kate.' I reach out my hand. 'I haven't told him anything.'

'Told me what?' Chip demands.

'I thought I could trust you!' Kate cries, looking at me. 'I thought you were my best friend.'

'Kate . . . '

'And you!' She turns on her husband. 'You have always tried to make me be different than I am. You have always insisted that I pretend to be better than I am, some cardboard figure of perfection. How could you do that? When all along you were sleeping with Lucy?'

'It wasn't all along, Kate. It was just twice.'

'You have been so pompous! So pretentious! Such a hypocrite! Both of you! I compared myself to you, I tried to live up to you, and all along you've both been liars and adulterers!'

'Just that one summer, Kate. Just twice that summer.'

Kate looks around the room so wild-eyed that I'm afraid she's searching for something to throw. She surprises me completely when she announces, 'I'm leaving.' She crosses the living room.

'Kate,' I say sensibly, 'you can't get off the island this late at night.'

She doesn't reply.

Chip says, 'What about the children?'

She turns to look at her husband. 'You deal with them.'

'But what shall I tell them you're doing?'

'Tell them I'm going to Garrison's,' she says, and rushes from the room and up the stairs.

Chip follows her, leaving me alone in the room.

Twenty minutes later, just before midnight, the taxi arrives. Kate's face is pinched as she comes down the stairs, a suitcase in each hand. Chip follows, looking drained, ill. He leaves the door open and follows her out into the street. The interior light of the large van shines on Kate's blonde hair as she settles in. Chip speaks to her. Grimly, she replies. The car door slams. The taxi pulls away from the house.

Chip returns to the house, closing the door behind him quietly. We stare at each other as if from across a great distance. His eyes are full of sorrow, confusion, and something else . . . concern? affection? If he tries to embrace me in an attempt at consolation, I will die of shame.

'Dear God, Lucy, what a terrible mess we're in.' He moves toward me.

Even speaking with him like this seems like a betrayal of Kate and Max, but my heart is so full that it's all I can do to choke out: 'We can't—'

He stops dead. Nods, clears his throat. 'I'll leave first thing in the morning.'

Tears steam down my face. 'All right.'

'If you want me to take Matthew and Abby back to Sussex, I will.'

'Leave them. It will be better for all of them.'

'I'll arrange to take the test as soon as possible.'

'Thank you.'

'I'm sorry about Jeremy.'

'I know.'

'Do you want—' His forehead furrows with pain and puzzlement. He doesn't know what to offer. But his eyes search mine.

I look at this man. Even now, at this terrible moment when my whole being is scourged with self-loathing, my eyes take pleasure in the sight of him, and something deep in my soul is satisfied. I have sailed with Chip to Tuckernuck. We have made love. I have succumbed to the dazzle and lure of an attraction as deeply beautiful and mysterious as the pull of the tides. I let myself be swept away, and I loved the sensation of surrender, of being *taken*. All my life I've resisted this force; I've been afraid of it. I've been right to be afraid of it. Look where it has taken me. Worse: Look where it has taken our children. Our families. My friends.

'I just need to sleep,' I say.

'Will you . . .'

'I picked up a prescription for sleeping pills on the Cape.'

'Good.'

I turn my back and climb the stairs, hurrying toward to the necessary oblivion, the silent numbing dark.

SUMMER 1991

I WILL NEVER know what happened between Max and the lovely young Vivienne. I did ask him. He retorted brusquely, 'Nothing happened, for God's sake!' But his face flushed and he didn't look me in the eye. Perhaps he didn't actually sleep with her. But *something* happened, if only in his mind. And whatever it was, it was enough to scare him, the way my brief entanglement – for it happened so quickly it could never be called an affair – scared me.

And stimulated me. No doubt about it, what had happened between Chip and me had been a kind of gift, reminding me of life's various delights. Reminding me of life: the pleasures of the senses, the good luck of what I had, who I loved. All at once, once again, I saw how wonderful my husband was, how infinitely amazing my daughter. I had not seem them clearly for the past few months; they had been distanced from me by a veil of grief. Now I wanted to love them the way they deserved to be loved.

Perhaps Vivienne did the same for Max. I think it's possible. Whatever happened between them, it worked as an emotional jump-start for Max. Of course I was jealous, and if I let myself dwell on his possible infidelity for very long, I could send myself into a rage. But I'd rather have Max unfaithful than lost in a cold despair.

That night, when I came home from Nantucket with Margaret and seduced my husband in the nursery of our home, marked the beginning of a new kind of relationship between Max and me. It was as if we were falling in love all over again. Getting to know each other for the first time. Perhaps it was simply that Max had considered divorce and had contemplated the consequences, the damage that would be done to his daughter, the chaos it would bring down onto our lives. As I had considered, and turned away from it.

MARGARET AND I stayed in Sussex with Max until the last few days in August then we packed up the Volvo and headed back to Nantucket. The Cunninghams were still in residence and they agreed to stay on for another day and night so that the M&Ms could have one last golden seaside day together. Then they would pack up and head back home.

The night before they left, we celebrated our annual 'Big Lobster Night.' Usually this came at the beginning of the summer, when we had just settled into our vacations. At the beginning of this summer the thought of any kind of celebration had been impossible for me. But now I was, if not mended, mending; I was back on the side of light and laughter and hope.

I was the one who said, 'We haven't had our Big Lobster Night. Let's have it tomorrow.'

All the windows in the rambling old house were thrown wide open, and the white cotton kitchen curtains filled and fell with the gentle breeze that brought in the tang of sea air and the calls of birds settling in the apple trees and in the tangled thickets surrounding the house.

The men, including Matthew, had gone off to 'Hunt the Giant Lobster,' while the women stayed behind to set the dining room table, make an enormous salad, and start the huge pots of water boiling. Baby Abby sat in a canvas swing chair, her head nesting on her chins, bright eyes watching the rest of us.

The front door slammed.

'Here they are!' Margaret shrieked with excitement and a little real terror. The sight of the hideous lobsters always unnerved her.

'Women, the hunt was successful!' Chip bellowed as he entered the kitchen, beating his chest with one hand, holding up the bag of lobsters with the other. Max followed with more lobsters.

'They went like this!' Matthew told us in his high little boy's voice, and he snapped his thumbs and fingers together as if they were claws, stretching them toward Margaret.

'Eeeek!' Margaret screamed, and raced from the room.

Matthew giggled and chased after her.

'All right, Women, let the Men do their work!' Max and Chip lifted the lids off the huge pots, and steam roiled up into the warm air.

They were dressed alike in khaki shorts, polo shirts and ancient, time-honored Dock-Siders. Chip was taller than Max by a good four inches, and he had an enviable thatch of thick blond hair, while my husband's dark curls were receding. But Max was just as handsome, and he enjoyed life more, and was a better person. He had more integrity. He cared about the state of the world; Chip pretty much only cared about making money. I was fond of Chip, but what had happened between us had been insignificant. No one needed to know; it was almost as if it had never happened. Let the universe fold over it like a wave over a ripple in the tide. It was over. It was gone.

'Ladies, start your shucking,' Kate said.

Kate and I sat at the round kitchen table, each with a brown paper bag at our feet, pulling the rough green husks and the silken threads off the fresh butter-and-sugar corn. It was one of the rules of Big Lobster Night that the corn wouldn't be husked until the last possible moment.

The screened door banged as the M&Ms raced shrieking outside. Like does sniffing danger, Kate and I automatically lifted our heads and called out, 'Backyard, kids!' In this isolated enclave on the cliff, traffic was slight and sporadic, but it was easy for children absorbed in their own fantasies to forget how, in the evening when the sun was still high and the air still shining with light, cars could speed around the corners, and shadows could play tricks with vision.

'The lobsters are ready!' Max called out.

Kate plunged the corn into the boiling pot. I filled the champagne bucket with ice and a bottle of Mumm's, and filled two champagne flutes with apple juice for Margaret and Matthew as they came tumbling into the house.

'Wash your hands!' Kate and I called simultaneously.

Last year we'd added a microwave oven to the ancient kitchen; I melted butter, poured it into small ramekins, and set them before each place at the dining room table. Chip and Max carried in the heavy platters of lobster and corn. When everyone was seated at the table, Chip rose and lifted his champagne flute high.

'To the summer of 1991!'

'To the summer of 1991!' everyone echoed, and raised their glasses.

We all reached to clink our glasses against that of every other person at the table. Arms crossed and recrossed over and under other arms. Chip had carried Abby's swing in and set it next to him; he leaned over and toasted his daughter, touching his flute to the pacifier clipped to her terry cloth romper. Abby shrieked with joy at his attentions. The M&Ms got silly, as usual, but this year no one spilt anything.

I looked around the room, and I was perfectly content. Big Lobster Night was an occasion with all the warm profound glow of any ritualized family holiday, when memories of past years provided an aura to the present. The seven of us were like family. We could all *be* one family, actually; we looked enough alike, healthy, strong, shining like polished apples from the day in the sun, our hair a gleaming woody palate ranging from Kate and Chip's sun-streaked biscuity blond to Max's dark chocolate.

Chip and Max distributed lobsters onto each plate. I buttered an ear of corn for Margaret, cracked open a claw, extracted the meat, and showed her how to dip it into her bowl of butter. Over the past few years both Margaret and Matthew had been disgusted at the first taste of lobster, so we'd made a pact: If they would *try* the lobster, they could eat whatever they wanted if they didn't like it. The lobster wouldn't go to waste but would be made into lobster salad for the next day, and eventually, we grown-ups thought, the M&Ms would develop a taste for it.

'I wonder,' Max said from his end of the table, 'if anyone has ever done a psychological study matching the way people eat lobster to their personality types. For example, look at Chip. He reached for the tail right away, broke it off with one powerful crunch, and has already eaten most of the meat. I, on the other hand—'

'You are anal,' Chip interjected, pointing at Max's plate where the claws and tail lay cracked open, not yet touched, as Max drizzled the butter in swirls over the white meat.

'I prefer to call it orderly,' Max retorted with fake hauteur.

'And the mothers,' Kate pointed out with a grin as she used the nutcracker on Matthew's lobster's claw, 'have not touched their lobsters yet, because they are unselfishly helping the children. Yes, I would say your psychological study might actually have some validity.'

'This is yucky!' Matthew announced, spitting out a chewed white mass onto his plate.

'You don't have to eat it,' I told him. 'What would you like?'

'A peanut butter and jelly sandwich?' he asked tentatively. He didn't want to be a problem; he knew this was a special night.

'Fine. I'll make it.' I rose.

Stepping into the silence of the kitchen was like stepping into another world. It was quiet, and steam still rose like whispers from all the big pots. On the windowsill above the sink was an old vase holding a wild bouquet of lush, heavy creamy roses from a rosebush I had watched Aunt Grace plant and nurture. The refrigerator was new, and we had added a dishwasher, but the stove was the same one Grace had used, and the kitchen counter where I stood making Matthew's sandwich was the original speckled green linoleum on which Aunt Grace used to roll out her infinitely delicate pie crusts.

Had Aunt Grace ever wanted a child? Had she ever been pregnant, had she ever thought for fourteen fraught days, I am going to have a child, then miscarried? Had she been so fascinated by Dorothy Wordsworth's life because Dorothy had also never married or had children but had lived with her brother and wife all her life, taking care of her nieces and nephews? As a child, in my naïve and innocent arrogance, I hadn't considered the possibility that Aunt Grace might have desires I knew nothing about. It had seemed to me right and natural that I should have this woman in my life who adored me, whom in turn I adored, who opened the world wide to me in a way my parents never could. And Grace must have known that I worshipped her, that my life was changed because of her; she had left me this house full of our summers together.

My aunt had spent hours telling me things. 'This is a mussel shell. This is a clam shell. Those little skittering creatures are spider crabs.' In the evenings she had spent hours reading poetry to me, introducing me to the English Romantics and the American poets as well. She'd taught me to knit and crochet. During the long hot summer days of my childhood when I drowsed in the hammock beneath the cherry tree, or sat at the kitchen table, pinching with great concentration the pie crust into perfect peaks and valleys, or sat across from her at a card table, playing gin rummy as rain tapped against the windows, I'd felt a sense of satisfaction so deep that it resonated in my bones and belly. It was as if I were at the very center of a green and gentle world, as if I needed to know nothing more, as if this moment in time was good and true and right and would last forever.

In my adolescent years and in the first extremes of sexual passion and jealousy and longing, such honeyed content-ment was so lost to me that I never even remembered experiencing it. And then one night after Max and I had been married for almost a year, I found myself lying in his arms after making love. His hand loosely clasped my breast, his breath stirred my hair. Moonlight fell through the window into our rented apartment bedroom, turning the room silver, blurring the boundaries of ceiling and wall so that we seemed weightless and boundless, swirled in an ethereal sphere where stars spent luxurious eternities sailing across the sky. And I felt that old, slow-moving, profound satisfaction eddy in my blood again, a kind of melting original magic.

Later, when Margaret was an infant, lying in my arms, hot and heavy, lashes brushing against her cheeks, drinking milk from my breasts, I felt that same contentment. I had so much milk, an endless supply, it seemed, and my daughter was growing fat on it, on my milk and nothing else. My breasts were enormous, blue-veined, the nipples round, dark, and protruding. I could feed the world, I thought, let anyone come, I would lie there like a drugged queen, sharing my illimitable wealth. Everything was so profoundly sexual. The skin of my arms and legs was as receptive and sensitive as the tender skin between my legs; all the world was a caress. I loved everyone; I held Max, I held my infant, and sometimes it seemed I was so blissed out that I would have welcomed anyone, and everyone, into my arms.

On that humid August night the moisture from the pots made my hair curl into ringlets as I made Matthew's sandwich. I carried it into the dining room and set it on the table before him, then sank into my chair. Chip and Max were discussing the Red Sox. Kate was opening a lobster claw for Margaret, who was winding Abby's swing. I loved Margaret and Max best, but I loved the Cunninghams, too.

They were such good friends. I dipped a piece of tender white lobster into my butter and put the succulent piece in my mouth. It was as if I were clothed in silk, as if this night were a shimmering firefly in the vast darkness of the world. I loved everyone at the table. The profound contentment had come again. Deep in my heart I suspected I was pregnant.

AUGUST 1998

THE MORNING AFTER our trip to Children's Hospital, I come awake all at once with a start, as if my sleep has been one long falling and I've just landed, smashing, onto the pavement of reality. My insides feel like jelly, wobbly and fragile. I lift my hand and am surprised to see that it is a whole thing, not lined with hair-fine fractures.

Tying my robe around me, I walk through the house. Chip is in his room, packing. I hurry past. Matthew is sleeping, snoring in rhythmic drones like one of the little prop jets that fly us over the sound. Margaret is lying in bed, reading. I smell coffee and head for it. Downstairs the Littlies are still in their pajamas, building a house out of dominoes and cards under the dining room table. They call out to me, their faces round and clean and hopeful as suns.

'What's all this?' I drop to my knees and scoot beneath the table. Jabbering, pointing, they explain the intricacies of their make-believe world. I could stay here forever.

The phone rings, spreading minuscule branches of alarm through my body. I back out from under the table and race to the kitchen to pick up the phone.

Kate says in a cool brusque voice, 'Could I please speak to Matthew?'

'He's asleep.'

After a moment of silence, Kate says, 'All right. Then Abby.'

Abby fingers a scab on her knee while she chats with her mom. Her thick brown hair, normally in neat braids, hangs down around her face.

Chip comes down the stairs, suitcase in one hand, coffee cup in the other. 'Is that your mother?'

Abby hangs up the phone. 'She says Garrison is really sick. She's got to stay in Sussex to help him.'

'Look, sweetie,' Chips says, kneeling and pulling his daughter to him. 'I've got to go, too.'

Abby twines her arms around her father's neck and pouts prettily. 'Oh, Daddy, do you have to?' But she's not truly upset; her attention keeps slanting off to the dining room, where, over her father's shoulder, she sees Jeremy building stairs with a deck of cards.

'You know I do, pudding,' Chip says. 'Give me a hug.' He pulls his daughter to him so tightly that she squeals, 'Daddy! You're breaking all my ribs!'

'Want us to drive you to the airport?' I ask Chip as Abby skips back to Jeremy.

'I can call a cab.'

'No, we'll drive you. The kids can come; we'll stop by the Downyflake on our way home and get doughnuts.'

'Well, then, all right,' he agrees awkwardly. On this sunny day so much that was dazzling about Chip seems dimmed; his shoulders slump, the lines of his face are elongated and deep; even his hair seems less golden. In one evening his life has been changed forever. He looks at me, holding my gaze in his, and a long slow flush burns from his neck, up his jawline, to his cheeks, but I don't believe it's a flush of anger.

He says, 'Lucy.'

My eyes fill with tears.

'Look. This is just too hard on you and it's not fair, all of us deserting you right now.'

'It wouldn't be right if you stayed.'

He considers this; he knows I'm right. 'It's not the end of the world,' he says softly. 'It might even be—'

'No.' Quickly, I turn away. 'Hey, Jeremy! Abby! Come on. We're going to drive Chip to the airport and then go by Downyflake!'

'Yay!' they both yell, and in their rush Jeremy hits his head on the table and Abby knocks over part of the card house and I yell up to Margaret that I'm taking the Littlies for doughnuts and in the ensuing commotion there's no way that Chip and I can exchange one more private word.

Jeremy and Abby chatter in the backseat. Chip and I ride quietly until just before we arrive at the airport Chip asks, 'What are your plans?'

'I guess I'll spend the rest of the week on the island with the children.'

'Do you mind? I mean having Matthew and Abby?'

'You know better than that. It's easier to have them all together. Anyway, the children were expecting to be here this week.'

'Yes, but you were going to have some adults to help out.'

I meet his eyes. Even a brief glance sparks a current between us, and I quickly look away. 'We'll be fine.'

BUT LATER THAT morning, as I organize snacks and towels and coolers and herd the children into the car and off for the beach, I wonder if that's really true, that we'll be fine. I feel numb, dumb, and confused, so that it's a kind of labor to decide to perform the smallest action. Driving to the Jetties, I drive right past the usual turn-off and we're two blocks down the road before Matthew yells, 'Uh, where are we going?'

'Oh, thanks, Matthew. I wasn't thinking.' I make a U-turn, go back to the right street. It's not that I wasn't thinking, but that overnight my mind has become cluttered with memories and fears that snicker and sway like gaudy beaded curtains, interfering with my vision of normal life.

The children don't notice; it's the end of summer and the air shimmers with heat and light. They tumble out of the car, run over the hot sand, and plunge, yelping, into the sea. I find a spot for all our stuff and set about the domestic task of unfolding towels, setting up our little beach home for the day. The water is as tame as a housecat, rolling on its belly to display the sleek pattern of its stripes, mostly just drowsing in the sun, waves lifting and falling like the breath of a sleeping beast. Jeremy splashes with Abby, rides on Matthew's shoulders and belly flops, whooping, into the waves, laughs maniacally, and does not cough.

What were they thinking, I wonder, how could Max and Kate and Chip leave *me* in charge of four children? While the sun slowly slides across the sky, I pretend to read a book, but really I'm watching their every move with a kind of desperate vigilance, as if I'm being tested, as if the truth is out now, that I'm a worthless, reckless, dangerous woman, a poor excuse for a mother, a fool. A menace.

I've forgotten my sunglasses. The sun on the water is so brilliant it blinds me, my eyes burn with the effort of watching the children in the glinting light, and I'm glad, the

discomfort pulls my mind away from the seductive
whispers of self-loathing that rose up in my mind yesterday
and threaten to multiply, obliterating all other thoughts.
Now I understand why young women burn themselves
with cigarettes, why troubled adolescents cut themselves,
because their very own body has become a stranger to
them, a traitor, a thing apart that acts of its own stupid,
stupid accord, and must be punished. Now for the first time
I understand how one pain desires another, and when the
memory of Max's face last night, or Kate's, or Chip's,
threatens to make me burst into a torrent of tears right here
on the sunny beach in front of the children, I dig my nails
into my skin as hard as I can, and that pain, pure and shrill,
draws my mind away and provides a stinging moment of
relief.

But I am the grown-up here. It's essential, I remind myself,
to be rational, competent, decisive. If only because the other
three have left us, these children are in my charge, and I can
at least protect them now. This moment. This moment. And
the next. So I track their every move in the water and slather
them with sunblock. At the end of the afternoon I round
them up and drive them home. We all shower and clean up
and the M&Ms help me chop veggies for tacos while Jeremy
and Abby return to their card house.

Tacos are a naturally messy meal, and at dinner, the four
kids laugh when the filling falls back onto the plate or a
crunched taco shell flies across the table. They joke and tease
and blast each other with obscene noises. They laugh so hard
they spit. I let them. They are silly, even unruly, but they are
safe.

. . . .

EVERY NIGHT KATE calls to talk to her children. The third night, when I answer the phone, Kate asks me, 'Are my kids driving you crazy?'

I miss you, Kate! I want to cry. I'm so confused, so lonely, so guilty, so bad, God, what I wouldn't give to really talk to you now. But her voice is chilly and formal. I reply, 'Not at all.'

'They can come home any time. Just let me know. And I've mailed you a check for groceries and stuff.' She sounds like a stranger.

Kate, I think, my Kate, Katie! 'That's not necessary.'

'I know. But I want you to cash it. I'll feel awkward otherwise.'

At this I can't help but burst out laughing. 'Well, God, I wouldn't want you to feel awkward, Kate.'

She doesn't reply for a moment, but when she does, her voice is softer. 'How's Jeremy?'

'Fine. He seems perfectly healthy. But I've scheduled a complete workup for him in September. How's Garrison?'

'Not good.'

'Perhaps you should talk to him about all this. He's wise.'

'Maybe.'

We're beginning to talk. Hope rises in me like a stream. 'I want you to know that I didn't tell Chip anything.'

'About what?'

'You know what I mean. The men . . . those first summers here.'

'That was a long time ago, Lucy.'

'Yeah, well, so was Chip's infidelity. And mine.'

'But you were my best friend, Lucy. That makes a difference.'

'I know. And I'm sorry. But you still need to talk to Chip.'

'Why? Because it suits you, because you want to get everything out in the open?' Her voice grows angry. 'I'm sorry about Jeremy, but don't use his illness to hide your shit.'

'Kate—'

'I've got to go. Call me if you want me to come get my kids.'

MAX DOESN'T PHONE me, so I call Stan, who has friends who work at the newspaper.

'What's up?' Stan asks lazily.

I start to tell Stan about Jeremy and find my throat blocked. If I tell Stan, that will somehow make Jeremy's illness more real. Will bring it closer. Jeremy doesn't even know about it yet, it doesn't seem fair to give this information to someone outside our family. Besides, I don't deserve the comfort of Stan's sympathy.

'Max and I have had an argument, Stan. A big one.'

'So Max's depressed?'

'Very. Could you just kind of keep an eye on him for me? Phone me if you hear rumors that they're worried about him at work?'

'Can do.'

'How's Write?/Right?'

'Everything's cool. You seen a doctor about those anxiety attacks?'

'You know Stan, they haven't been occurring lately.'

'Great. Maybe you don't have anything to be anxious about.'

'That must be it,' I say dryly.

'Take care of yourself, lady,' Stan says warmly.

'Thanks.' Unexpected tears sting my eyes.

. . .

A FEW DAYS later, I receive an envelope in the mail with the Write?/Right return address on it. Stan has sent me Max's editorial from this week's newspaper. It's all about CDA. Max declares that in the beginning he didn't know that Paul Richardson, the owner of the paper, was also a shareholder in the corporation that wants to build offices on the land, but he knows now, and he stands firm on his position: The land should be built on. It will be beneficial to the town. He'd be glad to debate this with anyone. I'm glad Max has taken this stand. I'm glad to know he's working, just as if his life has not been shattered.

I read the editorial to the children and talk with them about this, the issues of the town, the more private matters of fighting for what one believes in.

Margaret asks, 'When is Dad coming back to the island?'

'I don't know,' I tell her truthfully. 'Why don't you call him and find out?'

It's after seven. He doesn't answer at home. He doesn't answer at the office.

'We'll try later,' I tell her.

We do, but we still can't reach him.

IT IS PROBABLY the most beautiful August I've ever spent on the island. We go to the beach every day. The sun beats down, spangling the ocean with diamonds. We all swim, build sand castles, play Frisbee, search for shells. We turn as brown as filberts. Jeremy doesn't cough. At night we sit around the dining room table playing noisy games of Clue and Monopoly and poker.

A week goes by like a dream, the only reality the flashfire thought – Jeremy has cystic fibrosis – that wakes me in my bed at night and assaults me all through the day, flaring over my head, or exploding in my chest like a gunshot. There is nothing I can do, no way I can change things, but I can hope, I can pray, that when the tests come back, they will prove that Max is Jeremy's father, even if it means — terrible thought, I'm a traitor whatever I wish. Because of me, there's a fifty percent chance that Margaret carries the CF gene. It's so odd, not having anyone to talk to, not Kate or Max. It's lonely, and I hold the ache of loneliness close to me, pressing it against me like a sliver of glass or a razor, using it to punish me for what I've brought upon us all, knowing that as a punishment it is not nearly sufficient.

THURSDAY NIGHT I take the four children to see a comedy at the Dreamland Theater. About a thousand other families want to see this movie, too, but we take our place in the long snaking line and wait patiently, progressing by inches to the box office where we're at last rewarded with tickets. Matthew steers the Littlies in to get seats for us all; Margaret and I wait in line at the concession stand to buy candy and popcorn for everyone.

The movie's funny and brilliantly bright. When the lights come on everything around us seems slightly dim, as if we've faded or our vision has. This is exacerbated when we make our way with the crowd to the exit to find the dark night teaming with rain. Sharp needles of cold rain blow sideways in the wind; I pull Jeremy back into the shelter of the foyer.

'Wait a minute!' I call to Matthew, Margaret, and Abby, who are being swept by the crowd out the front doors. Stripping off my sweatshirt, I yank it on over Jeremy's head.

'Mom!' he fusses. 'Don't!'

'I don't want you to get a cold, honey.' I squat down to his level, surrounded by an army of knees and feet and legs, shoved and buffeted by the general movement of the crowd.

'I won't get a cold! I don't want to wear your stupid sweatshirt, I'll look stupid!' For a small boy, he's determined; as fast as I can pull it down, he struggles to pull it up and off.

'No one will see you.' When had he become so stubborn? Finally: 'Jeremy Maxwell West!' I snap, iron in my voice. 'We are not leaving the theater until you wear this sweatshirt, do you understand?'

A woman my age looks down at me, alarmed by my tone of voice, then understands the problem and gives me a sympathetic smile.

'All right.' Jeremy gives up and goes limp, so that I practically have to drag him by the hand through the crowd and out the door.

I parked the Volvo on Oak Street, next to 21 Federal. With Jeremy's hand tight in mine, I run across the street and up the sidewalk, open the car door, and usher him in.

Matthew and Margaret are already in the backseat.

'Where's Abby?' I ask.

'We thought she was with you.'

My heart explodes in my chest. '*You* had her! Damn! I don't believe this!' I scan the streets. Clusters of parents and children stroll run through the rain to their cars or into Yogurt Plus, but no small girl with braids is anywhere in sight. 'Jeremy, you stay in the car with your sister. Matthew, come help me look.'

'I can look, too,' Jeremy offers.

'You stay right there!' I scream, and he flinches, hurt by the shrillness of my voice.

I race back to the movie house. It's empty now. Only a few people stand in the entrance to the movie house, looking up at the sky, waiting for the rain to cease.

'Abby?' I call. '*Abby!*' I rush into the theater, which is empty except for a man picking up discarded popcorn boxes. 'I've lost a little girl.'

He looks around him, holding out his arms. 'She's not here.'

'Oh, God,' I murmur, turning back to the street and the rain, 'oh, God, don't do this, please don't do this, it's too much, I can't bear it . . .'

'Lucy?' Matthew's standing by the entrance, his hands on Abby's shoulders.

'Where have you been?' I shriek, falling to my knees, grabbing the little girl, embracing her. 'Where did you go?'

She's soaking wet. 'A man had a puppy—'

'*A man had a puppy!*' I cry. 'Don't you know better than to talk to strangers? Where did you go?'

'I didn't go anywhere. He was standing right there, with his baby, waiting for the mommy and his little girl.' Abby points, and there, materializing before my eyes, is a slender young man with a baby in a Snugli and a blond cocker spaniel on a leash and a woman with soft brown hair and a child in her arms.

'We're sorry,' the man says, coming forward. 'We saw that she was separated from her family. We waited . . . we would have called the police if you hadn't come back.'

'Thank you, thank you,' I babble. 'So nice of you, such a crush, wasn't it, it just gave me such a scare, we're all getting soaked in this rain, we'd better go, thank you again . . .'

Matthew, Abby, and I run to the Volvo and climb in.

'Where did you go?' Jeremy asks, and Abby answers, but all at once I can't hear their voices. A white mist rises up around me, and the roar of the ocean fills my ears. I lean my head on the steering wheel. I'm aware that I'm making a terrible moaning noise, but I can't seem to stop until Margaret asks in a terrified voice, 'Mom? Are you okay?'

'No, I'm *not* okay!' Turning, I glare at Matthew. 'Don't you ever lose sight of your sister in a crowd like that again, do you hear me? I thought you had more sense.'

Matthew glares back at me, stunned and insulted. 'I didn't—'

'Don't say a word!' I snap. 'Not one more word.' I start the car and with a shriek of the tires, peel away from the curb. 'I don't know how you can be so selfish. My God, she's your only little sister, you saw that I was dealing with Jeremy, it's not like you're mentally incompetent, it's just incredibly negligent and selfish of you to lose sight of her like that—'

'Mom!' Margaret says, leaning forward and touching my shoulder. 'Hey. What's up with you?'

Looking in the rearview mirror, I see that Matthew's jaw is clenched and his face red with suppressed emotion, while Margaret's face bulges with anger. Jeremy cows, wide-eyed, and next to me on the passenger seat, Abby weeps.

'Oh, God, Matthew, I'm sorry. Kids, all of you, I'm sorry, I'm sorry. Forgive me. I was just so scared. Abby, honey, I'm sorry to be so mean, I was just frightened. Matthew, I'm sorry.'

The rest of the ride is in silence. None of the children will forget this night. They'll never trust me again. They shouldn't.

.   .   .

THE NEXT DAY it's still raining. I take all four children with
me to the grocery store and we fill the cart with nothing but
ice cream, fudge sauce, marshmallow fluff, sprinkles, candy,
and Reddi-Whip. We pick up videos with Jim Carrey, with
Bruce Willis. We stop at the Hub and I buy junk reading for
them all, violent comics for Matthew, *Casper* and *Smurfs* for
the Littlies, romance novels for Margaret.

At home we spread out our purely sugar buffet on the
dining room table. We heat the butterscotch and hot fudge in
the microwave, pour sprinkles into a bowl, and make sundaes
of repulsive extravagance which we eat as we watch the
videos. I fully expect someone to have a stomachache, even
to throw up, but no one does.

WHEN THE SUN comes out, it slants differently, and that
night a cool breeze drifts in. Ads for back-to-school supplies
dance across the television screen. As she comes down the
stairs, Abby stubs her toe and bursts into tears. When I try to
console her, she continues to weep. God, I think, her toe is
broken.

'Hold my hand and hop into the living room,' I tell her.
'I'll get some ice to put on it.'

'I want *Mommy!*' she sobs.

I settle her on the sofa, dial Garrison's number, and give
Abby the phone. I can tell by her expression that Kate is
refusing to come back to the island, even for a day.

That night I call Chip. That weekend he arrives to pack
his children's things. I expect my own children to be sad and
cranky when the Cunninghams are gone, but to my
surprise, they don't seem to mind. In the evening the three
of us sit together on the back porch, watching the light flare

and fade in the sky. Margaret asks me what it was like here when I was a girl. Jeremy lies with his head in my lap, eyelids heavy, insisting he's awake. While I tell my daughter about my aunt and my childhood days in this house, I twine my fingers through my son's gold-tinged curls.

MAX DOESN'T ANSWER the phone at our house, so late the next afternoon when both children are in their room, conked out into naps by the heat and humidity of the day, I phone him at the paper.

'Look,' I say. 'You have to talk to me. Are you planning to come back to the island?'

'No.'

'The children miss you.'

He does not reply.

'Did you have the test taken?'

He does not reply.

'What can I tell the children? You're not being fair to them, Max. You're punishing them more than me.'

He does not reply.

'Max, please. I'm so frightened. I'm so alone.'

He does not reply.

'I'm coming home this week,' I tell him. 'It's too hard on the children, being away from you for so long.'

He does not reply, and I hang up the phone.

MARGARET AND JEREMY help me pack. Always before I've had another adult to help me lug the heavy suitcases out to the car. Now I miss what before used to make me impatient: Max or Kate saying, 'Did you throw all the perishables out?'

'Are all the windows shut and locked?' I need another adult to help me with even the smallest things.

Because we're leaving before the end of August, we make it on standby on the last boat to Hyannis. The kids are wired about going home, and probably they're nervous about their father's absence. They squabble on the boat and in the car until they both fall asleep, leaving me to make the drive through the dark to Sussex with only my thoughts to accompany me.

The Volvo's headlights flash over our front lawn. Max's van isn't in the drive. I turn off the engine and sit for a moment in the dark night, hearing the late summer clicking of cicadas. Max often works late, but it's one o'clock at night. He doesn't work *this* late.

'Are we home?' In the passenger seat, Margaret stirs.

'We're home, baby. Here, you unlock the door. I'll carry Jeremy.'

The moment we enter the house, I know: Max hasn't been living here. The air is hot and stale, oppressive. I carry Jeremy up the stairs. Margaret pulls back his sheets and I gently lay my little boy in his own familiar bed. I untie one sneaker; Margaret unties the other. We slip off his socks. He smacks his lips together and whimpers, but doesn't wake. I pull the sheet over him. Let him sleep in his clothes for one night.

Margaret helps me carry the luggage into the front hall, and then I say, 'That's enough for tonight, honey. Go on to bed.'

She looks at me, her dark brown hair a whirled shaggy mess, her eyes old. 'Mom, where's Dad?'

'He must be working.'

'Mom. I'm not a complete idiot.'

'Honey—'

'What's going on? Look, I won't tell Jeremy. But come on!' She can be so fierce, a tiger of a girl.

'It's complicated, Margaret. And I'm too tired to tell you about it tonight.' She looks at me, relentless. I have to tell her something. 'Your father and I have had an argument. But things are going to be okay. I promise.' How can I promise that? When do I stop lying?

She doesn't believe me. She still stands in front of me, obdurate.

'It's late, Margaret. I'm exhausted.'

She glares.

'Please, honey.'

'I hate this.'

'I do, too.' I reach out to hug her, but she wheels away from me, storms into her bedroom, and slams the door.

In the kitchen I discover that the cats' bowls are completely empty. When did Max feed them last, I wonder. While I put out dry and canned food, Midnight and Cinnamon meow and rub against my ankles. They eat ravenously. I watch, pleased by this sight of satisfied hungers.

The answering machine has sixteen messages, some for Write?/Right, some for Margaret, one for Jeremy, some for Max. All can wait until tomorrow.

I open our bedroom windows to let fresh air in and it comes, cool and dry, bearing the scent of apples, and with that scent the sense of autumn brushes over me, making me shiver. This is such an unsettled time, still as soft as summer, knife-edged with fall.

I slip beneath my sheets and try to sleep. Can't. Sitting up, I try to read, but the words seem smudged. I pad around the house, looking in on my sleeping children. I heat a pan of milk; it tastes awful. I pour a glass of wine and set it down untouched.

I know where my husband is. He's sleeping at the office, he's hiding from me.

I change into a pair of sweat pants and a loose T-shirt, slip my feet into sandals, grab up my keys. I scribble a note: 'Went to Dad's office; be right back; xoxox Mom,' and leave it on my daughter's bedside table, just in case she wakes.

It's after midnight when I pull into the parking lot at the newspaper offices. Max's van is parked in front.

Kate's Mercedes station wagon is parked in the shadows at the side.

My heart lurches, races.

They could simply be talking, I think. They could be sharing a bottle of wine and talking about all this, trying to figure out what the best thing is for both families.

My knee hits the set of keys hanging in the ignition and starts them chiming. Through the large picture window at the front of the building, I see the ghostly room, empty desks illuminated by one lonely light. They must be back in the staff lounge.

I have the key to this building. I want to know. I need to know.

Heat flares up my face, as if my heart is a fiery caldron. So it's true, that cliché, *my blood boiled*. My hand is shaking so hard I can scarcely get the key in the lock. I feel frightened and furious, and oddly enough, *guilty*. This is a shameful thing I'm doing, close to voyeurism. I feel like that awful-sounding word, that snakelike creeping thing, a *sneak*. I am sneaking. I am literally sneaking as I softly shut the door behind me and stand in the dark offices. Enough light shines in from the street to illuminate the various hulks of computer-laden desks and a soft gleam of lamp in Max's private office shows that the room is empty.

I walk back toward the staff lounge. The door is closed. My heart drums loudly in my ears, as if geysers of hot blood are shooting up my neck. It is a sickeningly uncomfortable feeling. I force myself to stop and take a deep breath. I put my hand on the doorknob.

I open the door.

FALL 1998

KATE AND MAX are lying on a blanket on the floor. Naked, they lie side by side, facing one another, Max dark, angular, and masculine, Kate blonde and feminine, her hip swelling up from her slender waist like the lines of a cello, the two of them curved together, a living yin/yang symbol.

They are not making love; they have finished making love. It was not spontaneous, accidental: both Max's and Kate's clothes are neatly folded on chairs. On the floor near their heads are two half-full glasses and a bottle of red wine. On several of the tables, candles flicker. Candles. I wonder who thought of this, this *romantic* touch, that makes the act seem not so completely about revenge, but about the two of them, together. Perhaps they have wanted to do this for a long time.

They have been talking, it seems that they have been lying here after making love and talking.

Kate looks up at me and smiles an oddly goofy smile, embarrassed and challenging at the same time and for a moment she looks just like Matthew. She doesn't try to cover herself. She says, 'Lucy.'

Max doesn't look at me but rolls on his back and brings his arm up to hide his eyes.

I close the door. Good, I think. Good. This is what I deserve. This is the least I deserve.

Back home, I walk through the dark house, checking on my children. Both sleep soundly.

I take two sleeping pills and lie on top of my bed, because that's what one does at night. I think: If Max was the one who brought the candles, then he's not depressed. That's not something a depressed person does.

I search my heart for jealousy, knowing that I should not have to search. Jealousy always comes unbidden, like desire. Perhaps I'm just too full of fear for Jeremy to feel much else. In an odd way, I'm grateful to Max and Kate, as if their act will balance out some eccentric scale, making me less culpable, or at least more forgivable.

On this thought I fall asleep.

WITH CHILDREN, SO much of life is routine. You just have to keep going. In the early days of September we shop, as always, for school clothes. After the freshness of the sun and sea, the electrically modulated glare and air of the malls are exciting. Margaret brings friends, who attend to her serious deliberations with much squealing and discussion. Jeremy is simply patient; he hates trying clothes on, he doesn't care what he wears, he just wants to get out of this store. He has gained weight and height over the summer. He has gone up a size in boy's clothing. I stand in the boy's section of Filene's, holding a size six polo shirt in my hands, staring at the label, wanting to fall to my knees with joy. He's growing normally. Perhaps they got the tests wrong, made a mistake, mixed up

his results with another child's. I've postponed our visit to
Children's Hospital for a week. He seems so healthy now; it's
as if he *will* be healthy if we can just keep away from that
hospital, those doctors. It may be irrational, but it's what I
need to do, for now.

'WHEN'S DAD COMING home?' Margaret asks as the three of
us sit around the kitchen table, eating spaghetti.

'I don't know. I wish I did.' I have told the children the
truth, or a version of it: Max is sleeping at the newspaper.
He's so busy, he doesn't have time to come home.

'I'm going to call him,' Margaret says, her face dark.

'Please do,' I respond. 'Maybe he'll make time to talk with
you. He's always too busy to talk to me.' That is the truth.
And Max *should* talk to Margaret. She shouldn't be punished
for what I've done.

'Can't we just go to the newspaper and see Daddy?'
Jeremy asks. 'Just drive down and surprise him?'

Little boy. Jeremy has lost another tooth and lisps now
when he speaks; it's kind of cute. He's insisted on wearing the
one outfit he chose himself, something the kids will probably tease him about at school: a blue and-white striped
button-down shirt and a navy blue sweater vest. He looks
like a miniature copy of his father.

Or, rather, his clothes are like his father's. After our month
in the sun, his hair is bleached almost blond. He looks much
more like Chip right now than like Max.

We should know any day now whether or not Max and
Chip carry the CF gene. We should know who Jeremy's
father is. If Max is his father, then I believe Max will be able
to get past all this, to forgive me, to come home, to help me

tell Jeremy about his illness. But if Chip is his father . . .

'Go ahead,' I prompt my children, letting irritation color my voice. 'Call your father at work.'

Margaret eyes me suspiciously but takes up the phone and dials. She hands it to Jeremy. 'You ask, Germ. He's always nicer to you.'

'That's not true!' Jeremy and I protest together. Then Jeremy goes quiet, listening. After a while, he says, 'Dad? This is Jeremy West, your son. When are you coming home?' He clicks off, hands Margaret the phone. 'Just the answering machine,' he tells us.

I rise from the table. 'All right, I've got some work to do in my study. Margaret, you rinse the dishes and stack the dishwasher, okay?'

'Mom, you haven't eaten anything.'

'Oh, sweetie, I ate tons at the mall.' I kiss the top of her head and hurry from the room.

SCHOOL STARTS, AND I'm grateful. Both children are preoccupied with thoughts about teachers, friends, schoolwork; they don't have time to worry about whatever idiocy their parents are up to.

Tuesday morning I watch Margaret and Jeremy run through the rain to the school bus, then turn back into the quiet of the house. Usually morning is a luxurious time for me, like a drift of new age music after a rock and roll opera. But this will be the first time in two weeks that I've been in the house without the children to protect me from my thoughts.

I take a mug of coffee into my office. Since I've been home, I've managed to sort through the month's mail and pay the necessary bills, but I haven't called Jared Falconer yet; my thoughts clog up whenever I consider such a decision. I *could* start thinking about Write?/Right. I could call Stan. I should call Stan. But I'm seized with a restless energy, like we feel on the island when a storm approaches. When we can see the black clouds rolling toward us. When we feel the shimmer of the air. When the leaves on the trees rustle nervously.

I want to board my windows, bolt the doors, and hide my family in the depths of the house.

But I am the one who caused the storm. I have brought the danger into the center of my family's life.

The doorbell rings.

'CHIP!' MY HEART stops. 'Come in.'

Meticulously he shakes the rain off his umbrella, folds it, and sticks it into our umbrella stand. He looks so *judicial* in his beautiful gray wool suit and wing-tip shoes. I'm in sweat-pants and a loose blue cotton shirt.

My heart hammers. I lead him into the living room. 'Would you like to sit down?'

He sits. We look at one another.

'The test results came back positive.'

I lick my lips. 'I see.'

'I carry the CF gene.'

I feel myself flushing violently from head to toe, as if just now, right now, I've been caught in some embarrassing act. 'Well.'

'Have Max's results come back yet?'

'I don't know. He won't talk to me.'

'It seems pretty unlikely that he'd carry the CF gene, too.'

'Unlikely, perhaps, but not impossible.'

'Kate's moved out of the house. She's living with Garrison. She talks to the kids on the phone but she hasn't seen them for two weeks. I had to take them shopping for school clothes.'

'Garrison is dying, Chip. This won't last forever.'

'Yes, well, when he dies, I'm sure she'll take on some other hopeless cause.'

'Why does that make you so angry? It's a wonderful thing Kate is doing. These people really need her help.'

Chip takes his time, considering my question. 'I suppose it makes me angry because she needs them as much as they need her. You'd think that having a husband and a home and two great kids would be enough to fill a life, but no, she's got to go be Florence Nightingale.' He runs his hands through his blond hair. 'It's like we're not enough for her.'

'Perhaps no one person is ever enough for anyone. We're all so complicated.'

'I want you to tell me about Kate's sexual infidelities.'

'For God's sake, what can it matter now?'

'I think it matters a lot.' Chip leans toward me, fixing me with his steady blue gaze. 'Lucy. If she had an affair, affairs, then that somehow makes me feel less guilty, but more important, it's a sign that our marriage isn't strong, not as complete, as I'd thought. It means that you and I—'

I stand. 'Don't do this, Chip.' I'm shaking and I lock my arms around my body, hugging tight. 'It's enough, what I've done to Jeremy, to Max, to all of us. Don't ask me to do any more damage to your marriage than I've already done.'

Chip rises, too. 'Lucy, you're looking at it the wrong way 'round. We did what we did because of something missing in our marriages.'

'No, Chip. Stop. I mean it.'

He moves toward me, as if to hold me. 'Lucy. You and I—'

I shake my head once, decisively: *no*. 'Please go. Please.'

He studies my face and something like pity softens his gaze. 'All right.' He walks to the door, then stops. 'You'll call me when Max finds out his test results.'

'Of course.'

When the door is shut, I rush to it and turn the lock. Chip carries the CF gene, I think. This is overwhelming. This is almost more than I can bear. I make my way to the sofa. Burying my head in my hands, I sit as stunned as if suddenly just hit by a car. I can't think. I can't feel. I'm numb.

THE SOUND OF knocking on the front door rouses me.

Stan sweeps in, shaking the rain off his poncho like a puppy. His long-strapped briefcase hangs from one shoulder; his gold-rimmed glasses and all his metal rings and studs glitter against his pale skin.

'What's up with you?' he replies. 'You look like shit.'

It feels good to smile. 'Thanks a lot.'

'I left a lot of messages on your machine . . .'

'I know. I've just been so busy. How are you? Have you had breakfast?' Stan is so *normal* I could hug him.

'I'll have a Coke if you've got one.'

I lead him into the kitchen. 'I've got that, and some bacon and eggs, too. Or English muffins. I've brought back some great wild beach plum jam.'

'Lucy. Forget the food. What's up?' He drops his briefcase on a chair with a thud.

I close the refrigerator door. I fight for composure, then turn to face him. 'They think Jeremy has cystic fibrosis.'

'Who's *they*?'

'The physicians at Children's Hospital.'

'Why do they think that?'

'They did a test. A sweat test.'

'Is it an accurate test?' Stan's a great believer in all things scientific.

'Yes.'

Stan looks at me. 'That sucks, man. Is there a cure? Can anything be done?'

'No cure. Lots can be done, depending on the case. The only hopeful thing is that it's one of these weird diseases that can be mild or severe.'

'And which is Jeremy's?'

'They think it's a mild case, but really they don't know. They can't predict. We can only wait and see.'

'How's Jeremy taking it?'

'I haven't told him yet. There are some other complications . . .' I'm dizzy. I sit down, suddenly, in a chair.

'You okay?'

'Yeah.'

'Not to be unkind, but have you looked at yourself in the mirror recently? You look like some kind of vampire has been at you.'

I touch my head. 'My hair . . .'

'You've lost a lot of weight, Lucy, and your face is drooping down like a bloodhound's.'

His concern undoes me. I wonder why Margaret didn't tell me that I look so bad; she's always my worst critic. My laughter gets out of control, turns to weeping.

'Hey, Lucy.'

'Everything's gone to hell, Stan, and it's all my fault.'

'Okay.' He pulls up a chair on the other side of the kitchen table and folds his hands on top of the table. 'That's a start. What's the rest?'

I take a deep breath, and tell him. My affair with Chip. Jeremy's illness. Max's anger, Kate's anger, the confusion that is about to fall over our children. When I'm through, Stan shakes his head. 'Man. This is kind of Biblical.'

'Yeah,' I snort, 'Old Testament version.'

'You know, you ought to come with me to AA.'

I blink. 'What?'

'AA. You know what AA is.'

'Yeah, well, I'm not an alcoholic yet. Although, give me time . . .'

'Or ACOA. Adult children of alcoholics. They've got some really good ways to help you straighten out your thinking.'

'Like "Let go and let God?" I don't think so, Stan. I'm not feeling like God and I have a great working relationship these days.'

'You might want to develop one. I mean, it seems to me, you've lost your best friend and your husband in one fell swoop—'

'You think I've lost them for good?'

'You can't predict the future. But you've lost them for today and probably tomorrow and you need some help. And you know what else? You should focus on work. Write?/Right is part of your life. Besides, it's not beyond the realm of possibility that Max and you will get divorced, that Write?/Right will become crucial to you financially.'

'What you say makes sense, Stan. But right now . . . today . . .' I meet his eyes. 'Stan, right now just doing this, sitting here, looking at you . . . it's the best I can do. It's all I can do.'

Stan's brow furrows with concern. His voice cracks when he asks, 'How can I help?'

'Just keep Write?/Right going. And give me some time.'

'I can do that,' he says.

WHEN STAN LEAVES I feel more in control. There are things I must do to keep the house functioning like a normal home; gratefully I run a load of laundry and begin to clean the kitchen.

It's Jeremy's first day of being in school until three o'clock; kindergarten classes were only half day. Will he be tired? Will he have picked up some viruses? Schools are swamps for viruses. I know I've got to be less cowardly about Jeremy's condition. It's just that I feel so overwhelmed right now, it's all I can do to keep my head above water.

I've got a basket of warm-smelling clean laundry in my arms when I see Max's van pull into our drive.

All right, I say to myself. All right. Breathe. I watch him slam out of the van and stride toward the house.

His face is so grim that I know what he has to tell me.

I open the door.

Surprised, he flushes. 'Are you going out?'

'No. I just saw you through the window, and I . . .' We're so awkward with one another.

A sheen of sweat dapples his upper lip. 'We need to talk.'

'Yes. Would you like a beer? Some tea?'

I'm so formal, acting like some kind of damned *hostess*, and it surprises me when Max walks past me, into our kitchen. He runs the cold water tap and fills a glass. He drinks.

I stand in the doorway, looking at my husband's back.

His voice is rough. 'I don't carry the CF gene.'

There is no good way to do this. And I have to do this.

'Chip was by earlier. His results came back. He does carry the gene.'

'Well, there you are.' Max slams the glass down on the counter. 'Chip has two sons. I have none.'

'That's not true.'

'It's as true as black and white, Lucy.'

'Max, will you sit down? Can we talk about this?'

'There's no point hashing it over,' Max says. 'We can't change things. What's done is done. We need to go on from here.'

'Yes,' I say eagerly, leaning toward my husband. 'Exactly. And we need to think of Jeremy—'

'I'm filing for divorce.'

'*Max.*'

'I want joint custody of Margaret. All our assets split fifty-fifty, except of course you keep the Nantucket house.'

'But what about Jeremy?'

'What about him?'

'Max, God damn it! He's your *son.*'

'Okay,' Max says brusquely, 'I'm out of here. I really just stopped by to pack up some things. I'll stay at the newspaper until I find an apartment. You'd better be prepared; we need to put the house up for sale.' He brushes past me, just inches away, as he goes by out of the kitchen and up the stairs to our bedroom.

I follow him, torn between anger and disbelief. Max takes a duffel bag down from the closet shelf, tosses it on the bed, begins to fill it with underwear, shirts, socks.

'Come on, Max,' I say softly. 'You can't stop being Jeremy's father. Not just like that. Not like flicking a switch.'

'But that's exactly what happened,' Max replies, shoving

his clothes in together ruthlessly. 'And *you* flicked the switch, Lucy. *You.*' His face flushes as he speaks.

'I know that. I know. And I'm so sorry, Max, I can never tell you how sorry I am that I've hurt you. But we're still a family, and we've got to think about Jeremy first of all. He's only a little boy. He's going to have enough to deal with this damned condition. You can't desert him now.'

'Yes,' Max says, 'I can.' He pulls the zipper so fast it shrieks. He hoists it and turns to leave.

I block the doorway. 'Remember that summer, Max. Remember the things you said to me. You didn't know if you loved me. You implied that you were going to leave me, because you wanted a son.'

'God,' Max says quietly, his face bleak. 'Isn't it ironic.'

A sob catches in my throat and tears course down my face. 'Oh, Max. Please. Don't leave me. Don't leave us. We need you.'

Tears rise in Max's eyes. 'Every time I look at Jeremy, I see living proof of the affair you had with Chip. You can't expect me to live with that.'

'Max, Jeremy isn't, isn't *evidence!*' I sputter, fighting for the right words. 'He's a little boy. Our little boy.'

'*Your* little boy,' Max says. His face is wet with tears.

'Oh, God, Max, I'm sorry.' I cannot bear the pain on his face, the pain that radiates from him in a sheen like a kind of cramped energy, almost a visible light. I want to hold him, to try to diminish that pain. I reach out.

'Don't, Lucy,' Max says, and steps sideways, away from me, as if my touch is distressing. He walks around me, down the stairs, down the front hall to the door.

.   .   .   .

I NEED MAGIC. I want spells and incantations. I want someone to *help* me. I can't do this by myself. This is how a criminal feels when she has pled guilty and stands all alone, when the judgment has been given and the gavel dropped down. This is how she feels, full of self-loathing and a smothering terror, unable to breathe, choking on her very life.

I have lost my best friend. I've lost my husband. I will lose this house. My children's lives will be snapped in half. I want to scourge myself, to drag my nails down my face.

With trembling hands I punch in Chip's number at Masterbrook, Gillet, and Stearns. After waiting on hold for a few moments, I hear Chip say hello.

'I'm sorry to phone you at work.'

'Quite all right.'

'I thought you should know. Max got his results. He doesn't carry the CF gene.'

'I see. Well.' He clears his throat. His voice has the formality of one who is not alone in a room. 'We should get together to discuss this as soon as possible.'

'Yes.'

'I'll call you this evening.'

'All right.'

'Lucy. It will work out, you know. It's going to be okay.'

But he's wrong, it's not true, it won't be okay, my son has cystic fibrosis, my husband wants a divorce, and I am the one who's brought all this disaster down on all the people I love.

I pace through the house like a tiger, full of a terrible wrath, weeping, talking to myself in a voice I scarcely recognize as my own. When I pass through the living room, Midnight and Cinnamon crouch down, fur bristling, then streak from the room and up the stairs to hide.

I've got to get control of myself. Right *now*, for I hear the front door slam so hard the house seems to shake. I hear fierce whispers.

I compose myself, taking several deep breaths, then step out into the hall.

'Margaret?'

My daughter stands over my son.

'Go to your room, Jeremy,' she says.

'You're not the boss of me,' he shoots back.

'What's going on?' I demand.

Margaret glares at me with blazing eyes. 'Tell him to go to his room, Mom.'

I stare at her, dumbfounded.

'Or I'll say it all in front of him,' she says.

My heart sinks. My fear turns into despair.

'Jere-Bere, I've made some peanut butter crackers for you. And some grapes. Why don't you take them into the den? You can watch TV.'

He stares at me, suspicious. I seldom let the children watch television after school; he knows something is up. He also knows that Margaret and I are more powerful and in bad moods; he might as well grab this chance while he can.

'Okay,' he concedes grumpily. 'But Margaret is still not my boss.'

'Let's go into my study.'

Margaret follows sulkily. I shut the door and sit at my desk. She sits in what I think of as Stan's chair. She's wearing an old faded polo shirt of mine over a pleated plaid miniskirt and Doc Martens. She sets her school notebook on her knees and clutches it for all she's worth as she glares at me.

'What's up?' It could be about school. It could be.

She speaks in an angry rush. 'Matthew stopped me after school. Kate told him that you had sex with Mr.

Cunningham. He says Chip might be Jeremy's real father.'

I run my hands over my face. 'Margaret, let me explain—'

'Just tell me!'

'I will, if you'll give me a chance—'

'Is it true?'

I hesitate, then quietly admit, 'It's true.'

She flushes scarlet. 'That's disgusting!'

'I know, I know it's terribly upsetting. But I want you to—'

'Upsetting?' She's spitting with fury. 'Mom, it's *gross*. It's, it's *pornographic!*'

'Stop that.' I'm deathly quiet.

She opens her mouth, then shuts it so tightly she shudders all over.

'Listen to me, Margaret. Seven years ago I made a terrible mistake, it's true, but it wasn't a simple thing, and I'd like to talk to you about it sometime when you're calmer. I don't know if Daddy and I are going to get a divorce. He's pretty angry with me right now. That's understandable. He has a right to his anger. There's something much more difficult that our family has to deal with. Jeremy has cystic fibrosis. He doesn't know yet – and you mustn't tell him. He needs more tests; I want to discuss this with him when we have all the facts. I don't want him to be scared. I won't have him frightened, Margaret, do you hear me?'

Margaret sinks back in her chair. Her skin has gone from scarlet to white. Her eyes are wide. Her voice is tiny when she asks, 'Does that mean . . . will Jeremy have fits?'

'No, honey.' She is so shaken, all at once transformed into my child, my girl. I go around the desk and kneel before her and take her hands in mine. Her hands are freezing. 'It's not that kind of disease. It doesn't affect the muscles. It has to do with secretions. It's why Jeremy gets so many colds and can't gain weight.'

'Is he going to die?'

'No, no, honey, no.' She's so pale she frightens me. 'You know what, Magpie? I've got some iced tea in the refrigerator. I'm going to get you a glass. You wait right here.'

'No, Mom, I don't need tea.' She pulls her hands away from me. Her brow is furrowed, but color is returning to her cheeks.

'Margaret, the important thing right now is that we haven't told Jeremy yet. You've got to promise—'

'I won't tell him.' Her lip trembles. 'Am I going to get it?'

'No. Your father doesn't carry the cystic fibrosis gene.'

'So Chip *is* Jeremy's real father.'

'*Natural* father.'

Her face flushes. 'Why did you do it, Mom?'

I pause. Margaret's seen it all, I sometimes think, especially when I hear what videos she watched at a friend's house. But this is different. This is her mother talking. This is, as she said, pornographic. Which is worse: to tell my daughter that I felt love for another man, or to tell her I didn't?

'It wasn't really an affair, Margaret. It was just a very brief . . . liaison. When you were seven. Right after your father and I lost baby Maxwell. When we were both so sad. I guess I just needed a friend, and it was all more to do with friendship than with desire. Sex is a complicated thing, Margaret. Sometimes it's about true love. That's when it's best. Sometimes it's about other things.'

'Matthew says his parents are getting divorced. He says his mom is living with that Garrison guy.'

'Well, you know, that might just be a temporary thing. I

mean, everyone is mad right now.' I manage a little laugh. 'Well, *I'm* not mad. I'm the one people are mad at. The thing you have to remember, Margaret, is that your father and I love you, and we love Jeremy, and we're going to do the best we can for both of you, to keep you both safe and happy. We—'

But Margaret's face has hardened again. 'How can you say that? Why don't you tell me the truth? Are you guys getting divorced? Just tell me.'

I walk to the window and look out, gathering my thoughts. 'Dad has told me that he wants a divorce. But I don't think he really means it. You know how, when you're mad, you say a lot of things you don't mean? That's what he's doing right now.'

'He *should* be mad. Poor Daddy.'

'Poor Jeremy,' I say softly.

'It's all your fault.' Tears well in her eyes.

'Oh, Margaret.' I reach out to hold her. 'We'll get through this.'

But she recoils. 'Don't touch me!' she says. Her eyes harden. 'Don't ever touch me again.'

'Sweetheart . . .'

'I'm *not* your sweetheart! I don't want to be *anything* to you! You've ruined my life!'

'You're exaggerating just a little, don't you—'

'It's true! Everyone's going to laugh at me. Talk behind my back. Guys will think I'm a slut like you.'

I wince at her words. 'Margaret, please.'

She's wild now, standing, yelling, her face flushed with anger. 'I hate you.'

'Oh, Margaret, don't—'

'When you get divorced, I'm going to live with Dad!'

'No, Magpie, no. I won't let you.'

'Wait and see,' she spits bitterly and runs from the room.

'Margaret!' For a moment I'm stunned, filled with a white numbness, and then rage explodes in my chest and without thinking I yell, 'Come back here!'

Sobbing, Margaret rushes through the house. Hurtling after her, I race through the hall and up the stairs, just in time to see her slam her bedroom door. Filled with an insane, blood-pounding energy, I hurl myself against the door and half fly, half fall into her room. Margaret stands in the middle of her room, fists clenched, her face contorted with anger and contempt.

I grab her shoulders and shake her. 'Don't you dare walk away from me when I'm talking to you!' Somewhere in my heart I know that this anger is meant for Max, but I can't help myself; my fingers dig into my daughter's shoulders. 'Don't you ever walk away from me again!'

Anger bleeds from her face, replaced by a look of genuine fear.

Appalled, I drop my hands. 'Margaret, I'm sorry.'

She backs away from me, her chin quivering, her face melting back into a child's face, the face of my darling little girl.

'Margaret, honey, you've got to give me a break.'

We stand, both shaking, weeping, horrified at the wrath we've summoned up from each other.

My daughter glares at me, her entire body rigid with loathing. 'I *wish you were dead*.'

Wild with pain, I press my hands against my mouth to keep from shouting abuse at this furious, arrogant, relentless young woman. Something powerful within me surges, wanting to continue the fight with Margaret, wanting to escalate it, wanting to scream and hit in an ecstasy of anger. It's all I can do to get myself out of her room and into my bedroom where I stare around me like a madwoman, looking for something to destroy. This is how people get murdered, I think, this is how suicides happen, this is what makes a man gun down his entire family, this is what makes a woman slit her own throat.

Come on, Lucy, I command myself, do *something*. You've got to get in control. You've got to calm down.

What would I do normally? I'd call Max. I can't do that. I'd call Kate. I can't call Kate, but if I could, what would *she* tell me to do? I can almost hear her voice saying, 'Lucy, lock yourself in the bathroom where no one can get to you. Pour yourself an enormous Bailey's Irish Cream and drink it in a hot bath steaming with buckets of your best bath salts.' Maybe it will work. I don't know what else to try. I race downstairs and into the kitchen.

'Mom!' Jeremy calls. 'Mom! Come look!'

'Not now, hon. I want to take a bath.'

'But, Mom!'

Holding myself together so tightly I feel ready to shatter, I go, Good Mother, into the den. 'What's wrong, Jeremy?'

'Mom, look. A hurricane is headed toward Nantucket!' Like his father, Jeremy loves watching the Weather Channel.

'Don't worry, sweetie. It probably won't reach Nantucket. It's got lots of time and room to change its course.'

'But what will happen if it does hit the island?'

'Don't worry about the hurricane,' I want to scream. 'You're in much more danger from your own mother!' Instead, in a falsely calm voice, I say, 'Remember what they did the summer you were four? How they boarded up the windows on Main Street and put X's in tape over the windows in houses?'

'Will Mr. Findlay board up our house?'

'Of course.'

'Can the hurricane come here?' Jeremy asks.

'No, Jeremy. Hurricanes don't come this far inland. We'll just get lots of wind and rain.'

'Cool,' Jeremy says.

'Right. I'm going to take a bath.'

'Are you going out tonight?'

'No,' I sigh, exasperated, ready to weep. Why does everything always need an explanation? 'I've been typing all day and I want to relax my back muscles.' This sounds reasonable. At least it satisfies his curiosity, so I hurry from the room, grab a glass of creamy liqueur, and head back upstairs. Rushing through my bedroom, I lock the bathroom door and turn the faucets on high so that hot water plunges into the tub, quickly sending billows of steam into the air. Glimpsing myself in the mirror as I undress, I consider that the body reflected in the mirror looks far too normal to have brought about so much turbulence in the world, and this thought almost makes me smile. If I could share it with Kate, we'd both laugh.

I sink into the warm water, feeling it close around my skin like the silkiest of comforters, and I *am* comforted, it does accept me, this fragrant water. Silence. Peace. I take a deep breath. It has been a long day. The liquor and the easy heat release something within me, and with the thundering of the water to hide my noise, I'm free at last to surrender to the full, shuddering fury of my emotions.

What have I done? What can I do? Who will help me? Will Margaret, my precious beloved light of my life, my beautiful daughter, really leave me to live with her father? A well of grief and fear rises within me, ready to spill out. I bury my face in my hands and prepare to let it come.

'Mommy?'

I stifle my sobs. 'What is it, Jeremy?'

'I don't feel good.'

'Go lie down in your room, Jeremy. I'll be out in a moment.'

'But, Mom. I really feel ucky.'

I take deep breaths to control my shuddering breath. Not now, I think, come on, Jeremy, give me five minutes alone. 'Honey, go tell Margaret.'

'She won't open her door.'

'All right. I tell you what. Go lie down on my bed. I'll be out in just a moment.'

'But, Mommy.'

'Jeremy, please. I want to finish my bath.' I'm digging my fingernails into my knees with frustration. Jesus, can't I have five minutes to fall apart in peace?

'All right,' Jeremy agrees, his voice plaintive, and then I hear retching.

'Jeremy?' I rise from the tub, my skin scarlet, covered with suds.

'Mommy, I threw up.'

'Oh, sweetie.' Pulling a towel around me, I open the bathroom door. Jeremy sits by the door, thin shoulders heaving. A small pile of undigested crackers and peanut butter swims in a pool of mucus and phlegm. 'Oh, baby.'

Jeremy weeps. 'I don't feel good.'

I kneel next to him, suds dripping from my face and hair. 'Poor baby. Do you need to throw up more?'

He shakes his head. I lift him in my arms and carry him to my bed, settle him among pillows, then grab a moment to slip into my robe. I take his temperature, which is only slightly high, and change his clothes, dressing him in his favorite old pajamas. I give him ginger ale to sip. I clean up the vomit.

Jeremy lies listlessly against the pillows.

'How do you feel, kiddo?'

He shrugs. 'Would you read to me, Mommy?'

'Sure, hon.' I grab a pile of books from his room and settle him next to me. I can hear a rattle of phlegm in his chest as he breathes. Rain thunders on the roof and slides down the windows.

I READ FOR hours, it seems, while Jeremy squirms restlessly, unable to concentrate on the books, too uncomfortable to sleep. Right in the middle of a story, he asks, 'Mom, is Dad mad at me?'

'No, Jeremy. Of course not. He's just so busy.'

'But he doesn't come home any more. He never even calls me.'

I have to give him some excuse: 'It's this town meeting thing, honey. After tomorrow night Dad will have more free time. He's just so busy until then. Don't worry, your daddy loves you, I promise. Okay?'

Jeremy shrugs. 'Okay,' he replies.

THE EVENING IS endless. Margaret leaves her room to rustle around in the kitchen. She carries a plate of sandwiches and a glass of milk back to her bedroom, clicking the lock on her door loudly. For a while Jeremy and I stare at the television, because we're too exhausted to do anything else. Jeremy falls asleep at nine, his body hot and limp in the bed. I'm too drained for any thought or emotion. This day has been catastrophic. At ten o'clock, Margaret stomps from her room to use the bathroom, then returns to her bedroom and turns off her light. I slide down into my bed next to my son, eager for the escape of sleep.

I WAKE ALL at once, my heart pounding. 'Jeremy?'

It's twelve-thirty. My bedroom is dark. The nightlight in the hall glows steadily. Rain batters the windows; my God, I think, how much rain is there in the sky? I rub my hands over my face. Max's side of the bed is empty. My heart seizes up, clutches tight like a fist in my chest.

'Jeremy?'

Hurrying into the bathroom, I can *feel* no one is there, but I turn on the light for my eyes to verify that sensation. Perhaps Jeremy returned to his own bed; I hurry into his room, flicking on the light. He's not there. I rush into Margaret's room. Her blanket is up to her neck. Midnight is curled at her feet, a natural furnace; the cat narrows her eyes at me in a silent hello.

I run down the stairs and into the kitchen. The room is dark and empty. All the rooms are dark and empty. I run through them, flicking on light switches, scanning the rooms, expecting to find Jeremy curled up on the sofa, or in a chair in my study.

'Jeremy.' I do not yell it, not yet, I don't want to frighten Margaret, we've got enough going on in our lives, there has to be a reason, something I'm missing, something logical that explains where Jeremy is.

The kitchen door is closed and bolted.

The front door is closed, but the closet door is open to the hall, and at once I see what is missing: Jeremy's rain slicker and rain boots.

All right. *Think.* No one has kidnapped him, no one could have come into the house and lifted him from his bed and dressed him in his rain gear. He's not crazy, he wouldn't have gone out to play in the rain. So he went somewhere on purpose.

He went to see his father.

That has to be it. Jeremy is worried about his father, and confused because Max has been away for so long.

I race up the stairs and into my bedroom. I pull on sweatpants, sneakers, sweatshirt. I scribble a note to Margaret and stick it on her bedside table. Grabbing up my car keys, I head out into the rainy night.

Steadily the rain pounds down, banging on the roof and the hood of the car, like hundreds of evil spirits trying to get in. Most of the houses on our street are dark, with a porch light shining here, the blue flicker of a television screen shining through the window there, the steady glow of a stove light in a window further down the street. This is a safe town. It's a small town. It's only a matter of perhaps twenty blocks between here and the newspaper. A child could walk there. Which way would Jeremy go? These streets should all be familiar to him, but then again he's just a child, and it's dark, and rain obscures everything. We have walked from our house to the Little Red Schoolhouse, about eight blocks away. We have walked from there into town, to the library, the post office, the pharmacy where we buy ice cream cones. We have walked from there to the other side of town, where *The Sussex Gazette* is. Jeremy could figure it out. He could find his way.

It's a safe town, I keep telling myself. There will be no

perverts, no monsters lurking to steal a little boy, not in the middle of the night, not in a downpour like this. I drive six blocks without meeting another car on the streets. As I turn the corner onto Main Street, a blue pickup truck goes around the corner, a woman with bleached blond hair driving. She's driving carefully, concentrating in the heavy rain. People would be driving carefully, they wouldn't be speeding, the chances that they would accidentally hit a small child walking on the sidewalks are low. Really low, I would think.

Still I wish I had called the police. The police department is only three blocks away from the newspaper. They would be there by now.

And then I am there, pulling into the parking lot. No cars are parked there. Through the picture window a light gleams, illuminating the empty office. Rain pellets slam my windshield so furiously it's like a swarm of bees, splattering noisily, trying to break through the panes. Rain hits the pavement of the parking lot in pops, ricocheting back up in little bursts. The shrubs beneath the window and on either side of the front door shiver violently in the wind.

Between the bushes, sitting on the front step, head bowed over onto his knees, is a small figure, a little boy in a yellow rain slicker. He looks up as my headlights play over him. His face is streaked with tears and rain.

'I WANT MY daddy!' Jeremy insists as I lift him and carry him to the car. 'I want my daddy!'

'Daddy's going to be furious with you for leaving the house in the middle of the night.' I dump him in the backseat and fasten his seat belt. My teeth chatter with adrenaline.

'You were a very bad boy, Jeremy. You did a very dangerous thing.'

'I want my daddy,' Jeremy weeps. 'Where is he? I thought he was here. You said he was here.'

I pull a tissue from my pocket and wipe off Jeremy's wet hands and face, wishing I had a towel. Jeremy sneezes.

'Daddy's not at the newspaper tonight. He's at a friend's house.' I start the car, turn the heater on full blast.

'Is my daddy dead?' Jeremy asks.

'Dead? No! Where did you get such an idea?'

'My daddy would call me if he was alive.'

'Oh, Jeremy.' I turn to look at my frail, wet, weeping son, and my throat closes up with pity and remorse. 'I tell you what. I think I know where Daddy is. I'll show you his van, okay?'

'Okay.'

It takes only about ten minutes to drive through the dark night out along Route 16 to Garrison's house in the woods. We meet no other cars.

The porch light is on at Garrison's house, the rest of the windows dark. Kate's Mercedes convertible is in the driveway; Max's van behind it.

Is it anger? Is it jealousy? Is it idiocy? I park the car behind the van, storm around the side, undo Jeremy's seat belt, and lift him in my arms. He seems weightless as I stride up the front steps and pound on the door. It's as if I have three arms, four, I hold him and beat on the door while the rain plummets down all around us.

A light comes on inside. Figures move behind the curtains.

Max opens the door. He's wearing only a quickly tied robe.

'What the hell?' he says, blinking.

'Daddy!' Jeremy whoops, and hurls his entire body at Max with absolute unthinking assurance that his father will catch him.

Max catches him. Jeremy hugs his father's neck, clings to him like a wide-eyed baby lemur.

'Can we come in?' I don't wait for Max to answer. I step inside, out of the noise and assault of the rain.

Kate enters the living room clad in a pale cream negligee beautifully ornamented with lace. I am aware of my thoroughly drenched hair, my drowned-rat appearance.

'Daddy, you didn't come home, you didn't answer my phone calls, I thought you were sick. And I threw up tonight!'

'Jeremy sneaked out of the house,' I tell Max. 'He got up when I was sleeping, and dressed himself, and walked to the *Gazette*. In the dark. In the rain. Alone.'

'Mom said you were working, Dad. But why can't you come home at night like you always do? Why don't you call me on the phone? Are you mad at me? Why—' A series of sneezes overcomes the little boy.

'You're all wet, pal,' Max says.

'I'll get a towel.' Kate hurries from the room.

'Don't you love us any more, Dad?' Jeremy asks.

For one long moment the room is silent except for the plopping of beads of rain off my clothes onto the wooden floor and the steady drumming of rain on the roof.

Max looks so sad it breaks my heart.

'Of course I still love you, Jeremy,' he says.

Kate hands Max the towel. For a moment Max's dark head is bent as he rubs the towel over the golden-streaked hair of the little boy nestled between his forearm and his chest.

'Will you come home with us, Dad?' Jeremy asks.

Max doesn't answer right away but intently rubs the towel over Jeremy's legs. He's looking down; I can't read the expression on his face. I can hear Kate breathing and the crackle of Jeremy's raincoat as he shifts in his father's arms. I hold my breath.

Max says, 'All right.'

He sets Jeremy on the floor. 'I'll get my things.'

Oscar has been wriggling around our feet ever since we came into the house, and now the little dog stands on his hind legs and does a wriggling dance of ecstasy as Jeremy greets him. Kate follows Max out of the living room. I hear their voices but not their words.

Max returns, a duffel bag in one hand, a briefcase in the other. Without speaking, he hands me the briefcase, then picks Jeremy up with one arm. 'Okay, sport. Let's go home.'

Oscar whimpers and jumps at our feet. Kate walks over to pick him up; as she bends, the low neck of her negligee falls forward and I can see clearly her small high breasts. I think of Max touching those breasts. I thrust the thought away. Kate stands holding the dog to her chest.

Jeremy says, 'Is Aunt Kate going to come home, too?'

'Not tonight,' I reply. 'She's staying here to take care of Garrison.'

'Want an umbrella?' she asks as we open the door to the wind-blown rain.

'No, thanks,' I tell her. 'We'll be all right.'

BACK HOME, I stand in the shower, letting hot water scald down over me, until I'm warm again. Max is putting

Jeremy into dry pajamas, blowing his hair dry, and he's brought out an electric blanket for Jeremy's bed, and layered it above the sheet but beneath a quilt, so that Midnight and Cinnamon's claws won't snag a wire. I don't like using an electric blanket with the children, but I understand Max's logic tonight, to make the bed as warm as toast. And I'm so glad he's back I'm not going to fuss about a thing.

I blow my hair not completely dry – that would take forever, – but dry enough, and I pull on my flannel night-gown and knee-high cotton socks, a far cry from Kate's negligee, but I don't feel very seductive right now. I'm exhausted. It's 2:00 a.m.

And Margaret is awake; I find her sitting on my bed when I come out of the shower.

'Dad's home,' she says.

'I know. Did you see my note? Your dreadful little brother walked all the way to the *Gazette* in the dark.'

Margaret's eyes go wide with surprise. 'Oh, man, he's going to be grounded for life.'

'At the very least.'

'But he got Dad to come back from the newspaper.'

Something bitter stirs in me, longing to tell Margaret exactly where Max was tonight. Instead I say mildly, 'He would have come back sooner or later.'

She eyes me warily. 'Dad's thumping around in the guest room.'

'Well, we still have a lot of stuff to discuss. But he's here. So stop worrying and get some sleep.'

To my utter surprise, Margaret comes over and wraps her arms around me. 'I love you, Mommy,' she says, her voice muffled by my nightgown.

I hug her against me tightly. For a moment I can not even speak. Then my breath comes and I say as if I never doubted it, 'I know you do, darling. Now go to sleep. You've got school tomorrow.'

I walk her to her room and tuck her into bed. She's asleep the moment her head hits the pillow.

In his room, Jeremy sleeps soundly, too. Both Midnight and Cinnamon are on his bed; they like the warmth of the electric blanket.

The light is already out in the guest bedroom. I stand in the doorway.

'Max?' I can see that he's already in bed, turned with his back to the door. 'Thank you.'

'It doesn't change anything, Lucy. It's just for tonight.'

'Can't we talk?'

'I've got to get some sleep.'

'All right.' Still, I linger, waiting for him to say something else, wishing I could say one perfect thing. After a few moments, I say, 'I love you.'

He doesn't reply.

I leave him, go into our bedroom, and stretch out alone on our queen-size bed.

BUT THIS ISN'T my night for sleep. No sooner have I fallen into a deep doze than a noise wakes me: Jeremy coughing. I stumble through a familiar night-nurse routine, finding the teaspoon, the children's cough suppressant, the Vicks VapoRub, the cherry cough drops that probably don't do any good but help Jeremy to believe that not all medicines taste bad. Jeremy feels warm to me, no doubt because of the accumulated heat of the two cats and the electric blanket.

He's fussy and exhausted and doesn't want to let me take his temperature with a mercury thermometer and I'm out of tongue fever strips, so I turn off the electric blanket. I manage to get the cough medicine down him and prop him up on two pillows, then bumble back to my own bed, dizzy with fatigue.

I WAKE TO the smell of coffee. Amazing. An adult in the house again. I lie there, loving the aroma, letting it lull me into a sense that this is a normal morning like any other. I hear Jeremy cough; I hear Max talking to him.

I find everyone in the kitchen. Max is at the stove, preparing his famous scrambled eggs. Margaret flutters around him, handing him the salt and pepper, taking the eggshells from him and disposing of them, setting the table, pouring orange juice, fussing over Jeremy, so happy to have her father around that she can't stop smiling. She's dressed for school, and so is Jeremy, but after one look at him, I know I'm keeping him home.

'Morning, Glory,' I say to my daughter, kissing her cheek.

'Morning, Mom.'

'How do you feel this morning, Jeremy?' I bend to kiss his cheek, too, and let my own cheek linger against his forehead. I'm pretty sure he has a fever.

'All right,' he says and bursts into a series of coughs.

'You know what?' I speak casually, stirring milk and sugar into my coffee. 'I think I'll keep you home today.'

'But Dad's going to drive us to school!' Jeremy protests.

'Honey, listen to yourself. You're coughing. And you didn't get much sleep last night at all.'

'Mom, I want to go to school!'

'Better stay home, sport,' Max says. 'Better take care of yourself and get over your cold.'

'If I stay home from school, can I come to town meeting tonight?' Jeremy asks.

Max hedges. 'Let's see how you feel this afternoon.'

'Dad,' Margaret says, 'all the teachers are talking about town meeting. They said you've been writing editorials in favor of developing the Lamb property, but lots of people think it should go to conservation.'

A blob of egg falls from Jeremy's fork. I reach over to wipe his shirt. As he answers, Max stretches out an arm to shove Jeremy's chair closer to the table. 'That's true, Magpie. It's a complicated situation, and an emotional one.'

Margaret watches her father carefully. 'They say Mr. Cunningham is the lawyer for the ConCom.'

'Uncle Chip?' Jeremy asks.

Max doesn't flush or pause. 'Right. Uncle Chip.'

Margaret presses. 'Are you mad at Mr. Cunningham, Dad?'

Here it is, I think, the first test, and certainly not the last by a long shot. Jeremy senses the tension and stares from his sister to his father.

'No, honey, I'm not mad at Uncle Chip,' Max says evenly. Calmly he meets his daughter's eyes, speaking with the measured judiciousness that people have come to admire him for. 'Mr. Cunningham's a lawyer. It's his job to speak for the people who hire him. He and I might disagree at town meeting, but that's business, not personal. We've been on opposing sides of issues before, you know that. He's a Republican, I'm a Democrat, you must have heard some of the arguments we've had.'

'It's kind of weird, you being on the side of the developers.'

'I know. It's not my customary position. But I've done a

lot of research on this matter, and I believe that building the complex will be the best thing for the majority of people in this town.'

'I heard the principal tells Mr. Clarence that it's going to be like *Clash of the Titans*.'

To my infinite relief, Max throws back his head and laughs. 'Then it should be entertaining for everyone.' He rises. 'If you want me to drive you to school, Margaret, better hurry. I want to leave in five minutes.'

'Dad?' Jeremy twists in his chair. 'Are you coming home tonight?'

Max looks at his little boy. 'Yeah. Right after work.'

Jeremy nods to himself, once, sharply, like Max does, satisfied.

The rain has stopped, but the skies remain gray, and wind tosses the heavy leaves of the trees so that they occasionally fling their drops of water against the house, making a sound like someone tossing pebbles at a window. When Margaret and Max leave, Jeremy slumps in his chair like a balloon with all the air gone out of him.

'Hey, chum, I want to take your temperature.'

He fusses, but I insist, and discover that his fever has suddenly shot up to one hundred and two degrees.

I call Wally Calder, our pediatrician, then I bundle Jeremy up warmly and drive over to the clinic. We sit docilely in the waiting room, while other children with their own coughs, sneezes, itches, and aches, grumble and whine in their mothers' arms. People look at us sharply each time Jeremy coughs. I know the sound is impolite, irritating; I smile guiltily and remind him to cover his mouth. He sits on my lap, his skin hot, parched-feeling, as uncomfortably dry as a fish out of water. A new vein of dread has opened up within my heart and glitters at me like a metallic thread leading into a frightening labyrinth.

JEREMY KNOWS WALLY well and does not shy away from the doctor's various intrusive investigations. Wally is deft and humorous, a genius with children, and pretty great with mothers, too. He's calm and ugly in a kind way that makes him seem accepting of anything, a mother's greasy hair after a week with a sick child, a parent's neurotic need to bring a child in over nothing more than a little cough.

'Well, buddy,' Dr. Calder says. 'Do you know what we get to do today? We get to have a chest X-ray!'

'Will it hurt?' Jeremy asks.

'You won't feel a thing. I promise. It's sort of cool, like a *Star Wars* kind of gadget.' He looks at me, glasses glittering. 'I think we might have a little pneumonia going on,' he says cheerfully.

His office is in the same modern glass and stucco building that houses the hospital, and it's only a matter of walking through a maze of corridors to get to the X-ray room. Again we wait patiently. Jeremy sits on my lap without fussing, his head burning through my shirt.

After the X-ray, I pull Jeremy's shirt back on over his arms. We return to the hall, intending to walk back to the pediatrician's office, only to see the doctor striding toward us down the corridor, his white coat streaming out behind him.

'Hey, Jeremy.' Wally Calder has the X-ray in his hand. He squats down to be on Jeremy's level. 'You know what, buddy? You get to get some VIP treatment today. You know what VIP means, don't you?'

Jeremy shakes his head.

'It means Very Important Person, and that's just what you are. You get to check into the hospital today.'

'I don't want to,' Jeremy says, cringing.

'Come on, you haven't even seen it yet. You get to lie in bed and watch TV all day. Listen, I'd like to do that myself.'

'I don't want to,' Jeremy insists.

'Well, you see this X-ray here, Jeremy? It shows me that you've got pneumonia. Your lungs are congested. I would bet that you're having trouble breathing. Even more than that cough, I'd bet that you're working hard just to get breath into those lungs. That's making you feel tired, like you don't want to play ball or even go to school. Well, the only way we're going to get rid of that congestion is in the hospital, with some really powerful medicine that's going to zap the pneumonia. See what I'm saying?'

Jeremy nods warily.

'Let's go back to my office and get your admission organized,' Wally says. 'I need to make a few phone calls.'

Jeremy takes the doctor's outstretched hand and walks by his side. Stunned, I follow.

Once we're seated in the pediatrician's office, a pretty young nurse appears.

'Jeremy? Can you come with me? I forgot to weigh you.'

I rise, but Wally says, 'You can wait here, Lucy. He'll be right back.'

Jeremy obediently slides off my lap and takes the nurse's hand. She shuts the door.

Wally leans toward me, his face suddenly stern. In his white lab coat, with his thick glasses flashing like some kind of scientific equipment, his sharp scent of antiseptic and soap, he seems frightening and cold.

'Lucy, Children's Hospital called me three weeks ago to tell me that Jeremy has cystic fibrosis. I'm so sorry.'

'Is he terribly sick?'

'He's got pneumonia, as I said, and with cystic fibrosis, infections in the lungs are always much more dangerous. Look, I'm not trying to scare you. I want him in the hospital because we can get better antibiotics into his system faster than with oral medications, and he needs some fluids, too; he's becoming dehydrated. Have you told Jeremy he has cystic fibrosis yet?'

'No. I wanted Max to be with me when I tell him, and we've just been. . . .' How do I explain these past three weeks? 'So busy.'

'So you haven't gone to any of the clinics at Children's Hospital?'

I shake my head. 'We were on Nantucket . . .'

Patches of red blotch Wally's face; he is angry with me, or frightened. 'There are all sorts of things you need to learn. *Soon.* Things that can prolong Jeremy's life. That can save his life.'

I nod meekly.

'Lucy, this is not the end of the world. Jeremy can have a good life. He can have a long life. But you can't be a coward about this.'

'I know.'

'All right. Let's get Jeremy into the hospital. I'm going to call ahead. You take this X-ray with you.'

I PHONE THE newspaper. Max is out and not responding to his cell phone.

I ask to speak to Roland Cobb: 'Tell Max I'm taking Jeremy

to Children's Hospital. He's got pneumonia. I'll call him from there.'

'Is there anything I can do?' Roland asks.

'Yes, please. Call the high school. Someone needs to tell Margaret where we are. Perhaps after school she could go over to—' My mind stops dead. 'Matthew Cunningham's' is what I usually would say, have always said. Ordinarily I would have spoken with Kate a hundred times by now, arranging for Margaret to be picked up, driven to piano lessons, fed, and tended to. Without Kate there, it's as if a void opens up beneath me. I can't even think.

Roland says, 'I'll have Andrea go to the high school and get Margaret. She can stay with us this evening, and as long as necessary.'

'Thanks, Roland.'

JEREMY SLEEPS AND coughs during the ride into Boston. Even though it's the middle of the day, the traffic along Route 2 is heavy, eight lanes across of rushing vehicles, vans, trucks, cars, Jeeps, swerving in and out of lanes, honking, braking, speeding past. The sun flashes off all the metal hoods and roofs like emergency signals. A red pickup truck cuts in front of me, missing my left fender by inches, and the driver leans out his window and gives me the finger. Startled, I focus on the road. I'm between the lane lines. I'm going sixty-five. What am I doing wrong? Why did that guy give me the finger? I want Kate with me. She'd lean out her window and shout, 'Moron!' Or Max would say, mildly, 'That wasn't directed at you, Lucy. He's just having a bad day. Don't take it personally.'

But *everything* feels personal right now. My heart thumps

in my ears, the steering wheel is sticky in my hands, the traffic alarms me, we're going too fast, we're going too slow. I want to be there, where Jeremy can be helped; I want to stay away, because once we're in that hospital, there'll be no more evasion: Our lives will change for ever.

There's valet parking at the entrance. Brilliant. Jeremy clings to me apprehensively as I carry him into the emergency room, but he perks up as he spots all the extravagantly colorful giant cardboard fish dangling from the ceiling, seeming to float in the air above our heads. The novelty of the bright rooms and the cheeriness of the nurses carry us through the admissions process and up to the fourth floor where we're greeted by a cheerful nurse named Cindy who chats with us so pleasantly it could almost seem that we were here to have fun.

Jeremy flushes with alarm when he sees his room. Max and I should have prepared him, we should have told him about his condition before now. In spite of the mural of animals ringing the ceiling, it is still very much a hospital room, with a high bed set next to a panel of equipment. A whip of self-loathing lashes me. Cindy and I settle Jeremy on the bed, remove his street clothes, tuck him into a hospital gown. Dr. Potter, as lean and leathery looking as a whippet, examines Jeremy, then tousles his hair.

'Okay, Jeremy, here's the deal. We're going to put a shunt in your arm, right here. It will pinch for a moment, but that's all, and then we'll be able to hook you up to an IV tube that will provide your body with antibiotics and fluids that will help you get rid of your fever and moderate your coughing.'

Jeremy's lip quivers. 'Mommy,' he cries. 'I don't want to do this.'

'Sure you do,' I say with false enthusiasm, wrapping my arm around him, wishing I could press him right back into the safety of my own body. 'They're going to make you well. You want that, don't you?'

'I want to go home.'

'You will, baby, but first you've got to get all well.'

He cries, just as I nearly do, when the shunt is put into his vein, but mercifully the nurse is adept and swift, and before we know it, Cindy is attaching a tube from the wall to Jeremy's arm.

Cindy smiles. 'There. You did really well, Jeremy.'

Tears spot the ends of Jeremy's eyelashes, but he studies the IV tube snaking from the wall with some curiosity. 'This is kind of like being a deep sea diver,' he says.

My brave little boy. 'Right! Like the oxygen tubes going into their face masks.'

'Kind of.'

The nurse asks, 'Do you want to be a diver?'

'Maybe.'

'We'll get you in practice for that,' she says. 'but now the best thing would be for you to rest.'

Jeremy nods obediently, leaning back against his pillows, looking infinitely small and pale. He is very tired.

'You've got your own bathroom, Jeremy.' Cindy opens a door to show us. 'And see that big purple chair? That turns into a bed. Your Mom can stay here in the room with you tonight. And I'm sure you've noticed the television. It's got a VCR so you can watch your favorite videos.'

'This is a cool room, isn't it?' I ask Jeremy.

'I guess.' He closes his eyes, then opens them. 'Mommy?'

'I'll stay right here with you, Jeremy.'

I stand near him, holding his hand. I'm surprised at how

quickly he falls asleep. He's sick, I realize. He's really sick. My heart plummets.

Dr. Potter enters the room, a chart in his hand. 'Mrs. West?'

Jeremy's asleep, still I stand close to Dr. Potter, wanting to shield my son from the man's verdict.

'Okay. I've spoken with Dr. Calder. I've seen your son's X-ray. As you know, he has pneumonia, and with cystic fibrosis, it can be a real problem. I'm recommending that Jeremy stay in the hospital for a two-week course of IV antibiotics—'

'Two weeks!'

'This is not unusual with a CF patient with pneumonia. Jeremy's lungs are badly congested.'

'But two weeks!'

'Perhaps, if you desire, you can learn to administer the IV yourself, three times daily, in which case, if things go well, it is possible that Jeremy could go home in about a week.'

So many *ifs*.

The doctor continues. 'We can help you find a home care company who would arrange for a nurse to help you learn how to change the dressing and so on.'

'I need to sit down.' I sink onto the large purple chair.

Dr. Potter pulls up a chair. 'He'll only be actually hooked up to the IV three times a day, when he gets his dose. That will take about thirty minutes. Then we cap it off and he can get up and run around, play with the other kids, use the activity room. A physical therapist will be in soon to start Jeremy on chest percussion therapy. She'll perform it three times a day. You can watch it so that you can do it when Jeremy's home.'

'Three times a day?'

'For thirty minutes. It loosens the mucus, the child coughs it out, it frees the lungs. Your husband will want to learn it, too.'

'I can stay with Jeremy.'

'Yes. Twenty-four hours a day. Or his father can stay with him. Where do you live?'

'Sussex.'

'About an hour's drive, then. Often our parents stay at the Best Western next door, take turns so they can shower and change clothes and so on.'

'Can his sister visit?'

'How old is she?'

'Fourteen.'

'Certainly.'

'And friends?'

'Anyone younger than twelve is screened at the front desk for health purposes. And of course all visitors are allowed only at the parents' discretion.'

'Jeremy's going to be all right, isn't he?'

'We'll be able to get this pneumonia under control. But cystic fibrosis is unpredictable. We take one day at a time around here. But I assure you, the more you learn about CF, the better for your child.'

I BEGIN TO learn. Late in the afternoon, when Jeremy wakes, a physical therapist begins the chest percussion therapy on Jeremy that she says will become a normal part of our daily lives, as basic as brushing teeth. We tell Jeremy only that it will help loosen the mucus in his chest. I want to wait until Max is with us to tell Jeremy about his illness. Jeremy dozes while I'm visited by a social worker and a nurse. They speak of glands. Secretions. Antibiotics. Enzyme supplements. Medications. Physical therapy. I ask questions, each question leading to ten others. It's more than I can comprehend. They give me brochures to share with my family and friends and with Jeremy's teacher. I stare at the brightly colored covers, illustrated with what looks like children's drawings. Inside, the information is printed in a variety of types and colors, lots of white space, with pictures drawn by children. The information is direct and precise, presented in an unintimidating manner and I'm surprised to find myself wondering who created these brochures. Then I focus on the words.

I'm reading when our phone rings. I snatch it up. 'Max?'

'How's Jeremy?' he asks. He's at his office, I can tell by the general commotion of ringing phones and shouts around his voice.

'He's got pneumonia. He's on IV antibiotics. They say he'll be here for two weeks.'

'Two weeks! My God.' He covers the mouthpiece, but I hear him snap at someone: '*Not now.*' Back with me, he says, 'I'm coming in right away. Do you want me to bring anything?'

'His book. *Caleb's Friend.*'

'All right. I'm on my way.'

THIRTY MINUTES LATER, the phone rings again. I hear the cultured, slightly British tones of Phil Bergshon, the minister of the Sussex Congregational Church and a good friend.

'Lucy. Roland told me about Jeremy. How is he?'

Phil's concern flows around me like balm. We're not alone, I think; our family's part of a community.

'He's got pneumonia. He's on IV antibiotics. He'll be in here for a while.' Talking about this makes it a little less terrifying.

'Is there anything I can do? Anything at all? I thought I'd

stop by tomorrow or the next day. I'd like to bring Jeremy a kind of magnetic puzzle that caught my eye in the toy store. It might help pass the time. When he feels up to it, of course.'

Tears mist my eyes. 'Phil, that's so kind of you. You don't have to bring a present, but we'd love to see you.'

Phil's voice changes slightly. 'I was wondering . . . about Max . . .'

'Yes?'

'I know Max is on his way to the hospital now, as of course he should be. But frankly, Lucy, to be blunt, I'm calling to express my most sincere hope, and I know that the entire community joins me in this, that Max return to Sussex tonight.' When I don't reply immediately, he adds, unnecessarily, 'For the town meeting.'

You fuck, I think. This is the real reason you called. Wearily I reply, 'I don't know what Max's plans are.'

'I don't mean to appear callous about this, Lucy, when Jeremy's ill and all that, but you've been such a wonderful part of our town for so many years now that I'm certain you appreciate how imperative it is for Max to appear at town meeting tonight. If you and Jeremy could do without Max tonight for just a few hours, you know it will make an inestimable difference in the way the town votes.'

'Phil—'

'I know Max has written editorials, and thank God he has. But his *presence* is so necessary, I'd venture to state that it's essential. He speaks so well, and is so much respected by the community. He—'

I don't want to hear any more. 'Phil. I know. I'll tell Max you called.'

There's a brief silence, then Phil's voice grows honeyed

again. 'Of course. Thank you, Lucy. My prayers are with you and your family.'

JEREMY'S STILL SLEEPING at five o'clock when Max arrives. He leans over the bed and stares at the little boy's face, then looks at me.

'How is he?' Max looks exhausted. The skin beneath his eyes is nearly violet, he needs a shave, his clothes are rumpled.

'He's had a busy day.'

'I brought the book and some other stuff.' Max settles in a folding chair, placing a large bag between us. 'Did you tell him about . . . ?'

'Not yet. I wanted you to be with us.'

'All right. Thanks.' His forehead furrows. 'I guess.' He studies my face. 'How are you?'

'Tired. This is all so complicated, Max. It's not like Jeremy will be cured by one hospital visit. We're going to have to deal with it every day. Several times a day. There's a ton of stuff to learn. How to do percussion therapy on his chest. About medications.' My voice wavers.

'Okay,' Max says. Reaching out, he takes both my hands in his. 'Okay, Lucy. We can do this.'

I stare at him. 'You said *We*.'

'Yes.'

'You mean you don't want a divorce? You're staying with us?'

Max takes a deep breath. 'Yes. I'm staying with you. If that's what you want.'

'*Max*. You know it's what I want.' I'm whispering, as if any change in the atmosphere might scare him away.

Max rubs the bridge of his nose. 'I've been thinking and thinking about Jeremy, trying to sort out what would be best for him. He's the one who matters most, he's the one we have to protect. Right now, he's just a little boy, and he believes that I'm his father, and I don't think it would be right to take that away from him. He's going to have enough to deal with, with his illness. He doesn't need the confusion of all the rest of this.' Max looks at me levelly. 'Does this make sense to you?'

'Yes.'

'But someday we'll have to tell him about . . . Chip.'

'Yes.'

'If Jeremy wants to change things later, he always will have that opportunity. We won't keep anything from him.'

'All right.'

'We have to talk with Margaret about all this now, though. We can't ignore her.'

'I know. Oh, Max—'

On the bed, Jeremy stirs and wakes. 'Daddy?'

'Hey, sport, look at you!' As Max stands by the hospital bed, I can see in every line of his body how he wants to pick Jeremy up. Instead he gently smooths Jeremy's hair.

'Your bow tie is crooked, Dad,' Jeremy declares. 'I have pneumonia. Look at my arm. They put a needle in my vein. It hurt.'

'Wow.' Max's voice trembles. He clears his throat. 'Does it hurt now?'

'Just a little. And a lady came in and pounded on my chest and back!'

'Did that hurt?'

'No. She was funny. It made me cough.' Jeremy leans back against his pillow, suddenly tired.

'I brought *Caleb's Friend* in. Want me to read to you?'

'Okay.'

'Great.' Max undoes his tie, opens his collar, rolls up his sleeves, his movements efficient, masculine, yet domestic, each movement making this room more *ours*, more comfortable in our lives.

'Max,' I say, 'Phil Bergshon called. He wanted to urge you to come to town meeting tonight.'

Without hesitation, Max replies, 'I can't.'

'Well, you *could*.' I begin, reasonably. 'I'll be here.'

Max stares at me. 'I think this is where I should be tonight. Don't you?'

'Yes. Absolutely.' We gaze at one another. There's so much I want to say.

'Daddy?' Jeremy chirps. 'Where's the book?'

Max smiles at me. I smile back.

'Right here, son,' Max replies, and settles on the bed, pulling Jeremy firmly against him. He begins to read.

THE TELEPHONE RINGS. I answer it; it's Martin Reid, the town counsel, wanting to speak to Max.

Annoyed, Max takes the phone. 'Right. Yes, pneumonia. No, I won't be able to make it tonight. Roland Cobb will speak in my place. I understand, Martin. Martin, look. I'm not going to change my mind.'

After that the phone rings continually. Almost as soon as Max disconnects from one person, another calls.

'This is ridiculous,' Max says. 'Don't they understand they're calling a hospital room?'

'I could tell them you're not available,' I suggest.

'I've got a better idea.' Max lifts the phone off the cradle and stuffs it under a pillow.

WHEN THE NURSE arrives with Jeremy's dinner, Max takes his cell phone out into the hall while I sit with Jeremy, cajoling him into trying a bite of the mashed potatoes, another spoonful of Jell-O. He eats listlessly, and falls back asleep when he's through.

Max is still on his cell phone, talking in terse determined tones. I phone the Cobb's house and ask to speak to my daughter.

'Hi, darling. How are you?'

Margaret's voice is shaky; she cannot say it fast enough. 'Is Jeremy going to die?'

'No, no, sweetie. He's not that sick. He's got pneumonia, and they can get antibiotics into his system more quickly when he's in the hospital. They have an IV in his arm. He's asleep right now. He'll need a lot of rest. You can come visit him tomorrow if you want.'

'Where's Dad?'

'He's here with us. He's on his cell phone right now.'

'Is he going to miss town meeting?'

'Yes. Max wants to be with Jeremy tonight.' For a moment we're both quiet, assimilating this startling fact. 'How was school?'

'Okay.' Her voice is lighter.

'Are you going to spend the night at the Cobbs'?'

'Yeah. They've given me their guest room. It's awesome. I've got my own bathroom, plus my own TV. Andrea says I can watch all I want.'

I respond like a normal, dutiful mother. 'That's great, but

don't stay up all night and forget to do your homework.'

'Yeah, Mom, like I'm going to turn into an airhead.'

'Can the Cobbs take you home tomorrow to get clean clothes?'

'Gee, what a good idea! We hadn't thought of that.' With each second my abrasive, testy, secure adolescent returns to me and to herself. 'Andrea already drove me over. I've packed up a bag.'

In the background someone speaks. Margaret says, 'Mom, we've got to go. I mean the Cobbs are going to town meeting and I'm going with them.'

'I'll talk to you tomorrow then, sweetie. I love you.'

'Love you, too, Mom. Kiss Jeremy for me. And Dad.'

BY SEVEN THE phone calls have stopped. Town meeting has begun. Jeremy watches television and dozes, often wakened by his cough.

'Let's make a plan,' Max suggests quietly. 'We can't both spend the night with him. We've got two weeks ahead of us and Margaret to think about, not to mention work.'

'I'll stay here tonight.'

'You were here all day. Don't you want a break?'

I hug myself. 'I just feel like *I* need to be with him tonight. His first night in the hospital. While he's so sick.'

'All right, then. Why don't you go home now and get some things, toothbrush, nightgown—'

'Gallon of Scotch,' I joke. 'Yeah. That's a good idea. If he wakes, tell him I'll be right back.'

'I'll be here.'

. . .

THIS DAY HAS been so filled with terrors and wonders and strangeness that I feel as if entire months have passed. People could have landed on Mars for all I know. There could be a new president. I ride the elevator to the main floor, follow signs back to the entrance, and it's as if I'm leaving the heart of a labyrinth, walking out from an enclosed, claustrophobic maze into the real world, an open space full of lights and noise and good ordinary life. But I know the hospital will become more and more real to me.

The lobby is not as full as it was during the day. A bearded man sprawls in a corner chair, reading a book, looking as if he's waiting for a plane. An Indian family huddles together, chairs pulled into a circle, talking intensely, the women's saris sparkling with gold and silver threads. A plump older woman in vivid yellow sweatpants exits Au Bon Pain, wearily lugging a heavy shopping bag across the floor. Magazines to read while she sits by someone's bed? Knitting?

I get my car keys from the valet and, pushing through the revolving doors, I step out into the night. The air is cool, and it's raining. I stand for a minute, dumbfounded, surprised by the fresh scent of the wet evening, brought right into the moment by the small drops of rain pelting my head, my feet on the hard cement pavement. I hurry across the sidewalk toward the parking garage.

A handsome man, tall and lean in a Burberry raincoat, strides toward me.

It's Chip.

His face is grave. 'Lucy.' He reaches for my hands.

I step back. 'What are you doing here?' When I look up at him, rain splatters my face.

'Roland told me that Jeremy's sick.'

'Yes, but aren't you supposed to be at town meeting?' Rain

streams down all around us, sinking into our clothes, sizzling when it hits the pavement.

With a brusque movement of his hand, he brushes that away. 'Someone else can deal with it. How is Jeremy?'

'He has pneumonia, but he's stable. It's that the cystic fibrosis complicates everything.'

'I brought him a present.' He's got a box in an F.A.O. Schwarz bag. 'We should get out of the rain before it gets wet.'

I put my hand on Chip's arm, forestalling any forward motion. 'Only family members are allowed to see him tonight.'

Chip looks down at my hand, puzzled, then looks directly at me and holds my gaze. 'I believe I qualify.'

I gasp, dumbfounded. When I find my voice, I stutter, 'Well, uh, Max is with Jeremy now. And Jeremy's really very sick.'

'Max is with Jeremy.'

'Yes.'

'He's staying with you?'

'Yes.' Rain runs down my face, feeling like tears.

'And that's what you want?'

'What I want—' My throat closes. I want too much, I think wildly, I want the impossible. 'Yes. It's what I want.'

'Let's get out of the rain.'

Chip takes my arm and leads me across the street and into the glassed foyer of the parking garage. It's warmer in here, quiet and orderly, with lights shining calmly on the stairways and doors.

Chip gently pushes my wet hair away from my face. 'Are you all right?'

'I'm just so worried about Jeremy.'

'How can I help?'

'I don't know. Just let me go, I guess, so I can hurry home and get my things and get back to him.'

'All right. I can do that.' Chip stands a moment, looking terribly sad. 'I do need to tell you one thing, Lucy.'

'What?'

Chip clears his throat. I feel something very much like danger in the air. Outside in the street cars pass, their lights flashing and winking, their tires sighing on the wet pavement. The street light turns yellow, red, green. Rain streaks the windows, making the shadows fall over us in arabesques.

'According to Massachusetts law, the natural father of a child has paramount rights to the child. It's very difficult for the nonnatural father to establish his claim on a child.'

'I don't understand what you're saying.'

'I'm saying that *by law* Jeremy is *my* child. By law the fact that Max is living with you in what is called a parental relationship does not give him the rights of custody.' He speaks quietly, but with authority, standing there in his polished wing-tip shoes, his elegant raincoat, his blue eyes dark with emotion.

I'm so surprised I laugh. 'Chip, you've got to be kidding me.'

'I'm not. I'm telling you, Lucy, that if I took this to court, I would win full or partial custody of Jeremy.'

'But you wouldn't do this. To Jeremy. To Max. To me!'

'Jeremy is my—'

'Jeremy is Max's child. You know that. You've seen him with Max. Come on, Chip, have some compassion. We've got so much to go through with Jeremy's condition, it's going to be hellish. Don't make it worse by trying to take Jeremy away.'

'You think that Max is the best father for Jeremy.'

'Yes. There's a powerful connection between them, Chip. It may not be "natural," but it is real. They are father and son.'

Chip doesn't move, but it seems that a light in his eyes dims. He takes a deep breath. 'You're sure.'

'I'm sure.' Something catches in my throat. I want to tell him more. I desired this man. I loved him. In a way, I love him still. I regret all the pain we've caused, but I will never regret that desire, and what it brought to us. But my son waits for me and right now that's all that matters. 'I need to go home.'

'Lucy . . . I don't know how to say this, but if you need any money for Jeremy . . . I want to help. If I can help financially . . .'

'Thank you. I think we'll be okay.' I start up the stairs toward the car.

'Lucy?' Chip calls. 'Later? In a year or two? When Jeremy's older? I do want to tell him that I'm his genetic father.'

I stare down at him. 'Yes, of course. Max thinks so, too. Just not yet, Chip, please.'

'Okay. Okay. I want to be clear about this, Lucy. Because you want me to, I'm backing off.' In the shadowy blue light of the foyer, with the rain-streaked glass behind him, with his raincoat hanging in folds past his knees, Chip looks like a creature underwater, almost like a merman, and I realize how he, too, is a creature caught between worlds, a man who cannot be a father to his natural son.

'Thank you.' This time I go up the steps without looking back. I do not hear steps coming after me. I find my car, unlock it, climb in. I drive to the exit, pay the ticket, then steer my car out into the night, into the falling rain.

. . .

THE HOUSE SMELLS like apples. The answering machine blinks imperiously. Midnight and Cinnamon materialize when I turn on the kitchen light, insinuating themselves around my ankles, scolding me with stereophonic mews for my absence. I dump great cups of dry food into their bowls and give them each a plate of canned food which they set upon ardently, purring and waving their tails as they eat. I take the time for a quick shower, grateful for all the bourgeois comforts that refresh my body, the sharp scent of the soap, the grassy green drift of shampoo. I hurriedly dress in clean clothes and pack a bag to take to the hospital. The house is unnaturally quiet with everyone gone; I'm not surprised that the cats are following me from room to room.

'Max will be home late, kids,' I tell them.

Cinnamon protests by rolling on her back, showing me her seductive stomach. How, she suggests, looking at me upside down, could you leave someone as gorgeous as me, alone? I stop to pet her luxuriously striped silky fur, then hurry back to my car, back to Children's Hospital.

BY THE TIME I've parked and traced my path back through the hospital, it's after eleven, and Jeremy is asleep. The lights are off by the bed, but enough light illuminates the room so that Max, sitting in a chair in the corner of the room, can read the brochures I read earlier.

He looks up at me, his face sad, weary. 'How are things at home?'

'There are about a million messages on the answering machine. I didn't even bother to listen to them. How's Jeremy?'

'The nurse was in about thirty minutes ago. She said that his temperature's down.'

'Good.' I stare down at my sleeping son.

Max stretches and looks at his watch. 'It's almost midnight.' He yawns and pulls on his jacket. 'I'll go into office in the morning, then come in. I should be back here by ten.' When he looks at Jeremy, his face is tender, full of emotion. Then he inhales deeply and straightens his shoulders, steeling himself to leave.

I walk with him to the door of the room. It's as if this hospital bedroom has already become a kind of home for us, like a tiny apartment.

'All right then,' Max says. When he looks at me, the tenderness has left his face, replaced by a cold flatness. This is how he looks when he's depressed, and his jaw bristles with a day's growth of beard. It's that beard that sets me off, and that look. 'Good night.'

It's the way he walks away from me without kissing me, without touching me, without seeing me.

My heart begins to race double-time. Something explodes in my belly, something hot and bitter rises in my throat. I can't breathe. Hot blood drums at my ears, yet my fingers have grown cold. I can scarcely stand.

A panic attack? Yes. *This* is what my panic attacks are about.

'No,' I say. I don't shout it, but I don't whisper it either, and at the far end of the hall a nurse looks at me sharply.

Max turns.

'No,' I say, more softly, but my passion makes the one word vibrate. Leaving Jeremy's room, I stride out into the hall. Taking Max by the arm, I pull him away from the medical unit and into the open corridor where elevators and telephones line the walls. 'No, Max, you can't leave like that. I won't let you.'

'What are you talking a—'

'You said you'll stay with us.'

'I did. And I meant it.'

'Do you think you're doing us a favor?'

Max runs his hand through his dark curls. 'Come on, Lucy. I'm beat.'

'I don't want to live like this, Max.'

'Lucy, the boy is—'

'I'm not talking about Jeremy. I'm talking about *you*. I don't want to live with you acting as if you're doing us a great big stinking favor with your presence.'

'Lucy, this is hardly the time or the place—'

'This is absolutely the time and the place!' I'm not yelling, but I'm shaking all over, and my voice trembles. 'If you stay with us, Max, then damn it, you've got to do it right. You can't hang around Jeremy and Margaret and me with the dead fish, hang-dog face you've given us before.'

'Come on, Lucy, I can't help it if I'm miserable.'

'No. But you can *show* us your misery! You can let us help you deal with it! And Max, you've got to see a psychiatrist and get some antidepressants!'

'Lucy, it's not necessary.'

'Yes, it is necessary. I mean it, Max. You've got to change. If you want to stay with us, you've got to really want to stay. And you've got to show us you want to stay. You've got to show *me* you want to stay. This is going to be *hell* we're headed into with Jeremy. This is only the beginning, and it's going to be scary and heart-wrenching and the most difficult thing I've ever even heard of. But you know what? I can do it, and I can do it without you, and I'd *rather* do it without you than with you dragging around depressed. It's too hard on me, Max, I get lonely, and afraid and full of a useless anger, and the children and I feel like you love everyone at the paper and don't care for us at all—'

'That's not true. That's never true.'

'All right, but that's the way it seems to us. Max, can I tell you what it's like when you're depressed? It's not just that you don't talk to us. You don't even *look* at us. You snap to attention whenever anyone from the paper calls, but when we try to talk to you, you stare into space, or you slam out of the house or you hide in your study, and you pretend you don't hear us, or maybe you really don't hear us, and that's pretty damned scary as well as insulting, don't you think?'

I'm pacing now, and the words are rising up out of me as if carried on a geyser that's been capped and covered over for too long. Miserably, Max bows his head; he looks like he'd cover his ears with his hands if he could.

'Do you know how I feel when you're depressed? When I have to ask Roland how you are because you won't tell me, and Roland is *kind*, he understands, he's not like some of the secretaries or bright young girl reporters, those disingenuous little hypocrites who make it clear that *they* understand you when your old rhino-hided wife can't, who smile at me with such fucking compassion in their eyes that it makes me want to vomit on their shoes! When you're depressed, Max, you're like a black hole in our house, and everything revolves around you, all our lives absolutely stop while we try to figure out what's going on with you and how serious it is and how long it's going to last and whether or not by any miraculous chance one of us, your son or your daughter or your wife, could possibly matter enough to get through to you. It's why I turned to Chip, for God's sake!'

At the far end of the corridor, a pair of nurses eye us. Max and I glare at one another, the air between us absolutely shimmering with tension.

After a moment, Max rubs the bridge of his nose. 'I didn't know,' he says softly. 'I'm sorry. I'll . . . I'll try.'

I turn my back on the nurses and modulate my voice. 'Try. What does that mean?'

'It means . . . all right. I'll see someone about antidepressants.'

'You promise.'

'I promise.'

'This week.'

'When I find time . . .'

'No! Not when you find time. Max, I'm not waiting. I need your help now. I need your love. I need your *passion*. It's the only way I'm going to make it through this. For God's sake, Max, we have to *love* each other if we're going to love Jeremy and Margaret.' I can't believe I have any more tears left in me, but I discover that I do. My face is suddenly wet, and tears fall on my shirt, on my hands.

Max squints, holding back his own tears. 'I was here tonight,' he reminds me. 'I skipped town meeting to be here.'

'That's good. I know. I'm so glad. I'm so – impressed. But I need more, Max. I need your love. I need your touch.'

He looks down, and the slant of his head, the way his features droop, making him look old and vulnerable, tugs at my heart.

'It's you I love,' I whisper. 'Don't be afraid.'

He flinches, as if I've struck him, and perhaps I have. I've touched him where he's most sensitive. The most terrible thing about marriage, I suppose, is that we know and understand one another's weaknesses and fears as much as we know our strengths and desires.

'I'm afraid, too, Max, for Jeremy. I'm *terrified*. But we should be. This is scary stuff we're dealing with. But think how brave Jeremy is going to have to be. You have to be brave, too. You have to be brave first. If you're going to stay with me, with me and Jeremy, you can't do it halfway. You can't do it and expect me to be grateful. You have to do it with all your heart and soul and body, Max. You've got to conquer your fears. You've got to show Jeremy and me you're doing it. You've got to show us how to do it.'

'You're asking a lot.'

'I know.'

'What can I say?' He looks tired, drawn, old, and as young as the boy I fell in love with in college.

'Say you'll call a psychiatrist tomorrow.'

He looks at me bleakly. Then he nods, once. 'I'll call a psychiatrist tomorrow.'

'All right then.'

We are facing each other like adversaries, our faces tense, our bodies taut. And all at once Max looks at me, really looks at me. A tenderness falls over his face. 'I do love you, Lucy.'

I dissolve at these words. I can't go on. I'm nearly crouching on the floor when Max reaches out to catch me. He holds me against him as we cry together, and the weeping hurts, but the embrace sustains us both.

TUESDAY MORNING I wake to good news: Jeremy's fever is down. He eats the breakfast the nurse brings him, and asks for more.

That afternoon, Max and I tell Jeremy that he has cystic fibrosis, emphasizing its effect on his lungs. It is why he coughs so much, we tell him, and the coughing is good. In fact, we're going to learn, all three of us, and Margaret later, how to perform the chest percussion therapy that loosens up the mucus in his lungs. It makes the mucus jump off his lungs, we tell him, so that he can cough it up and spit it out. If it stays there, it makes it easier for Jeremy to develop lung infections. So we want to get it out, and we'll pound on his chest and back for thirty minutes three times a day. Also, he'll have to take enzymes every day, to help him digest his food, because the same mucus that troubles his lungs also prevents proper digestion.

That's enough information for now, we think. We'll have the rest of our lives to tell him more. We'll be learning along with him.

Jeremy doesn't appear frightened or upset when we talk to him about all this, and afterward Max and I congratulate each other. We haven't shown our fear, so Jeremy isn't afraid. And when the flowers and candy and gifts arrive from his friends and his teacher and the *Gazette* staff, he begins to see that being in the hospital does have its positive side.

WHILE JEREMY NAPS, Max and I phone a Sussex psychiatrist and make appointments. Then Max drives out to Sussex to organize his papers and the necessities he'll need for spending the night here.

He's only been gone minutes when Andrea Cobb arrives, with Margaret in tow. There's much commotion, it's like a birthday party, especially because the Cobbs have bought Jeremy a present: the expensive dual-control Space War set that he's been yearning for.

'Andrea,' I exclaim, 'you shouldn't have. It's too much!'

'No, it's not, Mom!' Jeremy cries, and we all laugh. 'Wanna play, Margaret?'

'Sure, Germ.'

Margaret and Jeremy settle on the bed, all attention focused on the game.

'I'm going to stretch my legs,' I tell them.

Margaret waves a careless hand: Go.

I stroll around the hospital halls with Andrea. It feels good to walk.

'Jeremy looks good,' Andrea says.

'They've got the pneumonia licked, I think, but we'll be living with the CF every day.'

'How are *you* holding up?'

'Well, to be honest, I'm tired and scared and heartbroken. And I'm thoroughly sick of the inside of my own head. Let's talk about something else. Tell me about town meeting.'

Andrea chortles malevolently. 'It was pretty colorful! It lasted till midnight.'

'You're kidding.'

'I'm not. And several of our, shall we say more *distinguished* town leaders – Cory Richmond and Daniel Swartz, among others – had to be reprimanded for using profanity and shouting.'

I laugh, imagining it. 'It must have been wild.'

'You've probably heard: We voted to let the CDA Development Corporation build its building. All this,' Andrea points out, 'without either Max or Chip Cunningham to lead the battle. We know Max was at the hospital, but we don't know what happened to Chip. He just didn't show up. His assistant was good, but not as good as Chip. In fact, that might be why his side lost. But maybe not.'

'Mmm,' I respond, ambiguously.

We turn the corner, following the bright floor tiles back to the medical ward. Andrea says, musingly, 'I hear the Cunninghams are getting a divorce.' Andrea would like to hear what I think about this, I'm sure. Everyone knows that Kate and I are best friends. *Were.* I owe Andrea something, at least an explanation for why I've sent Margaret to her house instead of the Cunningham's.

'I haven't talked to Kate recently,' I admit. 'I've been so busy with Jeremy, and of course Kate with Garrison.'

As we turn back toward the medical ward, Andrea goes off to buy some cookies and coffee. I'm alone as I approach Jeremy's room, and so I hear my children talking to each other.

'Am I going to die?' Jeremy is asking.

I freeze outside the door.

'Get out of here!' Margaret responds. 'No-oo. Duh.'

'But I'm in the hospital.'

'That's because you have pneumonia, Germ. If I had pneumonia, I'd have to go to the hospital, too, maybe.'

'But I've got cystic fibrosis.'

'That doesn't mean you're going to die. It just means you have to do special things. It just means you're special, Jeremy.'

'But I could die.'

'We all could die. Would you stop talking about dying? Mom and Dad would kill you if they heard you talk like that. Let's play Space Wars again.'

Her voice is sharper than it should be. Give him a break! I mentally chastise her, and then I think: She's frightened, too. Max and I need to spend some time with her.

I sweep into the room to see them bent over the electronic game, thumbs clicking. 'Hi, guys.' They're too engrossed to do more than mutter a reply.

· · · ·

ANDREA TAKES MARGARET back to Sussex; Margaret has homework to do and it's a long drive. Jeremy's tired and falls into a light doze while watching television. Later tonight Max will come in to spend the night here and I'll go home to look at my mail, listen to the answering machine, and sleep in my own bed.

The corridor is busy tonight with families and friends visiting the other young patients. Laughter rises and falls in the air and footsteps beat eagerly against the floor. I look out at the lights of the city, feeling melancholy and lonely. I try to read but my mind won't settle. Tomorrow I'll call Jared Falconer to tell him I can't take the job. I could call Stan right now; I'm not sure he knows we're here. Probably he does, because everyone knows everything about everyone else in Sussex. But just in case he doesn't, it wouldn't hurt to call him. I should find out how Write?/Right is, even though I've only been away from the phone for two days. But I don't want to talk to Stan, not really. Write?/Right seems frivolous, part of another life. I can't get my thoughts to settle on work. Every path in my mind leads to Jeremy.

'Auntie Lucy?'

I look up to see Abby in the doorway, holding a present wrapped in paper covered with balloons. She looks great, with her long brown hair brushed out around her shoulders and held back by a pink headband that matches her pink dress.

'Abby!' God, how I've missed this child with her sensible freckled nose and her smile.

Kate stands behind her, unbelievably perfect in her plain fawn-colored dress and shoes. Her summer tan still glows so that she's caramel all over, head, skin, and clothes, and burnished, like a well-polished lamp. Cool as ice, she greets me. 'Hi, Lucy.'

'Kate.' I'm too stunned to say more.

'I brought this for Jeremy.' Abby holds up a package. She blinks rapidly as she takes in the formidable equipment of the room, the height of the hospital bed, Jeremy's bandaged arm.

Jeremy's eyes flutter open. 'Abby!' Suddenly he's a packet of six-year-old eagerness. 'Look at my arm! I have a shunt! I get antibiotics twice a day from a tube that comes out of there! I have cystic fibrosis! And the Cobbs gave me Space Wars!'

Abby climbs up on the bed and kneels facing him. 'I brought you a present.' She watches while Jeremy tears off the paper to find five videocassettes of the latest children's movies.

'Thanks!' Jeremy explodes in a spasm of coughing. Kate and Abby freeze, and I put my hand on his back and hand him some tissues. When he's through, he says confidently, 'I'm supposed to do that. I'm supposed to cough. I have to get all the yuck out. Want to watch a video?'

Abby eyes the Space Wars set. 'That's cool.'

'Wanna play?'

'Yeah,' Abby says eagerly.

Kate's looking a little white around the edges.

'Let's step out into the hall,' I suggest.

'I hate hospitals,' Kate mutters.

'I used to. I guess I'll learn to love them.' I steer her toward the far hall by the elevators and the telephones.

'How long will Jeremy be in?'

'Two weeks.'

'Two weeks!' Kate goes pale. 'Jesus. That's awful.'

'Well, it looks like it's going to become part of our lives.'

'This is terrible. I'm really sorry.'

'I know.' Up close, Kate doesn't look so perfect. She's lost weight, and beneath her makeup her eyes are shadowed. 'Tell me, Kate, how are you?'

She eyes me warily. 'You really want to know?'

'Of course.'

Heaving an enormous sigh, she slouches against the wall. 'The truth is, I'm just one great big emotional snarl. Garrison's really sick. I spend all day taking care of him and trying to keep his spirits up and hiding in the bathroom weeping, then Abby comes home from school, so I plaster on a fake smiling face and act like Donna Reed.'

'You do it so well,' I interject wryly, as if this were old times.

'Yeah, thanks so much,' she shoots back. 'And then, there's all the rest of it—' She glares at me.

'Chip, you mean.'

'Chip. I'm furious at him, but to be completely honest, I'm glad that something finally happened that enabled me to change things. I've wanted to do this for a long time.'

'This.'

'Divorce.'

'You're really going through with it.'

'I really am.'

'So I did you a favor,' I say, only half joking.

'Yeah, right.' Her face is grim. 'I'm seeing a therapist.'

'Which one?'

'Sam Campbell.'

'Max has an appointment with him. For antidepressants.'

'You're kidding.'

'I'm not. I'm going to see him, too.'

'Good God,' Kate says. 'How bizarre. Sam's head must be spinning.' We stare at each other and we can't help it: We connect; we grin. Then Kate's face grows somber. 'Chip's put the farm up for sale. Although you probably already know that.'

'What about Abby and Matthew?'

'You mean, how will they deal with the divorce? They'll survive. I mean, Matthew's already had a lot thrown at him. He knows Chip had an affair with you. He knows Chip is Jeremy's father. If he can absorb that, he can handle anything.' She takes a deep breath. 'He's got a girlfriend.'

'Chip?' I gasp, incredulous.

'No! Matthew!'

'*Matthew?*' I don't know why I'm so surprised. And irrationally insulted and jealous; I want him to like Margaret. 'Who?'

'Cecila Clark. The little tramp.' Tears well in Kate's eyes.

'Kate, Cecila is a perfectly nice young woman.'

'Cecila's a slut. She wears the tightest—'

'Kate. Get a grip. Remember what it was like when you were their age.' In a softer voice, I add, 'Remember what it was like when we first met?'

Kate looks at me, and for a moment I hope she's seeing not me, exhausted, harried, frightened, guilty Lucy West, married mother of two and adulterer, but the Lucy West I was that long-ago spring afternoon when our eyes met at the baseball game. When Matthew and Margaret were three years old and we were not yet even thirty. When the air was sweet with the fragrance of new-mown grass and with the sight of so many young daddies coaching and cheering on their young sons. When lust was something to grin about, and mischief only reminded us that we were still young.

Kate's blue eyes darken. 'I remember how we used to joke about living in a retirement home together. Max would write a newspaper and Chip would sell stocks and you and I would sit on the front porch in wicker chairs and gossip.'

'Yeah.' An elevator opens, ejecting a nurse who hurries past in the opposite direction from Jeremy's ward.

Kate looks at her watch. 'I've got to go.'

'Wait, Kate. About you and me. Do you think . . . ?'

Kate stares at me levelly. Her voice is tight with control as she says, 'Do I think we can still be friends? I don't know, Lucy.'

'I think we need each other, Kate.'

'You could be right. It's too soon for me to judge,' Kate says quietly. Then, as if she's conceded too much, she straightens. 'Anyway, I should go. I just wanted Abby to see Jeremy, I didn't intend to get into true confessions.' Abruptly she turns and strides back to the medical ward.

Following behind Kate, I notice a few especially pale hairs sweeping down to her immaculate collar: gray hair! Kate has gray hair. Shocked, I find myself patting my own curly mop, thinking not of vanity but of the relentless passage of time.

Back in the room, Kate announces, 'Time to head home, Abigail.'

'Not yet, Mom!'

'We've got a long ride and you've got school tomorrow.'

'But Mom—'

Kate kisses Jeremy's forehead. 'Bye, guy. See you.'

'Good-bye, Auntie Kate.'

I hug Abby. 'Good-bye, Abby. Thanks for the gift.'

'Good-bye, Aunt Lucy,' the little girl says, pouting as her mother ushers her toward the door.

Kate's shadowed eyes, her sulking child dragging at her

arm, her thinness, all make her appear so vulnerable, even frail.

'Kate—'

Kate stops in the doorway and looks back at me guardedly. 'Yes?'

I love you, Kate, I want to say, but she looks too stern, too defensive. I'll have to wait until she's ready. 'Thanks for coming.'

She nods. 'Goodbye, Lucy.'

They go off down the hall, Abby tired and still protesting all the way to the elevators that she doesn't want to leave yet. Jeremy's tired, too, and crabby with it, and more than ready to collapse back into the comfort of his bed watching *The Little Mermaid* video. I pile the new videos on a table, ready for tomorrow. The rest of the ward is quiet now. Visitors have left, patients are asleep.

I stand at the window, looking out into the night. This room has a view of the parking garage, and suddenly I see Kate and Abby, four floors below, crossing the street.

They seem both far away and near. Kate's head shines golden, no gray visible from this distance, in the glow of the street light. Kate is holding her daughter's hand and after they've crossed the street, they still hold hands, so Abby has already forgiven her mother for taking her away from Jeremy. I can imagine the conversation they will have in the car on the way home. Abby will want to know about the hospital room, Jeremy's shunt, cystic fibrosis. Kate will explain it all to her in simple terms, then she'll change the subject, guiding Abby's thoughts to more cheerful matters so that Abby won't have trouble falling asleep. Perhaps during the drive to Sussex Kate will sing songs to Abby, songs that we once all sang together as we drove down to Hyannis to begin our August vacation.

Kate and Abby walk across the sidewalk and through the glass door of the parking garage where only last night I stood with Chip. My window provides me with a view of my friend and her daughter as well as a reflection of myself and Jeremy in this hospital room. The futuristic-looking components of the Space Wars game lie at the foot of Jeremy's bed Jeremy rests, eyelids heavy, watching the television screen. Overlaid, blurrily, are the hem of Abby's pink dress, her white socks, the gleam of her black dress shoes, then it all disappears as Kate and Abby head into the cavernous building.

I feel so alone.

Suddenly they come back outside. Standing on the very edge of the sidewalk, they tilt their heads, looking up, counting the floors, scanning the lighted windows, and then all at once they see me standing pressed against the glass. From here it looks as if Kate's face is wet, but perhaps that's a trick of the light. Kate and Abby are holding hands, and with their free hands they wave at me. They wave and wave and wave. When I wave back, making great sweeping arcs with both my arms, Kate drops her daughter's hand and presses the tips of her fingers to her lips, then cups her hands beneath her mouth and blows, as if sending an invisible balloon of kisses into the air all the way up to where I stand. I can almost feel them arrive. I clap my hands together above my head, as if catching the kisses. And from all this distance away, I can see Kate smile.

Acknowledgments

I want to thank the many people without whose generous assistance I could not have written this book.

At Children's Hospital, the brilliant, dedicated, and absolutely awesome Mary Ellen Beck Wohl, M.D., Chief, Division of Respiratory Diseases, and Harvard Medical School Professor of Pediatrics; social worker Judy Bond, who responded to my questions with knowledge, patience and humor; physical therapist Ann Gould; Annemarie Fayemi, staff nurse; Robin Emmerling, staff nurse; Adam Courchaine, pulmonary technologist; Mark Dovey, M.D.; Donna Giromini, secretary, Division of Respiratory Diseases; and Allen Clapp and Lillian Shulman, who gave me my first tour of Children's Hospital.

I am grateful to all those connected with Children's Hospital for taking the time from their busy schedules to talk with me. Children's Hospital is a wonderful place; its staff is knowledgeable and generous. Any mistakes in this book about the complicated disease of cystic fibrosis are mine alone. For information about cystic fibrosis, call The Cystic Fibrosis Foundation at 1-800-FIGHT-CF or check out the CF web site on the Internet.

The Sea Man, by Jane Yolen, is published by Philomel Books, New York.

I also want to thank: the authentic Nantucket woman, the beautiful Toni Ramos, who helped me begin; Attorney Kevin Dale, who is humane, thorough, and wise; Susie

Robinson, who showed me Tuckernuck and who knows how to steer a boat through dangerous currents; Susan Pitard, head, Weezie Library for Children, Nantucket Atheneum, for researching literature about mer-boys; Maryanne O'Hara, for her insights and support; my superlative editor, Jennifer Weis; my excellent agent, Emma Sweeney; and my wonderful family, Sam Thayer, Josh Thayer, and Charley Walters.